Praise for t[...]

A bolt of lightnin[...]
McCanless to 18[...]
woman with a madd[...]

"A wo[...] joy of a book."
—bestselling author Judith O'Brien

"Susan's love scenes are rich and sensuous . . . and the plot is
exciting and full of wondrous discoveries. Ms. Plunkett has
all the promise of becoming one of the superstars of romance."
—*Under the Covers*

Silver Tomorrows
An earthquake thrusts wealthy socialite Emily Fergeson
back to 1882 Colorado—and into the arms of the man
she belongs with . . .

"Fans of the Western romance and the time-travel romance will
get more than just the silver, they will get the gold, if they read
this tale."—Harriet Klausner

MAKE TIME FOR THESE EXCITING TIME PASSAGES ROMANCES NOW AVAILABLE FROM JOVE!

Titles by Susan Plunkett

REMEMBER LOVE
SILVER TOMORROWS
HEAVEN'S TIME

HEAVEN'S TIME

Susan Plunkett

If you purchased this book without a cover, you should be aware that this book is stolen property. It was reported as "unsold and destroyed" to the publisher, and neither the author nor the publisher has received any payment for this "stripped book."

TIME PASSAGES is a registered trademark of
Berkley Publishing Corporation.

HEAVEN'S TIME

A Jove Book / published by arrangement with
the author

PRINTING HISTORY
Jove edition / June 1998

All rights reserved.
Copyright © 1998 by Susan Plunkett.
This book may not be reproduced in whole
or in part, by mimeograph or any other means,
without permission. For information address:
The Berkley Publishing Group, a member of Penguin Putnam Inc.,
200 Madison Avenue, New York, New York 10016.

The Penguin Putnam Inc. World Wide Web site address is
http://www.penguinputnam.com

ISBN: 0-515-12287-4

A JOVE BOOK®
Jove Books are published by The Berkley Publishing Group,
a member of Penguin Putnam Inc.,
200 Madison Avenue, New York, New York 10016.
JOVE and the "J" design are trademarks
belonging to Jove Publications, Inc.

PRINTED IN THE UNITED STATES OF AMERICA

10 9 8 7 6 5 4 3 2 1

For Denise Silvestro with my thanks and admiration

Chapter 1

"WHERE THE HELL did they come from?"

"Damned if I know, Colonel. They're just . . . there. We didn't pick them up until a second ago," Carl Hank said.

"Why the hell not?" Colonel Greg Brighton seethed. "Major Fuller, return to the shuttle."

Fastened to a satellite high above Earth, Major Melissa Fuller hesitated for a fraction of a second. "Problems?"

"We've picked up a small cluster of meteorites. Calculations show intersect in . . . seven minutes, eighteen seconds." Carl Hank's calm, unemotional tone conveyed the danger louder than if he had shouted.

Hurtling through space at more than 17,000 miles an hour, Melissa ignored the sudden lurch of her heart. The clock in her head began the countdown.

Seven minutes.

Only a miracle would get her back to the safety of the shuttle in that short time.

The pending situation did not deter her from completing her mission. "One more bolt and I'm ready to replace the cover." She torqued the bolt, satisfied with the repair.

"To hell with the cover," Carl practically begged.

"Leave the damn bolt and get back here on the double. Move, Major!" Colonel Brighton's booming order reverberated in the confines of her helmet.

"Yes, sir," she answered in her normal, unflappable tone. "The repair is complete. I'm sliding the cover into place but will not bolt it. Repeat. Cover is not bolt—"

"Forget the satellite! Get the hell back here, Major Fuller. Now!"

"Yes, sir." Melissa secured the tools. "Preparing to disengage from the satellite."

"Thank God," she heard Carl breathe through the speaker near her ear.

With calculated movements designed for efficiency, Melissa angled for the safety line securing her to the antenna struts. Relying on her NASA training and a self-discipline honed by four years at the Air Force Academy, she focused on carrying out Colonel Brighton's order. Panic led to mistakes. Melissa Fuller did not make mistakes. Nor did she yield to useless or destructive emotions.

"Move faster, Major. You'll be in the meteorite zone in less than six minutes."

Melissa acknowledged the order. A good officer followed procedure and avoided unnecessary risk. If Colonel Brighton thought she could clear the meteorites' path, she could. He wouldn't have given the order otherwise.

The time for worrying about the dangers had passed long ago. She had known the risks when she fought for and won the privilege of being an astronaut.

The crisis of the moment prompted questions. How had they not detected the approaching meteorites? Was there a larger problem aboard the shuttle, adversely affecting the instrumentation?

She unhooked the tether. Later she'd pursue the answers.

Five minutes, twelve seconds.

"Life line detached. Satellite free," she reported.

"Reattach, Major."

At Colonel Brighton's authoritative tone she immediately secured the line.

"You can't make it back, Major. We've reasoned your safest course is to remain with the satellite. Use it as a shield."

"Yes, sir." She gauged the distance between the shuttle and the satellite yawning in the corner of her eye. Too far. "Trajectory of impact, sir?"

"From your vantage point, at intersect they'll look like they're coming straight out of Orion's belt."

Concentrating on maneuvering against the satellite, Melissa released a small sigh of relief from her tightly guarded emotions. The housings for the adjustment boosters, used to control and correct the satellite's position with jets of dry nitrogen, flared at angles. The housings gave the structure bulk. In turn, that meant more protection from the menace approaching at incredible speed.

"Looking good, Mel. Can you get a second safety line attached?"

The tremor in Carl's voice made her glad she couldn't see the impending peril. She withdrew a secondary line and fastened it to an exposed eyelet. A quicker than normal tug on the rope flowing through the lock in the weightlessness of space tested her grip.

Three minutes, nine seconds.

"I've never seen anything like this come out of nowhere so fast." Colonel Brighton sounded calm, in full command. "They might miss you, Major."

"Yes, sir. They might." And they might not. How had they escaped detection? What had gone wrong?

Wedging her cumbersome legs and feet against the antenna struts and satellite framework, she double-checked the safety lines.

Two minutes, twenty-seven seconds.

Ready for whatever came next, she turned her head.

Millions of stars glittered like distant Christmas lights in the black void. They seemed close enough to touch. Since childhood, she had dreamed of walking among them. Now she was. The dream had sustained her during bleak times. Regardless of what life dealt, the stars waited for her every night. Their faithful presence kept her focused. High above the Earth, they were safe from all of the heinous things people did to one another.

The stars never disappointed her, never demanded the vile or the impossible, and never punished with the cruelty the strong inflicted upon the weak. They had accepted the names of the innocents she had given them one by one a long time ago, before she knew that most stars already had names derived from mythology or a numerical index.

She focused on Delphinus, a cluster of stars shaped like a small kite. "Chandra, Kate, Delvin, Rashad, Pacho," she murmured. The stars bore the names of companions who had shared the hell of her early childhood. She had chosen the tiny constellation because of its tight formation.

Chandra, beaten to death before her fourth birthday.

Kate, left alone, except for Melissa and Delvin, who did not know what to do when her fever spiked. They risked the beating sure to follow and called 9-1-1. Kate died in the hospital, too weak to fight the infection from a ruptured appendix.

Delvin. Dear Delvin. Aching to belong somewhere, anywhere, he joined a gang at age ten and never saw eleven.

Rashad, in the wrong place at the right time, caught a stray bullet on the way home from seventh grade.

Pacho. Oh, sweet Pacho. Gallant defender. Protector of the littlest children. He gave that bastard Horace Freeland a taste of what tiny Cindy had endured under the whip of a belt buckle. The system had abhorred Pacho's retaliation. It had labeled his method of deterrence a vicious crime and treated him as an adult. In an ironic way, their assessment had merit. At fourteen, Pacho had never been a child.

Remembering Pacho carried a sadness. Melissa doubted he'd had a vicious bone in his body until Horace and Annie Freeland taught him how to really hate. Pacho never made it to trial. He never made it out of his cell to the infirmary after being stabbed.

Social workers had removed Cindy from the Freelands' home. Soon after, they deposited eight-year-old Melissa into the next way station in a series of temporary stops on the road to adulthood.

As though knowing she thought about him, the star she had dubbed Pacho twinkled brighter.

Two minutes.

Early in life, Melissa learned the futility of fear. In striving to achieve her goals and surmount the enormous obstacles that she faced, she consigned all forms of useless emotions to the guillotine of ambition. Each night, the stars lured her into working a little harder, stretching her ability, and strengthening her tenacity until she succeeded.

"How are you holding up, Mel?"

A flicker of surprise widened Melissa's eyes. Colonel Brighton always called her by her rank, never employing the familiar name preferred by civilians. It was one of the things that made him easy to work for—he epitomized the consummate professional.

"Doing fine, sir. When the situation is over, I'll secure the cover plate and complete my mission."

"You have nerves of steel, Major. No one would hold it against you if you screamed."

"No need, sir. I haven't screamed or cried since I was six." She had screamed then. Loudly. No one cared. Wasted emotion changed nothing. Better to tuck it away than release it and pose more obstacles. There had been enough of those in the foster homes she bounced through with other kids who refused to accept the basic laws of nature. The bureaucrats made the rules. The tough, or lucky, kids survived the system rife with atrocities committed by society's enforcers without penalty. Twenty years ago, no one had cared if she went to school with bruises and scarcely spoke. That is, not until Mrs. Hanson substituted in her third-grade class for a month.

As she had done for the past two decades, Melissa said a prayer for Eileen Hanson. Because of her, the system placed eight-year-old Melissa with the Tibbenses.

Henry and Melva Tibbens became both redemption and salvation, angels in a world that had lost all hope. With the patience of God, Henry Tibbens opened doors and showed her the way out of the mire. Together, they watched *Star Trek*. As a family they attended movies and visited museums.

Several weekends a year, Henry took her to his office at the aerospace company where he worked. The marvels he revealed in vivid pictures of space, satellites, and drawings had enthralled her. After one visit to the cavernous building where she saw a rocket engine being assembled, she knew she had found her dream—the goal that shaped her life: One day the powerful booster rocket would send her into space. She would walk among the stars that Mr. Tibbens dreamed of exploring with technology. She would be his legs and eyes, and she would share every glorious moment of it.

Henry and Melva taught her many things during the five years she had with them before the winter when an automobile accident took their lives.

Her gaze shifted toward the star known as Polaris. To her, the bright star visible year-round was Mr. Tibbens. Staring at Mr. Tibbens amid the millions of bright points in the black void, Melissa felt satisfaction settle over her. She had achieved her dream of walking in space.

After the deaths of Henry and Melva Tibbens, she survived the bad foster homes and excelled in the better environments. Now, she had all she hoped for: an education, rules that didn't change when authority left the room, and value. Colonel Brighton valued her. He gave her the mission.

One minute, nine seconds.

"Have you ever ridden a bucking bronco, Major?"

"No, sir. They were in short supply where I grew up."

"Just as well. Hold on with both hands. We don't need a hero." Colonel Brighton cleared his throat. "Hang on for eight seconds. Cling to that satellite as though he was your first lover."

The analogy made her frown. Tony Landis, her first and only lover, was not a man she could count on for anything, let alone cling to. She had loved him as deeply as she knew how, but never managed to share more than her body with him. It hadn't been enough. He had needed something from her she didn't have, and he would not settle for less.

In retrospect, she owed him an apology and perhaps more than one thank-you. Since Tony had walked out of her life, she had concentrated solely on her career. Personal relationships got in the way. She wasn't any good at intimacy. Trying to be good at it hurt, and heartache never changed anything for the better.

Forty-one seconds.

For the first time, Melissa thought about dying in space. Her situation here was life or death; alone, clinging to the satellite, middle ground did not exist. What remained after achieving her lifelong goal of floating among the stars? *Plenty,* her logical mind affirmed. Her career had just begun.

She had loved her time at the Air Force Academy. To gain entry she had needed a sponsor. She had patiently camped in the reception area of her congresswoman's home office until she got an appointment. When she left the building, she had an advocate and a mentor to guide her through the maze of paperwork that followed.

The academy had been heaven. The strict rules never changed. All she had to do was play by the book. The physical demands toughened her, and she welcomed it. She devoured every academic crumb she could find and all the golden insight she discovered in herself. She needed it all to get to the stars.

"Fifteen seconds and counting," Carl said softly. The worry in his voice as the numbers ticked down tensed every muscle in her body.

"Ten."

"No matter what happens, you hold on to that hunk of metal, Major."

Colonel Brighton became her mentor early in her astronaut training. He lived and breathed by the book. He accepted no excuses and made none. Gender, race, religion made not a whit of difference. Performance, dedication, and the ability to follow orders were all he cared about. And he did care. She saw it in his eyes each time he addressed those in his command. He was proud of his people and insisted that they continue giving more than their best and making him proud.

As her commanding officer, Greg Brighton had earned her respect and the modicum of precious trust she rarely afforded anyone. Better to trust herself in all other aspects of life. She knew what to expect. Above all else, Major Melissa Fuller was a survivor. If any way existed of avoiding disaster, her sharp instincts would find it and turn it to her advantage.

"Seven."

"Yes, sir. I'll hold on until it's over." In quick succession her fingers flexed and reassured her grip. The practiced calm she always found in the most crucial part of any mission tucked the last tendril of excitement into an invisible, impenetrable vault. The time of waiting ended. Clearheaded and confident, she finished the countdown.

Three.

Two.

One.

Impact.

The satellite shuddered against her body. She clung tighter, trying to meld her skin through the space suit with the satellite.

The rasp of her rapid breathing increased as she watched a piece of booster housing disintegrate. Instinctively, she turned her head to track it. The housing tumbled away like a dandelion puff before a spring storm.

"Hold on, Mel."

"It's almost over," assured Colonel Brighton.

The entire structure flexed. The safety lines pulled her tight against the struts.

"Oh, shit!" Colonel Brighton seethed over the rasp of her breathing and a flurry of voices in the background.

Melissa barely heard them. The satellite vibrated, then lurched. The motion tilted the structure, pointing the top of her head at Earth.

Static crackled amid the shouts and Colonel Brighton's colorful expletives filling her helmet. The tremors against her space suit increased. Needing to assess her situation, she changed her grip and angled sideways.

The booster jets near her foot spewed nitrogen. Propelled by the nitrogen gas, the satellite teetered, then began moving against the starry backdrop of space.

Her mouth instantly became a desert. *Shut it off! Shut it off! Where're the external controls?*

Her labored breathing sounded loud in her helmet. Frantic, she twisted around to the opposite side.

The entire control housing was gone.

Without the controls, the adjustment booster would continue firing until the nitrogen supply was exhausted. By then, it wouldn't matter. She'd be dead. Trussed as she was to the shaking satellite, she had no hope of shutting down the booster or freeing herself.

"Damn," she murmured, lifting her head and straightening. The jet blast propelled the satellite out of its stable orbit. Given the angle of the structure, and the power of the adjustment booster, she and the satellite would reenter Earth's atmosphere together.

She really was going to die in a blaze of glory clinging to what would soon be a billion-dollar hunk of debris. And anyone looking up at the sky on the dark side of the planet would see the flare of her death.

An early childhood dream of happiness seized her thoughts. Though irrational, it escaped the tomb she had consigned it to long, long ago. The vision of herself as a woman holding a baby, standing beside a faceless man, whose love she felt filling her like the warm rays of the sun in springtime.

Anguish for all the dreams that had died so early without even a tear erupted from her soul in a cry of protest. She had tried to love but failed miserably. And gave up. Now she loved no one and no one loved her. Not a single person would miss her.

In the moment she faced death, she held a cold, impersonal satellite in arms that had never known the delight of holding a baby. With sudden urgency, she wanted all those things in her innocent childhood dreams: a man to love, a child to nurture, a heart that knew more than isolation and suspicion.

In a burst of hysteria, she demanded that the Creator of the Universe experience the same displeasure with the outcome of her life and holler, "Cut!" She needed another chance to get it right, to balance . . . to . . . what?

Ahead, the lighted crescent of Earth looked tranquil and inviting. From the dark portion of the planet, a spot of light flared. The needlelike burst climbed straight toward her.

Did they see it in the shuttle?

She shouted a warning, her teeth chattering with the vibration of the propulsion boosters. It seemed surreal for an instant. Sound did not carry in space. Outside the world of her space suit, no one heard the chatter of her teeth or the repercussion of her helmet banging against the satellite. The safety lines holding her in place battered her limbs. The force of the shaking increased, making it harder and harder to hold on.

An awkward glance to the right sent her heart into high gear. Her odd angle afforded barely a glimpse of the shuttle fading into the oblivion of distance.

Alarmed, she sought the light beam racing toward her. What was that? What the hell was that racing up from the Earth? A weapon? What else could it be?

The absurdity of being shot out of orbit by a secret weapon struck her. It was a comedy of circumstance and error, but Melissa didn't laugh.

She waited for the first bite of fear—and felt nothing.

She waited for her life to flash through her mind. The expectation met an emptiness as great as the void of space behind her.

She waited for the brilliant white light she had read about to appear and lead her down a tunnel where peace and joy embraced souls free of mortality.

Instead, a cloud formed where no clouds could exist. Stretching from a dark spot on the Earth, it enveloped her, soothing her for a final glimpse of her beloved stars.

Anguish, regret, and anger burst forth in a wounded scream. Emotions she had repressed for most of her life found a primeval outlet. In the silence of space, the scream reverberated inside her helmet and expanded, filling her head with a cacophony of sound and color. She continued screaming until the bolt of light from Earth seized her.

The satellite entered the ionosphere. On Earth, a brilliant falling star streaked across the sky.

Chapter 2

RORY MCCULLOUGH STRAIGHTENED behind an expansive walnut drawing table obscured by layers of architectural plans. Sensing a familiar presence, he glanced beyond the massive desk beside him.

Shelan stood in the office doorway. Her wizened countenance was full of life and color. The bright fringed shawl wrapped around her thin, age-wrinkled arms caught a ray of sunshine streaming through the office skylight. Reds, lavenders, and blues shimmered, as though dancing with anticipation. Green and yellow flowers bloomed on the blue background of her skirt.

"There are things we must speak of, Rory, and something I must do for you." Excitement glittered in Shelan's eyes, scrubbed nearly as colorless by age as her gray-white hair.

"You have done enough. I could not have built what we have without your help." He tossed his pencil on the drawings strewn across the table, then rounded the desk. The familiarity he and Shelan enjoyed spoke louder than words. Her rare appearance at the sanctum of his office while he worked boded importance.

"My contributions have been small. Very small in comparison with my rewards." She captured his hand in both of hers.

Rory ran his thumbs over the translucent, spotted skin on the back of her bony hands. Since receiving an enigmatic answer shortly after they met, he had not asked her age. The years between then and now had curved her spine and hunched her once proud shoulders. However, her mind remained sharper than a well-honed pruning knife.

"You planted the gardens with flowers and herbs." Rory gave her hands an affectionate squeeze and felt her fragile bones.

Shelan's laughter rippled with a youthful vibrancy belying her advanced years. "*You* built the gardens. I did little beyond advising on how and what to plant." A touch of pride kept a bright smile on her colorless lips. "The herb garden has thrived, hasn't it?"

"Yes. Would you like to walk through it with me?" Whatever she had on her mind would bloom amid the serenity of the plants and flowers they both prized.

Rory tucked her thin fingers into the crook of his arm. The disparity of their size required her to lift her hand nearly to her shoulder. He led her across the office to the veranda door. The whisper of a calm ocean caressing the shore at the bottom of the bluff lent tranquillity to the sun-dappled afternoon.

He opened the gate leading into the private garden sheltered on three sides by the house.

"It is not good for a man such as you to be alone. You need a wife," Shelan said, gazing beyond the blushing rose perched on the edge of her fingertips.

Rory grinned. "Short of pulling one out of thin air, there isn't much chance of finding one."

"You work too hard." Shelan bent and examined a queen of the meadow for the first sign of blooms.

"If I don't, I won't be able to keep us going." He lifted the rose she had fingered and inhaled the rich fragrance. "But after I deliver these plans in Seattle, money won't be a concern." He glanced up from the aromatic flower and smiled. "For a while, anyway. They are paying me very well."

"Will you seek a wife then?"

Rory chuckled and avoided Shelan's omniscient eyes. He knew better than to speak anything other than pure truth to the old woman. "I may want to, but I probably won't. What woman would live out here . . . the way I live? She would want changes I'm not willing to make. And if I found one willing to take this on, she'd probably demand more care and time than I could spare. The unfairness of it would make us both miserable. There's enough guilt in the world without me creating more."

Shelan nodded thoughtfully; her nearly colorless eyes grew distant before she spoke. "You have thought about a wife, then?"

Rory raised an eyebrow and wondered about Shelan's intentions. "You know I have. I have long suspected you read my thoughts."

She dismissed his speculation with a wave of her arthritic hand. "But you have never spoken of marriage."

"Why indulge in futile dreams?"

Shelan wandered deeper into the herb garden, stroking plants on the way. The heady aroma grew stronger each time she brushed a leaf or a stalk. "What do you wish for when you think of a wife?"

Rory stared at the tranquil sea. In the distance, a bank of fog hugged the blue water. "Intelligence. Independence. The ability to share the vision we've begun to make into reality. A helpmate who wouldn't talk me to death with useless questions and impossible demands."

"You mentioned neither love, nor lovemaking, Rory." Shelan touched his arm, her head tilted in sympathetic certainty. "Are these not important to you?"

Rory laughed. Damn, Shelan allowed him no privacy. She never had. "Very—but I'd settle for a wife who respected me, if she met the rest of my wish list. As for sex . . ." His voice trailed. He could not speak of the unsatisfied drive that found fleeting relief in the sophisticated bordellos of Seattle. Revealing the dark side of his nature made him more vulnerable than he cared to feel, even with Shelan.

In the weak moments of his dreams, the wife he craved made love with him with a consuming passion that quenched the hunger in his soul. The love in her eyes when she gazed at him in the throes of ecstasy fed the ardor swelling his heart to the bursting point. She shared his dreams and his work with a zeal rivaling his own.

But she was not real, merely a figment of imagination wrought from errant moments of loneliness.

"Perhaps she would not find it offensive to share my bed occasionally." For a foolish instant, he wished the woman in his dream existed.

"And give you children of your own?" Shelan nodded thoughtfully.

The game of dream indulgence seemed to knit the clouds into a depressing grayness. "Enough of this. I must go back to work."

"Stay."

Whether it was a request or a command, Rory acquiesced. "Why do you speak of things that are impossible? I'm content with the life I have."

"I am not content for you, Rory. You are a good man, the best I've known in many, many decades. However, my decade with you is approaching an end. Tomorrow, I will have been with you for ten years. It is time for me to leave."

Alarmed, Rory took a step toward her. Herbs rustled around his legs. "Leave? Why?"

Some of the vibrancy always surrounding Shelan faded. "That is how it must be for one such as me. Ten years and ten days. That is all I can spend with one person."

Leaving? Life without Shelan? At her age, where would she go? How would she take care of herself? And if she left . . . Who would he confide in? Share his plans for Freedom House with?

"Ah, Rory, not once have you allowed me to speak of my magic, let alone use it."

Rory stiffened. The only magic in the world came from the heart. Black magic. White magic. It all came from the place where each person created their own miracles. Except for Shelan . . . There was something special—no, *mystical*—about her. He had known it the moment they met, and he'd helped her anyway. As he grew to love her, he ignored her difference the way he overlooked Elmira the housekeeper's deformed ear and Marvin the handyman's shortened right leg. Now, she wanted him to look at who and what she was in the light of day. He did not want to acknowledge how extraordinary she was.

"Shelan—"

Her crooked fingers waved him into silence. "You know what I am. You have asked for nothing and given all. You have sheltered me, protected me, fed and clothed me. You have indulged every whim I've voiced."

The intensity of her pale eyes froze him. The pain of losing his dearest friend and confidante flowed through him. He knew the resolve behind her implacable expression. Nothing would change her mind.

"Ah, Rory, Rory my heart's delight and comfort, I cannot change what must be without forfeiting my life. It burdens my soul to leave you alone. However, it would break your heart if I stayed, as you wish, and died, would it not?"

Fighting the torment welling from his toes, Rory broke the hold of her beseeching gaze. "Are you dying, Shelan?" Though he spoke softly, the words bit hard into his heart. "I will not permit you to sneak off and pass from this world without my attendance."

The sadness emanating from her deepened the lines in her weathered face. "We are all dying, but I have many decades ahead before I join my fellows—unless I abandon the covenants. Should I do that, death will claim me within days. No power on earth can alter the vows I took more than two centuries ago. When we part for the last time, you will see me only in the memories of our years together. That is how it must be, Rory."

As he realized the impact of her longevity, he sank onto a boulder. "Two centuries . . ." The words barely fit in his mouth, let alone his comprehension. No one lived for two centuries.

Gazing into her age-bleached eyes, he saw the certainty of truth. It burned belief into his heart. Shelan had never lied to him, nor he to her. Regardless of how impossible it sounded, he could not deny her claim. "Two hundred years?" he echoed, struggling to reconcile truth and logic.

"Aye. And for the last decade, you have bid me to save my magic." A knowing smile brought out the laugh lines etched around her eyes. "I must repay your kindness. Had you not rescued me from the vermin on the wharf, I might have died then."

She exhaled sharply. "In the months before you found me, I lived dangerously. My companion of the previous decade, a young woman, lived amid dark forces. Helping her thwart the evil intentions of those who should have cared for her required great strength from both of us.

"It is sufficient to say, by the time she was safe and happy, I had spent too much time in the presence of dark powers. Although I won my battle for her freedom, the effort temporarily weakened me. Then I was much as you see me now, a spent old woman vulnerable to anyone stronger. I needed a protector, a champion while I regained my strength.

"You were my rescuer, Rory. Like those who attacked me on the wharf, you knew nothing of what I am. They knew only that I had a gold coin they wanted for themselves."

He recalled his rage at seeing three men assault an old woman on a San Francisco wharf. "They were fortunate I did not kill them."

"Initially, I feared they might kill you. But what we speak of is history. What we must concern ourselves with now is the future. I have a debt I must pay and no choice but to pay it."

"Why didn't you tell me you'd have to leave?"

Shelan casually lifted a shoulder. "You did not wish to speak of it, nor would either of us have changed anything we have done."

Straight to the core of the matter. That was Shelan. The accuracy of her words struck him with the force of a bullet.

He had not wanted to know anything of her past. She spoke to rocks and plants with the same tenderness she showered on distraught children. She made plants thrive where they had no business growing. Unusual things about her crept into his awareness, like the way she healed the sick with herbs and mumbled prayers.

"I find it difficult to think of you as a witch," he breathed, giving voice to his thoughts. He hadn't wanted to acknowledge the mysteries of the little miracles she had quietly performed over the years.

"Aye, it is not the most flattering description, but it is accurate, nonetheless. You should know, Rory, I have used no magic with you these last ten years."

He knew about her magic, though he would never have acknowledged it even to himself before her admission. Magic was a convenient scapegoat for success or failure. Recognizing such ambiguities at work on his behalf would have led to questions concerning his ability and judgment. The hard work Rory had poured into the last decade left no such questions.

The calm certainty Shelan had never influenced his business made his bleak acceptance of her inevitable departure even more difficult. But as always, he would help her in any manner she wished. "What would you have me do to assist you in this, Shelan?"

"Pack what you need for a week. We leave at dawn. There is something we must do before I leave you."

The soft touch of her hand on his shoulder forced him to raise his head. Tears brimmed in her pale eyes. He swallowed the thickness in his throat, then nodded.

Two days later, Rory sat in the center of a stone circle abutting a blue mountain lake. Curls of aromatic smoke rose from ten small fires around the ring. The crystal hanging on a thong around his neck felt hot. Absently, he reached for the transparent quartz pendant. Tiny sparks of static electricity prickled his fingers.

Shifting to hide his surprise, he studied Shelan. Dressed in white, she glowed against the blue-black lake reflecting the colors of sunset streaking the sky.

He believed in the old woman and she believed in this magic. From the beginning of their friendship, he had trusted her like no other. A decade ago, she told him she had to leave San Francisco. Sensing her specialness, he had closed his offices and journeyed north with her. The remote house he built above Bellingham Bay made reestablishing his architectural business in distant Seattle seem nigh onto impossible. Fortunately, however, Seattle enjoyed steady growth, and the excellent reputation he had earned in San Francisco followed him north.

Expanding cities needed good plans for new, permanent buildings. Rory was a master at turning what people thought they wanted into something they loved. The first year in northern Washington, clients came in dribbles. Word of his peculiar interpretative talent spread. By the third year, clients sought him out at a steady flow that kept him busy. In retrospect, the transition did seem like magic.

"There is nothing mystical in your success," Shelan had assured him when he marveled over his good fortune. "It is the reward that a man who does what he loves cannot help but reap. Your sorcery is in your head and in the way you listen to the words and find the meanings of what your clients don't say."

Now, there were words left unsaid between them, yet everything necessary lay revealed. She had ten years of magic bottled inside her and a debt in need of payment. What could it hurt if he accepted the gift she chose? Regardless of the outcome, he knew with certainty that she would do nothing to harm anyone. Years spent in the same house and discussions consuming uncounted evenings instilled an unflappable confidence in the gentleness of Shelan's nature. He cherished those hours and her keen insight. The evenings ahead promised only silence and fond reminiscence.

As still as the stones forming the circle, Rory sat facing the pristine lake. A fire blazed between him and Shelan. Since dusk, Shelan had hummed and chanted in a lyrical, unfamiliar tongue. Her voice rose and fell with a full spectrum of emotion. At times it sounded as though she was pleading with an invisible deity, then becoming angry, and finally contrite and cajoling. The intricate sequence fascinated him.

A long time after the full moon climbed the ladder of night

and crossed directly overhead, Shelan rose. In the firelight, she appeared years younger than when she had begun the elaborate ritual. Rory watched, enthralled by the changes in her appearance that the fire tricked him into seeing, and curious about what came next.

She removed the pendant from around her neck. In the firelight, the fractured quartz pieces glowed rose-red. At one time it had been part of the crystal he wore.

"I will not depart leaving you bereft of companionship, Rory. Your woman will come. She has known little of the gentle side of life. Open your heart. Let her discover the joy and serenity found only in risking her heart and trusting others. Help her redeem herself, and in so doing, you will have found your soul mate."

Shelan folded his fingers around her pendant. "When you are ready, give this to her. Be sure, Rory. Even your patience and gentle heart may not be enough." She blinked slowly, holding her eyes closed for several heartbeats. Color the hue of a summer sky flooded into her eyes when her thick lashes lifted. "The woman is all you said you wanted, and you are all she needs." A twinkle in her bright-blue eyes banished the heavy lines around her temples and mouth.

As Shelan straightened to her full height, the markers of age melted into the night. Fingers of ebony stretched through her gray-white locks, playing in the breeze. The age spots faded from her hands, which now appeared strong and supple.

Stunned, Rory watched the old woman he knew as bent with age transform into a strong, vibrant woman not a day over thirty-five. With a thumb and forefinger, he rubbed his eyes. When he looked again, she appeared even younger.

"Your eyes are not playing tricks, nor are you hallucinating. I am young again. It's the magic," Shelan whispered, then gave him a conspiratorial wink.

"I'm sorry. I didn't realize . . ." There were so many things he had not realized until tonight. Had denying her the open practice of her arts harmed her in any way? Guilt settled on his shoulders with the impact of a fallen tree.

"No, Rory, limiting my use of magic helped build my

strength these ten short years. What you see now is the manifestation of the love we bear one another. My changing body is a reflection of your beautiful spirit. Together, we have shared joy and built hope. You allowed my participation and thereby enriched me. My restoration is a gift you unknowingly gave and I knowingly accepted without hesitation and with great joy."

Her dazzling smile made his jaw drop. Lord! The changes continued before his very eyes. He blinked quickly, not wanting to miss the evolution, not sure he believed what he was seeing.

"Believe in me, Rory. Believe in what I am and my powers. Your future and her fate rest in you." Shelan knelt in front of him and took his hands. She traced the lines on his palms with young, straight, fleshy fingers. Her skin felt like warm velvet, smooth and unblemished. "Such big hands—to match your heart."

Shelan cupped his unshaven face and planted a parting kiss on his lips. "Good-bye, Rory. Believe in me. Remain near the circle for three days. No harm can breach its barrier."

Rory rose on shaky legs and started forward. "Shelan?"

She paused at the edge of the circle, then turned slowly. In the brilliance of the full moon and the blazing fire, he marveled at the image of loveliness she presented. His eyes were not playing tricks. She had become a beautiful young woman, shedding her clothing as she left the sacred ground.

"You cannot follow me, Rory. Do not look for me, for you will never find me." Sadness touched the sparkle in her eyes. "Should you be foolish enough to try, you will lose the marvelous challenge of the woman you said you wanted." An enigmatic smile mingled anticipation with sorrow as she discarded the last of her filmy white robes.

Rory stared long after Shelan's shapely, naked body disappeared among the trees. The sounds of the fire, the water lapping at the shore, fish jumping, and night creatures playing on the wind in the trees filled the night.

Shelan was gone. He would never see her again. What had

seemed like a death sentence a short while ago lightened somewhat with the aspect of her rejuvenation.

Were he to believe his eyes, she had indeed spun magic within the circle. An old woman stooped with age had become a strong, beautiful young woman within the stone boundaries.

He considered that it might be more comforting to believe himself delusional, but he knew he was not. Practical men wise in the ways of the world did not embrace delusions. However, he knew the world held many inexplicable mysteries. And Shelan was one of them.

Now she was gone. Forever.

He rubbed his chest over his heart, where an ache had begun with her announcement in the garden. He loved the old woman, magic or not.

After a time, Rory sat beside the fire. Doubt about what he had witnessed crept in with the night chill. Shelan might be a magic woman . . . no, she *was* a magic woman. He ceased denying her abilities.

He gathered a handful of stones and threw them into the lake one at a time. Moonlight glistened on the ripples undulating across the water. The more stones he tossed, the greater the confusion of circles.

Witches. Spells. Incantations.

The scope of his new knowledge proved more vast than his logical mind could grasp. He focused on the results.

Shelan's sage wisdom in a youthful body . . . The unfinished thought almost brought a smile. Magic or not, she would fare well wherever she chose to go.

Fingering the crystal around his neck, he stared at the fading ripples.

She'd said he would have a woman. A wife.

The hint of a smile softened his stoic expression, then disappeared in a wave of incredulity. How would he find a wife by spending three days near the confines of a stone circle?

Believe in me.

Hearing Shelan's voice echo inside his head, he scooped another handful of pebbles and rose.

Until a few days ago, he had managed to ignore her magic. It wasn't as though he disbelieved. He had purposefully not given the matter serious thought. Now . . . now, he either believed wholeheartedly or committed himself into the care of saner individuals.

Believe in me.

By the time he had tossed the last pebble into the lake, he bowed to reality. Shelan had invoked a spell. The tingling of the crystal against his chest bespoke the working of it.

He would do as she asked and remain near the circle for three days.

He fed the fire, then undressed and settled within a nest of warm pelts he'd brought as sleeping pallets.

The crystal bit into his palm as he clutched it tightly. Seeking escape from the loss of his friend, mentor, and companion and the incredible display of her power, Rory indulged in the fantasy that often filled his lonely dreams. He wondered how a wife would appear within the circle.

Rory stared absently at the stars. One glowed brighter, and brighter still. The crystal in his right hand warmed as the star streaked toward Earth.

Rory sat up cross-legged. The damn star was falling out of the sky and on top of him.

The night lit with the brilliance of a noon sun. The lake glowed from below.

As quickly as the star had brightened, it winked out. Only the sound of water lapping the rocks and the snapping of the agitated fire filled the night. Even the insects ceased their noise.

Rory continued blinking at the heavens. Ghosts of light played across his vision. Was the shooting star a sign? Was the woman Shelan promised really coming? He laughed aloud at the absurdity, yet relished the excitement of seeing Shelan's promise fulfilled.

Drawn by a force he neither denied nor understood, he abandoned the warmth of the furs and walked toward the lake. Squinting, he peered into the darkness.

The water lapped at his toes.

Something was out there.

Chapter 3

MELISSA SCREAMED UNTIL the fires of outrage burned the sound from her throat. Still she railed at the injustices experienced during a life over too soon to right any wrongs. Once anger broke the shackles of her rigid self-control, nothing short of death could cage it again.

The bolt of light rising from the Earth struck her like a cloud. Blue-white swirls caressed her, cooling the heat, prolonging the silent scream contorting her face into a gargoyle of anguish. Even staring down the throat of death, Melissa vented her rage until a vortex of light sucked her into oblivion.

When a smattering of awareness returned, the searing heat evolved into bone-chilling cold. Water held her nude body in pulsing suspension. Her aching limbs felt as heavy as tree trunks. The burning in her lungs allowed no time for rumination. She opened her eyes to a liquid darkness thicker than the inside of a sealed coffin. Instinctively, she clawed her way upward. The blackness swam inside her head as she flailed toward the surface. Fireflies of light darted through her vision with each movement.

Just when her lungs threatened to explode, she broke the surface. Splashing, she gulped air, trying to push herself higher, desperate for a clean breath. She coughed and gasped. The shimmer in her vision matched the pulse reflexively closing her throat.

Breathe.

The command charged her entire body with life. Gasping, she sucked in another sweet lungful of cool, life-giving air. She steadied herself, treading water and regulating her breathing until her head cleared.

A full moon revealed the boundaries of the water. Dimly, she realized the size of the lake. Not far away a fire burned on the near shore. Coughing, sputtering, Melissa trained her gaze on the light and swam toward it.

Each downward stroke threatened to drag her to the bottom. Fatigue added a millstone every time she lifted an arm. Her legs could barely move. Each stroke seemed to gather weight from the bottom of the lake, as though she were dragging the far shore behind her.

Despite her determination, the water closed over her head. Melissa commanded her arms to reach, her legs to kick. In a final betrayal, her limbs went slack. Resigned to a battle lost, she almost welcomed the satin oblivion of the dark water. The lake embraced her with the possessiveness of a jealous lover.

Suddenly, powerful hands gripped her naked shoulders. Instead of sinking, she was surging upward with the force of a geyser spewing from the depths.

Frantically, she tried to seize the heaven-sent rescuer and hold fast. Her arms dangled uselessly from her shoulders. Trapped in a warm vise forged of flesh, she could not offer an iota of assistance. Gratitude flowed through the haze of her awareness. Salvation was a man powerful enough to defy the water and strong enough to cradle her helpless body.

Drawing one raspy breath after another, she blinked her stinging eyes and tried to see him when he lifted her from the lake.

Water sluiced from their naked bodies as he approached the fire. She wanted to walk, but her muscles, weak as a newborn babe, refused even a feeble quiver. Limp in her rescuer's arms, she had no choice but to let him dry her with a shirt. The tender way he toweled her battered body soothed the ghost of something raging in a distant place, and it faded into nothingness. With it fled her anxiety.

Fighting the lethargy of exhaustion, she lifted her heavy eyelids for a glimpse of her savior. Although he appeared mortal, he felt like an Olympian god. Eyes the color of gentle summer rain clouds regarded her with a reverence that sent a ripple of awe across her chilled skin.

With the care of a mother handling her newborn babe, he buried her in a mound of furs as silken as the water, but warm. So warm. Empathy shimmered in his vigilant gray gaze as he molded the furs around her shivering form. When her eyelids dipped again, an exhausted sleep claimed her in a restful, dreamless cocoon.

Rory marveled at the woman in his furs. Crouched beside her, he could not tear his gaze away from the damp head peeking over the edge of the bear pelt surrounding her. If he looked away, she might disappear. So he remained where he was until the cold night air seeped into the marrow of his bones.

He dressed slowly, all the while watching the furs rise and fall with her breathing. When she coughed, every muscle in his body tensed.

The woman Shelan had promised lay before him. Real. Breathing. Flesh and blood. Entrusted to his care.

The crystal around his neck tingled in confirmation. Absently, he gripped it through his shirt. Warmth filled his hand.

Magic. What other explanation existed?

Excitement coursed through him. He wanted to laugh, to shout his good fortune at the night, to jump high enough to embrace the entire world. A grin that refused to fade covered his face.

Her impossible, fantastic presence seemed a dream. He wanted to hold on to it for as long as it lasted.

The feminine form beside the fire would fill the lonely nights. Perhaps she would take him to her bed. Perhaps she would even greet his lovemaking with the passionate response he craved. Perhaps . . .

For just a moment, he closed his eyes and reveled in the remembered feel of her chilled flesh against his when he carried her from the water. Then, he had longed to give her the warmth of his body. Although she was not a small woman, the contrast of their sizes and her vulnerability had made her seem so.

Only a blind man could have missed the lush details of a body ripe for a man's adoration. At present, he considered the bulky bear pelt hiding her delectable femininity a prudent barrier.

Protecting the gift Shelan bestowed had been an obligation met without forethought. Remembering the way in which the woman had regarded him made him feel almost godlike. Yet all he had done was fetch her from the water.

A man could become lost in her hazel eyes with their flecks of color changing in the dancing firelight. He liked the short, dark-brown hair framing her oval face. Leaning closer, he noted with satisfaction that a healthy color had replaced the blue tinge of her lips. Full, even lips parted slightly in sleep. Kissable lips.

He swallowed and looked away. His giddiness at being the recipient of the impossible forced him to look back at her. Her high cheekbones and smooth olive skin belonged to the woman who filled the dreams and fired his passions during cold winter nights.

Ah, sweet dreams. Once they began weaving their spell around his heart, he could not halt them. Reveling in them, he envisioned her as the helpmate he had yearned for, sharing his life and work. Together, they would nurture the gardens and the children. Together, they would turn the haven he had built into a heaven. That, indeed, would be magic.

Magic.

His heart lurched with a memory of Shelan imploring his belief in her. He had believed—or at least he had not disbelieved. Shelan's transformation from an old woman bent and wrinkled by age into a vibrant young beauty played through his mind again.

The change was real. So was the woman nestled in his furs.

What could he have possibly done to deserve the gift before him? For ten years he had been the beneficiary of Shelan's company, her friendship, her sage advice, and most

cherished of all, her unflagging belief in him. He had bene-
fited ten times tenfold for an act of violence he committed
because he could not tolerate the strong battering the weak.
He had nursed her back to health as he would an injured
child. Under her tutelage, he learned the healing arts of touch
and the potency of nature's bountiful plants.

Awed by the magnitude of powers Shelan commanded on
his behalf, he watched the woman she had selected for his
wife.

The sun rose over the mountain, and still he watched the
woman sleep.

By noon, he was halfway in love—and he did not even
know her name.

The sun cast twilight colors above the shadowy mountains
when Melissa woke. For a few disoriented moments, she
watched the colors play and evolve into the gathering night.
The first stars of evening twinkled in friendly welcome.

"I'm glad you have awakened. You had me worried."

From her prone cocoon, Melissa watched her rescuer pour
a cup of steaming coffee. *Who was this man clad in work
boots, thick gabardine pants, and a black-and-red-plaid shirt
heavy enough to serve as a jacket?* He seemed enormous.
The breadth of his shoulders blotted out the firelight and
stole the radiant warmth.

She didn't know him.

He set the coffee aside and bent over her.

Why am I sleeping outside?

She inhaled wood smoke, soap, and the unmistakably
masculine scent of the man watching her with undisguised
awe.

Where did he come from? Of greater importance, how had
she gotten here?

He cradled her in one arm as though she was a piece of
fine china and pulled a log up behind her. Before laying her
back, he checked the thickness of the furs over the wooden
bolster.

"Is that comfortable?"

Melissa stared at him, trying to separate reality from dreams.

What was she doing here?

"If it isn't, let me know. We'll try something else." He picked up the cup steaming beside her. "Coffee? I make a good pot."

Melissa continued staring until recognition flickered. He was her rescuer. The realization brought a strange consolation.

Although he was not a classically handsome man, his generous features and open expression fascinated her. A hairline scar ran through the center of his left eyebrow, marring the otherwise perfect arch. The glow from the fire danced in hair that was shades of auburn, gold, and nutmeg, promising to feel as soft as the furs surrounding her. She thought he must have shaved the thick stubble that hid his square jaw and the cleft in his chin last night. Or had she imagined it? Nothing seemed clear, except the gray eyes watching her as though he expected her to sprout wings and soar with the angels.

"I'll fetch one of my shirts for you. It will be cumbersome but easier to manage than trying to keep the bearskin around your shoulders." He glanced across the lake. The last strains of light glimmered over the horizon. "It gets cool up here when the sun sets."

Lying perfectly still, she felt a dull ache inside her body. She released her gaze from the man, who seemed friendly, yet nervous, and stared at the coffee. She would have to move to drink it. The alluring aroma made her mouth water. She swallowed . . . and winced at the pain, then winced again at the ripple effect in the rest of her muscles from wincing.

"Are you ill?"

The concern that knit his brow over the bridge of his straight nose made her flinch. A brief head shake was all she managed, and even that sent a shock of pain down to her toes and back.

"I'll help you with the shirt." Without waiting, he cupped the back of her neck and drew her forward. "Relax. You're safe with me."

She did relax. Any movement extorted too much effort and hurt more than letting him dress her. The blue-and-green-plaid flannel shirt, although large on her smaller frame, felt soft and warm on her sensitive skin. The shirt smelled of soap and her rescuer.

He rested on his heels, studying her for a moment while she returned the scrutiny. With effortless grace, he reached behind him and pulled a broken tree stump underneath him for a seat.

Steeled against the pain bound to fire each nerve she disturbed, she reached for the coffee. Cradling the cup in both hands, she brought it to her lips. It smelled wonderful. She sipped noisily, then swallowed, nearly dropping the cup from the sudden stab of fire in her throat.

He unwound her fingers from the cup and set it aside. "Look at me."

She obeyed, blinking back the sting in her eyes. The persistent, gentle probing of his fingertips along her neck and throat eased her fleeting anxiety over a stranger's touch.

"I won't hurt you," he assured. "Not intentionally."

His concerned gaze roamed with his hands.

Something was wrong. Terribly wrong. The sensation crept into her awareness with the stealth of fog rolling over a forest before sunrise.

"Do you understand me? Speak English?" A flicker of uncertainty clouded his eyes.

She nodded.

"Is your throat sore?"

She yearned to rail that of course her throat was sore or she'd be able to swallow the coffee she wanted so badly. Instead, she afforded him only a curt nod.

"Can you speak?"

She opened her mouth to give him a demonstration of caustic eloquence. And could not utter a syllable. The words were there, but the sound never passed her throat. Refusing to believe she had no voice, she tried again, straightening despite the shards of pain slashing at her muscles.

"Sh-h-h-h." He placed his fingertips on her upper lip and

drew her jaw up with his thumb. "Save the effort. I'll fix something to help you swallow easier."

Shaken, she beseeched him with her eyes to make it good. In response, he caressed her cheek before rising.

"I was taught how to blend herbs and prepare concoctions by a master—or I should say a mistress. She could work magic . . ." His step faltered as his voice faded. Without another word, he rummaged through his packs and selected a variety of pouches. Within minutes, odd-smelling herbs steeped over the fire, and the task of concocting the aromatic elixirs absorbed his attention. Not once did he glance in her direction.

She wondered at his pained expression when he mentioned the woman. Was the mistress of medicines his lover? Was she his wife? Regardless, she was someone he deemed important.

Melissa gazed beyond the man diligently crushing bits of a fragrant array of leaves and stems with a mortar and pestle. Ripples from jumping fish and errant kisses from a fickle breeze disturbed the mirrored surface of the lake. She stared at the water for a long time, her mind drifting in a haze of ambiguity. Finding neither fear nor peace there, she leaned against the fur-padded bolster and stared at the stars. Her eyelids grew heavy.

"Don't sleep yet. There are things you must help with first."

Melissa's eyes popped open. He sat beside her, a bowl in each hand.

"Gargle with this. I have no honey with me, but I doubt it will taste too offensive."

Hoping salvation rested in the bowl, she straightened and reached for it—then hesitated.

"It won't hurt you, I swear." As though understanding her reluctance, he smiled patiently. "I only hope it helps, if not to restore your voice, at least to ease the pain enough for you to eat and drink." Doubt clouded his eyes and erased the last traces of his smile. "You could speak before you came, couldn't you?"

She looked at him for a long time, then nodded. Could she? She shook her head. Why would she expect to if she could not? Her shoulders shrugged, forcing a grimace.

"Your entire body is in pain?"

A light snort conveyed that she did not appreciate his gift for understatement.

"I can alleviate some of that, too."

The confidence he radiated lacked any form of threat. She drew a heavy breath and reached for the bowls. The brew smelled of cherry and other vaguely familiar herbs. The first mouthful stung the back of her mouth, then soothed it. The second sent relief tingling down her throat. Soon, she realized the act of gargling and spitting might be something best performed in private. Yet he seemed unaffected while wiping her chin with a cloth until she finished.

He fetched a bottle from his pack, a piece of flannel, and a square of supple hide.

Her eyes narrowed in question when he hunkered down beside her.

"Castor oil isn't just for swallowing," he assured her with a knowing smile. "You're going to wear this."

Wear. Castor oil. Skeptical, she frowned.

He chuckled. "Go ahead and doubt me. At least you won't have to eat your words. Or the castor oil."

She exhaled loudly, ignoring his attempt at humor.

"Tilt your head back as far as you can."

She complied, stiffening when he wrapped the flannel around the slender column of her neck. The smell of castor oil tickled her nostrils. A mild, pleasant scent, it seemed benign. She let him fix the wrappings, hoping he knew what he was doing.

"I'll help you lie down." He supported her shoulders and rolled the log bolster away. "Comfortable?" He gestured toward her throat.

Surprisingly, it was. She nodded her thanks.

"We haven't finished. Shelan did not explain how you were to arrive, but from the looks of you, I suspect you've been through a great deal."

If she looked as bad as she ached . . .

Who was Shelan?

After slipping the fur pelts away from her right leg, he poured a spot of oil into the center of his palm. As he rubbed his hands together, a pleasant aroma of wintergreen filled the air. The first contact with her thigh nearly electrocuted her shrieking nerve endings.

She stiffened, recoiling from the effect it created in her sore body.

"Try to relax. This will ease the ache. Tomorrow morning you'll feel better, maybe even good enough to stand." With long, gliding strokes, he massaged the oil into her skin. The warmth touched the marrow of her bones. Effortlessly, he worked her knee, then kneaded oil into her calf. She was liquid when he started on her foot. The spots he rubbed on her sole and the pad of each toe turned her into jelly. The skill in his fingers seduced the soreness and replaced it with torpidity.

Enthralled by the miracle he was performing, she watched him work around her ankle and knead her instep. It felt strange, yet comforting, to see her rescuer's big, gentle hands massaging the aches from her limbs. She wondered who he was and how she came to be here with him. What was she doing in the lake? How did she get there? And from where did she come?

"I'm Rory McCullough." He flashed a smile at her. "I guess I'll learn your name when you can talk." His eyebrows rose in hope.

He finished with her right leg and started on her left. Braced for the initial shock of the stinging balm, his soothing hands rewarded her immediately. Her right leg felt remarkably better. The marvelous elixir and his skilled fingers removed most of the ache.

A fine sheen of perspiration beaded his forehead. The way he watched her watch him made her wonder if his interest extended beyond relieving her discomfort. A vaguely familiar warmth budded low in her abdomen.

Rory turned his head and peered into the darkness, but not

before she saw the flash of desire turn his gray eyes into storm clouds.

Melissa's eyes narrowed. First her voice, now her vision played tricks. Or had she misinterpreted his look? Surely she must have.

"Do you recall meeting Shelan at any time?"

Shelan again. Should she know the woman? If so, something else was terribly wrong. She shook her head, denying his question and her elusive memory. Whether the muddle in her mind came from the wonderful sensations radiating from his hands or not, she needed to straighten it out. Soon. But not before he finished the massage.

Rory drew the silken pelt over her legs, then straddled them, careful to settle his weight on his heels. After pouring more oil into the hollow of his palm, he slipped his hands under the pelts.

For a split second, she saw his eyes darken with passion. Then it disappeared.

This time she was sure of what she read there. She inhaled very slowly. The warmth in her lower abdomen rose to her breasts. What was happening to her? The glide of his hands along her hips, around her waist into the small of her back, deepened the ache at the juncture of her legs.

"Put your arms around my neck." He bent low over her.

Hesitant at first, she complied.

"Hold on." He rocked back on his heels, taking her into a forward sitting position.

Melissa closed her eyes and laid her head on his shoulder. Anything this man wanted to do with her was marvelous.

The sinuous pressure of his fingers along her spine turned her bones to mush. Wherever he touched yielded whatever ache her body had harbored. Reveling in the absolution from pain, she tried to recall the last time a man had touched her. And could not. Yet as sure as she was that she couldn't remember, she knew there had been a man. Shaking off the lethargy, she tried to recall one single thing about her life before Rory McCullough plucked her from the lake.

She struggled out of the comfortable embrace, frantic. She

searched Rory's narrowed gray eyes and felt the tension of his concern. *Why?* she tried to ask.

Desperate for answers, she leaned around him, smoothed the dirt beside the fur pallet and printed with her fingertip.

Where am I?

"We're in the mountains above Bellingham Bay."

Bellingham Bay. Bellingham Bay. Concentrating, willing recognition, nothing surfaced from the cavern of her mind. If she didn't remember it . . .

She smoothed the dirt and wrote in large letters, *How did I get here?*

He drew a deep breath, then released it slowly. "Shelan brought you to be my wife."

Chapter 4

Melissa gaped at Rory, hoping she had misunderstood but knowing she had heard him clearly. Someone named Shelan brought her here to marry a man she had never seen? Ludicrous. Melissa shook her head in disbelief. The enormity of her incredulity rivaled that of her unvoiced questions.

Why couldn't she remember what she had been doing moments before finding herself nude and drowning? For that matter, why couldn't she recall anything at all before Rory McCullough had hauled her aching body from the lake? And why did she feel as though someone had shaken her until her back teeth loosened?

One question at a time, she told herself. With a self-discipline wrought from years of practice, she garnered an aura of calm and set aside her tumult. Answers came easier if she didn't become confused with useless emotions. A deep-seated confidence bolstered her belief that she was not her worst enemy; the answers locked inside her head would reveal themselves in due time. For reasons unknown at the present, she had consigned those memories into a remote corner of her mind. When whatever had caused her to do so passed, they would come forth. She was sure of it.

Meanwhile, she refused the lunacy of becoming a stranger's wife. Denial gushed from the haze hiding all the things she knew and was.

"Please, don't look so worried. I wasn't implying anyone would force you into marriage. Besides," he added, "we may not like one another."

The tightness in his voice distracted her from the questions rolling through her mind. Belatedly, she realized his mar-

velous hands had continued to ease the soreness from her
shoulders. She relaxed, staring at him with unabashed curiosity, as he laid her back onto the furs.

The longer she examined him, the more she saw of his
character. He hid nothing, wearing his emotions as comfortably as he grew whiskers. The disappointment she sensed
from him evolved into resignation. Perhaps he had wanted a
wife. But certainly not her. How could he want her when he
didn't know her?

He took her left hand, turned it palm up, and studied the
calluses and lines. "Shelan said a person's hands reveal their
character . . . how hard they work, how careful they are . . ."
He ran a finger over her thick calluses, then turned her hand
over and examined her nails. "You know how to work hard,
and you're healthy. Your nails are clear and strong."

The assessment made her wonder if he planned to take her
to a market or a preacher. Neither appealed. Given his size
and strength, she might not have a choice. Anxiety set her
searching for avenues of escape.

"There's no cause for alarm, nothing to fear. I promise
you, no one will force you to do anything not of your choosing."

Fear? The notion was alien. She wasn't afraid, and wondered if she should be. Yet the gentle way he handled her
body and melted the aches denied the slightest reason for apprehension. Her head tilted, her eyes narrowed in an attempt
to understand why he treated her with such reverence.

The faint smile parting his well-defined lips carried a sadness. "You look as though you don't believe me."

Melissa softened and shook her head.

"Is that no, you don't believe me?"

Again, she shook her head.

The breadth of his smile remained unaltered, but it
reached his eyes and became genuine. She liked what she
saw.

"Your trust is well placed."

Instantly, her eyebrows shot up. Trust? She hadn't implied
that she trusted him, nor did she. Why would he think she'd

trust a stranger? Unless . . . he trusted easily. In that case, she had to decide whether a gullible man or a fool sat beside her.

His smile dimmed. "No, you don't trust me, do you?"

Slowly, Melissa shook her head, wondering if he read her thoughts.

"It shows in your eyes. I think you have not trusted much, and perhaps with good reason."

Melissa met his inquiring gaze without an answer for either of them. Instinctively, she kept her own counsel and refused her trust even though he had done nothing to abuse it and, thus far, much to earn it.

"For now, it makes little difference whether you trust me. However, you might sleep better if you could find it within yourself to believe you're safe within the circle."

Circle? What circle? Seeking an answer, any answer at this point, she turned her head away from the firelight. Several large boulders twelve to fifteen feet away stood like sentries in the shadows. Columns of carefully stacked rocks filled the voids between them to form an evenly picketed ring.

She pointed at the stones and looked a question at him.

"Yes. They mark the boundaries of the fairy ring." Rory shifted off her, straightened the furs to keep her warm, then settled on the stump he used as a bench. Forearms braced on his spiked knees, his loosely folded hands flexed restlessly without her flesh to massage.

"Before we leave this circle, I'll tell you all there is to know." A flash of a smile sent him peering into the darkness across the lake. "That is, I'll tell you what I know. Whether you believe it is up to you."

She touched his hand. Frustration at her inability to speak grated on her nerves.

Rory shook his head. "Tomorrow. It is a long story and you need rest to heal your throat." He tucked her hand beneath the furs. "I would like to know your name."

Surprised she knew it, Melissa rolled onto her side and printed her name in the dirt. She wasn't about to question the small gift of knowing her own name. At least, not yet.

"Melissa Fuller," he read. "Melissa—a pretty name worthy of your beauty."

Nonplussed, Melissa stared at him. Although she wasn't sure of much, she knew she and beauty were never in the same mirror, unless someone looked over her shoulder. Yet the sincerity of his compliment conveyed his belief.

"Good night, Melissa Fuller." Rory rose and turned his broad back to her. The action removed him from her reach as surely as a solid wall with a closed door.

Too many years of speaking his mind and the unvarnished truth had robbed him of tact. Yet there seemed no way other than directness.

Melissa Fuller oozed skepticism. Not once had she smiled. Judging by her attitude, he doubted that she smiled often even in the best of times. A pity. She had such an inviting mouth. The wariness she wore like a cloak thicker than the bearskin covering her reminded him of other distrustful souls he knew well.

Unless he looked at her, doubt that she was real crept up on him and threatened to turn her into a dream or a figment of his imagination. But the tingling in his hands served as a testimony of reality. Melissa Fuller was solid, breathing, and silent.

Perhaps, like most things, magic had flaws. The imperfections made it more acceptable. But he couldn't help wondering what had happened to her throat, why she couldn't speak. Clearly, she had expected to converse with him earlier.

Restless, he walked to the water's edge and scooped up a handful of pebbles.

He hadn't asked the right questions. He hadn't believed in Shelan's magic, not with the zeal of a true believer. If he had, he would have asked from where, and how, she would bring the woman. What sort of trauma had Melissa Fuller endured because of the magic? Because of him?

Angry at his selfish negligence, he chucked a pebble far out into the lake. He should have asked if Shelan knew what sort of torment awaited the woman she summoned. The knots in her lean muscles provided testimony of an ordeal that would test a strong man.

Even so, he refused to believe Shelan had caused the woman any harm. More likely, she had rescued Melissa from some dire circumstance.

When he carried her out of the water, Melissa had looked soft. But when he massaged the knots and aches from her limbs, he discovered few soft areas. What made a woman mostly muscle and sinew? What sort of life had Shelan taken her from? Had she wanted to leave?

Feeling the questions too large for his comprehension, Rory tossed the last pebble into the dark water. Without a backward glance, he walked into the night beyond the enchanted circle.

Outside the fairy ring the chill of the air nipped at him. The guilt nagging at him grew heavier with each step. The unhappy woman hadn't volunteered to leave everything behind and become his wife. No woman worth having would do that.

His natural optimism dimmed with the inexplicable certainty Melissa Fuller wasn't given a choice in the matter. "Why not?" he muttered, running his hand down the flank of his packhorse. He patted the horse and checked the hobble. Shelan had assured him that nothing would bother the horse so close to the circle, and nothing had, though he had heard wolves and cougars in the distant night.

He ambled along the lake shore, pausing occasionally to gather stones and skip them across the water. Away from the circle, his thoughts became sharper, his thinking clearer.

Their strange predicament must have favorable aspects for Melissa. Lord knew, few women would view sharing his chosen path as one of them. All things considered, he owed it to her to help her find something that made her happy, or at least brought a smile to her sensuous lips.

Recalling Shelan's parting words—"The woman is all you said you wanted, and you are all she needs,"—gave him pause. Would Melissa realize she needed him?

Rory skipped a stone. It bounced five times before sinking.

Once Melissa's throat mended, why would she need him? He had little to offer a woman and even less for a wife. He had known the truth in the garden when Shelan first spoke of leaving. He had known it for years. How had he forgotten so easily?

He skipped the last stone over the water and returned to the circle. As soon as he crossed the stone barrier, his worry melted and the situation assumed a cheerier outlook.

Lack of sleep sapped his energy. He poured a cup of coffee and settled onto the stump. Without hesitation, his gaze drifted to Melissa.

She looked back, waiting, watching expectantly.

Rory laughed in spite of the ghost of guilt balanced on his shoulders. "I thought you were sleepy."

Melissa shook her head, then pointed at him.

"Yeah, I'm tired. It's been a while since I got a night's sleep."

She pushed up on an elbow. The effort deepened her perpetual frown.

"What are you looking for?"

She patted the bearskin, then pointed at him.

"My bed furs? You're in them." He sipped the steaming coffee, content to watch her expressive features wrestle with a solution.

"Don't be concerned, Melissa. When I get sleepy enough, I'll curl up beside the fire."

She regarded him for a thoughtful moment before directing her attention on the stones forming the circle.

"This is the first time—and undoubtedly the last—I've built a fairy ring."

The way her wide eyes scrutinized the boulders made him chuckle. "That's what Shelan said it was. Given what has happened, I believe her more now than ever." He glanced into his cup, then at her. She regarded him with an intensity that reached into his heart. "Maybe if I had given her more credence . . . more thought, or questioned her intent . . . you wouldn't be here. You would be safely tucked in your own bed somewhere, maybe even with someone you wanted to be with. It didn't occur to me before, but I must ask: Are you married? Do you have children? Will someone miss you?"

The vaguest hint of an irony he wished he understood softened her expression. She shook her head, and he wasn't sure if she was quietly lamenting her plight or laughing at him. Damn, he wished she could speak.

Melissa leaned on her left elbow, found a twig, and scratched in the dirt, *Who is Shelan?*

Rory shook his head slowly. Giving voice to what Shelan meant to him posed an enormous challenge. Words could not describe her place in his heart or the integral role she played in realizing the dream they shared. "Shelan is many things to me . . . a true friend, a mentor, a critic, a supporter, a port in a storm . . . and she left because she had no choice either."

Dead? Melissa asked with her stick.

Again, Rory shook his head. Shelan was dead only in the sense that he would not see her again. Recalling her rejuvenation, he drew comfort from knowing she lived on, strong and vibrant. "Oh, no, Melissa. Shelan is very much alive."

With a mixture of amusement and trepidation, Rory met her curious hazel eyes.

"Perhaps if I start at the beginning, things will become clearer." He sipped his coffee. "For both of us."

Melissa settled into the warm heaviness of the furs and curled her left arm behind her head.

"Ten years ago, I lived about eight hundred miles south of here, in San Francisco." Rory braced the coffee cup on the fingertips of both hands framed by his upthrust knees. "I'm an architect."

Seeing Melissa's raised left eyebrow, he nodded. "A very good architect.

"It seems only last year, but it was a full decade ago that I went to the wharf to keep an appointment with a prospective client. He was scheduled to arrive on the *Fortune's Bride.* The ship was late, which was not unusual. While I waited, I walked and reviewed the requirements he had sent to me.

What he wanted and what he needed were at odds. That's often the case in life as well as in business." The vivid details of the fateful day burst with clarity. He sorted through them, picking only the relevant points for her ears.

"While waiting, I wandered farther down the wharf than I had planned. That's when I found three men attacking a very old woman. She didn't stand a chance. Seeing those men beating and robbing a frail woman filled me with rage. I confess, I damn near killed all three."

His fingers flexed one at a time around the top and bottom of the cup. "I'm not a violent man. Hell, before then, I had never been in a fight. My size is a deterrent, I suppose." He glanced up and caught her rapt attention. Lord, he didn't want her afraid of him or believing he possessed a violent nature or a volatile temper. "Shelan said only a drunk or a man tired of living would take me on. I seldom drink and I try like hell to avoid deranged people. Consequently, no one has tested me.

"However, you asked about Shelan and I digressed."

As he straightened in preparation for continuing the story, Melissa touched her throat.

"Your questions will have to wait. It is difficult enough telling this with you silent. I doubt I could do it otherwise, but I will hold to the word I've given you."

Resolved to finish the explanation, he rolled his shoulders in an attempt to relax. "I carried Shelan to my home. That evening she began my long education with the healing plants. She had great recuperative powers. After she mended, she told me she had to leave San Francisco. I sold my business and my house, packed up, and we headed north."

Melissa sat up, startled.

He shook his head. "Yes, quickly, and without question. My friends speculated that I had lost my mind. Some thought Shelan and I were lovers despite the great disparity in our ages. However, you'd have to have known Shelan to comprehend why I never hesitated to give her what she needed. I have never had a doubt or a second thought, Melissa.

"On our quest to find where we would live, she told me

she was a magic woman." Rory gazed into the night, wondering why he had harbored such an aversion to believing the old woman's professed difference. "I did not want to hear it. I did not care. I told her she had to exclude me from whatever she wished to do. I wanted no part of it. She agreed and we never spoke of it again—until three nights ago."

He avoided Melissa's gaze while recounting his conversation with Shelan in the garden. Obligated to divulge the whole of it, he omitted nothing and endured the discomfort of revealing so much about himself.

Telling her of building the circle and what he witnessed within the stones flowed easily. The wider her eyes grew when he described Shelan's transformation, the faster he spoke.

"This morning, I searched for Shelan's robes, figuring you might wear them. They had vanished along with her sleeping furs and everything else of hers. When, where, I don't know."

Some of the tension holding him rigid on the stump eased. "It is an impossible story, isn't it?"

Melissa nodded.

"It is the truth as I know it. Do you believe it?"

Melissa shook her head, nodded, then shrugged her shoulders. Confusion and frustration at not being able to ask questions twisted her expression. She picked up the stick and scratched on the ground, then erased the message and tossed the stick at the fire.

"You didn't lie. That's something. You probably don't know what to believe, do you?" He identified with her quandary and ached to do something, anything to soothe the clash between belief and logic.

Melissa shook her head in resignation.

"You're here and neither of us knows how she brought you. I haven't the knowledge to send you back the same way." An image of pulling her from the lake made him frown. The ordeal had carried serious consequences. "I will book passage on any ship you wish and arrange transportation on any railroad you need to get home."

Irritated by a sense of honor dictating that he return her to her life, and possibly the arms of one she loved, he fed the fire. "Shelan didn't ask if you wanted to come, did she?"

Melissa shook her head with a certainty that added to the guilt heaped on his spirit.

"She brought you here for me, and I let her." He stood, glancing around for something with which to make a pallet. "It is difficult to explain. I did not disbelieve her, yet . . . This is my fault."

Finding nothing suitable for a bed, he returned to the stump. "There is something else you should know." He meant only to glance at her, but he could not tear his gaze away. She gave him her complete attention. "The circle. There is still magic within its confines. As impossible as all that has happened seems here, it is far more disruptive to the spirit outside these boundaries."

She pointed at him, then in the direction where he had wandered earlier.

"Yes. I felt it and didn't much like it. Shelan bade me to remain here for three days. You slept through today. We have two more left. All things considered, I think it wise to do as Shelan said I should. Have you any objections?"

Melissa's mind spun with a dozen objections. The entire scenario Rory had revealed smacked of the fantastic. Yet listening to every word he said and watching the play of deeper emotions on his guileless face made it just as impossible to deny. Although she questioned the validity of the story, his sincerity conveyed his belief.

The truth as he knew it. Truth had as many hues as those who professed to own it. Certainly she couldn't account for her presence in the lake, nor could she recall where she had come from—yet. Until she did, the fairy tale seemed as plausible as any explanation she could conjure up.

The quagmire of impossible answers to fantastic questions allowed no room for logic. Dimly, she considered rational pursuit useless until her voice returned.

Melissa set aside the dilemma. Rory McCullough's generous offer of returning her home touched her. She hadn't a clue where *home* was. Unless she remembered, she and Rory McCullough might share more time in each other's company than either liked.

She scooted to the edge of the furs, tucked them around her, then pointed at the empty spot beside her. The pallet belonged to him. Her sense of fairness would not deny him a place to sleep, even if it meant he would be next to her. Besides, sleeping on top of the furs near the fire would be more comfortable for him than on the bare ground.

"What are you doing?" Rory's head tilted with interest.

Melissa pointed at him, then at the space she had created.

"You would not be afraid if I slept beside you?"

The amazement lighting his tired eyes captivated her for a split second. She shook her head. If she knew nothing else, she knew Rory McCullough would not hurt her, nor would he force himself on her in any way. He backpedaled too easily, a characteristic she recognized as insecurity or a sense of unworthiness about something of tremendous importance. She couldn't decide which attribute fit Rory—insecurity or unworthiness—and she wondered why a man like him would have either.

"I accept." He pulled off his boots and set them aside.

Rory lay on his back at the far edge of the pallet, as still as the rock circle itself.

For Melissa to get comfortable beside a heat-radiating body took some adjustment. She tried lying on her left side. Her knees hung over the edge of the pallet and let cold air in under the bearskin. Gingerly, her body protesting each move, she tried lying on her right side and curling her arm as a pillow. Her elbow poked Rory's shoulder. Nothing seemed right.

"Use my arm for a pillow."

Lord, he sounded weary. She lifted her head.

Rory put his arm around her and drew her close. She nuzzled her cheek against his shoulder, comfortable at last. When he tucked the edge of the bear pelt around her, it felt as though they had cuddled for the night a hundred times before. She closed her eyes wondering why lying in his arms felt so right.

Chapter 5

THE DREAM WORLD of sleep turned fantasy into reality. Tongues of flame burned Melissa from the inside. Wanting relief from the heat besieging her secret places with eroticism, she sought the source. At the same time, she reached out in her dream, her hand stretched across the heavy masculine body beside her.

The barriers of elusive taboos disintegrated in a shower of glittering stardust. A delicious taste of freedom heightened her bravado. The fire burning in her veins leaped. The brilliance banished the cobwebs of inhibition. The clear light of the pyre incited a delicious hunger. Appeasement lay within reach. She sensed it on all levels. Pulsing flesh rose and fell beneath the power of her avid touch. The scent of male, virile and hard, perfumed the air, filling her nostrils. The faint taste of perspiration salted the tip of her tongue.

The heat intensified, drawing her into the vortex, where sensual fulfillment waited. The solution breathed under her touch. Yielding to the seductive promise, she pressed closer.

A barricade thwarted her from reaching what she coveted with such frenetic desire. Her entire body writhed, pushing, tugging until she vanquished the impediment. Still, she wasn't close enough to the bliss that promised to extinguish the blaze consuming her.

Floating in the surrealistic obscurity of dreams too long denied by practicality, she recognized the final impediment as clothing. So simple. Get rid of it. Seize what she craved to the depth of her soul. Kissing, tasting, caressing, she gloried in the flavors and textures of sweet, dangerous dreams.

"Melissa."

The object of her desire responded with a summons of his own. The yearning in his voice encouraged an instinctive craving to know all of him. That pleased her. His response fed her hunger. She redoubled her efforts for possession.

"Melissa."

In the dreamland where every instant brought something new, her hand lost all sensation. Greedy fingers flexed in thin air, still searching for the elusive response she hungered for. Her breath sounded in rapid gasps. She wanted the man beside her more than she had wanted anything.

"Melissa."

The strident call of her name shattered the tendrils of the dream, leaving her aching, feverish, and breathless. She opened her eyes to an exposure of flesh patterned with silken chest hair. Immediately she squeezed her eyes shut, shocked that her subconscious could produce such a vivid carnal fantasy.

"Melissa? Are you awake now?" The rumble of his voice in his chest reverberated against her parted lips tingling with the taste of his skin.

Please, God, make this part of the dream, she prayed. She forced her eyelids open, then slid her gaze sideways. Frozen with shock, she stared at the powerful fingers wrapped around her wrist. As the last shreds of sleep faded, reality crashed down. The startling evidence of the dream's intensity lay before her. For a heart-stopping moment she tried to deny that she had acted out the dream with the man beside her. The erotic play of her subconscious had become all too real. Her potent quest for release had found a fulfilling answer in Rory McCullough. If he had not awakened her, would she have continued undressing him? Then what?

Rory's unbuttoned shirt revealed a broad chest sprinkled with golden-brown swirls of hair that glistened in the morning light. His chest rose and fell in the quickened pace of arousal.

"Do you want this as badly as I do?"

God help her, she did and knew she'd regret any answer she gave.

She raised her head and looked down the length of his body. Her naked inner thigh rested on the proof of his desire. Rory held her hand above the gaping top button of his fly. A different kind of heat rose from her toes. The flush of passion became the mortification of embarrassment.

Stricken, her gaze flew to Rory's face for the full impact of his reaction. What could she say after undressing him? Exploring him? If he ridiculed or laughed at her, she'd crawl into a hole and pray for death.

Not a hint of a smile eased the tension evident in the fine lines at the corners of his mouth. Gray eyes filled with hope and hunger regarded her without blinking as he brought her limp fingers to his lips and kissed each one with a tenderness that made her ache.

What kind of man rewarded her unforgivable invasion of privacy with kindness instead of revilement? She preferred his anger. That, she understood.

Gingerly, she slipped her leg off him. When he released her hand, she drew the bearskin over her hips. "I'm sorry," she mouthed, hoping he understood her regret, even if she did not.

"You're sorry?"

Her solemn nod cast a sorrow in his enigmatic gray eyes.

"So am I, but for very different reasons." Without another word, he rose, shedding his few clothes with each step he took closer to the lake.

Melissa gawked. Though certain she had seen many men in scant clothing, she was just as positive none had ignited the libidinous desire now surging through her.

The long stride of his muscular legs continued into the cold water. Within a heartbeat, the lake caressed the tight moons of his buttocks and closed on his narrow waist. Not a splash broke the still air when he lifted his powerful arms and surged forward.

From amid the furs, she watched long, even strokes propel him toward the center of the lake. Incredulity dulled her agitation. She wanted him, desired him, with an abandon that consumed her. The delicious slivers of promised fulfillment became aches in her lower abdomen. It seemed crazy. Not only had she lost most of her memory, she'd lost control of her body.

Last night, she'd hoped clarity would accompany the cool light of morning. She'd have even settled for a modicum of logic to emerge from his outlandish story. Instead, the morning brought a maelstrom of erotic passion and more confusion. Whatever caused the dream had seared her with near-lethal desire.

She had undressed a stranger. She had kissed and intimately explored him. And at the moment, she wanted to do it again and continue caressing him, loving him—making love with him—until the hunger inside her was satisfied.

The base excitement become one more thing defying her comprehension. A woman who instinctively relied on logic, not emotion, to guide her, Melissa found no middle ground where her actions made sense. In a short time, the rules of life and the laws of nature had crumbled around her. What was this place and who was the man who affected her in such bizarre, wonderful ways?

Finding only more questions, Melissa stood up. Rory's plaid flannel shirt hung from her shoulders to the middle of her thighs. Absently rolling up the sleeves, she scanned the water until she spotted him approaching the far shore.

She started toward the edge of the lake. The soles of her tender feet registered every pebble and sharp twig. The soreness lingering in her muscles seemed nothing in comparison to what it had been before Rory's healing oils and hands.

The simple act of washing her face quelled some of her disquiet. Running damp fingers through her short hair, she saw Rory in the middle of the lake now, swimming toward her. She gritted her teeth, gathering her bravado. She'd face him and the aftermath of her actions when he emerged from the lake. Nobody ever died from humiliation, she told herself. It will pass—not comfortably, not easily. Wryly, she admitted that her inability to speak absolved her from bungling any attempt at an explanation she didn't understand.

Unsure whether she could sustain another potent dose of

his masculinity, she fetched his clothing. With his trousers beside her, she tucked her knees under her chin and pulled the big shirt down like a flannel tent over her legs. From her perch on the boulder nearest the water she monitored Rory's approach.

Rory stood up a dozen feet offshore, his gaze finding hers. Water streamed down the triangle of darker chest hair that narrowed to a small line disappearing just below his navel and lapped at his abdomen. Spikes of wet hair clung to his face and neck. He pushed at a cluster draping his left eye and shook his head. Droplets flew in all directions.

The water was cold. She held up his clothing as an invitation.

"Are you sure you want to watch me dress?"

His deep intonation shattered the spell. Yes, a voice answered from behind the haze in her brain. She had been anxiously waiting for him to emerge from the water, ready to feast her eyes on all of him. Already, the heat of desire danced in her veins.

Drawing a calming breath, she shook her head, believing she'd lost more than her good sense in the last day or so. A lance of guilt pierced her fresh embarrassment. She placed the clothing on the rock and turned her back.

Eyes closed, she listened to his approach. He stood so close she heard him breathe and the soft rustling of his clothing as he dressed. Her mouth went dry as she imagined every detail she'd glimpsed of his fully aroused body. Her breathing quickened. She drew her knees up a little higher on the boulder to collect herself and adjusted the shirttails over her feet. Instead, a fleeting fantasy rolled through her mind. In it, he wanted her as badly as she wanted him. Naked, they tasted, kissed, and writhed with uninhibited passion.

"Don't think about it," Rory whispered, resting a cool hand on her shoulder.

The fantasy evaporated into a cloud of sexual frustration.

"I can feel it rolling off you and it's burning me. There is more happening within this circle than either of us understands." He traced the cords of tension between her shoulder blades.

Melissa hugged her knees. If she turned and saw the patient understanding she heard in his voice reflected in his eyes, she'd lose what little remained of her rational mind.

If only he would become angry, or ridicule her in a tirade, her defenses would rise in response. Harsh edges and verbal retaliation came automatically. She understood how to fight for and defend herself. But kindness? Understanding? Nothing had prepared her for that.

The manipulation of his strong fingers on the knots in her shoulders eased the physical tension. Slowly, she let him seduce her into relaxation. She clung to the illusion of choice, all the while suspecting she had none when it came to him.

"I have an extra pair of pants we can cut off for you. We're going to have to walk out of here in a couple of days. Will you be up to that?"

Lethargic, she nodded. She'd walk to the moon and back if he gave her another massage like last night's.

His thumbs rode up her spine, working out tiny muscle knots and tensions. "I'll make a pair of moccasins for you. They'll do until I get you home. To my house. We'll get some practical clothing for you in Fairhaven."

She started to tell him she didn't know where home was. The words never got past her throat.

"Hungry?"

She nodded, savoring the marvelous way he worked the kinks out of her muscles below her shoulder blades. If magic existed, it lived in his hands.

"How does your throat feel? Better?"

Again she nodded, hoping he'd continue massaging the knots from her back.

"Can you speak?"

The hope in his voice added to her disappointment that she could not.

"Perhaps it will take a while to recover your voice. I'll prepare another gargle and freshen the castor oil poultice." He squeezed her right shoulder, then turned away.

The absence of his touch left her as isolated as the rock upon which she sat. When she bowed to the inevitable and straightened her legs, the trousers he promised lay beside her. She pulled them on and looked for a way to hold them up.

"Here," he called, cutting a length of rope from a coil beside the provision packs. "I don't have a spare belt. This will suffice."

She threaded the rope through the heavy twill belt loops, then tied it. Not a muscle twitched while he trimmed the long pant legs with a Bowie knife.

"That should do for now." He slipped the big knife into its scabbard, then grinned up at her. "I'll see what we have for moccasins after breakfast. Think you can eat something?"

Right on cue, her stomach rumbled at the mention of food. Melissa shrugged, then pointed at the cold coffeepot beside the fire.

"We'll try it."

She watched him, certain she had never met a man like Rory McCullough.

Melissa wiggled her toes in the comfortable moccasins Rory had fashioned. He had measured, cut, and stitched the hide with the precision of a gem cutter. Most amazing was the tiny stitching in even rows. Tracing the lines, she glanced at him, amazed by the nimbleness of his big fingers with the small needle and tough hide.

"It is only sewing as women must do all the time," he murmured.

She shook her head, then accepted the herb broth he had prepared.

"You do not sew?"

His amazement almost made her smile. Instead, she fingered a button, raised an eyebrow, and cocked her head as an explanation of her expertise with a needle and thread.

"You can sew on a button?"

Nodding, she blew on the broth. It smelled like medicine. Whatever it took to restore her voice, she'd wear, drink, or do. The countless questions clamoring for answers demanded that she speak soon.

He offered a twig, then flattened the ashes rimming the fire. "Let's learn what we can about each other. You start. Ask whatever you want. I'll answer."

After the briefest hesitation, she bent to the task of printing in clear block letters. *Where are we?*

"Washington Territory, about twenty miles inland from Bellingham Bay. When we leave, we'll travel west, to the home I built a little south of Fairhaven. Shelan and I searched long, nearly a year, before finding that spot. It took me another year to finish construction on the house."

The pride he emanated made her wish he'd elaborate. Before she could ask more, he changed the subject.

"My turn. Where is your home?"

She had deliberately tried not to think about the enormous hole in her memory. She stared at the ground, at a loss for a response. The stick dangled in her hand. The forces obscuring her memories lacked the symptoms of amnesia. If she'd had a true case of amnesia, she wouldn't have remembered her name. No, this was different. She knew what was missing, but not how to get it back.

For a moment she studied Rory and considered fabricating an answer. Instant shame denied the lie. Rory McCullough's openness and honesty demanded that she treat him with the same respect.

"Do you trust me so little that you will not tell me?"

Hating the disappointment in his voice, she pressed the stick into service. The first letters bit hard into the fragile gray ash. The ashes crumbled, nearly obscuring the words. *I don't remember!!! I try. Don't know.*

Perplexed, Rory touched her shoulder. "What don't you remember? Where you live, or how to get there?"

Both, she wrote, staring at the ground. *Each time I feel near, a haze shuts everything out.* She didn't want to see his face during the long silence that followed.

The written admission brought greater vulnerability. Unable to speak, alone with a stranger in the middle of a pristine forest, with no idea of where she came from or how she got here—defeat reared its head. She had beaten the monster back countless times in the past. Of that, she felt certain. The trouble was, she couldn't recall those times or the reasons.

She turned her head. Rory seemed absorbed in thought, staring right through her. Again she wondered who he was and how he made her feel she could tell him anything. The sensation smacked of trust, but she knew it could not be. Instinctively, she trusted no one, except herself. Herself. Someone she no longer knew . . .

"Do you recall anything before you arrived here?"

Melissa shook her head, then wrote in the ashes. *Impressions. Feelings. Snatches of memories. No sense. Nothing makes sense.*

She smoothed the ashes, then continued. *Something happened. It will come back. I'll remember. Know why, how, I got here.*

"That's probable. With a little time, your voice and memories will strengthen. I've seen memory loss before."

Rory drew a heavy breath. "A couple of years ago, friends in Seattle brought a ten-year-old boy to me. Darin was quiet and very battered. With Shelan's help, I cared for him. After his physical injuries mended, he worked hard and showed great promise in his studies.

"One day I took him into town as a treat. He asked to see the ships, so we visited the harbor. Something he saw there terrified him. I don't know what it was, nor could he tell me later. Shortly after the incident, his memories started returning."

Rory's gray eyes hardened with an intense anger that froze Melissa. Whatever Darin told him still held a fierce grip. She never wanted Rory's cold ire focused on her.

"It was not pleasant for him, then."

She scratched with the stick. *Or for you.*

The statement etched in ashes said what he would not.

"He had nightmares for a while. With Shelan's gentle touch and patience, he learned how to take some of the sting out of the dreams. Eventually, their horror faded and they went away. When he needs to speak of some new thing he remembers, we do so."

He lives with you? His regard for Darin lay clear, just as his deep love for Shelan also shone in his eyes at the mention of her name

Melissa had trouble reconciling her desire to blame Shelan for her plight with the tenderhearted woman Rory had described. Of course, to blame her meant she believed Rory's incredible story. The trouble lay in not being able to disbelieve it.

"Not exactly. My point is that Darin was a child and less equipped than an adult to deal with the aftermath of terrible things that happened to him. You're strong, healthy, and older. If Darin, a frightened child, regained his memories, it seems likely you may have an equal or better chance of remembering."

Encouragement?

"You want to remember. Darin did not."

Better not to?

Rory stiffened, causing her to do the same. The man wore his feelings outside his clothing.

"Regardless of what the truth is, it is better to know the whole of it. Half-truths, omissions, and lies can haunt you. Intentional ignorance hurts you and helps those who mean you harm. Ugly or pleasant, there is no weapon against fear like the truth."

Is experience talking?

Rory smoothed the ash slate. "Sometimes secondhand experience is harsher than firsthand action. The lesson, once learned, isn't easily forgotten. Speaking of which, what do you remember—besides how to read and write? A man? A husband and family?"

Melissa's respect for him grew. He provided glimmers of soul-baring insight, then changed the subject before she pressed for more. If she could speak . . . but she couldn't, and he had answered more questions than she.

No man.

"Hmmm."

She glanced at him, wondering at the meaning of his almost-comment.

No children. Wouldn't forget.

"You're sure?"

Jaw clamped, she shot him a withering glance. She was not her mother or her father. She'd never forget she had a child, let alone throw it in a dumpster because it proved inconvenient.

Melissa paused, feeling another tiny piece of her past slip from behind the haze and fall into place. The realization of being tossed into the trash like so much garbage filled her with revulsion.

"Okay. You wouldn't forget you had a child."

No family.

"I'm sorry," Rory whispered.

Inexplicably irate, she printed in bigger letters. *No sorry—can't miss what I never had.*

"Yes, you can."

I don't. Futile. Stupid. She threw the stick down and walked across the circle to a mossy boulder near the lake. Carrying on a conversation via a stick was difficult. Arguing was impossible. Who was he to tell her what she did or didn't miss? She didn't know which bothered her more, not having a family or having him feel sorry for her. The last thing she wanted from him was pity. She detested pity from anyone, especially herself.

"Are we having a disagreement or are you having a temper tantrum?"

Melissa spun on her heel, her arms locked across her chest, and glared at him. She'd never thrown a temper tantrum in her life! That she knew. If the vile monster of injustice escaped the tight cage she held it in, she'd scream and not stop.

A sensation of screaming in anger, helplessness, and outrage flashed across her mind. It disappeared before she collected herself enough to seek details.

Stunned, she touched her throat. Had that happened? Had she let it out, and now could not gather the million, invisible tendrils to put it back? Had she screamed so loud, so hard, that her vocal cords went silent? Why?

The questions tumbled unmercifully. Out of the chaos came more uncertainty. If the tumult would quiet just a little, she might divine whether whatever brought her here caused the horror or rescued her from it. Every problem had at least two sides. Figuring which side faced up was the cornerstone of a successful starting point for any solution.

"Family is important to me. I apologize for assuming it was important to you too."

She wanted to rage at him not to expect her to care what he thought, but it did matter. And she didn't know why. That admission further rankled her.

Resentment for her inability to express the myriad conflicting things crying for release stiffened her. She tried to speak. No sound emerged, and still she tried to force the words.

"Don't." Rory's stern command left her jaw hanging. "You'll undo what little healing has occurred if you strain your throat again."

Glaring at him, she knew he was right.

"Frustrated?"

She continued glaring, not dignifying the question with an answer.

"I suspect that you tend to speak your mind." Curiosity twinkled in his probing gaze.

She folded her arms across her abdomen.

"You're angry, too. Why?"

She gazed across the lake. The mountains cast long shadows as the sun dipped behind the peaks. Yes, she was angry. Livid.

"Do you know why?"

Melissa slowly gave him her full attention. She extended a hand and tilted it back and forth. The true source of her anger eluded her. Just as puzzling was the breadth and depth of the anger. Nothing changed because of it. Useless. Like guilt. Unproductive.

"Do you know how to fish?"

What on earth did that have to do with—?

"I'll teach you."

She didn't want to learn how to fish. She wanted her voice back, her memories, her life.

"Sometimes fishing has nothing to do with catching fish," he explained, while roaming the camp and gathering his paraphernalia. "Sometimes it is more about feeling like you're doing something while your mind sorts through what's bothering you. It has proved beneficial for me many times. I've fished for hours and drowned a lot of bait without catching a fish. Then, I wasn't fishing because I was hungry; I was fishing for solutions. More often than not, I found them in the form of little voices whispering details or secrets I may have forgotten in the mayhem of daily living. Want to give it a try?"

The man possessed the patience of a saint, but she didn't want to drown anything. Nor did she want to hear the dozens of little voices in her mind. She wanted to hear just a single, clear one. Shaking her head, she walked to the furs and sat in the middle.

Unaffected by her refusal, he stood on the boulder farthest out in the lake and proceeded to fish.

Melissa stretched out on the furs, her gaze trained on Rory until her eyelids grew heavy. Through the long, slow blinks, he remained steadfast at the lakeshore, seemingly oblivious to her scrutiny.

Her eyes closed a final time as she bowed to sleep. Maybe the whole thing was a dream and she'd wake up where nothing strange touched her. Maybe.

Chapter 6

THE FIRST RAYS of morning sun woke Rory. The fire at the center of the stone circle burned low. Relief flowed through him. He had slept on his side and facing the lake all night. He doubted that he had the fortitude to stop Melissa if she had another dream like the one that woke them both yesterday. Careful not to disturb her, he rolled into a sitting position.

She had tried to say that she was sorry she had set him on fire with her exploration. *Appalled* better described her reaction.

He was sorry, too, for a different reason. Selfishly, he wanted her to desire him with such fervor while she was awake.

Watching the deep rise and fall of the bearskin hiding her breasts, disappointment gave way to shame. Her depleted physical condition required all her energy to mend. The kind of lovemaking she had initiated in her dream state would have drained her.

The phantom trails of her hand and mouth across his body warmed in anticipation of her touch. The rock-hard arousal straining his trousers accompanied the quickening in his breathing.

Disgusted by his response to an incident best forgotten, he left the pallet. He undressed and waded into the cool lake, which welcomed his overheated body.

The second time he pushed away from the far shore, physical desire yielded to a rational line of thinking. Melissa faced monumental obstacles. Until she recalled her origins, it was impossible to restore the fabric of her life. It might be too late already. Telling anyone that a magic woman had spirited her off to become a stranger's wife would land her in an asylum.

Melissa became his responsibility the moment Shelan summoned her. He marveled that he had been a part of Shelan's plan for getting a wife. He sure as hell had not thought it through.

Some helpmate, he thought testily, wishing Shelan would return for five minutes. Melissa could not cook on an open fire. She could not even make coffee. And the thought of making love with him while awake scandalized her.

Ever the optimist, Rory tried to find a positive side.

Midway across the lake, he grinned into a face full of water. Although she didn't fish, she couldn't scare them away with idle chatter while he had his hook in the water.

Encouraged, he sought another bright spot.

Considering her frustration and anger the previous evening, her silence might be a blessing. The way her eyes had pinned him with an exhausting fury had revealed a feisty spirit and a hot temper. Together, they might have flayed the hide from his body if she had succeeded in speaking.

He glanced in her direction before leaving the lake. Melissa lay on her side, the bearskin hiked up over her shapely thigh.

When he was dressed, he fueled the fire, made fresh coffee, and replenished the gargle and tonic for her throat. Upon hearing her stir, he departed the circle and checked on the packhorse. He took his time, then chopped firewood, stopping only when he realized they had enough for a week.

When he returned, Melissa sat beside the fire, her stick in hand.

He glanced at the message in the ashes.

Sorry. Angry at myself yesterday.

Rory cocked an eyebrow, skeptical. "I could have sworn you were angry with me."

Her head dipped toward her rising left shoulder. He recognized the fluttering tilt of her hand from yesterday.

"So-so?"

Nodding, she dropped the stick and fetched their coffee cups.

"Is your throat better this morning?"

She nodded, poured coffee and handed over his cup.

He took in every fluid motion of her body. The baggy clothing hanging from her shoulders and waist couldn't hide what he knew moved beneath it. The marvelous parts of her that his hands had not caressed, massaged, and rubbed held mysteries he ached to explore.

Rory gripped his hot cup tightly for a moment. "There's something we need to do today."

Her head lifted.

"Remember what I told you yesterday about being inside and outside the circle?"

She nodded, then waited.

"I'm taking you outside the circle today. We'll walk far enough to negate the effects of whatever is going on here." He sipped his coffee, his gaze locked on hers. No sign of last night's anger showed in her countenance. Satisfied, he set his coffee aside. "All right. Think you can eat something?"

It took a moment before she nodded.

"Good. Do your gargle and drink a cup of the tonic I made for you. After that, anything I fix will taste good."

An hour later, she finished washing the dishes in the lake. Rory threw a few provisions into a knapsack and picked up his rifle.

Melissa dried her hands on her shirttail. Curious, she reached for the Winchester.

Rory's grip tightened on the weapon. "Do you know how to use a rifle?"

Nodding, she glanced from the rifle to him, then back.

"Are you going to shoot me if I give it to you?"

Startlement brightened her features. The first glimmers of amusement lifted the corners of her mouth. It faded as quickly as it had come.

Rory was serious. He had no inkling of her intentions. A loaded gun in the hands of any woman made him nervous. Melissa had provocation. Shooting him might blunt the sharp edge of the unfairness she perceived in the circumstances thrust upon her.

The hint of mirth returned as she shook her head, crossed her heart, then raised her right hand.

The choice to trust her came with apprehension. Watching her closely, he gave the rifle to her. "It's loaded with a bullet in the chamber."

She unloaded it and cleared the breech so quickly that Rory had trouble following her actions. With the breech open, she checked the barrel for cleanliness. Satisfied, she lifted the rifle against her shoulder and stared down the sights. She tested the trigger but did not engage the hammer.

She admired the workmanship of the stock. After running her finger along the twenty-four-inch barrel, she hefted the rifle in her right hand and found the balance point. Studying the smooth magazine action, she loaded all fifteen .44-caliber cartridges. A final quick action sent a bullet into the chamber. She appeared satisfied and beamed with approval when she returned the rifle.

Most soldiers Rory knew couldn't handle a rifle half as well. What kind of life had Shelan plucked her from? He could think of nothing on this side of the law that made a woman firmer than most men and required weaponry expertise. The questions kept building. The sooner she remembered and recovered her voice, the better for both of them.

He took the Winchester and picked up the knapsack. "Let's go." For the moment, he preferred to remain ignorant of her marksmanship ability.

Melissa had awakened with bits and snatches of words from an old prayer rattling through her head. "Accept the things I cannot change." The phrase clung like the castor oil and flannel at her throat.

Practicing her credo of accepting whatever surfaced from the mire hiding the truth, she sought no answers concerning how or why she knew about the Winchester. After examining it, she decided that Rory McCullough owned a fine rifle and kept it clean and ready. She afforded him an admiring glance.

Thoughts of the rifle vanished when they crossed the circle boundary. The day grew sharper, the colors in the trees, grasses and lake brightened. Noises from the forest sounded closer, crisper. Overhead, an eagle cried and swooped toward the center of the lake. Wings flapping hard, it climbed at an awkward angle. A fish squirmed in the death grip of the eagle's talons.

The scenic world outside the strange circle of rocks assumed an ambience worthy of respect. In response, her senses sharpened as a benign veil lifted from her eyes. The breeze on her skin had a bite that belonged in the mountains surrounding them.

"Do you feel the change?" Rory's hand settled on her shoulder in solid reassurance.

The intensity of his expression made her wonder if the sharpness of color and sound affected him differently. She closed her eyes for a moment and drew a long, slow breath. Pine and the scent of grasses and damp earth filled her lungs.

She bared her left wrist, expecting to see the time of day. A faint band of paler skin ringed her arm above her wrist. A flicker of urgency rippled through her, then quieted. The time did not matter. She had nowhere to go and no way to get anywhere, except walk. Glancing at her companion, she held no doubt about who set the timetable or the destination.

The longer they walked among the trees and small meadows skirting the lake, the more niggling, evasive bits of thought flitted across her mind. They disappeared without leaving anything for her to grasp. The teasing put her on edge. Frustration deepened the sense of loss pressing harder with each step.

Rory gestured to a line of rocks jutting into the lake.

She sat, pulled one leg up and wrapped her arms around it. The contrast of the blue sky and lake against the countless shades of green relaxed her. The scene of mountains, heavy forests, and water felt vaguely familiar, yet not comfortably so.

"Are you strong enough to walk out of here in the morning, or should we wait another day?"

Head cocked, she looked at him. Anxiety tightened his features and deepened the faint lines at his eyes. She held up one finger.

"One question at a time." He settled beside her. "Do you want to stay another day?"

Part of her wanted to stay forever. The valley felt like an island in the heart of chaos. The sad response came from deep inside. She shook her head. Escape was not her way.

"You took a long time to answer. Are you sure?"

She looked around for a writing instrument.

"Wait." Rory brought the knapsack around. "I brought a pencil and paper." He grinned as he offered them. "Write small. That's all we've got."

She braced the paper on her uplifted thigh and started writing in the far left corner. *Very pretty here. Ready to travel. Aches almost gone. Thank you.*

"We'll leave tomorrow after first light and take it slow." The splash of a jumping fish caught his attention.

Two days to your house? She held the paper up to attract Rory's attention.

"Yes, if the weather holds. Longer, if it does not." He gathered a handful of stones from between the boulders.

Then what?

She studied him while he took his time answering. Whatever distracted him had nothing to do with the lake or their surroundings. He seemed uncertain of how to answer her question.

"What we do next depends on you, Melissa. I'll help you any way I can, but at the moment neither of us seems to know what that might be. Until we figure it out, you'll stay with me." The intensity of his gray eyes denied argument.

The idea held more appeal than wandering through the mountains without a destination. She shrugged, then sent her pencil into motion. *When voice, memory, return . . . I'll repay—*

His hand dropped on hers. "It is I who is duty-bound to repay. Caring for you while you mend is the least I can do. You're my responsibility."

Melissa shook her head. She was her own responsibility, not his. A deep self-confidence assured her that she could handle any situation, regardless of physical limitations.

"Yes, you are. You became my responsibility when Shelan brought you from . . . wherever you were. The only reason you're here is because of me. If I neglected that responsibility, it would dishonor all three of us and place you at a greater disadvantage than you face now."

The way he searched her face as though seeking an answer for an unknown problem warmed her more than the sun rising to its zenith.

"Besides, I want to care for you. It is also a way for us to learn about one another. We might like each other enough to get married."

She ignored the teasing light in his eyes. *Abhor marriage.*

"Do you know why?"

Melissa thought about the question. Images filled her mind. She almost caught a name. The rejection of a man who had once made her heart beat faster and her body tremble in anticipation flickered. Before she grasped the details of the vision, it fled.

Even as she accepted that someone she had cared for had hurt her deeply, she understood that the source of her aversion had much older roots. The sensation seemed more a validation than a reason.

They sat in silence while she sifted the glimmers of insight and snatches of memory rolling through her mind. Patiently, she waited for the emergence of a dominant motive. She straightened when a familiar isolation enveloped her and quelled the roil.

Trust.

"Trust? You don't trust people in general, men, or me in particular?"

Trust no one.

"I see." Rory picked a pebble from the cluster in his left hand. He sent it skipping across the lake surface. "Trust can be earned."

A heaviness that cast doubt on his optimism lingered from her exploration of the fickle memories hiding amid the haze. *Maybe you trust too easily,* she wrote.

Rory read the last entry, then chuckled. "It's possible, even probable. After all, I trusted you with my rifle. You didn't shoot me, so maybe my trust in you is justified."

Maybe. The day isn't over.

Rory's laughter boomed across the lake. She marveled at his good humor and the genuineness of his mirth. A stab of envy shot through her. Dolefully, she sensed that she had never been quick to laugh or find humor in a dour circumstance. Watching him, listening to the warmth and delight he found in her sarcasm, she felt a softening.

Accept what I cannot change. The phrase rippled through her awareness. The memories refused to come forth. She could not force them. Accepting that Rory McCullough wished to care for her even though he knew she did not trust him—that settled with the comfort of a new pillow in need of adjustment. Almost like trust, but not quite. She'd be on her guard for betrayal. Sadly, she realized that she expected it.

Rory removed the pencil from her hand and stuffed it and the paper into his shirt pocket. "Come on. Let's work out some more kinks from your legs. We have a long way to go tomorrow." He tossed the pebbles into the water and stood.

She let him pull her to her feet and left her hand in his as they walked. In truth, he had been kind and gentle with her. Although strange, it felt good having a protector during a vulnerable, chaotic time.

The warmth of his hand around hers permeated her body. The cool breeze did little to alleviate the radiant heat. Desire flowed through her veins like molten candy simmering on a low flame. She glanced at the hand holding hers. Big and calloused, it seemed incongruous for it to be the same gentle, masterful hand that had worked the knots out of her body.

They strolled through the woods near the lake for a long time before Rory changed direction. His easy explanations of the forest and its inhabitants enthralled Melissa. She stole glances at him, amazed by how much she enjoyed his company. She felt new, fresh in virgin territory with Rory as her guide.

Birds called and darted among the lofty branches in search of their nesting places. Occasionally, small animals rustled the underbrush. Melissa watched everything with a fascination that supplanted her preoccupation with the shroud hiding her past.

They entered a secluded glade dominated by a dark rock formation blanketed with moss and small bursts of ferns. A narrow creek gushed out of the base of the monoliths. The swift water had carved a crevasse in the forest loam. Farther down the watercourse, emerald-colored moss softened the boulders detouring the creek.

"Drink, then we'll eat something."

Melissa braced against the mossy, dark rocks and sipped from the source. The chilled water soothed her throat, which had become dry without her realizing it. She drank slowly, letting the cool balm work its magic before quenching her thirst.

They settled beside the creek in peaceful silence. Melissa ate a biscuit, washing down each bite with more water. At Rory's insistence, she chewed on a piece of jerky until her jaws tired.

"You did well." He rummaged inside the knapsack and withdrew a tin can. "So well that you deserve a treat." With a strange contraption that looked more like a prying tool than a can opener, he worried the lid open. Inside, the golden enticement of peaches awaited in heavy, sweet syrup.

A treat. A reward. Images raced through her mind too quickly to grasp, then disappeared.

With a thumb and forefinger, she fished a slippery peach half from the thick syrup. She tilted her head back and let the juice dribble from the peach into her mouth. When the trickle of sweet syrup slowed to a drip, she sucked the bottom of the peach before taking a dainty bite. Delicacies this delicious disappeared too quickly if each bite wasn't savored.

She swallowed. The syrupy fruit slid past her tongue without so much as a twinge from her throat. Instantly, the peach

formed a juicy pearl of nectar where her teeth had broken the
smooth surface. She flicked out the tip of her tongue to catch
the drip, then sucked at the ends before nibbling more. She
took her time and enjoyed every morsel.

When finished, she licked her fingers one at a time. She
paused with her forefinger in her mouth when she glanced at
the tin of peaches propped on Rory's knee. The pressure of
his whitened fingertips had dented the can. A peach half dangled from the fingers of his right hand. The syrup had
dripped onto the ground. Her gaze lifted in wonder.

The intensity of his dilated eyes radiated a controlled
hunger from his rigid body. No easy smile softened his
sculpted features. His chest rose and fell with slow, deep
breaths.

Melissa refrained from allowing her eyes to seek proof of
what her instincts proclaimed. Rory wanted her with a com-
pelling ferocity. Slowly, she lowered her hand from her
mouth, her gaze never straying from his. The desire simmering in her flashed to full boil. Unbidden, she slipped from the
rock and knelt before him. Using both hands, she lifted his
wrist until the peach hung just above her mouth. Bite by
small bite, she consumed it. With a deft motion of her
tongue, she drew his thumb and finger into her mouth. As the
last bit of peach slid down her throat, she sucked the remnants of syrup from his fingers, unsure which tasted better,
the syrup or Rory. Eyelashes lowered, she wondered if he
tasted this good all over. Instead of fighting the dangerous
speculation, she let it flow with the desire pulsing in her
veins.

"Good God. I thought the circle . . ." Rory's voice faded
when she removed his thumb from her mouth.

This close, his voraciousness lured her on a primal level.
Her breathing quickened. If she didn't regain some control,
she'd make a fool of herself again.

Seeking diversion, she stood and fished a peach from the
can, then tilted his jaw up. The shadow of his beard prickled
the sensitive web between her thumb and forefinger. Syrup
dripped on his chin until he opened his mouth. She lowered

the peach enough for him to take a bite. Fine lips that looked hard, like his hands, and promised an equal capacity for tenderness moved slowly as he chewed.

She fed him the rest of the peaches in small bites. Each time a drop of juice strayed, she longed to lick it off or kiss it away. Staring at a bead of juice in the hollow between his lower lip and chin, she wondered at the taste of his skin and the texture of his whiskers against her tongue.

Rory's powerful fingers closed around her wrist and lowered her hand to his mouth. She met his gaze and felt the heat searing her veins rise to another level when he slowly, sensuously drew one finger after another into the promised sweetness. The marvelous sensation of his tongue, teeth, and lips gleaning the last of the syrup from her thumb and forefinger shortened her breath. She licked her lips, her dry mouth suddenly salivating with the ravenous hunger to kiss him.

She swallowed hard and locked her knees to keep them from buckling.

"You taste sweeter than the peaches."

He drew another finger into the heat of his mouth. The velvet caress of his tongue against her fingertip sent a wave of desire rushing through her. The second wave left her lightheaded and aching.

Time held its breath while she contemplated the taste and texture of his mouth on hers, his tongue stroking hers, and the fiery flavor of passion. Regardless of the past lurking in a haze, she knew no man had affected her in such a potent manner.

"Melissa." The torment in his flinty gray eyes leaked into his voice. "It might be wise if we . . . if we walked again."

She stumbled in her retreat. He steadied her with a hand that trembled through her shirt. With great effort, she lowered her gaze. The tin can in his left hand was crushed to a nearly unrecognizable metallic mass coated with sticky syrup.

She watched the bunch of Rory's shoulders as he rinsed his hands in the stream. The play and ripple of his back under the flannel drawn tight enough to fit like a second skin begged for her touch. All she had to do was reach for him. Clearly, for reasons of his own, he wanted her; she wanted him just as badly.

That wasn't enough—or was it?

Straightening, she warned the whispers leaking through the veil hiding her memories that she would not walk away next time. Until she discovered a solid reason not to, she'd accept and explore whatever came her way. There was a niggling chance that she might never penetrate the mist obscuring the mysteries of her past. If so, she needed new memories.

Maybe she needed better memories, ones worth keeping.

Chapter 7

"WE'RE GOING TO fish for our dinner tonight and hope we catch enough for breakfast." Rory had followed the creek as it meandered through the forest, then back to the lake near the stone circle.

Crouched amid the paraphernalia emptied from the knapsack, he glanced at Melissa, then continued baiting two hooks. "Fish is easy to swallow. Good for you, too. Do you like it?"

She shrugged, unable to recall whether she'd ever tasted anything pulled from a lake.

"At least you're not predisposed to dislike it." He handed a baited line to her. "Watch. Then do as I do."

She complied, noting every ripple and nuance of his body with an intensity that had nothing to do with fishing. Mimicking his cast, she watched the cricket at the end of her hook sail into the still water near the burbling creek inlet.

"Slowly pull the line in." He spoke just above a whisper.

She followed his example.

Without warning, he jerked. "Got one."

Fascinated, she watched him play his line, her own forgotten and slack in the water. Moments later, he landed a good-sized fish. As it gasped and flopped, he ran a stringer through the gill and returned it to the water.

Rory baited his hook and cast again. The great arc sent the hook well past the center of the still water.

The glee twinkling in his eyes reminded her of a little boy delighting in the warmth of a late-afternoon escapade. It occurred to her that he enjoyed whatever he did. She marveled at the notion. Watching him from the corner of her eye, she wondered how he managed to have fun so easily. She wanted that secret revealed almost as badly as she wanted the fog lifted from her memories.

Perhaps if she studied him closely, she'd solve the mystery. Preoccupied, she pulled her line in when he told her to and let him bait it when the cricket was gone.

The sun had slid behind the mountains when Rory landed the last fish. "Pull your line in, Melissa. I think the cricket has drowned."

Realizing she was staring at him, she began retrieving her line. It had gained weight. She kept pulling, curious about what she might have snagged. Weeds, she figured. It felt like dead weight.

She yanked hard to free the hook. Without warning, the line came alive. Rory coached her, laughing, encouraging. "Let him have some line. He's a fighter."

The line played out between her fingers. An infectious excitement charged through her.

"Now haul him back. Hard."

Easier said than done, she decided. After several minutes, she wasn't sure who was playing whom. It seemed the fish was winning. She moved closer to the edge in anticipation of landing her catch.

In one great heave, the fish flew out of the water and flopped at her feet. Hopping from one foot to the other, she tried to get out of the way without stepping on the big, shiny mass thrashing around her ankles. The wet rocks turned to glass under her moccasins. Her feet slipped out from under her. Off balance, she teetered, her left arm windmilling before she unceremoniously tumbled into the water. The fish followed.

She broke the surface with a splash. Triumphantly, she raised her hand clutching the fishing line.

Rory's booming laughter echoed across the lake. "You have the makings of a true fisherman, Melissa. Take my hand."

She shook her head and thrust the jiggling line at him.

"Land your own fish."

Exasperated, she thrust it at him again. She needed both hands to climb out of the lake.

Chuckling, Rory took the line and landed the fish. "You caught the biggest one, Melissa. Beginner's luck?"

Grinning from ear to ear, she slapped her moccasins onto the rock one at a time. As long as she was already in the cold lake, she may as well bathe. She loosened her clothing, careful to tie the rope belt so she didn't lose it.

"From the looks of you, you'd rather play in the water than help me gut and clean these fish."

If that was the choice, he was right.

His halfhearted attempt at being stern delighted her. She held her nose and folded her knees until she sank. When she resurfaced and pushed the hair and water out of her eyes, Rory remained unmoving on the rocks above her. The grin that had danced across his features and in his eyes had disappeared. In the fading light, Melissa couldn't tell if he was concentrating on something or perplexed.

"Your smile is more beautiful than I imagined. I suspect you do not use it much."

The truth fit with something in the haze. Perhaps little in her previous life had warranted smiles. That also felt right. She wondered if she had the fortitude to make what lay ahead better than the life obscured by the mist.

Watching Rory gather the contents of the knapsack, then retrieve the fish stringer, she vowed to smile more. It seemed important to him. The small concession of a smile cost nothing on a personal level and seemed easy enough.

She took her time bathing, climbed onto the rocks and wrung the water out of her clothes. A chill rode the night air. Shivering, she dressed and worried her water-wrinkled feet into the wet moccasins.

The fire in the heart of the circle promised warmth. She hurried across the boundary—then stopped short.

Warm, thicker air leached the chill from her skin. Had the distinction not been so sharp, she might have attributed the change to the nearby fire. Other changes crept into her awareness. The line of trees seemed more distant and the lake darker. Something intangible settled over her.

"The spell Shelan placed on the fairy ring strengthened during our absence."

Her eyes followed the sound of Rory's voice. Crouched on the opposite side of the fire, he was barely visible in the flickering flames.

Like a moth, she gravitated toward the light. Embers flew on the heated smoke curls into the dark sky. She watched, savoring a buoyant serenity that quieted every uncertainty.

"Take the wrap off your throat. I'll fix a new one for you after we eat." Rory shoved the biscuit pan into the embers.

Content, she did as instructed, amazed by how wonderful she felt inside and out. She removed her soggy moccasins and set them near the fire to dry.

Rory's intense gray eyes met hers. The sight of him pleased her more than words could express. The sensation became a smile as natural as the air she breathed.

She raked her fingers through her wet hair. Wordless, Rory found a comb and offered it. She mouthed a thank-you, then dragged the comb through her tangles. Relying on the habit of years, she gave no thought to styling her hair, nor to anything else about her appearance.

Sitting beside Rory and the fire felt like riding a cloud in the Garden of Eden. Peaceful. Marveling at the utter sense of calm, she wondered if she had died. Grinning, she cast the absurdity aside. She felt too good to be dead, unless the Bible had overlooked the Archangel Rory.

"Eat as much as you can." Rory offered a plate of fish and biscuits.

Tonight the food went down easier. She decided she liked fish.

Rory nodded at her plate. "That's the one you caught. So is most of my dinner. It was at least a three-pound trout. We'll have the other fish for breakfast."

She savored every bite of food and washed it down with coffee. Meanwhile, she feasted her eyes on Rory. It would have been easier to stop breathing for all eternity than look away. He drew her in the same undeniable way a spring flower lured an industrious bee on a warm day. The desire denied in the afternoon crept back with undeterred tenacity.

She washed their dishes while Rory straightened and packed what they didn't need tonight or in the morning.

"Sit here." He gestured to the stump he used as a stool. "I'll make a new castor oil pack for your throat. After I'm done, climb into the furs and take off your clothes. I'll set them out to dry."

She followed his directions, relishing the feel of his hot fingers on her cool skin as he applied the poultice to her neck, aching to know his touch in more intimate places.

Tucked into the furs, she handed off her clothing.

Rory draped the shirt and pants on sticks pushed into the ground. He kept his back to her as he fed the fire. "That should keep you warm tonight."

Expecting him to join her on the fur pallet, Melissa scooted over to make room.

"You can have the furs tonight. I'm sleeping out there." He gestured at the darkness beyond the fairy ring. Without so much as a glance in her direction, he started for the dark perimeter.

A sharp sense of wrongness stung her. He was abandoning her.

The wildfire of desire blazing through her sent her into motion. Desperate to find appeasement in the only way possible, she sprang up from the fur pallet and ran after him.

He couldn't leave. Not when she needed him so badly. All logical thought fled. The barest hint of inhibition quailed in the depth of the potent, uncontrollable tide rising higher with each ragged breath she took.

She grabbed Rory's arm with both hands and yanked hard. Desire radiated from him and shot through her. He became essential to her next heartbeat. He couldn't, wouldn't leave her alone in the circle with this mounting need only he could assuage.

*   *   *

"Good God, woman! Get back in those furs!" Rory curled his hands into fists to keep from touching her. Since the episode with the peaches, he'd ached to strip her bare and taste every luscious inch before sinking into her. Lust and a blinding need to possess her slammed into him again. Each time, it hit harder than before and chipped away at his resolve to allow her to mend.

The heat from her hands flowed through him with an electric force. He tried to turn away, to save her from the need ravaging him. His boots felt nailed to the ground. In a quick motion, he unbuttoned his shirt, tugged it off, and wrapped it around Melissa's shoulders. If he gazed at her tempting naked body another second, he'd melt. Or he'd lose the last shred of his fragmented control and take her in the heat of passion.

Defiant, Melissa poked him in the center of the chest, then pointed at the pallet.

"Dammit, Melissa. I can't lie down next to you. Not without . . ." Defeat tiptoed across his resolve. "I'm trying to tell you, I want you too much to be trusted to sleep beside you and leave you alone." Had she no idea how he burned for her?

He inhaled sharply as she took his hand and tugged toward the pallet. Desperate to make her understand, he pulled his hand free, then cradled her face. The madness burning in him shone in her eyes.

"It's the circle, Melissa. It seems to intensify . . ."

The touch of her finger on his lips tested his willpower to the limit. A flick of his tongue would bring it within his mouth.

"I don't care what it is. I want you," she croaked in a whisper so faint that he thought he'd imagined it. She inched closer to him. The fine hairs on his neck rose. The sudden lurch of his erection straining his trousers became almost painful.

"It's the circle, Melissa. Shelan's spell is very strong. Tomorrow, when you're thinking straight, you'll rue—"

Again her finger pressed against his lips to enforce silence. The heat radiating from her fed the glowing force mushrooming inside him.

"Not tomorrow yet."

He turned and bent until his ear was inches from her mouth.

"Selfish. Don't care. Just know I need you, Rory."

"God help us both," he muttered between clenched teeth, then gave up the fight. With a will of their own, his arms slid around her. In that instant, he didn't care about tomorrow either. Just this moment and this woman.

He took her expectant mouth in a searing kiss. When the tip of his tongue delved between her teeth, there was nothing shy or restrained about the way she drew him further into her. Eager, hungry, she deepened the kiss, her body surging against his in the frenzy of an age-old rhythm.

Fire leaped through his veins. Needing her closer, he tightened the embrace. The shirt covering her shoulders slipped to the ground. The press of her breasts against his flesh became heaven and hell. Yet he needed much more than her delicious kiss and the voluptuousness of her breasts against his bare chest.

With eager hands, he explored the naked territory he ached to claim, needed to possess with a totality that would consume them both. The swell of her buttocks filled his hands. His fingers pressed into her flesh with the rhythm reflected in their kiss.

Need overwhelmed him. In a single motion he broke the kiss and swept her off the ground. For an instant he remained rooted, captivated by the neat, dark triangle of curls at the bend of her hips and thighs. The curve of her waist and indentation of her navel teased his appetite. His heart leaped at the sight of her aroused nipples proudly awaiting his touch, his mouth.

She regarded him with a forced patience. The dilated pupils of her hazel eyes met his in a way that made him believe she saw into his soul and hungered to devour it.

"It will be deep and hard, and all night, Melissa. Nothing gentle."

Her arms tightened around his neck. She twisted around until her mouth touched his ear. "Yes . . ."

Rory groaned when she drew his earlobe between her teeth and nibbled on it. He moved then, unable to get to the furs fast enough to suit his raging passion. On his knees, he laid her on top of the pelts and took her hands from around his neck.

"My boots," he managed in a shaky voice.

As soon as she released him, he tugged off his boots and socks, then pushed to his feet and removed his pants. Naked and on fire with as much lust as he thought the entire world possessed, he stood before her.

He understood the aching need and raw passion in her shining eyes. Beneath the surface, he saw the pit of her loneliness yawn as wide and deep as a river. He wanted to fill it, to mend her and heal his own aching loneliness. He wanted her on levels that surpassed his lust for her body.

Melissa lifted her open hand to him. Her left knee rose in invitation.

It was all the savage tempest inside him needed. He covered her body with his, sensitive to every inch of her soft flesh. Taking his weight on his elbows, he seized her mouth and let her devour him. His left knee slid between her thighs, which spread wide to accommodate him.

Her hands became flames flitting across his back, shoulders, and buttocks.

He tore his mouth from hers and found her hardened nipples. She arched into him, giving freely. If heaven had a taste, it was Melissa.

The smooth skin along her inner thigh pulsed in response to his erection gliding closer and closer to the paradise he sought.

Then she was tugging at him, trying to pull him upward. Reluctantly he abandoned the delicious rosy nipple. A wildness in her eyes conveyed a desperate ferocity that spoke louder than any words.

He shifted, allowing her to move her leg, then settled in the cradle of her thighs.

"Melissa," he exhaled, then claimed her mouth and drove into her.

The invasion wrung a sharp inhalation from her. In response, her legs rose and clamped around his waist as though to prevent him from fleeing. Given a choice, he'd never leave.

He wanted to go slow. He wanted to pleasure her to the depths of her soul. Instead, he consumed her while she devoured him. The need they shared drove him deeper and faster, and she met him with an intensity that carried them higher.

He felt the walls tighten further around his erection and curled his hands over her shoulders. Breathing hard, he broke the kiss and watched her intense expression and passion-darkened eyes.

"Let go, Melissa," he rasped.

Her climax brought on his in a shattering splendor of bliss that became death and rebirth into paradise. Nothing in his life had felt so beautiful, so elemental and all-consuming. The ethereal beauty of their union filled him with an intense joy so bright he surely glowed in the night. Melissa was the light, the source of fullness, and the other half of his soul. In that instant, he knew she was the only woman he'd ever love.

Feeling her tremble under him, he rolled them onto their sides. He enfolded her in his arms, unable to relinquish her nearness. Tenderly, he kissed her hair, her forehead, tilted her face up and kissed every bit of it, saving her mouth for last. He traced her lips with the tip of his tongue, then kissed each spot.

"We've just begun," he breathed, brushing his lips over her kiss-swollen mouth. "Before morning, there won't be any place on your body I haven't kissed and tasted."

The soft touch of Melissa's mouth at the hollow of his throat grew bolder as she explored and tasted him.

The magic was strong in the circle, he decided. The shimmy of her hips brought fresh life to his erection. How could he want her so soon after such complete satiation?

Melissa toyed with his ear, her hands leisurely exploring the contours of his ribs and shoulders. "My turn," she whispered, then she pushed him onto his back and sat with him buried all the way inside her. Her sudden, deep breath thrust her lovely breasts forward.

Rory grinned. All her treasures were exposed to his masterful, eager hands.

The small adjustment of her folded legs played against the slow rise of his hips. Melissa exhaled slowly, a smile growing broader with each little motion he made.

"You light up the night when you smile." Rory closed his hands around her hips and lifted her a few inches.

Melissa's eyes widened in surprise, which melted into silent laughter.

"Yes, Melissa, laugh with me. Make love with me." He brought her down as his hips rose and drove him into her. "Deep and hard." He lifted her higher, almost withdrawing, then held her.

The smile faded from her features. The lean specter of hunger gleamed in her eyes. She waited, her palms resting on his chest, her fingers pulsing into the wall of muscle beneath his heated flesh.

"Are you ready for me again?" He felt the spasms of her moist desire reaching for the head of his erection, clutching at him, trying to draw him inside the doors of heaven.

Melissa nodded and arched, throwing her head back, surrendering herself entirely to his whim. The show of trust humbled him.

His hips rose as he brought her down. Then nothing short of death could have stopped him from taking her to ecstasy. If the night didn't last forever, the memories would. Rory made sure of it.

True to his word, he made love with her until the first colors of dawn lit the eastern horizon and neither of them could move.

Chapter 8

DOUBT CREPT IN with the noon sun. Melissa lay still and pensive. Inhibitions shed like dandelion seeds in the night wind returned one fuzzy seed at a time.

The rise and fall of Rory's chest against her back reminded her of the abandon they had shared hours earlier. During their lovemaking, nothing else had mattered. She had given everything, including her trust, and had received more than she thought possible.

But last night wasn't real. The powers that brought her to the lake had changed the world inside the circle and her reality. No other explanation fit. The notion of physically restraining Rory and demanding that he make love with her . . . all night . . . it went against something lurking behind the veil hiding her true identity.

Determined not to repeat last night, she started inching away from Rory.

A calloused hand slid across her hip. His fingers spread over her lower abdomen and drew her closer. The flex of his erection against her back sent a thrill through her.

"Regrets so soon?"

The sorrow in his question added to a deep shame that refused any verbal acknowledgment.

"Sweet Melissa, we're the same people we were last night," he whispered with assurance into her ear.

Shaking her head, she denied it. Last night, she had been a wild woman who would not allow him to leave the circle and who cared nothing about consequences. She had taken what she wanted without consideration of the future. The irrationality of her actions perplexed her. How could something

that felt so right last night feel so wrong, so shameful, now?
It made no sense.

"Last night, we couldn't hide from who we are and what
we wanted." The tender caress of Rory's lips on her ear
added to her confusion. "No inhibitions clouded our desire."

She wanted him to stop touching her, stop talking, and
stop making her body crave his. "Last night . . . ," she managed in a raspy whisper that burned her throat, "That wasn't
me."

"Who else could it have been? We wanted each other then,
and we want each other now."

A tight, quick shake of her head deepened her denial.
Other than a bout of insanity, she had no explanation for her
irrational actions. Simultaneously, she possessed a certainty
that her behavior had been out of character.

To her chagrin, she did want him again. Heat coiled in her
tense body. The anticipation of having him inside her unleashed a subtle ache that increased with each breath. All she
had to do was shift her hips just enough to allow his powerful erection to slide into the cleft begging for him. Her
breathing quickened, but she remained still.

In the clarity of the bright noon sun, she found strength in
rationality. Whatever had happened to bring her to this place
made last night possible. It was over now. She would not be
ruled by desire. Succumbing to temptation led to disaster.

"What started here between us isn't over, Melissa, and it
isn't going away when we leave the circle. Neither am I.
After what we've shared, I couldn't. Not any more than I
managed to leave you last night." Rory's warm lips trailed
across her exposed shoulder.

"A great deal has happened. Undoubtedly, you need time
to adjust. We'll go slow from now on, if that's what you
need. When you want what we had last night again, you'll
only have to reach out to find me."

Melissa bowed her head and closed her eyes. At the moment, she didn't know what she needed, beyond the marvelous escape found in making wildly erotic love with him.

Even if she gave in to the desire raging through her, she would eventually have to face the consequences.

Last night she'd had no scruples, no control over anything except a means to assuage the inexplicable need for Rory McCullough. She didn't know him. Worse, she didn't know herself.

When he backed away now, loneliness crashed in on her with the force of a typhoon. It required all her resolve to keep from crying out or turning and reaching for him.

The gentle touch of his hand on her shoulder nearly destroyed her. "What we shared was as beautiful as it was wild. I didn't know a man could get as close to heaven without dying as you took me last night. Shelan's spell may have cast aside our reservations, but that was us, Melissa. Make no mistake about it."

Motionless, she listened as he rekindled the campfire. Moments later, he waded out to swim.

She rolled into a sitting position and looked out at the lake. Sunlight sparkled on the rippling blue water. Strong and sure, Rory swam toward the opposite shore. She pushed to her feet, not wanting to think about anything beyond washing up and dressing.

Melissa was grateful for Rory's silence as they ate a quick breakfast, then packed up the camp. When he brought the horse through the wide pickets of boulders, she realized that the fairy ring had become nothing more than rocks arranged in a circle. The magic had dissipated in the heat of passion.

Following Rory and the horse into the forest, she glanced over her shoulder. Rocks. Just a bunch of rocks. Nothing magical or even special.

But something inexplicable had brought her to the lake. If it wasn't magic, what was it? Where had it gone?

"Tomorrow we'll have to push hard to make it home before dark." Rory stacked another log on the fire roaring in the sizable clearing where he had set up camp for the night. "It's a hard trek, and I don't mind taking a couple of days if you need it."

"I'll make it." Her throat hurt, and her voice sounded like a frog whispering.

"I know you'll make it. That's not what I'm asking."

The sharp edge in his tone created a stillness in her. The change charged her senses. She dropped the furs she was spreading for pallets. Straightening, she turned very slowly and faced him. Her left eyebrow rose in question.

Rory stood beside the fire and brushed ashes and wood chips from his trousers. "I get the feeling you would walk through hellfire rather than admit you needed a rest or a drink of water. Since you give no indication of being tired, hungry, or thirsty, I don't know if I'm pushing you. I can't read your mind, Melissa."

Though she gave no outward sign, she tensed when he approached. Part of her was ready to run at the first indication of discord, another part ready to fight, and a third part remained a dumbfounded spectator waiting to see who would win.

Rory halted a step in front of her. His hand rose, then dropped to his side. "You're bruised all over your body. You have to be tired and sore. Is it so hard to say something?"

There wasn't anything to say. Complaining wouldn't ease the aches. Only time would heal the bruises sustained before he had pulled her from the lake. Meanwhile, life went on making demands. Surely he knew she wouldn't fall behind. She hadn't a clue to where she was or who she was, beyond her name and a few erratic, disjointed memories playing hide-and-seek with her awareness.

"I guess you think I'm a real bastard for last night. You're right. I didn't think about your bruises then. I didn't think about anything except that you wanted me as badly—"

Not wanting to hear the rest, she put her fingers on his lips, silencing him. "I'm fine. Tougher than you think."

His hand closed around her wrist. The tender way he kissed her fingertips melted a layer of her resolve to maintain a distance between them.

"I'm not fine, and not nearly as tough as I thought I was, or you apparently are. I've watched you all afternoon. You possess a daunting tenacity to push yourself that few men have." A sad smile touched his lips when he released her wrist. "Including me."

Nonplussed, she watched him turn away. There was something refreshing, yet startling, in his honesty. The revelation of his perceived inadequacy required a form of courage she lacked. Awed and more than a little humbled, she resumed laying out the pallets.

Within the confines of the fairy ring, she had thought him a straightforward man with simple ideals because of his openness, but suddenly the simplicity Rory McCullough embodied had become very complex. The man was a paradox. His admission of weakness required uncommon strength, a stength unrelated to the muscle and sinew of his powerful body.

Melissa fetched water from the creek dividing the tree-pocked meadow while he prepared the evening meal. With time to spare, she perched on a boulder and watched the forest shadows blend into darkness. The fascinating changes diverted her from thoughts of more pressing issues devoid of solutions.

"Come. Eat something."

Startled, she flinched, then caught herself before slipping off the rock. The man moved as silently as a breeze over the water. She grabbed a tree limb and swung her legs around the giant boulder.

"Would you like some help climbing down?"

She shook her head, wishing he was less solicitous. Such concern made her uncomfortable. Not knowing why it did irritated her.

"I'm fine," she rasped, then swallowed hard from the stab of pain in her throat.

"A simple nod will suffice. After you eat, we'll treat your throat." He stood aside, allowing her a path to the blazing campfire. "Stay close to the fire. We're in wild country and there might be wolves in the forest."

Night came quickly once the sun disappeared behind the mountains. Dropping temperatures warned of the coming cold. Overhead, a few clouds scudded over the stars winking in a lavender and gold sky.

Melissa sat near the fire, noting a cup of stew and clumps of bread masquerading as biscuits.

"Eat. There's plenty." Rory filled his cup with coffee and settled on a rock well to her right.

"Yours?"

"I ate. You didn't come when I called you. You seemed so preoccupied, I hated to disturb you." He sipped the steaming coffee. "It's getting late. We need to be on the trail by dawn if we're going to reach home before tomorrow night."

Melissa picked up the stew and ate in silence. Her throat hurt each time she swallowed. She reached for the canteen and found it in Rory's extended hand. For a man who couldn't read her mind, he was doing a pretty good imitation.

Later, she laid on a pallet of cushy pine boughs and wrapped the bearskin around her. Although she was physically exhausted, sleep eluded her. Rory's steady, deep breathing showed that he had no such problem.

Melissa rose, careful not to make any noise, and slipped into her moccasins. The night chill reached through her shirt. She hugged herself and stared at the heavens.

The stars drew her like old friends at a reunion. Seeking a better view, she ventured out into the darkness. As her eyes adjusted, fainter sparkles appeared.

Soon she found the boulder she had used as a perch near the creek. She felt her way and climbed on the top. Clutching a raised knee for balance, she arched her head back.

A quiet excitement calmed her disturbed thoughts. The peace it imparted surprised and delighted her. What was there about the stars looking down with a patience older than time? Their constancy soothed her unrest.

The constellations twinkled, as if greeting her. The summer triangle rode high in the night sky. The archer, Sagittarius, dipped into the treetops.

Her gaze rose to the star at the western point of the triangle.

I know you. The recognition made her smile. It took another moment before the name came. "Vega in Lyra," she whispered at the constellation, then grinned at the three bright stars forming the summer triangle.

High in the northern sky she found another friend. The heavens pivoted on Polaris, bright and clear. A second name flitted through her memory.

Tib? Tibia? Tibbin . . . Tibbens.

She also knew Polaris by the name Tibbens. How strange. Why would she have called the polar star such an odd name?

Melissa exhaled loudly and relaxed her balancing leg. For a long moment, she sat perfectly still and let her gaze drop to the creek rushing at the base of boulder.

Reluctant to hope, afraid to analyze, she let the tiny tendrils of memory reach inside the haze and pull out one bit of knowledge after another.

When she lifted her eyes to the heavens again, she knew every constellation pattern and star name. The longer she stared at Vega, the more memory gems glowed in the light of awareness. Her gaze flitted across the sky. One by one, she classified the stars into categories ranging from white dwarfs to red giants. Almost as quickly as she identified them, some winked out, their dim light overpowered by the rising full moon.

The triumph of recalling a whole body of information sent adrenaline surging through her. The rest of her memories might return the same way. Something would trigger them a chunk at a time. Optimism fueled her hopeful excitement. Patiently, she waited, but nothing more emerged from the fog incarcerating her past.

Somewhere, she'd had a life filled with dreams and normal problems. If she remembered, she might also know how she came to be with Rory McCullough in the middle of nowhere. *Magic* seemed a poor explanation.

A menacing scream sounded across the creek.

Startled, Melissa peered into the darkness. Rory's warning of wolves summoned unexpected apprehension.

Groping for handholds, she eased off her perch with only one thought in mind—returning to the safety of the fire.

Downstream, something splashed in the creek.

She bent into a patch of rocks glistening in the dappled moonlight. When she straightened and glanced over her shoulder, each hand held a rock.

Stupid, she admonished. How was she going to defend herself against something she couldn't see? Caution kept her moving.

The roaring campfire beckoned her to hurry into the safety of the light.

A twig snapped on her side of the creek. Whatever stalked her was moving closer.

Melissa halted, then slowly turned to face the peril. The creature would not bring her down from behind like a fleeing rabbit. She'd do all the damage she could with her rocks and wits. She resumed walking backward in the direction of the campfire. All the while she listened, her gaze searching the shadows hiding the menace.

Finally, it breached the edge of the darkness. Moonlight reflected in two luminous eyes tracking her. She stared back. Her heart skipped a beat, then slowed to a calm that left her in full command. She continued a measured retreat. The eyes followed and maintained a constant distance.

Each step drew the creature closer to a patch of light. When it entered the moonlit clearing, Melissa's heart slowed even more. She knew she couldn't outrun the cat, even though she had an easy fifteen yards' head start.

Out of the corner of her eye she spotted a shattered tree limb. She inched toward it, seeking a better weapon than two rocks. The predator matched her movements. The subtle change of direction illuminated a stain on the cougar's shoulder. It stretched down the golden fur of his foreleg.

"You're wounded," Melissa croaked, unsure whether that made the cat a more formidable enemy or gave her a slim chance.

She halted.

So did the cougar.

Slowly, never taking her eyes off the luminescent orbs gauging each move she made, Melissa sank into a crouch.

She set the rock where she could easily retrieve it, then groped for a club-size piece of the limb.

The cat snarled and crept closer. From the far side of the meadow, the horse whinnied in terror.

Melissa hefted the club in her right hand and straightened. All emotion fled, leaving a calm that allowed her to concentrate on the smallest deail: the stench of infection wafting on the scant night breeze, the dark tears running from the cougar's rheumy eyes, the unnatural rasp of its breathing, and the stillness of the night surrounding them. Calm, confident, she was conscious of only one thought—she had to kill the enemy determined to kill her.

The cry of an angry cougar brought Rory out of a light sleep. He sat up and pulled on his boots. The cat was close. Had Melissa heard it?

A quick glance at her empty pallet confirmed his worst fears: She had left the camp. She was wandering in the darkness with the cat.

He shaded the firelight and scanned the meadow. His sharp eyes caught movement in the direction of the creek.

The Winchester filled his hand. He surged to his feet and took off at a run, his heart beating a terror-filled staccato as he raced toward her. The meadow seemed three times as large as it had earlier.

On a dead run, he fired the rifle in the air.

The cougar held his ground for an instant before closing the distance on Melissa.

"Get down," Rory shouted from a few yards behind her. He tipped the rifle and put another round into the chamber.

Immediately, Melissa dropped to the ground.

The cougar lunged, bounding over Melissa and straight at Rory before he could bring the rifle around. The impact of the snarling cat sent the rifle to the ground. Fangs and claws flew at Rory. He caught the cougar's forepaws and hurled the cat aside.

"Run, Melissa!"

Snarling, the cat twisted to his feet and sprang.

Again, Rory deflected him. This time he did not escape the cougar's sharp claws. Three long gashes opened from his right collarbone to his solar plexus.

The third time the cat attacked, Rory stayed clear of the claws and delivered a hard kick to the animal's belly.

The cougar screamed, his fangs bared, eyes wide, and ears flat against his head.

For an instant Rory thought the cat was hurt severely enough to retreat, or at least to allow him to do so. Then the animal sprang.

Braced for the attack, Rory jerked at the sound of the rifle, then watched the cat flip away from him.

The cougar's upper body writhed as he screamed and tried to rise. The dead weight of his hindquarters thwarted him. A spot of blood on his spine mushroomed with each futile attempt to launch another attack.

A second shot left nothing but echoes in the silence of the night and the thunder of Rory's heart beating in his temples. The cougar's sightless eyes stared into the grass. A small hole appeared below his exposed ear.

Rory turned his head to the right. Melissa cocked the rifle into readiness. Not a trace of emotion showed in her expression or her demeanor. The lack of reaction made him shudder. He had expected her to run back to the safety of the fire, save herself. Instead, she stood her ground and killed the crazed beast. The notion befuddled him.

"Are you all right?"

Melissa cradled the rifle barrel over her left forearm with a grace typical of one familiar with firearms. She nodded, then swallowed and lifted her chin. "You're not."

It took a moment before her meaning registered. He glanced at his bare chest. When he saw the gashes, they began burning.

Melissa inclined her head toward the cat. "He was sick."

"I know. He wouldn't have attacked that way otherwise." The cat posed no puzzle; Melissa did. "Were those lucky shots, or do you shoot that well?"

Thoughtful, she hesitated before answering in her frog

whisper, "Not luck." The castor oil wrap at her throat shifted when she swallowed.

"Don't talk. Don't hurt yourself." He went to take her arm, then thought better of it. Blood from the open gashes on his chest ran down his torso and arm. What the damp waistband of his trousers failed to absorb ran along his forearm and dripped from his fingertips.

Using his foot, he turned the cougar over. A cursory examination of the cat's infected shoulder wound incited a weighty dread supplanting the relief of escaping with his life. Although the cat was sick, maybe his own wounds had bled quickly enough to keep the poison out. But then, maybe not—only time would tell.

He washed up at the creek. The cold water did little to stem the blood flow. "I'm going to have to stitch these," he murmured.

A soft tap on his shoulder diverted his attention. Melissa tipped her head toward the clearing. "You're right. The quicker, the better."

Bright moonlight lit the meadow. Rory eyed the rifle she carried, but he did not reach for it. At the moment, it rested in more capable hands than his. Ignoring him, she scanned the trees and walked backward for a few steps as though protecting their rear from another attack.

When they reached the camp, Melissa put water on to boil in every container Rory had.

"What are you doing?" Seeing her adjust the wrap on her throat, he lifted his hand. "No, don't talk. Never mind." He found his shirt beside the pallet and wadded it into a ball. Before he could press it against his wounds to absorb the blood seeping across his belly and soaking his pants, she grabbed his wrist and shook her head.

"Not clean."

Reluctantly, he let her take the shirt.

"First aid kit?" she croaked, her expressive eyebrows rising in hopeful expectation.

"I don't know what that is."

Crestfallen, she nodded.

"There is a pouch with herbs, bandages, and a stitching needle and thread in one of the packs. I'll need that." He glanced at the packs.

He settled on a rock near the fire. The night air alternately chilled and heated him. He'd welcome a little of Shelan's magic right now if it would ease the pain from the wounds and hasten their healing.

Melissa returned with the pouch and draped his jacket over his left shoulder.

"Tell me what to do."

Surprised that she didn't recognize the basic healing herbs, he drew a deep breath and began a concise and somewhat lengthy explanation. She asked no questions and followed directions with a sense of urgency that made him wonder about her haste. The questions remained silent. The effort it cost Melissa to speak was greater than his curiosity.

Competency marked her every move. Nothing touched the bloody wounds without being boiled first. Throughout the ordeal, he sat in stoic silence.

Had the situation been reversed, he doubted Melissa would have given any indication of her pain. It bothered him that she kept such a tight rein on her feelings. Wherever she came from must have imposed a harsh code of living.

Curious and needing a distraction, he formed simple questions.

"Have you tended wounds like this before?"

Instead of the nod or head shake he anticipated, she shrugged, undeterred from her labor to mix the herbs in the proportions he had indicated.

"This is a little more complex than sewing on a button, Melissa. Do you think you can sew me up?"

She nodded without looking at him.

"Are your hands steady?"

Again she nodded.

"Are you sure? Mine are still shaking." His extended left hand had a slight tremor.

She glanced at his fingers, then at him. Her expression made him feel foolish for asking.

"Damn, you weren't afraid out there, were you?" The realization escaped before he had time to analyze it.

Melissa shook her head.

What kind of woman faced down a sick cougar with a rock and a club without being afraid? Rory looked away. Either she was lying or she had little regard for her life. Believing that she lied sat more comfortably, but it felt wrong.

"Fear gets in the way. Useless. Clouds thinking. Can get you killed in confrontational situations."

She met his gaze when he turned back. For a moment, he saw surprise, confusion, and something he couldn't define in her eyes.

Holding her gaze, he asked, "Do answers like that materialize out of thin air?"

Nodding, she pressed a hot, herb-laced cloth to his wounds.

Rory sat a little straighter and inhaled sharply through his teeth. He endured the medicinal cleaning with an impassivity born of sheer determination. A trio of cat scratches wasn't going to kill him; neither was the pain of cleaning and sewing them up.

He hoped she used small stitches.

Chapter 9

MELISSA WORRIED WHILE she tended Rory. The economical manner in which he gave instructions made following them simple. He knew exactly what he needed and how much of each strange herb to use in the mix. Reminding herself that she caused him pain for a greater good, Melissa held her chaotic feelings in check.

When Rory fought the cougar, her first consideration had been her fate in this unfamiliar place. From the pit of the fog enveloping her memories, a deep certainty that she'd survive with or without him added confusion. The realization of how selfish her interests for survival were shamed her and increased the depth of her discomfort. The only saving grace she found was acting instinctively to kill the cougar.

Rory had been injured because she had ignored his warning about staying close to the fire. The last thing she had expected was for him to charge across the clearing and put himself between her and the cat. Her failure to heed his warning and his sense of nobility wound up jeopardizing them both. She had been ready to defend herself and face the consequences of her actions.

He seemed to think she should have been afraid. Perhaps she should have been. However, her only concern had been for Rory when she realized the tenacious cat wouldn't give up until one of them lay dead.

Later, when the critical situation passed, an emotional surge would exact a heavy toll on her. But not now. The invisible wall holding it back would not crumble until the crisis was over.

She pointed at Rory's pallet, picked up the sterilized container of bandages, needle and thread, then stood. From the corner of her eye, she watched him rise from the rock. He seemed steady enough.

"Anesthetic?" she asked when he lay on his pallet.

"I don't have any opium powder."

The mention of opium startled her. A fleeting, black implication conjured a sinister sensation. Like the countless elusive impressions before it, the scant glimpse of the other side evaporated.

Earlier, she had expected a first aid kit, now anesthetic. Neither existed.

Yet, came a small voice from the fog in her mind.

She wanted to dwell on the single word. Yet. It implied that the haze hid more than her identity. Could it hold secrets of things yet to happen?

Confused, she focused on Rory and caught the glint of worry in his gray eyes.

"Pretend you're sewing on buttons, except you only need one stitch. Tie each one off so if one breaks, the whole thing doesn't come apart." The heavy breath he drew sent a fresh wave of precious blood oozing out of the deep gashes. "Just sew the big holes up and stop the leaks."

Examining the wounds, she saw that the deepest of the gashes cut through the pectoral muscles. Above and below the diagonal slashes ranging from his collarbone to his belly, the wounds tried to close on their own. A good bandage would help seal them.

She threaded the needle. "It will hurt."

"Have you changed your mind?"

A quick shake of her head firmed her resolve. "Just a warning. I want to do this right." She cleaned her throat, then winced at the sudden dryness added to the usual pinch each time she swallowed.

"I trust you, Melissa. Put the stitches in tight enough to close the skin. Start with the middle one."

He trusted too easily. Of course, if the tables were turned, she'd have had no choice but to trust him. However, giving voice to his trust placed an added burden on her to live up to the implied expectations.

She began stitching.

Rory didn't flinch as the needle pierced his skin time and time again.

Melissa stopped to wipe her face on her sleeve. Although the night was cold, she was overly warm and perspiring from the strain.

"You're doing fine, Melissa. One more hole, and we can both take a nap."

She glanced at his face. Beads of sweat coalesced and formed rivers that dampened his hair. He was the one in pain, so why did it feel as if she was?

When she finished the last stitch, she straightened and arched her back.

"Thank you." Rory dragged his left hand over his sweaty face.

"Bandage," she reminded.

"Smear on some boiled lard first. Blue tin." He pointed at the pouch of herbs and medicines.

She fetched the tin and applied a liberal coat to keep the bandage from sticking. He needed to sit up for her to wrap his chest and fix the bandage over his right shoulder. The wounds seeped a small amount of blood, but the stitches held.

She brought the canteen and waited for him to drink his fill. "Sleep."

"Sure," he said, closing his eyes.

Satisfied she'd done the best she could under the circumstances, she waited until he fell asleep before adding wood to the fire. Next, she found the shovel he had tied to the packs that morning.

Armed with the rifle, the shovel, and a torch, she checked on Rory again before heading for the dead cougar. If she didn't throw dirt on it, she might have wolves to contend with, too. In the morning, she'd spread embers over the places where Rory had bled near the fire.

She did not question the reasons behind the actions that seemed imperative, but merely carried on, knowing there would be no peace or emotional release until she did.

At dawn Melissa fetched water and set coffee on to boil. She made it extra strong. The couple of hours of exhausted sleep she had managed had taken the edge off, but had not rested her.

Rory slept fitfully after sunrise. She watched him closely, wondering how to help him. His face felt warm, but not feverish.

The sun told her it was midmorning when Rory woke. He sat up very slowly, then swayed. Grimacing, he squinted at the sky.

"We need to pack up and move."

Melissa shook her head.

"We can't stay here."

She carried a cup of coffee to him.

His left hand ran through his hair, then over the whisker stubble along his jaw. "We have to get on the trail."

When he didn't take the coffee, she started to pour it on the ground. He took the cup left-handed.

"I'm too tired."

The simple statement sent him choking on the coffee.

"Today you're too tired? Not yesterday?"

"Maybe tomorrow too." She feigned a yawn. If he didn't have the sense God gave a gnat and know he was in no shape to walk through these mountains, she'd impose it.

"You're saying that so I'll stay here."

The accusation made her bite back a smile. It mattered little whether he knew she lied. If she refused to leave, he'd stay; he would never abandon her, defenseless, in unfamiliar country. Under different circumstances, she'd never have used so noble a quality as his deep sense of obligation against him. She suspected that it was too rare a characteristic to abuse lightly.

"My throat hurts," she whined in a rasp.

"Your throat hurt yesterday, too. That didn't slow you

down, let alone force you to indicate when you needed a rest."

She shrugged and tried to look pathetic enough to evoke sympathy, a ruse she wasn't particularly sure how to pull off. "I'm tired. It's your turn to stand watch."

Rory tossed his empty coffee cup at the pots beside the fire. "Are you telling me you stood watch all night?"

The awe in his voice almost wrung the truth from her. Not willing to give the lie a real voice, she nodded.

"No wonder you're tired." He searched the area around his pallet. "Where's my shirt?"

She pointed at two sticks holding the shirt out to dry. Dampness clung to the seams, collar, and cuffs of the shirt she wore. The thicker fabric of his shirt needed another hour in the sun.

She helped him to his feet and noticed they hadn't removed his boots last night. Some nurse she was. When she glanced up, she saw pain darken his flinty gray eyes as he stood. A tremor rippled his warm skin beneath her fingers. She held his arm tighter, unsure she could hold him if he fell. Guilt strengthened her resolve to protect him from further harm.

"Easy," she whispered. "Stand still a moment."

He made no protest but gingerly touched the stained bandage over his wounds with his left hand.

Just looking at the wrapping brought back the ordeal of sewing him up and made her chest hurt. She winced at the thought of removing the bandage and checking the wounds. The wrappings needed changing and given the limited supplies, she'd have to boil them for reuse. "Hurt?"

"Like the fires of hell."

She pressed the back of her hand against his whiskered face. "You're warm."

"Figures." As though reaching a decision, he straightened, his head rising proudly. "We have to make as much distance as possible, Melissa. I'm not likely to feel any better as time passes. If we can get down the mountain, you might be able to find help if we need it."

It made sense, but she was not convinced. Traversing the steep terrain required strength and energy. He had neither.

He studied the campsite. "We'll travel light."

A hundred arguments clamored in silent protest. Before she could voice the first, he caught her chin, forcing her to look at him.

"You're going to have to trust me, Melissa. We have to get as far down the mountain as we can today. Help me."

Dumbfounded, she gaped at Rory. The entreaty for her trust and help in the same breath tore at her. *Help* was exactly what she was attempting to do by keeping him in one place long enough for his wounds to start mending. Beyond that, she had no idea of how best to help him. She focused inward, but nothing emerged from her foggy past.

"Let me think. You eat." Time—she needed time to figure out how to reason with him.

"I'll eat, then we leave."

She headed toward the fire, intent on warming up the breakfast she'd saved for him. "And if I don't want to leave?"

"You leave me no choice but to start down without you and hope you follow close enough to shoot any sharp-nosed predator that catches a whiff of this." He pointed at the stain broadening on the white bandage. "If you don't . . ."

"You'd leave the rifle with me?" The intense way his troubled gray eyes stalked the trees told her that he wasn't bluffing.

"Why the hell not? I can't use it left-handed. I wasn't that good with it before I got hurt. Why do you think I fish instead of hunt?" He eased onto the rock beside the fire and lifted the lid on the iron skillet. He found a fork and settled in to eat a lukewarm breakfast.

How neatly he'd turned the tables on her. The man professed his weaknesses and shortcomings as easily as he smiled. In so doing, he gained the upper hand and put the burden of acquiescence on her. Guilt did the rest, for it wasn't a question of going their own ways in the mountains, merely a test of whose way they would go.

"We've been lucky, but those clouds are a warning. I'll

compromise with you. There's a cave about half a day's trek down the mountain. Let's get that far and see what the weather does." He tossed the fork into the skillet. "Rain, most likely."

A quick glance at the clouds gathering overhead promised that much. In the open, keeping his bandage dry would be impossible once the rain fell. Maybe his way was best. A cave offered easy shelter from the elements and a defensible position against curious animals. Compromise took the edge off her apprehension. "Okay. Can you ride?"

Rory shook his head. "We need the horse for our gear."

Melissa raised her hands in resignation. They'd do it his way and for now, she'd have to trust him. There didn't seem to be any other option.

An hour later, Rory led her and the horse into the trees. Worried, she watched him for signs of fatigue. Today he walked slower and selected the easiest trails. By the third hour, his gait was still steady and relentless. His silence spoke of his grit and stamina louder than any words.

They found the cave late in the afternoon. Signs of earlier fires proclaimed it an haven for those who knew the mountains. Melissa was just glad they finally reached it. She wondered how Rory had remained on his feet the last few miles. Her tongue was sore from biting back pleas for him to rest.

She took the lead rope from Rory's hand and guided the horse to the mouth of the cave. Quickly and efficiently, she unloaded the packs from the horse. Inside the shelter, her first chore was to fashion a place for Rory to rest. She untied the furs and spread them into a single pallet. "Lie down before you fall down, Rory," she croaked, noting his glazed eyes

He obeyed without protest.

She hobbled the horse as she had seen Rory do previously, then foraged firewood from the deadfalls in the brush. As soon as she got a fire going, she fetched water from a nearby brook and filled every container they had packed.

Rory lay fast asleep across the pallet. Touching the inside of her wrist to his forehead sent her heart down to her toes. He was burning up with fever.

"We're going to be here a while, Mr. McCullough," she whispered to him while pulling off his boots. "I'll be back."

By dusk, she had enough wood for a couple of days stashed inside the dry cave. The first drops of rain splattered on the leaves and evergreen boughs arching over the entrance. She hoped the horse would be all right. For now, her hands were full. Much as she dreaded it, she had to change Rory's bandage. In his present state, he represented 220 pounds of dead weight.

"How long . . . how long have we been here?"

"Two days." The cool, damp cloth in Melissa's hand faltered when she saw the pain reflected in his eyes.

"Give me the paper and pencil."

"Water first. As much as you can hold." Her voice was little more than a rasp. She dropped the cloth in to the pot beside the pallet and reached around for the canteen.

With great effort, Rory drank until it was empty. The exertion exhausted him.

"Tell me how to help you, Rory. Is there something I can do with those weeds to fight the infection?"

"Not weeds. Herbs. Help me sit."

Anxious, she supported his shoulders and pushed until he sat. The bandage over his wounds fell onto his leg.

"Where the hell are my pants?"

Since removing them, she'd washed them and him. Melissa pointed at the packs.

"Paper," he reminded.

At the fire, she dipped a coffee cup into a pot of warm broth. She wiped the sides with her fingers, which she dried on her pants, and took it to him. "Drink this first."

"What is it?"

"Broth from a rabbit I caught, and a few leaves I recognized as edible."

He sniffed the contents, then sipped. "It's good. This all that's left after you shot it?"

Melissa smiled, relieved that he still had a sense of humor.

Perhaps he wasn't as close to death's door as she had feared. "I caught it in a snare."

When he started to ask a question, she raised her hand. "I don't know how I knew to set a snare. I just knew. During the past couple of days, I've discovered I know a lot of other things about surviving off the land. The memories come when I need them."

He finished the broth and handed the cup back. "Your voice is stronger. Throat still hurt?"

Nothing compared to what he was suffering. That he thought of her discomfort at all touched her in an inexplicable way. "I'm still doing the gargle, the tonic, and the castor oil wrap."

Eyes closed, Rory bowed his head.

"Rory?" She set the cup aside and quickly scooted behind him. With her knees braced against the small of his back, she rolled his shoulders against her. "Please, don't go to sleep without telling me how to help you. Please, Rory," she rasped into his ear.

The soft brush of his beard against her cheek was his response. "Cut the stitches," he murmured. "Cauterize me."

Paralysis gripped Melissa. Surely the fever had addled his thinking. Did he even know what he was asking? The pain?

"Pencil and paper." His labored breathing nearly obscured his words.

Dry-mouthed, Melissa exhaled slowly, not sure what to do. Anger at the injustice of his suffering and her circumstances flashed through her. For two days she had beseeched him to awaken and tell her how to help him. This was not the answer she anticipated. It was not acceptable.

"I can't stay awake much longer." With a moan, he straightened, lifting his weight from against her thighs and abdomen.

Not knowing what else to do, she scrambled to the packs and found the small cache of paper and bit of pencil.

With great care, he closed the fingers of his right hand around the pencil and wrote a single sentence in shaky letters, then signed his name. He turned the paper over and began to make lines and circles.

"Listen close. At first light, follow the stream to the sea. It's rough, but you won't lose your way. Go north. You'll find someone. Go to my house." Exhausted, he dropped the paper and pencil. "If I don't make it, the house is yours. This paper says so. Take it."

She pushed his hand away. "I don't want your house."

"Leave me. Go down the mountain."

Melissa had no intention of leaving at any time without him. How could he even consider it? He'd die without—

"I'm dying anyway."

Why did he do that? How did he know what she was thinking? "I won't let you die. Dammit, Rory, you and that magic woman brought me here. She's gone to heaven knows where. You, Rory, you are not going to leave me alone in this place. That's just too unfair. I swear, if you die on me, I'll haunt you."

He coughed, doubled over, and stopped just short of grabbing his wounds. "You can't haunt me if I'm dead."

Tenderly, she eased him back until he was lying again. "Maybe not. But you'll haunt me whether you mean to or not. I don't need any ghosts. I don't want your house. And I'm not leaving."

"Then heat my knife and cauterize these so I can make love with you again as a man instead of a ghost."

Melissa stared at him. How could a man in his condition even think about sex? The rapacious hunger they indulged in the circle shone clearly in his fever-bright eyes. He was thinking about sex. With her. "You want to make love, huh?" Head shaking, eyes narrowing, a hint of a smile escaped. "You're not in any shape for it. The spirit, ghost or not, may be willing, but the flesh"—her gaze raked the bandage on the way down his body—

"Is not weak," he concluded.

Incredibly, the proof of his desire was clearly evident. "In your case, the flesh is strong and the mind is weak. Get it all together and I'll think about it. Just remember, I don't make love with ghosts."

"You keep arguing with me, and you will. Then you'll wish I was a man again."

"You stay alive and I'll make love with you again. Someday."

His left hand closed around her wrist. "You have to do this, Melissa."

She would rather have walked barefoot across hot coals than remove the stitches and cauterize his infected wounds, but from the tumult of denial roiling through her, a kernel of certainty crept from the fog. *It's his only chance.*

The clarity startled, then dismayed her. In her mind's eye, she understood the steps required as though she recalled them from a book in a classroom.

"I'll do it," she croaked to the fog as well as to Rory. She'd hate it, but she wouldn't defy both forces.

Resigned, she added wood to the fire and set water on to boil. Thankfully, Rory dozed while she made the preparations. Twice, she walked outside the cave and inhaled fresh air until the trembling in her hands abated. Each time she returned, the stench of infection assailed her. She battled nausea and fought for control over her squeamishness.

When she had everything ready, she roused him. The soft hide wrap that she had removed from her throat dangled in her hand.

"Bite on this." She put the folded leather between his teeth. "Feel free to yell. This is going to hurt like hell. I'll need to get the wounds as clean as possible before I cauterize."

She bent to place a kiss on his fevered brow. "Do us both a favor and pass out. I'll do the best I can whether you're awake or unconscious."

"I trust you," came his muffled words.

When she would have said more, the invisible wall first experienced when confronting the cougar rose silently into place. All emotion raced to a cage behind the fog. Her hands stopped shaking and her stomach settled. Whatever had taught her such control in her past taught her well.

She cut and removed the first stitch.

Chapter 10

RORY WOKE WITH a fire raging across the right side of his chest. Gingerly, he touched the bandage over his wounds. The pain now was different from that of infection. He inhaled deeply, slowly, recalling the stench of his flesh burning under the glowing blade Melissa had laid against his wounds to cauterize them.

Even though she hadn't wanted to, she had done what was necessary. The trust he placed in her reaped the reward of his life. Satisfied, he let sleep overtake him.

When he woke again, Melissa slept beside him. In the flickering firelight, he saw the dark rings of worry beneath her eyes. The deep sleep conveyed her exhaustion. Rory watched her curled next to him, her lips slightly parted, and a gentle peace stole the sharp edge from his physical pain. It did not matter where she came from, she belonged right where she was, at his side. The rare courage she showed in facing the cougar paled in comparison to that of sewing him up, then later removing the stitches and cauterizing the wounds.

Content that Shelan had chosen well, he gathered her hand in his and closed his eyes. Healing sleep claimed him instantly.

Incredible thirst roused him. Damn, had he ever been so thirsty?

Like an angel sent from heaven, Melissa hovered over him.

"Drink," she encouraged, slipping her hand behind his head and lifting his mouth toward the canteen.

Water had never tasted so good, nor had a simple thing like drinking it demanded so much strength. After he sipped from the canteen, he settled back on the furs, exhausted, and caught his breath.

The soft side of her wrist on his forehead felt like cool velvet.

"It feels as though your fever is down some. Are you in much pain? How do your wounds feel?"

"I am painfully alive, but you look tired."

"I'm fine." She busied herself at the fire. "Can you drink some broth?"

"How long this time, Melissa?"

"Oh, this is a different rabbit."

"How long have I been out?"

She approached with a cup of broth and knelt beside him, her relief evident in the softening of the strain around her eyes and mouth. "Three days this time."

He accepted her help in sitting and let the bandage fall from his wounds. Each movement ignited new fires in his chest. He examined the results of the cauterization curiously. "Nice work," he breathed, impressed by the healing burns that streaked his chest. Cautiously, he checked the mobility of his right arm and found it severely limited.

"Don't ever ask me to do that again." The cup of broth she offered shook in her trembling hands.

The torment in her features made his heart heavy. He'd had only to place his fate in her hands and endure; she had faced the burden of carrying out the noxious task. The stubborn streak he had detected in her had not allowed her to perform anything short of a lifesaving miracle. "It is my sincerest wish that you never have to, especially on me." He checked the temperature of the broth, then drank the entire cup. "Is there any more?"

Without a word, she refilled the cup and continued doing so until he drank the last spoonful.

She gathered the cup and pot, then rose and looked toward the cave entrance. "It will be dark in a few hours. I'm going hunting. You'll need more than broth to regain your strength."

She picked up the rifle propped nearby, then deposited the

cup and pot on an empty canvas pack. "I'll be back before dark."

"Melissa."

She paused at the entrance, but did not turn around.

"Thank you."

After a curt nod, she left him alone with the sounds of the crackling fire.

Five days, he thought. She had kept both of them alive for five long, difficult days. Small wonder she seemed taciturn.

He laid back and stared at the cave's ceiling. The throbbing of his wounds matched his heartbeat and accelerated with the painful exertion of movement. Much as he hated it, regaining enough energy to travel might take a day or two.

Fatigued, he closed his eyes and thought about the promise she had given of someday making love with him again. A wry smile touched his mouth. The only thing sweeter than her body would be winning her heart. There were no richer fantasies to carry him off to sleep than the memory of making love with her in the fairy ring.

"What happened to your clothes?" Rory asked two days later when Melissa entered the cave wearing his pants rolled above her knees.

"I washed them. They're drying outside." The banners of her diligence lingered as faint half-moons below her eyes. She stood near the fire and combed her damp hair straight back from her forehead. The austere contrast highlighted the angle of her cheekbones.

"What happened to your leg?" He rose from the furs and adjusted the red-flannel underwear bottoms he'd worn for the past two days.

She licked her finger and wiped away a line of blood drying on her calf.

He pointed at a series of small scabs forming on both calves. "Did you walk naked through a thorn patch?"

"Ah, no. I borrowed your razor and shaved my legs." Shrugging, she withdrew it from her pocket and tossed it on his folded shirt. "I don't think I'd ever used a straight razor before."

Shaved her legs? "Why would you do that?"

"Because it was the only razor available and I hadn't shaved since . . . a long time. I couldn't stand it anymore. In a few days, I'd have had to braid my leg hairs."

Rory tried to imagine a feminine leg with tiny braids from the knee to the ankle—and failed. "I'm afraid I don't understand why you'd want to shave your legs in the first place."

"I just do. Maybe I'm a masochist and want the mosquitoes to have easier access to a meal." Balanced on her heels, she glanced down. "I think I've just always shaved my legs."

Rory grappled for understanding. "Like a custom? Or a ritual?"

She shook her head. "I don't know. I needed to shave my legs, so I did, and it felt right. Okay?"

"With my razor." He tried to imagine the pearl-handled straight razor gliding over her naked calf.

"You probably didn't notice, but I also used it to cut the stitches I removed from your chest."

Instantly, a twinge of pain shot through his wounds. He touched the healing trio, glad he'd lapsed into unconsciousness after she removed the nineteenth stitch.

"I'm getting very good with your razor. Would you like me to shave your face now that I'm experienced?"

The mischievous glint in her eyes made him wary. "While I appreciate the offer, you've done too much for me already. I couldn't impose such a personal task on you."

"Oh, please, it would be my pleasure."

A half a dozen forms of pleasure raced through his mind. None involved a razor. "Maybe after you've shaved your legs a few more times, I'll consider it."

"Aw, come on, Rory. I need all the practice I can get." She lifted her pant legs a fraction and examined the razor nicks on her knees. Tiny cuts scabbed at every curve. "See? I improved on the left knee after practicing on the right."

She did need practice, but not on him. "I, ah, think I better keep all my blood."

A smile that lit the cave like a beacon transformed her features. "Touché."

The lady enjoyed a test of wits and verbal sparring. Her intelligence warned that he had best wait until he was clear-headed before taking her on in a full joust. Meanwhile, the exchange provided valuable insight to his already considerable knowledge of her. An irrepressible sense of humor was her Achilles heel. Tired, angry, or under the weather, she could be cajoled into a lighthearted mood through humor with an occasional touch of sarcasm. At those times when he successfully coaxed a smile out of her, he doubted he would ever find the strength to let her go home. She belonged with him.

Lost in thought of how he might keep her, he clutched the quartz pendant hanging from a thong around his neck.

"Why do you wear that piece of quartz? Does it have some significance?"

"Yes, Shelan gave it to me a long time ago." He admired the irregular, oblong crystal cradled in his palm and thought of the old woman. When he lifted his gaze to Shelan's latest gift, sorrow dampened his spirit. Melissa possessed no mementos of the important people in her life.

"Crystals," Melissa murmured, her gaze fixed on the quartz in his hand.

"Does it remind you of something?"

"I don't know."

Her fingertip stroked the warm pendant. A veil clouded her eyes as though she listened for something he could not hear.

"A window. I remember a window made of quartz." Abruptly, she shook her head. "It's gone." She dropped her hand to her side.

"Is that how it happens? Little bits of the past come to light like pieces of a puzzle?"

"Yes, and it's damn frustrating. When I reach for more, a door slams in my face. Yet when I least expect it, I discover I know things I need to survive." Perplexity glittered in her hazel gaze. "I remember things . . . how to do what feels like things I've done before or maybe studied for a long time. But not people. I can't recall a single person. I don't understand that. I've known you such a short time, but I'm sure I'd never forget you."

"Could it be because I'm the most handsome, desirable, and entertaining fellow you've ever met?"

Silent laughter shook her shoulders and brought tears to her eyes. Holding her ribs, she lifted her free hand, waved at him, then doubled over in mirth until she sank to the floor. A single glance at him made her laugh even harder.

Grinning, Rory wished he could hear her laughter. Watching her made him chuckle in delight, even if she was laughing at him.

"Look at us," she managed through a silent fit of laughter.

They were a pair, him unshaven and in his baggy red underwear bottoms, her in clothes that drowned her and bearskin moccasins.

"Cinderella and Prince Charming we are not. Hell, I don't have a stepmother, let alone a wicked one or a pair of mean sisters." The merriment dimmed. "I don't even have a mother or father." Color drained from her features. "I never did."

The revelation stole the gaiety from the air. A heavy weight settled on Rory. "Perhaps they are hidden in your memories."

"No. I know this the same way I knew I had no children when you asked at the circle. There is a certainty, in here, I cannot describe." Her fist pressed against her heart.

Rory hunkered down beside her. "I am sorry."

"Don't be." Her chin lifted sharply. "You had nothing to do with whether or not I had a family. I survived."

The shell built by her words and reactions reminded him of other injured souls dear to his heart. "I want more for you than mere survival, Melissa."

"So do I. I want to know where I came from, how I got here, and where I'm going. I want to know where I belong."

The feel of her damp hair cooled his fingers. "You belong

with me. I won't leave you. And I've already proved I won't die on you."

"I don't belong with you. Right now, I'm stuck with you, just like you're stuck with me. As for you not dying on me, if you ever do anything so foolish as to step between me and a danger I brought on myself and get yourself hurt again, I'll shoot you."

Rory chuckled. "You won't shoot me. And I will always put myself between you and any threat of harm. I'm bigger and stronger, and it is my duty to protect you, Melissa."

"I don't want to be your duty or obligation. I don't want to be your anything. When I think about relying on someone, I get a strong sense of disappointment. I'll take care of myself, thank you."

"You don't want to care about anything or anyone who might hurt you, do you, Melissa?"

"I'm done talking." She sidled away.

"We'll leave in the morning. There are some people I want you to meet."

"We won't leave in the morning. You need another few days before we set out."

"I'm fit enough to make it down the mountain. We're out of the herbs for your throat, the castor oil—"

"I don't care." She wheeled on him, anger flushing her cheeks with color. "We're not leaving tomorrow, or the day after. You need more time—" Her mouth continued forming syllables after the words ceased to flow. When she realized her voice had deserted her, frustration balled her hands into fists.

He glared at her, angry. In a moment of pique, she'd undone all the healing of the potions and poultices. "You are one strong-minded, stubborn woman. You don't know your own limits, so don't presume to know mine. We're leaving in the morning."

Melissa walked beside Rory. They might be going down the mountain at his insistence, but she chose the frequency and sites for their stops.

By noon she suspected that he had begun discovering the very limits he professed to know and accused her of breaching. Though he kept a distance, his glassy eyes bespoke the return of his fever. Still, he wouldn't consider stopping.

And he had the audacity to call her stubborn! If she had her voice back, she'd throw a few words in his face. Under the circumstances, Rory McCullough had better count her silence as one of his major blessings in life.

The rugged terrain gentled into sloping forests and wide expanses of meadows as the afternoon passed. Overhead, birds marking their progress soared on the wind currents. Melissa watched Rory closely, expecting him to falter and collapse at any moment. The man kept going. He could out-stubborn exhaustion much longer than she had thought possible. When they stopped for a quick trail dinner, he refused to let her check his wounds.

"We're close." He raised the canteen to his mouth and drained it.

Eager to keep liquids flowing through him, she refilled the canteen from the creek, then handed it back. To her great relief, he drank more. From the looks of his sweat-dampened shirt and pants, the fever was moving into a steady burn.

"Another hour." He set the canteen aside. "I can make it from here with my eyes closed."

The gentle slope of the next hill rose to a crest lower than the one they stood upon. Beyond, the sea beckoned as a definite end of their journey, and clouds formed a steely ceiling overhead. In another hour, he'd have to be able to find the path home with his eyes closed; it would be dark. She slung the canteen over her shoulder and offered assistance.

Rory glanced at her. "Still angry, aren't you?"

She nodded, finding it easier to admit anger than the worry grating her nerves. Heaven help her, she cared more about him than any woman in her right mind should care about a stranger. Except—he wasn't a total stranger. He'd been her lover and knew her body with an intimacy that made her crave making love with him again.

"Let's go." He took her hand.

She pulled him to his feet and wrapped the packhorse's reins around his left hand.

They walked steadily after dark only because Rory refused to stop. When the lights of a house appeared, Melissa breathed a sigh of relief. Salvation lay a scant half mile away.

Rory staggered, dropped the reins, and stood weaving back and forth.

Melissa slung his arm over her shoulder. She carried the rifle left-handed and used her right for balance around Rory's waist. Lord, but the man was heavy, and the heat of his fever had the intensity of a blast furnace.

Together they shuffled toward the light.

He'd better not die on her. He'd promised he wouldn't. He'd promised he wouldn't leave her. Why couldn't he have waited one more day? Just one day.

She stopped short, staggered, then braced herself when he faltered. They needed help. Anyone. If Rory's legs gave out completely, she'd never be able to support him. She raised the rifle and fired it.

Silence.

With the rifle stock braced between her legs, she cocked it. A second shot brought someone with a lantern out of the house.

"I can make it. Marvin can't help." Rory shuffled forward, paused, then straightened.

Melissa understood the body language. Even if he fell dead on the veranda, he'd make it home. His determination commanded respect and admiration. She understood the kind of commitment to a goal that excluded any possibility of failure and consumed every iota of energy. Even if his weight crushed her spine, she'd make sure he reached his beloved home.

Melissa alternately watched the lantern carrier draw closer and Rory's footing. Given the speed of the approaching help, whoever was coming must be crawling on all fours.

Straining under the off-balance burden of Rory's weight, she crossed half the distance to the house by the time the help arrived.

At the sight of a gnomelike man limping toward them, Melissa nearly laughed. His lopsided gait promised she would have to carry him, too.

"Mr. McCullough! Mr. McCullough, you're ill! Come, come to the house. Right this way."

What did he think they were trying to do? Disbelieving, Melissa tore her gaze away from the excited gnome and looked up at Rory. Some of what she felt must have shown, because he gave her a thin smile.

"Melissa, this is Marvin, my butler and handyman."

Her disbelief became incredulity. While she wasn't certain exactly what a butler should look like, she knew it wasn't like Marvin. Handyman? Perhaps he had talent with his hands, for clearly his fragile, deformed body possessed little strength.

However, Marvin's presence seemed to help Rory pull a grain of energy from a silo scraped bare hours earlier. He didn't lean as heavily on her shoulders and he stumbled less.

"We have been so worried, Mr. McCullough. Shelan did not say how long you would be gone, but we had not thought it would be this long. Oh, we will miss her dreadfully.

"What has happened to you? My goodness, are you hurt? Have you become ill? Did you fall? Is your arm broken? Where did you find Miss Melissa?"

Melissa envied his ability to speak and wished with all her heart he'd save a few words in the universe for her to utter. When they reached the veranda stairs, she thrust the rifle at Marvin.

Hands raised in protest, he leaped back, nearly losing his balance. "Oh, no. I cannot possibly bear the responsibility for so powerful a weapon."

Melissa left Rory balancing against a porch post and unloaded the rifle, leaving the breech open. Again she thrust it at Marvin.

"Take the rifle," Rory mumbled.

Marvin took the rifle and hurried up the steps. "Elmira. Mr. McCullough's home. He's home."

"Elmira is my housekeeper and cook," Rory explained, a wheeze evident in his breathing.

Melissa helped him into the house.

Rory guided them through the foyer, around the stairs and down the hall to a darkened room. Melissa supported him wherever he led and watched his feet for the first sign of a stumble.

"Sit." He crumpled backward. It took all of her strength to keep him from landing hard on what felt like a soft leather couch.

Elmira entered with a flurry, struck a match, and proceeded to make a circuit of the room, lighting lamps as she went. "Surely you aren't going to rest in here, Mr. McCullough. This office is hardly conducive to recuperation. You spend all your time amongst these drawings and plans of yours."

Ignoring the absurd chatter, Melissa lifted Rory's legs onto the couch, then eased his shoulders down. Damn, he was burning up.

He caught her hand and brought her fingers to his fevered lips. "Thank you."

Her growing soft spot for him expanded despite her anger. She bent until her lips were against his ear. "You promised not to die."

"I'll keep that promise. I'm just very tired, Melissa. That's all," he whispered. "Besides, I intend to collect on Someday."

Startled he could even think about making love when lying at death's door, she drew back. The hint of a smile faded from his pallid face as his eyes closed.

"Stay with me, Melissa." He licked his dry lips, then whispered, "Someday."

She stroked his burning brow until sure he was asleep, then set to work on cleaning him up and finding a way to treat his wounds and fever. If he made it through this crisis, she just might go to bed with him again. Someday.

Chapter 11

Too exhausted to sleep, Melissa ventured onto the covered porch outside Rory's office. The ocean breeze kissed her clothing with mist and cleared her head. She had done all she knew how to do for Rory. Now his recovery rested on his own shoulders. Judging by the swiftness with which he had regained his strength in the cave, his strong constitution would serve him well.

The faint light of morning grew stronger. A placid sea melted into the gray clouds blanketing the early-morning hour. The muted call of scoffing seabirds awakened the late sleepers nesting in the cliffs. Melissa left the porch and followed the rock walk to the edge of the bluff. Stairs carved into the cliff led to a small, sandy beach.

She wondered if Rory swam in the ocean with the same regularity that he swam in the lake. From the top of the bluff, she watched the seabirds scour the lethargic surf for their morning fare. Their cries of frustration became her voice.

As she started back, she assessed Rory's home. After he revealed his occupation and spoke of the home he had built, she had expected a sturdy dwelling reflective of his size and durability. It was that, and more. Something about the construction implied a dated design. However, he had said the house was less than a decade old. She wasn't sure what she had expected. It seemed an architect's home would embody a modern style.

Modern. She tried conjuring the meaning in terms of a house and failed.

Again, the sense of looking backward flitted through her mind. The uneasiness refused to clarify or go away entirely.

She studied the house. It was solid and pleasing to behold. The two-story structure, perched over at least a partial basement, was surrounded by fragrant gardens promising his creative side exceeded anything she had imagined.

The house radiated a permanence shared by the mountains and the unending tides of the sea. In keeping with the natural habitat, the simplicity of its design struck her as typically Rory McCullough.

When they had arrived, the beauty of Rory's home had escaped her. The place seemed more a madhouse. Between Marvin's and Elmira's chatter, she'd practically had to do physical battle to interject a written word concerning Rory's condition. She had penciled a list of what she needed for him. When they finally left her alone with him, she tried to fathom why he had considered it important for her to meet the couple.

Hugging her arms to ward off the chill, she returned to the house and checked on Rory. His fever seemed to have diminished, and he slept soundly. Amazed by his recuperative powers, she settled on the floor and drew a blanket around her shoulders. As soon as she closed her eyes, she succumbed to bone-weary fatigue.

She woke with a start. Two green eyes gazed sideways at her from a serious, freckled face. Melissa recoiled, only to meet the resistance of Rory's hand tightening on hers.

"She won't bite," Rory whispered.

For a moment, Melissa wasn't sure whom he addressed, her or the redhead in pigtails eyeing her with macabre fascination.

"Shelan said you're gonna be Rory's wife."

Apparently Shelan had said a number of things Melissa didn't hold with.

"Elmira said ya can't talk. That true?"

The second voice came from a boy of about seven.

"She will," Rory said, squeezing her hand.

Ignoring the six children crowding around them, Melissa rolled onto her knees and laid the inside of her wrist against Rory's forehead.

"I'm better," he assured her.

"Good," Elmira snapped. "You can get upstairs to bed, then, and sleep like civilized folks. Miss Melissa can eat something and get some proper rest, too. The poor woman has been sleeping on the floor when she wasn't fretting over yer care.

"Katy, Sandra, take Miss Melissa to the dining room. Supper is on the table.

"Darin, Tommy, you see that Mr. McCullough gets upstairs and into his bed.

"Orin, you see to straightening up in here.

"Roger, you come with me and fetch a tray for Mr. McCullough. He needs good food to recover from what ails him." Elmira clapped her hands twice and the children bolted into action.

Katy, the redhead with pigtails, and Sandra, an ebony-haired, brown-eyed child about the same age, each grabbed one of Melissa's hands and pulled her to her feet. The flurry of activity electrified the room.

Melissa glanced over her shoulder at Rory. For an instant, she caught his eye. The two largest boys closed in to help him up.

"Come along, Miss Melissa," Katy instructed, leading her out of the office and down the hall.

Curved-glass china cabinets and a sideboard with more cabinets filled walls edged with wainscoting and covered with crisp wallpaper. A long table with a dozen chairs dominated the elegant dining room. A single place setting indicated Melissa's spot at the table. Her stomach growled at the aromas of a real meal.

Katy and Sandra sat across the table and watched her eat.

"Do you speak English?" Katy asked.

Melissa popped an orange section into her mouth and nodded. Strange question. Rory had spoken to her in English, but perhaps Katy wasn't listening.

"Sandra had to learn English. She's Eye-talian, or at least the man who gave her to Mr. McCullough said she is."

"I must be. I like pasta. Mr. McCullough says it came from Italy," Sandra affirmed with confidence. "Katy and I are sisters."

"Well, not exactly sisters like you have a sister with the same parents. We don't have parents, but we decided to be sisters anyway."

Bingo! The children were the people Rory wanted her to meet. Other than their circumstances of being orphaned or abandoned like her, she wondered at his reason.

Melissa swallowed a bite of savory potato and reached for her coffee.

"Do you like children?" Sandra exchanged a knowing look with Katy.

Melissa managed a shrug. She hadn't been around kids since . . . since . . . The impression slipped back into the fog.

"Well, do you hate children?" Katy demanded.

Understanding the game, Melissa smiled, then shrugged again.

Sandra glanced at the door, then whispered, "Are you really gonna marry Mr. McCullough?"

Not wanting to dash their hopes either way, she shrugged and tilted her head to enforce her ambivalence.

"I hope not, because Katy wants to marry him when she grows up. But that's a long time to wait for a wife. Darin said Mr. McCullough will be an old man then, so maybe you'd better marry him." Sandra's elbow slipped when Katy nudged her.

"Are you going to stay here if you don't marry him?" Katy asked.

Again Melissa shrugged. Thinking of anything beyond the delicious dinner Elmira had prepared required effort. However . . . if she found a bathtub and a comfortable bed, the temptation to stay forever might lure her into a foolish promise.

"Do you know anything?" Sandra leaned forward on the table.

Melissa grinned, liking the temerity of the two girls, then shook her head.

"How come you're wearing Mr. McCullough's clothes?" Sandra tugged on Katy's braid. "She can't answer that."

"Oh. Sorry. Do you have any clothes of your own? I sure

hope so, because Mr. McCullough's are, well, kind of big on you." Katy grinned in triumph at the diplomacy of her new question.

Although Melissa hated disappointing Katy's sense of fashion, she took another bite of vegetables and shook her head.

"Mr. McCullough will buy you a dress so you can go into town," Sandra assured her with great sympathy.

"Even if you don't marry him," Katy added quickly.

Melissa couldn't suppress a grin. These two were more than a handful as a team.

"Are you going to tell on us for asking questions?" Katy twirled one of her braids.

Some of Melissa's enjoyment for the game evaporated. She shook her head very slowly. A conspiracy of silence imparted an ambiguous sensation that reached into the fog and disappeared. She pointed at the girls one at a time, then set down her fork and showed six fingers.

"No, we're ten."

"She wants to know how many children she has to like," Sandra said in a stage whisper.

"Oh. This is all of us. For now. I was the first. When I was three, Mr. McCullough bought me from some people and brought me here. Later, he built Freedom House. That's where we live and take our lessons. Tommy says we live in a palace compared to the orphanages he was once in. Sandra and I go to school, too. Mr. McCullough, he says girls have to make their way in the world. But I don't want to leave here ever.

"Mr. and Mrs. Lindstrom bring us over here lots. Sometimes we do chores. Sometimes we play and listen to stories. 'Course now that Shelan left to help some other kids, I don't know who will tell stories."

"Katy, Sandra," called Elmira from the doorway. "Say goodbye. Mr. Lindstrom will bring all of you for a visit tomorrow."

"Will you be talking by then?" Katy asked, twisting her pigtail a little slower.

Melissa shook her head.

"Too bad. We need a storyteller most desperately." She followed Sandra to the doorway where Elmira waited.

Melissa's appetite dwindled in the silence of the dining room. Their questions carried a refreshing openness. Yet something felt wrong. Try as she might, she couldn't pinpoint it.

She pushed away from the table and went to the window. Soon, twilight would give way to the night. Beyond the veranda and gardens, a tall, wiry man led the six children along a path winding through a stretch of evergreen trees marching to the sea.

The fog yawned. Katy. Katy . . . Kate.

The name conjured another green-eyed child, weakened by pain and fever. A sense of helplessness and something paralyzing in its horror crept out of her memory. Fear—an old nemesis of childhood she no longer empowered by acknowledging. Sorrow so monumental it weakened her knees until she sagged onto the floor as it overwhelmed her.

Staring out the window, Melissa saw a child's face dampened by perspiration. Pale freckles sprinkled the bridge of a small, upturned nose. Colorless lips parted revealing the gaps her permanent teeth had just begun to fill.

"Don't die. Don't die, Kate. I'll give you my favorite stuffed bunny if you promise not to die."

The child's voice echoed in her head. It was not just any child. It was her own voice, begging Kate to live.

"I called them. They're coming. The doctors will make you better. Don't die."

"He'll beat you," Kate wheezed, then drew her knees closer to her chest.

"I don't care if he kills me if you die."

The memory jumped.

Through the eyes of the child she had been, Melissa stared at an empty bed. Kate's bed. Soul-crushing loss sapped her will to live. Kate was dead. She was alone. Again.

Merciful fog closed the door on the past, leaving Melissa in a heap against the windowsill. She had not cried when she learned of Kate's death. Now, silent sobs wracked her body, for Kate, for the little girl who couldn't cry so long ago.

The sun had set when she lifted her tear-streaked face. A lamp burned over the dining table, which had been cleared of her unfinished meal. She got to her feet, agitated by her lapse of self-control. A need for space sent her fleeing through Rory's office to the outside.

A fine drizzle misted the evening. Impervious to the chill, she stood on the bluff and stared into the darkness. The restless ocean beat at the shore the same way bits of memory and wild thoughts pummeled her mind.

There had been others who joined Kate in death.

The certainty, born of sorrow, left her heart heavy.

Her eyes lifted to the heavens, hidden as thoroughly by heavy clouds as her memories were. In her mind's eye she saw a small, starry kite. As she focused on each pinpoint of light, names formed: Kate, Delvin, Chandra, Rashad, and Pacho. The awful circumstances of each death crashed through.

Helpless to stop the onslaught, she grasped her head in both hands. Her skull seemed too small to confine the torment without exploding. She sank to the ground and beat it with her fists. Their deaths were senseless. So much promise, thrown away.

Powerful emotions escaping from the cage of self-preservation accompanied the memories. No one had cared. No one had loved them. No one had wanted any of them. But they had needed and loved each other.

The hate that had become her ally in protecting the tender side of her from painful vulnerability roared through her in a red blaze. In that instant, she hated those responsible for the deaths of the childhood friends she had loved. The guilty ones had neither names nor faces. Cowards, they hid in the fog, using it the same way they used words and coconspirators to keep them safe.

Come out and face me now, she challenged those who lurked behind the defensive fog.

A desire to kill each and every one of them burned in the crimson anger illuminating the fog.

But they did not answer her summons. The shroud hiding her past remained unaffected by her impassioned demands.

Defeated, she rested her forehead on the cold, mossy ground. Nothing could change the past. Justice did not exist for the helpless, unwanted children of the world who had no champions.

She thought of Katy and Sandra, who seemed too damned happy to be orphans or abandoned children. The sisterhood they chose and shared had been denied her and Kate.

Melissa said a silent prayer beseeching Kate to guard and protect the girls from the fate she and Kate had suffered. The treasure of a loving friendship deserved nurturing and protection.

A strong hand lifted her crumpled body. For an instant, she thought it the hand of death come to join her with those in the starry kite. She lifted her face to look her fate in the eye.

Rory held her arm until her legs steadied. "Come."

The warm hand clasping her chilled fingers led her into the house. Depleted physically and emotionally, she accompanied him upstairs.

Standing beside a comfortable-looking bed, she peeled off her damp moccasins and unbuttoned her wet shirt. One-handed, Rory worried the soggy rope at her waist free. The pants fell to her ankles. Without a second thought, she climbed between the crisp white sheets and turned on her side, her back to him and the rest of the living world.

Rory tucked the bedding around her and left as silently as he'd appeared on the bluff.

A tear slipped over the bridge of her nose. He had left a light burning beside the bed to keep away the ghosts waiting to pounce in the dark.

The longer she stared at the low flame in the lamp, the more it seemed out of place. Alien.

Closing her eyes pressed more tears out of the corners.

Archaic. Obsolete. Historic.

The strangeness of the lamp enticed her tired eyes open.

Why wasn't there a light switch?

The question faded when she closed her eyes again.

Melissa rolled over and stared at the ceiling. Just before falling asleep, she'd thought of something important. Mentally stretching, she couldn't recall the gist, only the certainty of something being out of kilter. The warm sunlight streaming through the windows thawed the chill from her spirit.

Memories or no, she had changed little from the trauma of Kate's death. She grimaced at the irony of offering Kate her stuffed rabbit as an incentive to stay alive so many years ago.

The incentives had grown higher with age.

She had promised Rory her body for the same reason. Even without the memory of how Kate died, fever still held a mysterious power she thought she could forestall with a bribe. Of course, she couldn't thwart the ravages of a fever regardless of any sacrifice she willingly offered.

This morning, she questioned how close to death Rory had come on the mountain. He had thought very close when he coerced her into removing his stitches. When they reached his home, she had thought him near death with fever again, though he had assured her that he only needed sleep.

Sleep.

She gazed out the nearest window. Already, the day had slipped into afternoon. She rose and searched for her clothing. It was gone.

She stripped the sheet from the bed and wrapped it toga fashion around her. Somewhere in this house, there had to be another pair of trousers and a shirt.

An air of hushed solemnity pervaded the upstairs rooms. She padded toward the double doors at the front of the house. Her light knock when unanswered, and, curious, she pushed on the door. It swung wide on well-oiled hinges.

Rory.

The room screamed of his occupation. Sunlight streamed through a skylight over the bed, which, like everything else in the room, seemed oversized. Simplicity highlighted the fine wood grain of the furniture. The notion of sharing the enormous bed with Rory for a night warmed her. Nothing would be sweeter than to lose herself in the pleasure he offered.

However, without the strange, liberating effects of the fairy ring, she knew better than to expose herself to such frightening vulnerability. She had realized the next morning when the enchantment vanished that bowing to the desire roaring between them led to heartache. In the world outside the inexplicable glamour of the mountain circle, he'd share their exquisite passion, then cast her aside. A roil in the fog proclaimed her conclusion as a truth.

She picked up the trailing end of the sheet, draped it around her torso and headed toward the stairs.

There had been enough heartache and losses. Already she cared too much for Rory. Making love with him again would only deepen the hurt and hasten their inevitable parting.

Elmira met her at the bottom stair with an armful of clothing. "Back upstairs, Miss Melissa. You can't be traipsing around in a sheet."

Obediently, Melissa complied.

"Before you put these fresh clothes on, you need a bath."

The prospect of being clean and dressed buoyed her spirits.

For the next hour, she languished in a tub of hot water, shaved her legs with Rory's razor, and soaked every particle of dirt from her feet. The clothing Elmira brought seemed a bit odd, but easy enough to figure out. Melissa's preference for trousers prodded the feeling that things were not as they should be. Gazing at the dress and baggy undergarments, she thought none of it seemed familiar, as it should if she had worn clothing like this every day of her life. But if she had not, how could it be familiar?

She ate a hearty breakfast in the kitchen and listened to Elmira elaborate on the virtues of preserving everything growing in the kitchen garden while she made dinner preparations. After the meal, Melissa washed her dishes, then started on the small stack near the sink.

"Out. Out of my kitchen," Elmira scolded. "This is my job. If I need help, you'll be the first to know."

Two doors led outside from the kitchen, one out back toward the ocean, the other to a sheltered side yard bordered on three sides by the house. Curious, Melissa ventured into the garden alcove.

The garden fascinated her. Rocks and sculptured hills isolated plant groupings. Although she had no idea what sort of plants grew here, she knew they weren't the weeds they appeared.

"Shelan tended this garden. Most of the herbs growing here are for medicinal purposes," Rory said from the ocean side of a picket fence linking the two branches of the house. "Now that she's gone, I'll have to assume that task along with the side gardens—or hire another pair of hands."

Melissa hesitated, willing to offer her services if he taught her how to do the work. Perhaps he deemed this sacred ground.

Melissa surveyed him; other than his austere expression, he appeared the picture of health. Since she last saw him, he'd had a shave and haircut. She remembered the feel of his long, silky hair and envied the sea breeze playing in the auburn, nutmeg, and golden strands.

He opened the gate and came in. "Are you all right?"

A thin smile formed as she nodded.

"Yeah. I know, you're fine. Right?"

The smile took on life. She pointed at his right breast.

"It itches more than it hurts, so it must be healing well enough."

Given the opportunity, she would see for herself, but under the circumstances she had no choice but to believe him.

"Melissa, about yesterday. The children . . . Maybe I should have warned you."

Eager to disavow any notion the children were responsible for her cathartic behavior, she grabbed his hand and shook her head.

"Do you want me to keep them away from the house?"

She rolled her eyes, impatient to put his mind at ease. She took his hand and led him from the garden and around the back to his office door. Inside, she scanned the stacks of papers and drawings for something to write on.

"Here." Rory offered a fresh sheet of paper and pencil.

It wasn't the kids!!!! It was me! Memories. She paused, sure she could write volumes about last night's experience but not ready to relive it so soon. *Ugly. Painful. Beautiful. So sad.*

"The girls brought them on?"

Don't blame the girls.

"If seeing them brings back things you're not ready—"

Desperate to make him understand, she put her fingers over his mouth to silence him. When he stopped talking, she raised her finger in warning.

If you keep them away, I'll never speak to you again.

Tension flowed from Rory and he gave her a sudden smile. "You aren't exactly speaking to me now. How is your throat?"

She hunched over the paper so he couldn't see what she wrote until she finished. *It itches more than it hurts, so it must be healing well enough.*

Rory's laugh made her grin. How easy it was to see why Katy wanted him to wait until she grew up before taking a wife.

"I made more tonic and gargle for you."

I hope you added the honey this time.

Again he laughed. "You remembered."

I tasted it, remember? Definitely needs honey. Or chocolate.

"Chocolate, huh?"

She gave him her best angelic smile, then batted her eyelashes.

Chuckling, he flicked the end of her nose with a fingertip. "Honey for the tonic. Chocolate for dessert, after we put that castor oil necklace back on you."

I love being a fashion plate.

"Fashion plate? You mean stylish?"

Nodding, she rose from behind the desk. Rory's left arm caught her around the waist and drew her against him. Instant desire sent the heat of expectation coursing through her veins.

"You scared the hell out of me last night. If you had fallen off the bluff . . ." His voice faltered as his arm tightened, sending her quickly beating heart into a frenzy. "I don't want to lose you for any reason."

Astonished, she gaped up at him. It sounded as though he meant to keep her regardless of the demons that awaited in her fogged memory. She shook her head to clear it.

She had heard sweet words and promises before. Even if she could not recall who and when, the lessons learned carried a warning bite even the fog did not hide. All she had to do was convince her body that none of this was real.

Chapter 12

A WEEK AFTER taking up residence in the McCullough home, Melissa sat on the bluff, watching the sun set. Rory and his eclectic household made her feel welcomed and comfortable. If she didn't know better, she'd think she had found a permanent home. In odd moments she indulged in the fantasy of making love with Rory again. The memory of their uninhibited passion in the fairy ring haunted her constantly. Until experiencing it, she had scoffed at any such notions of overpowering physical attraction. Yet that was exactly what she and Rory had shared.

She shut out the erotic memory of their lovemaking and concentrated on the heavens. The clear sky promised a display of the stars in all their magnificence. She tucked the shawl borrowed from Elmira around her throat.

"You are a creature in love with the night, Melissa."

She smiled at Rory, glad he had not joined her earlier, when her errant thoughts had strayed into a realm that always made her too warm and quickened her breath. "I love the stars. I know them far better than I know myself." During the last couple of days, her croaking voice had strengthened to an audible whisper.

"Sh-h-h-h. No talking unless it's to tell me Someday has arrived."

Though he never pressured her, he was hopelessly focused on making love again. Each day in the warm light of his presence made her denial of the bliss she yearned to share with him more difficult. But indulging the fires of her body was sheer folly.

She looked over at Rory as he studied the sky.

Flexible and soft, his hair followed the playful whims of the ocean breeze. In sharp contrast, his profile was an unyielding silhouette against the starlit sky. The gentle curl of his mouth, ready for a smile or a heart-stopping kiss, fascinated her.

Not once since she'd known him had a hurtful phrase escaped those sensuous, gentle lips. The strength of his character showed in the firm set of his jaw and the straight line of his nose. Turned toward the sky, bent on serious study of the heavens, he echoed the intensity he showed anything, or anyone, that captured his interest.

A luscious shiver eased her frown. Being the focus of his attention was an incredible experience.

Someday.

He stood so still he could have been mistaken for a statue. None of the tremors of illness remained. But she knew the ordeal with the cougar had cost him dearly. She considered the way he favored his right arm. He lifted only light objects with it and used his left hand for everything except writing and eating. Even now, it was his left arm that he placed over her shoulder to draw her into his heat. Had she burned too deeply with the glowing knife and crippled him? The question gnawed on her conscience.

As if he read her concern, he captured her chin in his right hand and brought her face within inches of his. "You worry too much."

When she started to speak, his thumb slid over her lips.

"I see you watch me, your brow knit with anxiety when I do something left-handed. I'm mending just fine. Be patient with both of us." The tip of his finger traced her forehead. "All you have to worry about is you, and not injuring your throat again. We're both going to be fine."

With all her heart, she wished she could believe him.

He pressed his lips to her forehead, and though the shelter of his embrace loosened, it remained loving, yet possessive. "Watch the sky. Your starry friends are starting their show."

The patient gentleness he showered on her was becoming a narcotic. If she wasn't careful, Someday would arrive and she would lose everything. Yet even as she acknowledged the undeniable repercussions, her body responded to his sensual lure. She leaned against him and drank in the opiate warmth of his presence.

Together, they watched the starry cloak of night unfurl. The friends of her past soothed her questing soul with their unwavering fidelity.

The polestar beckoned, then captivated her. The fog emitted a flood of cherished memories surrounding the man who had given her hope when she had none. "Hello, Mr. Tibbens," she rasped. "I'll love you forever."

The years had dimmed his features, but not the impressions of his patient love for a tortured little girl angry at the world. Funny, the image in her mind had assumed some of Rory's features.

She laughed silently. Mr. Tibbens had barely topped five-feet-seven, yet he'd been a giant in her heart. Henry and Melva Tibbens had loved her until the day they died. The stars became her legacy of love.

Content with her friends in the sky, she looked at Rory. His head tipped back to see the stars. "Show me which one is Mr. Tibbens."

She pointed at Polaris.

"I wish your Mr. Tibbens could talk to me."

Melissa grinned, wishing the same thing for far different reasons, then started for the house.

Inside his office, Rory removed his coat and went straight to the drawing board. "Do you find Shelan's herbal—the book I gave you—interesting reading?"

She did. Shelan had recorded concise yet thorough explanations of the nurturing and use of each herb growing in the sheltered garden. The lists of treatments for ailments that Melissa had never dreamed existed amazed her. Shelan had carefully prescribed dosages and described side effects for every recipe. The detail of her drawings made them worthy of framing.

"You had best use the gargle again. It was cold outside." He smoothed a large sheet of heavy paper on the drawing board, then frowned as he examined it.

If it hadn't helped her heal, she'd gladly have poured the gargle and tonic into the ocean. Yet Rory made it fresh for her daily and always offered a piece of fine chocolate from the tin on his desk when she finished. She touched his arm.

He put down his pencil and looked down at her expectantly.

She curled her hand behind his neck and drew his cheek to her lips. After placing a kiss, she breathed, "Thank you."

Rory took a light breakfast in his office. The plans spread across the drawing table were near completion. Working from dawn until bedtime, he made up the time lost while he'd been in the mountains. Yet some things had taken longer than anticipated. The pull of the muscles healing in his chest limited his reach. Reluctant to severely test them, he continued expanding his range of motion incrementally.

Sensing a presence, he glanced up from the drawing table. Melissa stood with her hands behind her back, oblivious to the effect of the borrowed dress stretched across the top of her breasts. In a day or two, he would take her into Fairhaven and buy clothes that fit her. Sleep and good food had erased the dark circles under her eyes, but the haunted look remained. On those occasions when she wrote down the pieces she recalled from her past, she seemed at war with herself. The revelations painted a picture of a very different Melissa from the one he grew to know better each day.

She offered a scrap of paper from behind her back. *Can I help?*

"As a matter of fact, you can." At the desk, he cleared a writing surface. He opened a sheaf of papers holding the materials he'd calculated for the project. "Would you mind making a clean list out of these partials?"

She quickly rounded the desk and picked up the papers.

"They're in order. Start with the top sheet and go to the last." She must have discovered Shelan's assortment of oils. The subtle fragrance of roses clung to her dark hair. "Use this." He opened the side drawer and withdrew a stack of heavy writing paper.

She reached around him and quickly wrote a question on the message paper. He read over her shoulder.

"I usually make two copies, one at a time, then compare both to each other and the original notes. If you'll make the first, I can do the second when I finish these drawings." The half-finished rendering called to him. "These are the last. I hope to complete them today."

The eagerness she showed surprised him. He suspected she needed something more challenging than reading over Shelan's herbal or working in the gardens. She had thrown herself into those endeavors; he doubted any weed dared grow in the sheltered herb garden, she pulled them so quickly.

Rory returned to the drawing table, and work quickly consumed him. What some of his former colleagues in San Francisco had declared excessive detail, he loved for the precision of it. The more accurate his plans, the easier they came to life for his clients. Few of them understood the intricacies of architecture, nor did they wish to do so. Dollars were their forte. Rory took great care to show the wisest use of those investment dollars in each building he designed.

Shortly before dusk he laid down his pencils and rules. A great satisfaction settled over him at the end of every project. In those moments, he wondered if a master painter experienced a similar sensation after completing a work of art.

The scratchy sound of Lewis Waterman's newly marketed fountain pen on paper bespoke Melissa's continued diligence.

"The stars will be out soon. We can watch them through the cloud breaks," he said, marveling at her tenacity. When he thought about it, he realized he expected nothing less from her. She did everything without complaint and demonstrated a resourcefulness that never ceased to amaze him. No other woman he knew could have fared so well in the mountains. The survivor in her had conquered adversity and grown stronger with each challenge. Again, he wondered what sort of life had honed qualities most women loathed acknowledging.

Melissa waved her left hand and continued writing.

Patience. As his gaze drank in the visage that owned more of his heart each day, he smiled. He had plenty of patience, and he needed all of it when he lay in bed and recalled each tempting detail of their lovemaking. It was difficult to imagine what sort of demons had refused her more of their passion the next morning and every day thereafter.

Melissa set down the pen and handed him the stack of notes from which she had compiled the bill of materials. "Read out loud," she croaked.

"Wouldn't you rather watch the stars come out?"

She shook her head and arranged two piles of papers in front of her on the desk.

"You did both sets?"

She nodded.

And so he read while she checked the neat copies. The dryness in his mouth coerced him into pouring a glass of water from the pitcher on the side table near the couch. All the while, he read. After slaking his thirst, he refilled the glass and gave it to Melissa.

The clock on the desk read a few minutes past midnight when they finished. Smug satisfaction played over Melissa's lips. She slumped in his chair, bowing her spine, then straightened and stretched her arms high over her head. The arcing half circles she formed tightened the fabric of her dress across her breasts.

The motion riveted Rory's gaze and galvanized the hunger growing in his loins. Though he craved the fulfillment promised by her lush body, he now wanted more than the bliss they gave one another. She had as many moods as the weather and more facets than a fine diamond. He ached to explore all of them. The answers to his countless questions, questions never asked, remained locked within her nearly silent world.

"You saved me a full day's work. Perhaps more. Thank you." He pulled the chair away from the desk for her to rise.

"You want to check—"

"Sh-h-h-h. No. I trust you." He cupped her elbow and

helped her out of the chair and around the desk. The rose fragrance of her hair filled his lungs.

"But—"

The finger he laid against her kissable lips silenced her.

"No buts. I trust you." Unbidden, his arms drew her into an embrace. The curves of her body fit him perfectly.

"Trust yourself, Melissa." The erection growing in his trousers pressed her for more than trust. The uncertainty blazing in her searching hazel eyes cautioned him.

For all his admonitions and patience, he couldn't keep from lowering his lips to hers. With the lightness of a morning breeze, he brushed her lips with his.

"Kiss me." He savored the feel of her against him and the contours of her back and shoulders under his roaming hands greedy for the soft skin hidden beneath the fabric of her dress.

The subtle intake of her breath provided all the permission he needed. He captured her mouth in a tender kiss. Desire roared through him, quickening his pulse, though she remained rigid and did not return the kiss.

"Let me kiss you, sweet Melissa."

The slight pressure of her ink-stained hands on his shoulders eased. This time, he found her soft lips parted in submission. The glide of her cool hand along his shoulder charged his body with desire. The kiss deepened, drawing her into a hard embrace she welcomed with her splayed fingers at the back of his head.

Needing to taste more of her, the tip of his tongue ventured beyond the guard of her teeth. Nothing in life was as delicious as Melissa. To his delight, she teased him with the kiss, drawing him deeper into the vortex of passion.

A small sound escaped her. The sinuous motion of her belly against his erection fired his need. He wanted to tear away the cotton barrier between him and the delicious flesh of her shapely bottom.

He explored her mouth freely, letting the heady magic possess them. She wrapped both arms around his neck, holding him to the fire of the kiss. The magnificent pressure of her breasts against his chest sent his loins screaming. So sweet, so passionate and unselfish when she gave herself over to the torrential need that never went away, he took all she allowed, then reached higher.

The swell of her breast under his thumb made him shift. He captured her breast and thrust his thigh into the juncture he ached to unveil and possess. Her sudden intake of breath and tightening arms carried her higher onto his thigh. The heat of her hunger seared his leg through the layers of fabric.

He teased her tongue into exploring him, which sent her writhing against him until he thought he would explode. He burned to worship her body with all the love growing in his heart and free her from the demon denying them the glory found nowhere but in each other's arms.

Without warning, she stiffened, then drew back and pulled her hands from around his neck. His body lurched, his arms attempting to recapture the fire of her generous passion.

The touch of her hand on the left side of his chest deterred him. He relinquished his embrace by degrees until his empty arms hung from his shoulders in abject isolation.

Gazing into her dilated hazel eyes, hearing her quickened breathing, he knew the demon had fought valiantly and won again. His voice became a pained whisper when he spoke. "I am no better at tempering my desire for you than I am at not trusting you to know what you need. Do you not understand that I would willingly draw my last breath rather than hurt you?"

Tears pooled in her shining hazel eyes. "You don't know me." She blinked, sending a tear down her cheek. "I don't know me."

The slight quiver in her chin made him ache to gather her in his arms and kiss away her tears and turmoil. He stood motionless, not trusting himself to touch her while the fire in him burned his soul, aching for his other half.

"You will," he said with a sigh.

"You're so sure."

"I cannot be any other way. If you saw yourself through my eyes, you might understand." His fingers curled into fists when she lowered her head. Patience was a damn harsh taskmaster.

"Tomorrow, we will go to Fairhaven and buy clothes for you."

Her head shot up, her eyes wide with the protest ready to spew from her lips.

"We do this for me. If you are willing, I'd like you to accompany me to Seattle when I deliver this project. There is a doctor there I'd like an opinion from concerning your throat. That, too, is a purely selfish endeavor." He shoved his fists into his trouser pockets to keep from thumbing away the fresh spill of tears on her cheek.

"Will you do this, Melissa?"

She drew her lips between her teeth in contemplation and turned her head toward the window, where the stars peeked through breaks in the clouds.

It seemed a long time before her eyes met his. She nodded very slowly, then bowed her head and walked out of the room.

Rory listened until all sound of her departure faded. Sleep was a long time away for his aroused body. He decided to go outside and ask Mr. Tibbens if it would always be like this for them—all or nothing. The fire in him burned too hot with memories of her unbridled passion to settle for *nothing*.

Rory helped her onto the wagon seat. Again, the vague sense of recognition without experience struck her. She was sure she had not ridden in a horse-drawn wagon, yet she recognized it as familiar in a historical sense. Whenever the impression of gazing at herself in a different place in time flitted through her mind, it raced away, leaving an aftermath of disconcerting dread.

Tiny inconsistencies between the impressions leaking from the fog bank in her head and the world around her brought new, unsettling questions. Of late, she'd begun to wonder if she hadn't descended from the stars. The clothing she wore imparted an air of familiarity, but not on a personal level. It was as if she had seen it before but never worn it, though she could not recall what sort of clothing she *had* worn. Whenever she reached into the fog for that tidbit, she got the impression of sameness. That made no sense. Why would she wear the same thing every day? Or had she no choice?

Items she thought should be at hand were not. Some tasks, like creating the two copies of Rory's bill of materials, consumed an inordinate amount of time and effort bordering on exorbitant. How to minimize the task, she hadn't a clue.

She considered the questions and incongruities a progressive stride in discovering her true identity. Several days earlier, she'd had few thoughts about the inconsistencies between her past and present lives or why the familiar seemed strange. Now, for better or worse, the gap was widening. She had a feeling she wouldn't like the answers when they finally emerged.

"Would you like to visit Freedom House on our way to Fairhaven?"

Most assuredly she would. Each time the children visited, they came through the trees like visions in a dream, then disappeared the same way when they left. Believing they were as comfortable at the orphanage as they seemed proved difficult—yet she had found such contentment with Henry and Melva Tibbens. But she had been the equivalent of an only child with no competition for the affection and understanding they lavished on her.

Would that Kate, Chandra, Delvin, Pacho, and Rashad had received a modicum of the generosity Rory McCullough lavished on these children. Of them all, she thought perhaps Tommy appreciated it the most. His dusky skin tones and curly black hair contrasted sharply with his startling blue eyes. Something told her that a child of mixed race had a more difficult path than the others.

The road angled away from the path worn into the grass by the children and Mr. Lindstrom.

Melissa glanced at Rory. He possessed the tact of a saint. Not for a moment did she believe he wanted to buy clothes and take her to a doctor in Seattle for the purely selfish reasons he claimed. In truth, she knew it pleased him to do so, but he sought to please her, too.

"The curves of the road through the trees nearly doubles the distance between home and Freedom House."

The explanation broke her speculation.

"This road was already cut through the trees when we built a place for the children. There are projects more important than clearing the trees for a second, more direct road. Tommy and Darin do a fine job of keeping one clear for a carriage or wagon. Keeping two cleared is more than I would ask of them."

"They work for their keep?" The idea of child labor put her on edge.

"I guess you could say that. Each child has chores according to age and ability. It serves two purposes. The skills they acquire help them learn how to work together. The money they earn is theirs. They learn how to make the most of it. Tommy is a saver. So is Darin. Both love the outdoors. They talk about opening a logging operation and sawmill someday."

The grin lighting Rory's face bespoke a pride that raised the fine hair on Melissa's arms.

"Roger and Orin think only about their next trip to Fairhaven and the candy store. It took some persuading, but they save half of their earnings now." Laughter laced his words. "Perhaps they'll buy a candy store together."

"The girls?"

"Ah, the girls. They don't know what they want, other than never to leave one another. I have great hopes for Katy and Sandra."

The dynamics of Freedom House became clear. Not only had Rory chosen to rescue children from a cruel fate, he selected them as companions for each other. After brief consideration, she wasn't surprised he knew each child so well. She also realized the contented children she saw today were probably very different from those initially brought to Freedom House. The older children had the thickest shells around

their hearts; they were the ones who had endured the cruel,
dismal aspects of the world longer.

"Can we take the girls to Fairhaven?"

"I'll talk with Mr. Lindstrom about it if you promise to
rest your voice while we're in town. The girls and I can
speak for you."

The undeniable wisdom of the bargain he asked for made
her smile. She suspected his dealings with the children held
the same sort of gentle bribery.

"What if I don't like what you pick out in the way of
clothing?"

Rory laughed. "You don't trust my fashion sense?"

Shrugging, she had no idea of fashion and little choice but
to leave the selection in his hands. After all, it was his
money. She had only to wear whatever he bought.

Rory cocked an eyebrow in her direction. "I have no doubt
you are extremely capable of making your wishes known
without speaking."

Conceding the truth, she looked ahead.

The road curved toward the sea. An arch of branches
yawned into the daylight. An enormous two-story Victorian
house dominated a patch of cleared land marked with smaller
buildings and a barn. The design of the structures reflected
Rory's fine hand.

"Why do you take on these children?"

Rory hesitated a moment. "I'd take more if I could afford
them. Not just in a monetary sense. Their needs go beyond a
place to sleep, clothes, and food. Sven and Olga Lindstrom
are wonderful at overseeing them. Besides tending the basic
needs of Freedom House, they care for each child as one of
their own.

"Shortly after I started building Freedom House, I also
began to look for a couple experienced with handling a passel of children. On the surface, Olga and Sven were an un-
likely match with what I wanted. They had no children of
their own. Both worked hard, and they donated their free
time to a rather unconventional orphanage run by a church.

They were saving every penny to buy a house large enough to take on several abandoned children.

"Pete Jacobson, the doctor I want you to see in Seattle, took me to see the Lindstroms. Watching them with the kids, I knew they were perfect for Freedom House."

He gave Melissa a lopsided smile. "It isn't necessary to bring a child into the world to love one. That's what these children need—love."

Silently, Melissa agreed, remembering Henry and Melva Tibbens, the childless couple with mountains of love in their hearts.

The small laugh lines around Rory's eyes deepened in serious thought. "The children need my time most when they arrive. Each child lived with Shelan and me for a while, some longer than others, depending on the circumstance. Other than Katy, the first child, Darin remained with me the longest. Living at Freedom House while he had nightmares and struggled to regain his memory seemed unfair to all concerned.

"Tommy lured him into asking for the change. Their friendship is very strong. They know where I am when they need me."

"You're incredible," Melissa breathed.

Rory shook his head. "No, I only listen and ask questions."

"The right questions, by the look of the children." What she wouldn't give for the faces from her childhood to have had someone like Rory. Henry and Melva Tibbens had been her angels. Chandra, Kate, Rashad, Delvin, and Pacho had not been as fortunate.

"Charles Markel tutors the children. He's grown fond of them, too. However, his position at the Fairhaven school limits his time at Freedom House. I am hopeful of finding help for him in his duties."

"My god, you mean you support all of this yourself?"

"It is my choice. You'll discover some in town who think I am daft. Others think only women should be concerned with children. The only approval I seek is that of the children and myself." He halted the wagon in front of Freedom House. "And I want your approval, Melissa. What you think is very important to me. I'm curious, do you view Freedom House and the children as an unmanly endeavor?"

The sudden lump in Melissa's throat kept her from speaking right away. Though she might not be sure of much, she was sure that Rory McCullough was without question the most virile, masculine man she'd ever met. She swallowed the sudden gush of emotion and desire welling into her throat. "What you've built . . . What you give these kids . . ." The emotion nearly consumed her. "Unmanly? The strength of a man isn't measured in his size, but in his character. You're the finest, most generous man I know."

"Correct me if I'm wrong, but aren't I the only man you presently know?"

He could tease the light out of a star. "What I say is the truth. I feel it here." She straightened and touched her heart. "And here." Her finger lifted to her temple. "You don't need approval or anything else from me for what you are doing."

"But I do, Melissa."

The glide of his thumb over her lips left the question of what more he needed from her unasked. She sensed it went beyond the frisson of perpetual desire searing them both.

Chapter 13

"I LIKE THIS dress because it makes your eyes green, like Katy's." Sandra indicated a light woolen walking dress fashioned in forest-green and moss-green stripes.

"But the blue one is prettier. Look at the lace on the cuffs and hem," Katy said.

Personally, Melissa disliked them all and preferred trousers. The strangeness of the garments paled in comparison with the bustle contraption strapped around her hips. Layers of heavy clothing accompanied the corset and bustle. Though Mrs. Denman, the proprietress and local fashion expert, assured her that no woman appeared in polite society without a proper foundation, Melissa knew she had never worn such torturous devices. Barbaric was the only description for the fashion demands thrust on women.

She locked her jaw, stifling the stream of protests railing inside her. Even if she had to bite her tongue until it bled, she would keep her end of the bargain with Rory for the girls. Without Katy and Sandra, she would have left at the first suggestion of a corset and would never have experienced the atrocity of a bustle. Their obvious delight and sparkling excitement was a generous reward for donning the beautiful, if uncomfortable and unfamiliar, clothing.

Held rigid by the constricting collar, Melissa wiggled a finger behind the high neckline pressuring her throat.

"Not that one," Rory said, entering the back of the store. "I don't want her wearing anything tight around her throat."

"Perhaps we can loosen the fabric," Mrs. Denman mused, examining the neckline of the russet-colored dress. "This particular toilette is most attractive on your fiancée."

Fiancée? Anger added heat to Melissa's discomfort in the oven of the heavy dress.

"My fiancée." The withering disapproval that Rory shot at the young girls sent them scurrying around the display table.

"Oh, dear. Have I made a mistake?" Distress paled Mrs. Denman's rosy cheeks.

"I hope not," Rory said, eyeing first Melissa, then their young chaperones. "However, the issue has not been decided."

Melissa forgot the physical discomfort imposed by the weighty garb. The hope shining in Rory's gray eyes touched a chord behind the fog. The urge to flee never reached her stiff legs. Not comprehending why she rejected the notion did nothing to diminish the certainty that she had never considered marriage with anyone.

Rory cleared his throat and lowered his gaze. "Have you arrived at a selection?"

"I believe so." Mrs. Denman glanced at Melissa. "Miss Fuller indicated a preference for trousers, though I believe she has changed her mind."

Melissa broke her inertia with a quick protest.

Rory cocked his head. "Do you want trousers?"

"Oh, surely not, Mr. McCullough. They are inappropriate under any circumstances," Mrs. Denman insisted.

Melissa nodded, not caring what else he bought as long as she had a pair of trousers and a blouse and skirt.

Since she disliked them all, she chose the two dresses Katy and Sandra preferred. Two outfits were sufficient for a trip to Seattle, considering the apparatus required.

"We'll take a pair of whatever trousers she wants, too. I assure you, she will not wear them in town." He winked at Melissa. "She also needs a coat, Mrs. Denman. And shoes. I have business down the street and will return shortly."

"I'll see to it," Mrs. Denman assured with a smile. "Even the trousers, though I cannot imagine her wearing them anywhere."

"Katy. Sandra. Stay near Melissa," Rory said, heading down the aisle.

Like genies released from a lamp, the girls reappeared on either side of Melissa.

"We have several dolmans with matching bonnets that would be lovely with your coloring, Miss Fuller. I'll fetch them." Mrs. Denman hurried away.

"Were we not supposed to tell anyone you are marrying Mr. McCullough?" Worry clouded Katy's elfin features and squeezed the freckles along her brow. "Shelan said you are. And Tommy said I couldn't marry Mr. McCullough 'cause then you wouldn't stay. He said you had to stay so Mr. McCullough wouldn't be sad. He told me to marry Darin instead, but I don't know. Maybe that would be okay. Darin is closer to my age, so we can grow up and be parents." Katy's worry sent her fidgeting from one foot to the other. "Tommy said—"

"Sh-h-h-h-h," Melissa soothed, then knelt on the padding of her skirts and drew both girls against her. Holding them, feeling the worry flow out of them as they hugged her, Melissa understood the frailty of the security Rory tried to give them. She would not be the one to chip away what little confidence they mustered. Instead of admonition, she offered a dash of the tenderness she had found in the Tibbenses' home.

The future would take care of itself. When her voice returned, there would be time to explain why she could not marry Rory McCullough.

The girls remained beside her through the final tribulation of being fitted with a jacket and shoes. Their silence soon gave way to opinions on what she should choose and why.

Melissa exaggerated her reactions to the garments offered, her facial expressions and body language sending the girls into fits of giggles. Even the serious Mrs. Denman joined the merriment. Melissa's first attempts to sit while wearing the bustle brought peals of laughter from all three, though she was quite serious in that endeavor. The awkward adjustment required a skill that she would need to cultivate. Wearing such elaborate clothes in public was definitely going to take practice.

"Miss Fuller, you are a delight." Mrs. Denman wiped tears from her lower lashes with a lacy handkerchief. "You will be a marvelous addition to the Fairhaven community."

The smile lighting Melissa's heart flickered. Doubt rippled the fog of her memories. Rather than dim the ebullient mood, she retreated to the back room that was used as a changing room. At the door, she crooked her finger at the girls. Escape from the restrictive clothing required help.

Each layer became a game. She dressed the girls in the clothing from the outside in. Their enjoyment made her giddy.

Holding the corset firmly under her arms, Katy paraded between boxes and barrels. "My foundation is building."

"Not as much as mine." Sandra wiggled her bottom. The bustle shook over her skirts. "I have good posture and an excellent foundation for a train."

Melissa caught herself before mimicking a train whistle. The antics of the girls made the torturesome attire more palatable. She pulled on her borrowed dress, then gathered the garments, saving the bustle and corset for last.

When they emerged from the storeroom, Rory was waiting. "From the sounds of you three, I'd say shopping has its fun side."

"Oh, indeed." Sandra exchanged knowing glances with Katy and Melissa, then covered her mouth to stifle a giggle.

"All this hard shopping has probably made you thirsty. What do you say to a stop at Mr. Benjamin's before we head home?"

"I'm very, very thirsty," Katy giggled.

"I'll take those, Miss Fuller." Mrs. Denman relieved her of the burden. "Will you be wanting this one?" She examined the interior collar of the russet dress. "It appears there is plenty of material to let out."

"If you can make her comfortable in it, we'll take it."

Melissa touched Rory's arm and gave him a beseeching look while shaking her head. His generosity would put him in the poorhouse. Besides, she preferred that he spend the money on finding help for Mr. Markel with the children's education.

"Two dresses aren't sufficient," he said quietly.

She opened her mouth to protest, caught the tilt of his head, then closed it and nodded instead. She could be as obstinate as he, and he knew it.

"I see where this is leading," he murmured, then turned toward Mrs. Denman. "The blue and the green toilette will suffice. Add the skirt and blouse she tried on earlier—and don't forget the trousers." The warning in the glance he sent Melissa's way promised she had not heard the end of the wardrobe discussion.

Rory took Melissa's hand and tucked it into the crook of his arm. "What say we see what Mr. Benjamin's has to offer while Mrs. Denman prepares our parcels?"

"That's a fabulous idea," Sandra said.

"Oh, yes, let's do." Katy hiked her chin and waved her hand in mock sophistication.

Melissa caught the exchange between the girls and forgot everything except their laughter. Her fingers tightened on Rory's arm. In a flash, she recognized happiness as a welcome stranger.

"You have two admirers who don't give their hearts easily," Rory said after they left Freedom House.

"Thank you for today. The girls. The clothes." *For showing me happiness,* she added silently.

"My pleasure. I haven't seen them laugh so much in . . . perhaps ever. Children should laugh and be silly."

She caught his sideways glance and let the grin dancing in her heart escape.

"So should adults," he added meaningfully.

Perhaps so, since it felt so good inside.

"Do you think you were ever silly as an adult?"

Melissa pondered the question. The certainty that she had never indulged in anything approaching the antics in the store surfaced without redress. Slowly, she shook her head.

"I thought not."

Lifting her head sharply, she looked a question at him.

Rory trained his gaze on the road. "Only since I introduced you to the children have you begun smiling regularly. A woman who does not know how to smile is not likely to laugh much. The only reason for silliness is laughter."

Melissa cleared her throat, amazed by his insight. "You smile a lot."

"That's because I enjoy laughing. Most of life is funny, though sometimes in a macabre sort of way. If you look for humor even in distressing situations, it is easier to laugh and enjoy the world around you."

So that was his secret. What she needed was an instruction manual to show her how. . . . The thought faded into the roiling fog.

Instruction manual. The phrase became a key turning an invisible lock. She recalled bookcases filled with instruction manuals detailing complex minutiae. As quickly as it had emerged, the impression slipped back behind the veil.

"Memories?"

The brief flicker from the past sabotaged the fleeting happiness she enjoyed.

The image of endless details contained in row after row of color-coded books lingered. Why would anyone need to know the voluminous contents?

She stilled, suspecting that she had known every word on every page. Why? For what purpose?

The fog bullied her with silence.

"You didn't like this one much, did you?"

Melissa shook her head, aware but unconcerned about her transparency to Rory's discerning eyes.

"Find something absurd in it."

Eyes closed, she recaptured the image. In her imagination, she withdrew a manual from the stuffed bookcase and opened it.

Gibberish filled the book. One by one she tore out the pages and folded them at precise angles. In the magic of fantasy, she soon had a mountain of folded pages in the bowl of her skirt, which she held at the hem.

The woman in her imagination stood atop the bluff beside Rory's house with Katy and Sandra. A strong gust of wind blew from the ocean, catching the folded papers. They turned into a rainbow of colors and soared in all directions.

Excited laughter caught the breeze of her imagination. Katy's. Sandra's. Her own. The sky filled with colorful triangles flying and spiraling in the sunlight.

Suddenly the intimidating memory lost its dour punch.

It was silly, and oh so easy to enjoy in her present mood, with Rory's encouraging guidance.

Melissa nudged him with her shoulder and grinned. The conquest of the unknown marring the shiny penny of joy she had found today delighted her even more than the animation she conjured up.

"Good," he breathed, putting his arm around her and squeezing. " 'That which we can laugh at has trouble disturbing us.' " This time his squeeze drew her closer on the rumbling wagon seat.

"Who said that?" she asked, searching her memories.

"That, my dear, is a quotation from McCullough the Smile Monger."

He was that, she agreed, snuggling beside him.

"I've booked passage to Seattle. We leave in three days." Rory reined the horses toward the carriage house that doubled as a stable. "Would you like to practice walking around in the clothes we bought you before we leave?"

Had he noticed what the three watchers had not?

He climbed down from the wagon and reached for her. "I believe wherever you came from, you didn't wear anything similar to what we got for you today."

Hands on his shoulders, she jumped down from the wagon. "Is it so obvious?"

"Only to me. You weren't close to showing that much bewilderment when we were in the mountains." Rory's hands lingered at her waist.

"I don't know where I came from. Things are familiar, but not—" At a loss, she shook her head. "Like I've seen them somewhere, or something similar, but not experienced . . ."

"Like a dream?"

"Stronger." Her fingertips registered the growth of whiskers on his cheek since his morning shave. "Maybe I fell into a dream."

"This is no dream, Melissa. You and I are very real. I know I promised to help you go home, when you remember where it is, but I hope you'll stay here. When you remember where you came from, I could ask you to stay for the girls, and maybe you'd consider it. Maybe you would even do it. But the truth is, I want you to stay for me."

"I'm not a dream, either. Not yours. Not Shelan's." She cleared her throat and felt the bite of soreness eased by her ritualistic gargle. "Be careful what you wish, Rory. Until I know better, I have to blame you for my being here and magic as the conveyance."

The cloud of sorrow descending upon Rory's expressive features proclaimed that her effort to find absurdity in a serious situation had sorely missed the mark.

Rory closed the case holding the project now ready for delivery in Seattle. All hopes for a clear night of stargazing fled when clouds rolled over the sea. If the stars Melissa loved could speak, what would they say?

"Where did you come from?" The question leaked from his thoughts. More and more, he doubted her origins held any familiarity for him. Her attitudes and habits seemed forged from an eclectic creed. The bits and pieces of memory she recovered offered hope of total recall. Then what?

Loss pierced his heart.

Never mind the repercussions of soothing Katy and Sandra, both of whom would cry harder the longer Melissa remained. Or Elmira, who took Melissa's occasional strange behavior in stride, treating her with the same autocratic affection as she did him. If Melissa remained much longer, and then left, all of Freedom House would mourn.

But their sorrow would never match his grief.

He fretted over the promise made with honorable intentions. Regardless how much it pained him, he would send her wherever she wished to go when her memories returned. The choice was hers.

Movement near the bluff distracted his morose speculations. He set the case on the floor and looked out toward the sea.

Clad in the trousers Mrs. Denman disapproved of and one of Rory's sweaters, which hung nearly to her knees, Melissa walked along the bluff. Where did a woman more comfortable in men's clothing come from? The question nagged at him. A well-read man, Rory could not recall any culture in which educated women assumed the dress and habits of men.

For a moment, he considered she may have developed the preferences early in life, then carried forth in her own way. It fit Melissa. She had strong opinions and the tenacity of an angry bull.

He stood at the window and watched the wind blow her dark hair around her head. That, too, posed an anomaly. Although he liked the shorter, unfashionable style, he'd never met a woman with hair shorn above her shoulders.

All afternoon he had caught bits of Elmira's strident tones and laughter. Melissa had practiced walking and handling the voluminous yards of material that constituted a woman's skirt. He had refrained from watching the exercise, allowing her privacy and the help of a woman who was wise in the ways of the world.

Through the window he watched Melissa turn toward the wind rushing in from the sea, then tilt her face to the darkening gray clouds.

Rory let his mind float across the mystery of Melissa. She preferred trousers, handled a rifle better than he did, and had kept both of them alive in the mountains.

"Instinct," he mused. "She did it all by instinct. Where does a woman refine savvy like that? Why? God knows what's hiding in your memories, but you're not afraid of it, are you, Melissa? Not once have you shown the slightest fear, not even with the cougar. Why not?"

Hands wrapped around her arms, Melissa resumed her stroll down the bluff.

It seemed unreasonable anyone could develop armor over

their emotions strong enough to negate fear. In the mountains, he had glimpsed a hard shell and deemed it obstinacy. He considered her protective layers may have formed from loneliness or neglect. Perhaps she had known rejection. Regardless, she had formed the armor an incident at a time until her isolation was complete and her heart fended off the soft emotions that might wound her.

Rory recoiled. Surely his assessment was wrong.

Or was it? A fist squeezed inside his chest. Had survival in the place she came from cost so dearly?

His head hanging, he considered the conditions in which he had found some of the children now at Freedom House. Hunger. Filth. Neglect. Abuse of the most brutal, rank order.

If she had endured such conditions until she was old enough to fend for herself, small wonder she trusted no one. Anticipating the enemy stripped it of the power to inflict damage.

He had helped five of the six children at Freedom House lower their barriers and learn trust. But they were children, not a woman with years of practiced distrust.

Yet the principle was the same. Melissa would succumb and trust him if he had the patience to show her the way.

The intimacy of making love, of exposing need and desire, engendered a vulnerability she loathed risking. "Shelan, Shelan, did you strip away all her inhibitions to give me a taste of all I wanted, or to show her how magnificent we were together? For one short night, the shell held no power over the woman hiding inside."

Disturbed, he grabbed his coat and headed for the bluff. When he caught up with her, he turned her to face him. "Do something for me."

Her head cocked in familiar question.

"Reach inside your past and tell me if you've ever trusted anyone over the age of twelve." The way she stiffened said he asked too much.

"It doesn't work like that."

"I'm not asking you to find memories. I know if you could, you would. You have sharp instincts. Call on them."

"I trusted the Tibbenses."

"What happened?"

"They died." She started toward the house.

"Melissa?"

She paused but did not turn.

"Anyone else?"

Her head turned toward the calm sea for a long time before she shook it.

"You trusted me."

"That wasn't real."

"What we found with each other in the circle was very real. But I was referring to the way you reacted with the cougar. When I told you to duck, you went to the ground."

"Reflex."

He closed the distance separating them. "You trusted me in the cave."

Again her head shook in denial. "You trusted me, not the other way around." A gust of wind tried to swallow the whisper of her words.

Rory folded his arms around her shoulders and held her back against his chest. "It must have taken a helluva lot of hurt to hide the woman you showed me in the circle." He rested his chin on the top of her head. "I want her back, Melissa. I will do everything within my power to help you find her again."

Melissa lifted his arms from her shoulders. "She doesn't exist." Without a backward glance she started for the house.

"She does," Rory promised, certain that he had discovered the one thing Melissa feared, if only she could acknowledge it.

Chapter 14

RORY PACED THE hall outside Dr. Pete Jacobson's offices. The optimist in him sought a simple potion or pill to cure Melissa's damaged throat. The pragmatist knew better.

He checked his pocket watch for the fifth time in ten minutes.

Pete Jacobson was the best medicine man he knew and an old friend. If anyone could arrive at an accurate prognosis, it was Pete.

"Come in, Rory," Pete called from the door as his assistant, who was also his wife, departed.

"Miriam," Rory acknowledged with a short nod. The dour turn of her full mouth told Rory all he needed to know.

Pete sat behind a desk piled with organized stacks of journals and books. Sharp blue eyes peered over rectangular half-glasses perched on the tip of his aquiline nose.

"Whatever you have been doing to treat Miss Fuller has done more good than anything I know of, Rory."

Rory settled in the chair beside Melissa and glanced at her. Her stoic features betrayed no emotion. "I see. Is the injury permanent?"

"I have no way of knowing. Cases like this are rare." He waved at the journals piled on his desk. "I began poring through the literature when I received your message. The best advice I can give is to continue with what you're doing. Miss Fuller, the less you use your voice, the greater the possibility it will return. You've severely damaged your vocal cords, though I cannot determine in what manner. Let the body heal itself. Medicine is limited and cannot do more for you than what you and Rory are doing presently.

"Please understand, I cannot promise that even silence will restore your ability to speak in a normal voice for as long as you wish. I would be less than forthright if I did not express my doubt that you will ever have a strong voice again."

"There goes my singing career," Melissa rasped.

"Oh, my dear Miss Fuller, were you a singer?" Dr. Jacobson plopped back in his chair, his blond locks flapping around his ears. "I am so sorry to be the bearer of such sad news. Perhaps I am wrong. I have never tended a case like yours."

Melissa shook her head and dropped her gaze to her fingers laced on her lap. A tinge of color brightened her cheeks. "Sorry. Not a singer."

"Well," Dr. Jacobson relaxed, smiling, "there is nothing wrong with your startling sense of humor."

"Will she ever laugh aloud?"

"I know laughter is important to you, but I can't say, Rory. Only time will tell. Meanwhile, Miss Fuller, silence." Dr. Jacobson thumbed through the papers on his desk.

"Ernest Shaw over at the university put me onto a young man who recently arrived from the East Coast. Calvin Brockbannon might be the person you need. He taught at the American Asylum for Deaf-Mutes in Hartford, Connecticut. Presently, he is trying to rouse interest in the political communities for such an institute here."

"Sign language," Melissa whispered, her expression blank as if listening to something that neither man heard. "A manual alphabet."

The fine hair on the back of Rory's neck bristled, as it usually did when he watched a memory slip into her awareness.

"Why, yes, Miss Fuller. I believe Cal called it sign language."

"What is sign language?" Rory asked, sensing Melissa's return to the present and a fresh enthusiasm.

"A number of years ago, Thomas Hopkins Gallaudet devised a method of communicating through gestures," Dr. Jacobson explained. "He devoted his entire life to the endeavor. Through hand motions it is possible to convey entire ideas, much like a spoken sentence. For those things new, strange, or difficult to convey, there is also a manual alphabet. Of course, for it to be of use one must master a basic level of literacy."

"Melissa is well educated," Rory murmured, trying to envision conversing with Melissa with his hands while clothed.

"It is truly amazing to see Cal conduct a conversation. His hands move nearly as quickly as his mouth, though I would advise not standing too close lest you be struck with an adjective."

Melissa's silent laugh firmed Rory's conviction she would do what was necessary to use her voice again without fear of losing it. "Can you arrange an appointment with Mr. Brockbannon?"

"I can do better. Miriam and I are having him over for dinner tomorrow evening. Why don't you join us?"

Rory chuckled at his old friend. "A step ahead of us?"

Dr. Jacobson did not smile. "His work interests me greatly—but I had hoped that introducing him to you as a potential help for Melissa would be unnecessary."

"Melissa?" Rory had gauged her reaction to the exchange from the corner of his eye. Her slight nod conveyed her awareness of his close scrutiny.

"Would you like to take the text Mr. Brockbannon left with me? It may make interesting perusal." Dr. Jacobson withdrew a hefty tome from a stack on the side of the desk.

Melissa reached for it as though he offered a miracle cure.

"If you wish to communicate with Miss Fuller, you will have to learn what she is saying with her hands," Dr. Jacobson told Rory.

Rory smiled a deeper meaning to his understanding. When she applied those expressive hands to his flesh, he thought they communicated very well.

Calvin Brockbannon proved a soft-spoken, scholarly man. Melissa sensed an intense singularity of purpose about him. Eyes that seemed too brown for his fair skin and blond hair missed nothing. During dinner, he spoke little, but here in the

Jacobsons' parlor with a drink in his hand, he presented an interesting blend of serenity and excitement. More often than not, a flurry of hand gestures accompanied his words.

"I assume there is a purpose for meeting you and Miss Fuller to which I am not yet privy?" Calvin's slight build accentuated his towering height, which approached Rory's. A warm smile softened the sharpness of his almost gaunt features. "You are a very quiet woman, Miss Fuller, though your demeanor belies any pretense of shyness."

Melissa set aside the glass of sherry in her hands. The difficulty of asking for Calvin Brockbannon's help increased when a voice cried out from the fog, *Do it yourself. Ask for nothing. Incur no debts.*

For an instant she wavered. She glanced at Rory. The hope of communicating freely, without worry for her throat or the pain that flared and ebbed, won out.

Slowly she formed the letters of the manual alphabet memorized from the book that her host had thoughtfully lent her. "Teach me," she signed by spelling out the words.

Calvin's pale eyebrows rose with interest. "Why? You are not deaf. You're interest in conversation denies a hearing impairment."

When Rory started to speak, she held up her hand, silencing him and defying the sulking fog.

"Yes, Mr. McCullough, do allow her to continue. This is most fascinating." Admiration lit Calvin's brown eyes. "Teach you what, Miss Fuller?" he both said and signed.

"Sign language." She concentrated on the formation of each letter and hated the prodigious time it demanded. Her mind flew while her hands moved at what seemed a snail's pace.

"You are not deaf, but you do not speak?"

She debated answering him outright. "Want to. Silence best."

"Ah-h-h," Calvin breathed, glancing at the three spectators.

"Miss Fuller has a throat injury. I believe her chances of

recovery are greater if she remains silent," Dr. Jacobson offered.

"You wish to be silent, but not silenced. Is that it, Miss Fuller?" Calvin nodded thoughtfully.

Melissa couldn't stop the grin spreading across her face.

"Learning to sign is like speaking another language. If no one understands, it is useless."

"That is why we would like for you to tutor us together." Rory crossed the room and took her hand.

"I see." Calvin retrieved his drink and sipped it. "Most of my students at the asylum were children."

Asylum? Heavens, did they put deaf children in an asylum? A familiar rage of injustice skittered through her. She bit it back and assumed a wait-and-see patience. Of late, the common usage of some words proffered meanings very different from her interpretations. She hoped that was the case now.

"Does that startle you, Miss Fuller?"

"Asylum?" She desperately needed to sign whole words. Complete ideas would be even better.

"Why, yes. Though there is no institute for you and Mr. McCullough here, it is not for my lack of trying. Thus far, my efforts to establish an asylum for deaf-mutes have found little support in Seattle. Perhaps Victoria will prove a more benevolent location."

"Are you planning to leave, Mr. Brockbannon?" Rory slipped a protective arm around Melissa's waist. "I am far from being a wealthy man, but we can offer compensation for your tutelage."

Calvin stroked his smooth chin in deliberation.

"Teach children," Melissa explained, her fingers flying through the letters.

"Yes, yes, my intention is to work with children," Calvin said absently while watching her hands.

"We." She pointed at Rory and herself. "Rory's children."

Calvin straightened, his face lighting with renewed interest. "You have deaf children, Mr. McCullough?"

"No. However, Melissa has an excellent idea. If the children learned to sign, they could communicate freely with her and she with them."

The squeeze at her waist lifted her head. The pride and tenderness sparkling in his gray eyes blended into a smile that she answered with one of her own. They would learn all they could and teach the children a new form of communication.

"We have six children who would like more than an occasional whisper or gesture from Melissa," Rory continued. "Of late, they have taken to carrying slates and chalk around her."

"Interesting, most interesting," Calvin mused.

"I'm not asking you to come to Freedom House, just teach us and we will work with our children."

"What is Freedom House?"

"It is a beautiful place near Fairhaven, north of here," Dr. Jacobson chimed in as he and Miriam joined them. "Rory built it for the stray children he's collected over the years. Were it not for the funds he shuttles into supporting it, he would be a wealthy man, Calvin. Our fledgling university has a school of architecture that has yet to produce anyone near the caliber of Rory.

"I've known Rory for almost ten years. He has extended his assistance to children who have been subjected to things you and I would find outrageous. This is the first time I've known him to ask for anything of a remotely personal nature."

Hearing Dr. Jacobson's advocacy confirm her beliefs in Rory's altruism filled Melissa with a warmth she did not comprehend. She embraced it with her heart and cherished the sensation.

"Perhaps we can work something out," Calvin conceded. "I assume you have limitations on your time, Mr. McCullough, just as I do."

"I will make the necessary time available. What can you allow us and when can we begin?"

"Miss Fuller has already begun by learning the alphabet. I sail for Victoria in a month and expect to remain there for another. Can you remain in Seattle until I depart next month, Mr. McCullough?"

"Yes," Rory answered without hesitation.

Melissa leaned against Rory. The arm at her waist tightened.

Today she had accompanied him for the delivery of the plans he had virtually slaved over. The admiration of his client was evident in the attentive way he listened as Rory spoke with him and the men who would construct the building. While they wanted more of Rory's involvement in the project, he had stood firm and put a limit on the time he could give them. He had other commitments. The men had seemed to understand and counted themselves fortunate he had agreed to anything beyond the plans spread before them.

In reality, he had saved the time for her and learning the hand motions of signing. The insight bespoke his commitment to learning all that Calvin Brockbannon could teach him.

"Excellent. Why don't we arrive upon a schedule?"

For the next month Melissa and Rory studied signing under the tutelage of Calvin Brockbannon. The demands of meeting with clients and working added hours to Rory's days. On those rare occasions when business denied him a session with Calvin, Melissa tutored him into the night. He savored their private, quiet times.

Calvin proved a natural teacher. He maximized their time and stretched the limits of their separate schedules. Their afternoon hours together often lasted into the evenings.

Long after Melissa retired to a room down the hall in the boardinghouse where they lodged, Rory worked on the sketches and briefs for the commission he accepted.

Two clients, for whom he had worked previously, refused the suggestion of finding another architect. Both espoused their willingness to wait for his time and offered bonuses if he completed the overview and projected materials requirements of their plans by the end of the year.

Rory contemplated the benefits and weighed them against

the realities of a twenty-four-hour day. The bonuses alone would keep Freedom House in fine stead for the next several years. Despite the grueling demands of the projects awaiting his attention, the profitability that they ensured would secure a financially comfortable future for those he loved.

The daily sessions with Calvin and Melissa made her eventual departure seem even more unreal. Yet when the possibility reared its head, pain filled Rory's chest. If she chose to leave him, she would do so with his heart in her hand. It belonged to her with a totality that he dared not reveal, though he burned for the Someday when his love would assume the fullness of physical expression.

She attacked the challenge of learning with the same depth of passion with which she made love. Never had Rory witnessed an ability to focus so intently. Her concentration on making the nimble gestures second nature excluded the rest of the world, including him.

At odd times during business discussions and while walking with Melissa along the hilly streets of Seattle, he found his gaze wandering to hands instead of faces when people spoke.

The evening time that he and Melissa spent conversing in sign became favorite islands of the day. Laughter at their inept attempts and false meanings staved off frustration. Rory found that he read her hands far better than signed. Their final week in Seattle, she refused to acknowledge his spoken word. His admiration for the tenacity of her silence since her first visit to Pete Jacobson's office deepened daily. Voluntary silence became a taxing discipline that forced him to concentrate on honing his manual conversation skills.

Rory gathered his notes and drawings into his traveling case. The single rap of Melissa's knuckles on his door as she passed signaled the time for their evening study in the boardinghouse dining room.

Downstairs, a lamp burned over the long table seating eight boarders for breakfast and supper. Melissa's generous smile sparkled in her gaze when he entered. His heartbeat quickened, as it did each time she regarded him with such eagerness for his company.

"We have come far," she signed.

Rory nodded. "Tomorrow afternoon we go home." His slower manipulations matched her precision. Often, he spelled out words for which he did not know the gesture.

"Children." Longing dimmed her smile. "Think we ran away."

Rory laughed. "They know we come home soon. Are you ready to leave?"

Nodding, Melissa signed, "Calvin left today. I am ready for home."

Rory withdrew a paper from his inside coat pocket and laid it on the table in front of her. "I ordered these materials from the American Asylum for Deaf-Mutes in Connecticut. Calvin thought the literature and reference would help us teach the children. I am not the teacher he is," Rory said quietly.

"Me neither. So much still to learn," she signed. Approval marked her expression as she scrutinized the list.

When she returned the paper and he slipped it into his pocket, she resumed signing. "We will master it together."

"Together," he murmured. Hope leaped inside him.

Melissa's hands dropped to her sides. The yearning he saw in her eyes when she watched the stars at home and silently pleaded with them to speak seized her expressive features.

Rory tensed in recognition of a familiar, silent battle she waged in the aftermath of a volatile memory bursting from her shrouded past.

Again, he admonished patience. That even part of her warred in his favor kept alive his hope of sharing her life.

After a moment her frown eased. "Why are you such a good man?"

The surprising question evoked a startled laugh. "If selfish is good, I'm good."

"Not selfish. You give, give, give. Gave me this." Her hands stilled briefly. "Voice without speaking. I give you nothing, but my thank-you."

"I do what I want. It pleases me."

She hesitated before unleashing a flurry. "Why do you take the children?"

"Why not?" Delving into motives he no longer examined was best done at home. Yet, in the quiet of late evening, their end of the spacious dining room was private. While speaking in sign, the errant wanderer crossing to the parlor would have no understanding of their conversation.

"Avoiding the answer?" Color brightened her cheeks and she waved away the question.

"Some people collect stray animals," he signed slowly. "I suppose I collect stray people."

"Elmira?"

Nodding, "I have known her since I was fourteen. She came with us from San Francisco." Wondering how much was wise to say, he hesitated, then forged ahead. There would be no secrets between them. "I met her in a store. She had just been released from prison and was looking for employment. No one would hire her."

"Prison? For what?"

"Manslaughter," he spelled out. "We were in need of a housekeeper. I hired her." A guilty smile spread into a grin. "I did not tell my father about her past, nor did she. Elmira has been with me since."

"Your mother?"

Feelings mellowed by time and maturity surfaced with a blunt edge.

An audible sigh escaped Melissa. "Sorry. You do not want to talk about your mother. Tell me why you have a soft spot for the children."

"When I was ten, my mother pinned a note to my shirt and left me on my father's porch. The first time I met him was when he came to the door. He read the note, stuffed it into my shirt pocket, then closed the door, leaving me outside," he said softly.

"I thought any place was better than where I'd come from and that he could not be crueler than my mother, so I sat on the stoop." Recalling the ordeal, he found a humorous side. "For three days."

"Three days?" Melissa's hazel eyes widened with astonishment.

Nodding, Rory resumed signing. "It was a lesson in patience and resourcefulness. Horace Sawyer did not want to claim me as a son, but I wanted to claim him as my father. Since then, the plight of other unwanted children has allowed me to think more kindly of my mother. It could have been far worse. Had I been a babe she abandoned at a church or a workhouse, I might not even have survived boyhood. As for education or opportunity, there is precious little of that in a workhouse.

"I showed the note from my mother to anyone who came to my father's door. Three days was all his reputation withstood. He took me in to save face.

"My father was an architect. I became one, too." He winked at her. "A good one."

Her fingers covered her parted lips. The awe shining in her eyes humbled him.

"Good enough," he added.

"You love it."

"Yes. I'm fortunate. But I remember what it was like to feel what some of our children experienced. Tommy and Darin have endured reprehensible abuse. If I can give them something positive, educate them, let them know there are those who care and are worthy of their trust . . . their affection . . ." Having revealed too much of what lay closest to his heart, his hands stilled.

"Like me?" she asked.

"No. I wish to send them out into the world. You, I want to keep with me always."

"When we both truly know me, you will send me packing."

Sorrow darkened her eyes and restored a slight frown.

"You have remembered?"

She shook her head. "Bits. Pieces. Impressions. But I do not think I like myself."

"Perhaps you will have a choice of being who you were or who you are now."

"Who am I, Rory?"

The woman I love. He remained silent.

Chapter 15

MELISSA GLANCED AT the leaden sky before following Rory into the depths of the *Northern Trader*. A gust of chilly air quickened her steps into the shelter of the stairwell. The narrow passageways lit by kerosene lamps smelled of saltwater and aged timber.

Rory opened a cabin door, then stood aside for her to enter. The tiny quarters offered a lone, stationary bunk, a small table, and two lanterns mounted on the wall. At the foot of the bunk there was barely enough space for their trunks.

"I reserved this cabin for you." Rory set down the traveling cases that he trusted to no one else, then lit the lamps. "If you don't mind, I'll leave these here. We sail in an hour. Once we're under way and have had dinner, try to get some sleep. We'll be stopping in Port Townsend, then sailing on to Fairhaven before you know it."

Confused, Melissa touched his shoulder as he slid the cases into the corner beside their trunks.

"Yes?" His gaze immediately sought her hands.

"Where will you be?" she signed.

"On deck or in the salon."

"Why not here?"

A grin parted his lips. "It is highly improper for an unmarried man and woman to share a cabin. We were fortunate to get this one, or we would have had to stay until I could book suitable passage home."

Protest welled up in her silent throat. "I will not take the cabin you paid for while you scrounge for a place to catch a few hours of sleep." Chivalry and propriety were one thing.

This was tantamount to deprivation; she wanted no part of it. From the moment he pulled her from the lake he had considered her welfare above his own. He had fed her, clothed her, ensured her education in sign language, and offered a home more comfortable physically and emotionally than anything imaginable. In return, he asked nothing.

"Please, Melissa. I can't spend the night in the same cabin with you without jeopardizing your reputation."

Her hands shot an angry retort. "I don't care. Sharing the cabin wouldn't harm yours, would it?"

"A man's reputation is not judged in the same light."

"Stay."

Rory drew a long breath. "I would find it difficult to spend a night here with you."

Melissa froze.

"Look around, Melissa," he urged, speaking softly. "Where could I go in this cabin without feeling the ache for Someday with every breath I take?"

Desire burned in his smoky gray eyes. When he continued, he did so silently with his hands. "Sometimes, signing is all that keeps me from touching you."

Her hands snapped a response that would never have crossed her lips. "You can have my body. It is the least—"

Anger narrowed Rory's flinty eyes. He caught her hands in one of his. "You insult us both," he seethed. "Don't cheapen the treasure I hold so dear by offering yourself as payment for what I give freely. If I wanted a whore, I'd visit a bordello. It shouldn't surprise you that I know where the best ones are."

Stunned, she watched him turn his back. The slamming of the cabin door punctuated the finality of his departure. Weak-kneed, Melissa reached for the edge of the bunk and settled onto it. Her stomach churned. Why, oh, why had she offered to go to bed with him?

The battered restraints containing the raging desire that leaped into heated readiness whenever he so much as walked into a room remained in place. Since succumbing to his last kiss, she had thought often of tearing them down herself. In

truth, she wanted to make love with him. Her cheeks colored
as she acknowledged that she rushed to sleep every night
eager to relive the memories of the stone circle in lush, erotic
dreams. If he kissed her now . . .

He wouldn't kiss her now. She had demeaned herself in
his eyes by offering services available in any bordello. He
did not want a whore. He wanted something that wasn't real.

Holding her drooping head in her hands, she wondered if
anything in the circle had carried a shred of reality.

True, something had brought her there. Something magical had happened between them. Whatever that something
was, it hid behind the safe veil separating who she had been
from the person she'd become. Instinct warned of a vast gulf
between the two.

If she indulged her growing affection for Rory, her only
lasting reward would be his revulsion once he learned her
true nature. Placing the bits of fragmented memory and impressions in a jigsaw puzzle with half the pieces missing, she
did not like the emerging picture: that Melissa Fuller cared
little for anyone or anything beyond an elusive goal. For reasons still hidden, she knew the woman she had been was callous toward those around her. She gave nothing of herself.

Worse, she had nothing worthwhile to offer.

She was a fraud who hid her emotions until they shriveled.

Only a fool would still want her once he realized that re-
capturing what they had shared in the stone circle was a hollow illusion.

She closed her eyes, hoping to shut out the world and drift
into oblivion.

The omnivorous fog swirled into a shape.

A handsome man in a dress uniform smiled at her, then
executed a crisp salute with the gleaming saber in his gloved
right hand. He turned on his heel.

Recognition struck with the force of a physical blow.

Abruptly, he snapped to attention, all traces of the alluring
smile gone. His hard, cold gaze penetrated the crumbling
shell protecting her heart.

Tony Landis.

As soon as the name popped into her mind, memories sucked her into an emotional vortex. She had loved him. Only because she had broken her own rule and trusted him. And only now did she understand that he had loved her too.

The delicious tension of waiting, waiting, waiting for the right time to consummate what she had thought was a once-in-a-lifetime love made her head spin.

With inexplicable dread, she recoiled from the euphoria of painfully sweet anticipation that was inundating her senses. Fighting against the obsessive tide churning out of the fog only heightened the intensity.

With no recourse, she bowed in defeat, steeling herself to endure another piece of her past moving inexorably into the light.

Her rigid body went limp. She became two people on the viewing screen of her mind: one watching with a discerning eye, the other glorying in Tony's embrace.

Floating above the couple who writhed in passion amid tangled sheets, she relived the last night they spent together. The longer the vision took to unfold, the more she suspected that something was wrong. No laughter or joy celebrated their lovemaking.

The page of memory turned.

She sat in the center of the rumpled bed and watched him dress. The elation of giving herself to the man she loved left her basking in a warm glow.

"I can't do this anymore, Melissa."

"Wh-what do you mean? You can't do what?" At the horrible sensation of having made a terrible mistake she reached for the sheet to cover herself.

"I can't make love with you anymore. Damn it, woman, you've got so much to give, but you hoard it." Tony fastened his trousers, then looked at her.

How could she have forgotten the sadness in his blue eyes, the torment in his handsome face, or the way his strong, broad shoulders slumped in defeat?

"Tony, I . . ." She stopped short of baring her soul and indulging in the futility of confessing her love for him again.

He knew she loved him. "Is there . . . Is there someone else?" Lord, she sounded pitiful.

Tony sat on the edge of the bed, his shirt hanging open. "Would it make it easier if I lied and said there was?"

"You just don't want to make love with me. Right?" The flatness of her voice hid the anguish shredding her heart.

"You're tearing me apart, Mel. We've been sleeping together for—what? Almost a year now?"

Melissa's nod confirmed the term of their intimacy.

"I've loved you for twice as long. I know you love me or you never would have slept with me." His hand rose, then fell on the wrinkled sheet. "I've tried not to pry into things you don't want to talk about. Damn, but you're the most private person I've ever met. You don't say anything, and I'm not asking you to now. It's too late for me."

"I don't understand what you're driving at, Tony." She suspected, but she didn't want to admit it. Maybe she was wrong.

"For us, love isn't enough. For a year we've made love every way possible for a man and a woman to do so. But not once have I satisfied you."

"That isn't important," she protested.

"It is to me." Tony rose from the bed and buttoned his shirt.

She gathered the sheet around her, suddenly cold in the warm room. The scent of their lovemaking mingled with the tang of the disinfectant used by the motel maids.

"Good-bye, Melissa. I envy the man you decide to trust with all of your heart and the gift of your passion. You'll both find great rewards. I just wish it could have been me."

Tony Landis walked out of the motel room and out of her life.

In the numb silence that followed, the muted ring of the ship's dinner bell sounded like a death knell. *Fool! Fool!* it chimed.

The grief she had tucked away as another layer of callus on her heart burst forth. Tears she had refused amid the wrinkled sheets long ago now streamed down her cheeks. Noth-

ing stopped them or the sad replay of Tony Landis's
farewell. She had loved him, but not enough to trust him.
She had thought him cruel and his priorities askew when he
left her. What did it matter if she had never reached orgasm?
She had enjoyed their intimacy, and Tony never lacked stim-
ulation.

Now she understood what he meant.

The suspension of reality she and Rory had experienced in
the fairy ring had shown her the beauty of giving herself
completely on every level. Without the magic or whatever
had changed the world within the circle, she'd not reach that
bliss again. Then what? Rory would look upon her with the
same sad reproach as Tony Landis had. He'd leave too—or
send her packing.

The gentle sway of the ship on the waves of Puget Sound
lulled her into emotional exhaustion. But still the tears
flowed.

Rory answered the dinner bell summons expecting Melissa
to join him. During the meal service he watched the door.
The emptiness of the place beside him angered him as much
as it made him ache for her presence.

How could she place such a meager value on what he
longed for with every fiber of his being? Yet that was the
crux of it. The desire ravaging him was his to control.
Melissa had done nothing to deserve the denunciation he
heaped on her. Her concern had been for his comfort. Comfort wore many faces. But not one of them was the compensation of her body in payment for a debt she did not owe.
Her spontaneous offer rankled him more each time he recalled it. Had she given it an iota of thought, she would not
have offered herself.

When they shared the sweet bliss of lovemaking again, it
would not be because she perceived a sense of obligation.
The fulfillment of taking her body while giving his would be
out of the completeness of his love for her.

In the moil of rumination his appetite fled, and the food
became tasteless. With deliberate ritual Rory lifted his fork.

His participation in the dinner conversation required an effort he loathed exerting. All the while he wondered why Melissa hadn't joined them. Perhaps she was tired or was experiencing mal de mer. Most likely she was angry and deemed his company unpalatable.

After dinner, he navigated the passageways to her cabin. His rap on the door went unanswered. Hesitant, he turned the knob, expecting the resistance of the bolt inside.

The door swung open. The twin lamps he had lit earlier burned away the darkness.

Melissa lay curled in a tight ball on the bunk. The bow of her crushed bonnet hung over her jaw; the folded brim hid her face. The toes of her sturdy shoes peeked out from under the hem of the voluminous blue skirt wadded between her abdomen and thighs. Gloved hands cupped her elbows below her updrawn knees.

Rory let himself in, then closed and bolted the door.

He knelt beside her and loosened the ties of her bonnet. Silvery tear tracks were dried on her cheeks and the bridge of her nose. The even rise and fall of her breathing bespoke her refuge in sleep.

"Melissa, sweet Melissa. I didn't mean to hurt you," he whispered. The remnants of his ire melted into compassion.

Heavyhearted, he worried her hands away from her elbows. Her tight grip further dismayed him with the realization of how deeply she had withdrawn into herself.

Careful not to wake her, he cradled her head and slipped the pillow beneath it. The blanket he folded over her covered her shoulders.

He dimmed the lamps and listened. The creaking of the ship punctuated her breathing. The key he had forgotten to give her weighed heavily in his pocket.

He locked the door and headed for the deck. The cool, salty air would help clarify his thinking. What could he possibly say to ease her torment?

Melissa woke, but remained motionless. The ghost pain Tony Landis had inflicted left her emotions raw. He belonged to the past. Old instincts warned her to shut out all memory of him and her vulnerability as thoroughly as the fog had. She had done it before, she could do it again.

She hesitated, unsure.

Questions played hopscotch in and out of the fog. One begged for an answer that eluded her. She had loved Tony. Why hadn't she trusted him? Why had she always expected him to hurt her—until he fulfilled that expectation?

The discerning eye that had witnessed the memory revealed unbiased impressions. Tony Landis had admired her intellect, albeit grudgingly. He had loved her. For a time.

The hiccups of a prolonged cry escaped when she drew a deep breath. The corner of the blanket fell onto her cheek. Absently, she reached for it and drew it tight against the cold growing inside her.

She would not relegate Tony Landis to oblivion without comprehending herself. Why had she abandoned a lifetime of safeguards and loved him?

Sweet words, positive strokes, came the impartial answer. He had loved her and made her feel desirable. She had wanted someone to love and to love her. But like every other tender emotion she'd endured, she cautiously measured the depth of her affections, expecting disappointment and trying to minimize the cost. She believed Tony's professions of love, but doubted that any man could truly love her. Consequently, she always held back a part of herself and never reached the glorious heaven Tony offered each time they made love.

Rory had spoken sweet words too. And she doubted his sincerity even when it invaded her crumbling defenses. He was not Tony Landis, yet instinctively she treated him as though he were. Hiding the memory, consciously or unconsciously, had not dulled the aftermath.

Confused, she sat up and dangled her elbows across her upraised knees. She vowed not to ignore the dark memories scurrying into the virulent cavern where they had festered for years. They embodied partially learned lessons. She needed them to understand the persistent, unsettling feelings revolving around her identity.

"Are you all right?"

Startled, she raised her head abruptly. Rory sat on the trunks, his forearms resting against his thighs.

"I'm fine." The sound of her voice reminded her of the forced silence.

"Are you hungry?"

Head shaking, she tried to define what she felt. Exhausted. Drained.

Rory cleared his throat. "I believe an apology is necessary."

"Truly sorry," she signed. The insult she thoughtlessly delivered had pierced his tolerance deeply enough to anger him. Regret weighed on her shoulders until they slumped.

"Not from you. From me. I'm sorry I angered so easily. I should have realized you didn't mean what you said. Frustration is a strong impediment to clear thinking, and it's no excuse."

A derisive chuckle broke into his words. "My frustrations are not your concern. I had no idea my actions would cause you tears."

Needing him to understand, Melissa scooted to the bottom of the bunk. "What I said to you was as wrong as it was insincere. If I weren't so empty inside, I would feel ashamed." Her hands stilled for an instant. "And undoubtedly will later.

"What I cried about had nothing to do with you. Not directly."

She turned her head toward the wall and debated the wisdom of unveiling the reasons for her angst. The raw impressions defied revelation.

"Unhappy memories?"

She nodded at his unintended understatement.

"Then I am doubly sorry for bringing them forth."

"I need them," she said aloud in a frog voice.

Rory stood and brightened the lamp. "I imagine that you do. They are the key to returning to your home."

The morose declaration stung. No home could be better than the one he gave those who won his affection. Already he had extended a rare generosity she could never repay. Imposing longer than necessary only made her inevitable departure more difficult.

She waited for him to turn away from the wall. The broad expanse of his shoulders hid the expressive features she had learned to read at a glance. "I have tried to drag the memories of my past into the light—"

"Sign—don't speak."

She slipped off the bed and stood behind him. "Then look at me, Rory. Or have I offended you so deeply you do not want to see me?"

He neither turned nor spoke.

"Why are you here? Surely not to ruin my reputation."

When he turned around, she retreated a step out of reflex. The hunger darkening his stormy eyes reached inside her and fired the desire that taunted her dreams and was barely tameable when she was near him.

"Do you not know how deep my feelings for you go? Or don't you care, Melissa?"

"I don't know, and I care very much." A flicker of something she recognized as fear rippled through her. "Sometimes . . . sometimes, I don't even know what I feel, so trusting what I . . ." Words failed to express the constant turmoil of her thoughts. "I want to believe what I see, but . . ."

"But you can't?"

She bit her bottom lip and shook her head in confirmation. The storm in his eyes receded, exposing the bedrock of the incessant desire tugging at them both.

A sudden heave of the ship sent her backward. She barely caught the edge of the bunk and then sat down hard. The bustle she wore bit into her lower back.

"The sea is growing rough. A storm must be coming through. We entered the Strait of Juan de Fuca earlier. It will be dawn soon."

"Are we in danger?" she signed, then braced against the pitch of the ship.

"No, I don't think so." A sudden smile eased the tension. "At least, little more than when we set foot on this ship.

From the looks of her, the captain and crew have had years of practice at keeping her afloat."

Melissa followed his gaze across the aging timbers. The turbulence of the rough sea intensified the creaks and groans.

"What happens if it sinks?" she signed.

"I'll do my damnedest to get us topside and safely to the nearest shore." The tender smile eased the strain around Rory's mouth and heightened the conviction blazing in his eyes.

"You would, wouldn't you?" The thought summoned distress. He would jeopardize his chances of survival for her.

"How do I make you understand there is damn little I wouldn't do for you, Melissa? Are your memories so painful there is no room in your heart for a little faith?"

"Faith is something that belongs in churches."

"And in people. If you cannot find it within your heart to place your faith in people who care about you, you are doomed to be alone regardless of how many surround you."

Had she believed in anyone besides the Tibbenses? Surely there must have been someone? Nothing emerged from her sequestered memories. A tingle ran down her spine. The notion of separatism in the midst of people added to her disquiet.

"I believe in you, Rory. I believe you would die trying to rescue me if this ship goes down."

Rory cocked his head and raised an eyebrow. "Progress."

She gaped at him. "Death is not progress."

"We weren't discussing death. Neither of us wants to die. Besides, the ship is still afloat." He changed his hold on the ceiling beam and widened his stance as the ship tilted at an oblique angle.

Melissa gripped the edge of the bunk until the worst of the pitch subsided, then began unfastening her buttons.

"What are you doing?"

"Maybe I'm paranoid. Or maybe I'm just afraid. It doesn't matter, because disaster strikes the unprepared harder than those who anticipate it. If there is even the slightest possibility of this ship going down, I want a fighting chance. In this armor, I'll sink like a rock." Her fingers returned to the buttons.

"The sea will ease once we enter the shelter of Vancouver Island." As though to belie his claim, the ship rocked hard to the left and sent his free hand reaching for a ceiling timber. "I'd best leave while you change."

"Don't you dare leave me alone on this roller coaster," she croaked. "If it bothers you, open the trunk and find my trousers and shirt."

Rory made his way to the trunk and sorted through her neatly folded clothing until he found what she wanted.

The severity of the rough seas increased the tumult of the ship and the haste with which she stripped away the layers of proper clothing.

"Socks," she whispered. "I need socks."

"Right here." He tossed a pair on the bunk.

Melissa dressed quickly and replaced her shoes, glad she had something comfortable and sturdy instead of fashionable. She swept up the discarded garments and tossed them over the end of the bunk.

Rory sat next to her. "I've made this journey countless times, and I admit this is a pretty bad storm. They blow in, raise havoc for a little while, and keep on going."

"I don't want to drown," she signed.

"I won't let you." Rory leaned against the wall at the head of the bed and stretched his legs behind her. "What is a roller coaster?"

She faced him and hooked her leg over his knee as a stabilizer. "Something fun," she signed, her eyes closed and she smiled at the memory of the amusement park she visited as a loved child of Henry and Melva Tibbens. Her hands flew while trying to describe each detail.

"Slow down," Rory said, laughing. "I can't decipher that fast."

A silent laugh escaped as she slowed. Midway through her elaborate explanation of an amusement park, the ship twisted wildly in the water. She clutched his calf to keep from tumbling off the bunk.

Rory insisted she switch places with him. He tucked her into the top corner and braced his arms against the cross beams.

Describing a roller coaster became only the first of the exciting rides she recalled from Walt Disney World with the Tibbenses. The ship truly did feel like a wild ride mimicking danger at every twist and turn.

"What was the power source for all those events?" Rory asked when her hands dropped into her lap.

"Electricity, of course," she answered without thinking.

"I see. Where is this place?" Rory asked softly.

"Florida," she spelled out.

"Melissa, Florida was ravaged by the aftereffects of the war. Discussion of the fantastic architectural wonder that you described would have filled the trade journals. I have not heard—"

Why did he question her? "I didn't make this up," she said aloud.

"I'm sure you did not. However, electricity in the quantities required for what you described is impossible." Wonder glowed in Rory's eyes. "From where did Shelan bring you?"

Melissa met his awe-filled gaze with fresh awareness. Again the sense of displacement descended. If the things she remembered were impossible now, when and where could they have happened?

Her stomach roiled.

Time.

Try as she might to remember, no sense of what year she had ridden the roller coaster came forth. Mentally she shrank from a frightening realization: if she was not in a familiar place, perhaps she was not in a familiar time either.

"It may take far more than a train to get you home—if you wish to go."

She shivered. If the niggling conjecture forming in the back of her mind had merit, she'd rather be who she was now than resume her old identity and habitat. "If I don't?"

"I would ask you to be my wife."

The marriage proposal barely registered before the world started coming apart. The ship rose from a trough in the sea.

They heard what could only be the wind ripping the sails from their gaskets and sending the yardarms crashing to the deck.

Melissa didn't need to hear more. She leaped off the bunk and worked her way to the trunks.

"What are you doing?"

"Getting out of here. Staying in this cabin with the ship lurching like this is scaring me down to my toes," she whispered as she donned her mackintosh, the rubberized cotton felt heavy enough to keep her dry. "If this ship goes down, the cabin is a death trap." She implored understanding with a single glance. "The night you pulled me out of the lake was as close as I ever care to come to drowning."

"Maybe a little fear isn't a bad idea." Rory removed his suit coat and vest and tugged on a heavy sweater. Before pulling on his mackintosh, he reached into the bottom of the trunk one last time.

When they left for the passenger galley, his knife was belted to his right hip.

Chapter 16

STEADYING MELISSA IN front of him, Rory braced against the stairwell walls halfway to the deck. The force of the storm's fury hurled the door at the top of the stairs wide, then sent it hammering at the bulkhead. A torrent of water gushed down the stairs. The wave slammed into them as though angered by their presence. Rory caught Melissa when the water knocked her backward.

"Stay below," bellowed a sailor from the upper doorway over the groan of straining timbers. On deck, wind howled through broken rigging. The fire in the stairwell lamps flickered, then died. Only the nervous passageway lamps glowed from around the corner.

The bow of the *Northern Trader* dipped, and the vessel scudded sideways. Rory pulled Melissa close. When he looked toward the deck, the sea had claimed the sailor.

A groan vibrated from the walls and floorboards. Afraid Melissa's instincts of doom were all too real, Rory got them up two more steps.

"No matter what, you stay with me, Melissa," he shouted into her ear. Her nod against his chin was all the reassurance she gave. Together they navigated another step before the next surge of water found the open door.

A screeching on deck answered the storm's fury. The ship shuddered. With an anguished cry from what surely had to be the gates of hell, a mast crashed onto the deck.

Rory folded himself over Melissa as she curled into a ball. They huddled in the shelter of the tilting stairwell. Water crashed over them and raced for the cabins belowdecks.

The teetering ship leaned farther to the port side. Rory held them in place and focused on the spot where the doorway let the storm in.

Behind them, the last of the passageway lamps went out, and they were engulfed in total darkness. Each surge of water down the stairs sent him ducking.

"Crawl up two steps," he shouted at her over the roar of the ship and the sea.

Hovering at her back, he followed, bracing her against the next deluge.

Shouts from the black passageway behind them rose over the maelstrom. Rory had no time to consider the rest of the hapless passengers. "Two more stairs," he barked.

Melissa crept forward until both of their heads cleared the top stair.

"Duck," he shouted, lowering his forehead onto her left shoulder.

A torrent of water swirled over them. Rory lunged and caught the doorjamb in time to keep them from being washed back down the stairs.

The ship lurched backward. The whine of timber splitting against rock pierced the storm. The stairwell shook like a piece of driftwood tossed into the waves. Immediately the deck listed starboard. The stern slid around to where the port side had been half a moment earlier.

Rory unleashed a stream of curses and pulled Melissa to her feet. "We've hit rocks. She'll break up for sure in this storm," he shouted into her ear. "Hold on to me. No matter what happens, don't let go."

He bullied them onto the shifting deck. A faint morning light illuminated the devastation. Wind whipped the ropes dangling from the yardarms of the fallen mast. He snagged one out of the air, pulled it taut, and wrapped it around his forearm.

Instantly, the ship tilted and dove in the opposite direction. The deck under their feet disappeared. Timbers and waves crashed against the rocks. Rory grappled with his one-arm hold on Melissa. Mercifully, her arms found his neck and held on.

The next wave yanked the ship around the rocks. The violent repercussions rolled the deck onto her side. The momentum hurled them into the air. Below, the turbulent sea reached for them.

Melissa clung to Rory. The fall into the angry black ocean seemed to last forever. The relentless water bashing the ship and racing up toward her gave voice to the woman imprisoned within the fog of Melissa's memory.

In a distant place she clutched another life raft, made of cold metal. Terrible noise roared in her ears. Shouts and broken bits of conversation penetrated the crackling static in frantic tones.

Ahead loomed the blue-white sphere of Earth. Then she was falling, falling closer and deeper into the vortex of certain death.

A white-hot rage shot through her. She recoiled at the familiar force. The woman in a cumbersome space suit screamed in outrage. The sound burned in her throat and echoed in her ears. Anguish at an unjust world railed against leaving it too soon.

Regret as powerful as the gravity pulling her toward the planet's atmosphere consumed her. Sensations she had glimpsed as she had faced death emerged from the protective fog shrouding her memory with a formidable power.

In the distant place of her past, no one loved her, nor did she love anyone. The realization had revealed a crater in her heart—in her life. The early childhood dreams of a family with laughter and love had not come true. But the dreams had not died, they had merely retreated into the dark place to which she had relegated all soft emotion and futile fantasies. The disappointment of unrealized childhood dreams stung.

Seeing herself as the monodimensional individual she had diligently forged by eliminating every scrap of illogical, emotional energy from her existence did more than sting. It appalled her. How had she survived without friendship?

Laughter? A child's smile? How had she shut out such a crucial part of the world around her?

The bitter recrimination lingered in the heated darkness of
her memory. The woman with her face, the one who lived
behind the fog in her brain, was a cold, unfeeling person.
The detachment from anything remotely emotional kept her
isolated from everyone around her. Worse, she had prided
herself on the ability to remain uninvolved, unaffected. No
wonder she had loved no one and no one had loved her—
never would love her. She had proudly achieved the status of
a severely emotionally crippled person but realized what she
was doing to herself. And it hadn't mattered as long as she
kept all those fragments of her threatening, vulnerable feelings locked away.

That wasn't me. Please, God, it wasn't me.

She didn't want to own the pain wrought from loneliness
and anger surging from behind the mist with the power of a
tidal wave. Desperate for any form of denial she was the
same woman, she reached for the truth within the fog. Behind it awaited the reasons for such pain. Her grip on the salvation keeping her from a watery death loosened.

The doors of her past yawned open, and the memories of a
lifetime exposed themselves. Now she saw them in the light
of missed opportunities instead of accomplishments. Never
before had she realized the significance of trading her hu-
manity to achieve a dream. Sadly, she realized she had imposed that unnecessary choice on herself.

The weight of dark hurts rushing out of an even darker
cavern crushed the air out of her lungs. Time rolled back further.

*Two little girls giggled over pictures they drew at a table.
Kate disappeared. The finality of death sucked the last bits of
joy from childhood.*

*Melissa cowered in a corner. Taunts, jeers, and vile in-
sults matched every lash of the belt that stung her arms and
legs. The seeds of anger flourished in her helplessness.*

*Henry Tibbens shouted at a man twice his size in a court-
room.*

A grave marker read "Tibbens." Familiar loss crushed her.

Isolation.

Schools. Escape in academics. Libraries. The Air Force Academy.

The stars and Colonel Brighton.

The impact of viewing her entire life in flashes that banished the fog overwhelmed her.

"Melissa."

Someone called her name, but she didn't want to answer. Not now. Maybe not ever.

"Damn it, Melissa. Help me help you!"

"No," came her harsh protest against her past stripped bare.

She was beyond help. The strident order meant nothing. She pushed away, lost in unraveling memories.

Once free, she floundered in the watery tempest. The need for physical survival sucked the tumultuous memories into retreat, where they waited like a predator watching its prey slowly bleed to death.

Giant waves lifted her above valleys of water. Horrified, she looked around. The bleakness of her situation crashed over her with a wall of water.

A strong hand grabbed the back of her clothing. Wind-whipped spume stung her face.

"Melissa. Damn it, don't—"

A wave choked off the words.

Rory.

She kicked through the water until she could touch him in the gray light.

"Hold on to this." He clutched her wrist in a death grip, then pressed her hand onto the broken planks keeping them afloat.

In a daze, she abdicated her physical responses to the woman trained in making quick decisions and obeying orders without question.

"The shore is straight ahead."

The spray blowing in her face made her squint in the direction he pointed.

She glimpsed the dark outline of the shore when the next wave lifted them. The wave crested, the sea foam caught the wind and slapped them, then broke over them. Melissa gripped the plank hard enough to send slivers into her palms.

"You'll have to let go of this before we hit the rocks. Use both hands and your feet to push away." He spit out water. "Can you do it?"

If she could survive falling out of the sky clutching a satellite, she could navigate the rocks. She nodded.

"Good. All you have to worry about is getting to shore. I'll be with you all the way."

Staring at a wall of water, she nodded again. For the moment, staying alive consumed her complete attention. Without warning Rory cupped the back of her head and drew her into a hard kiss.

"I'll race you to shore," he said, then gave her another quick kiss. "I'll even give you a head start."

The excitement of his challenge shocked her. She stared at him. The man found fun and adventure at every turn. One of them was crazy!

"Go," he shouted, pushing aside the debris they clung to.

She swam because she had no choice. Wind and water played tug-of-war with her. Melissa's heart skipped a beat at the sight of the rocks poking deadly fingers out from the shore. They were big and solid. Curtains of spray rose in the air with each wave hammering at them. Beyond the rock barrier lay a narrow strip of beach at the edge of a forested slope.

Angry water pushed her toward the rocks. Spitting, coughing, she rode the momentum, hoping to use it to slide away from the hazardous stacks. A crosscurrent swirled, dragging her into a collision course with the pillars before she was ready.

Without warning, Rory's powerful hand grabbed the clothing at the middle of her back. He shoved just hard enough for her to use the tide as a slingshot and propel herself off the rock toward the shore.

Her knee banged against a submerged rock. Tentatively, she tested for the bottom. The next wave lifted her. When she descended, she put her feet down, groped for crippling obstacles, and stroked her arms forward in crab fashion. Her heart thudding like a jackhammer, she focused her entire being on getting to the land. Safety.

Winded and exhausted, she crawled onto the shore, her gaze scouring the beach.

Rory wasn't there.

She got to her feet and peered into the dark, frothy sea. Relief sent her to her knees as Rory emerged from a cresting wave, groped on the rocky bottom for footing, then hauled himself out of the water and scrambled to his feet. He didn't slow until he dropped in front her. The next thing she knew was his embrace.

"We made it." His chest heaved from exertion.

Melissa closed her eyes and returned the embrace, her shaking arms tightening with the realization that she never wanted to let him go. The strength of Rory's iron will and powerful body had kept her alive when she would have perished. Once again she owed him her life, and that seemed too paltry a payment for his generosity and fidelity.

"I was afraid I'd lost you after we were thrown into the water."

Anguish laced the raspy whisper in her ear. How could she tell him that indeed he had? She wasn't who he thought she was. She wasn't even the woman she thought she was before the ship hit the rocks. She was displaced, neither the woman she could and wanted to be in this time nor the insulated, emotional cripple she had made herself in what was now the future.

She didn't deserve Rory's unstinting affection. Through the defensive habit of indifference, she would shred it like so much confetti and never think twice. Death didn't frighten Melissa, but tenderness terrified her.

Without her practiced defenses protecting her soft side, however, she thrived on Rory's generous spirit and unselfish

caring. Being with him opened her to the simple, beautiful
things in daily life and made her feel alive in ways she barely
understood.

"It's all right, sweetheart. We're safe here."

Her hold on him took on a desperation that mirrored the
turmoil bubbling against her heart. The disintegration of the
barrier to her past also freed the old nemeses of self-doubt,
guilt, and fear. Small wonder she had locked them away a
piece at a time.

In all the revelations besieging her, she had gained no idea
of how she had transcended time and wound up in a place
where newspaper mastheads read 1887. With the absence of
the fog came the realization of two warring factions from different times.

Major Melissa Fuller wanted her life back. Now. All her
sacrifice and hard work had no attainable goal in 1887. She
cared little about homeless kids. She'd been one herself. If
she could make it in the world, so could they. So the kids had
problems. She did too. Hers was how to get back to her old
life. Only death would keep her from trying, and she obvi-
ously wasn't dead.

By noon the storm had played out. Chilled by damp, gusty
winds and wet clothing, Rory and Melissa scoured the shore
for survivors. They found six, two of them severely injured.
Bereft of food, water, and warmth, Rory considered the
chances of the wounded surviving slim. Their own weren't
much better if they didn't find shelter soon.

Rory eyed the forested slope over the beach. "Does anyone know where we are?"

"Aye," answered a man in gray shirtsleeves, shivering in
the lee of a boulder. "Cap'n turned us for a run at Friday
Harbor. If we held course, this'd be the tip of San Juan Island."

"Or Lopez Island," offered his mate, slapping his hands
against his arms.

Encouraged, Rory gathered debris from the sunken ship.
"Melissa, get behind that rock and out of the wind." Not sur-

prisingly, she ignored him and continued to collect firewood and pile it near the injured men.

He kept a covert watch on her. His worry deepened when she made no attempt to converse and responded to his queries with no more than curt answers. He had dragged out her admission of a memory flash while in the water.

Damn, she had no idea of how close he'd come to losing her. Remembering made him shiver from dread more than from the cold. She owned his heart, whether she wanted it or not, and without her, the future offered only irreparable emptiness. The children and his work would not fill the black void of her absence.

Dismayed, he could see that since they had reached shore, the rush of memories seized her with greater regularity than ever. Her behavior warned that the things she recalled brought no joy; instead, they made her grow distant. And the more she remembered, the wider the distance grew. The barrier he couldn't penetrate cast a pall of helplessness over him greater than when he had asked her to cauterize his wounds in the mountains. He knew of no remedy for the invisible wounds festering within her.

Two men disappeared into the trees. Soon the sound of branches snapping from their trunks cut the air. With luck, they would have shelter before nightfall.

Melissa rose from the wounded sailors. White lines of strain and cold ringed her mouth. "Ask him if I may borrow his glasses for a moment," she signed at Rory.

"What's she doing?" asked the sailor in shirtsleeves.

"Speaking to me," Rory answered. He crouched beside the injured man and made the request.

"Won't be needin' 'em," the sailor rasped.

"Thank you." Rory carefully removed the man's spectacles and handed them to Melissa.

"Cain't ya wait 'til he's dead?" demanded a stocky man as he came out of the forest dragging a pile of evergreen branches.

"Do any of you know how to snare an animal?" Rory asked, ignoring the barb.

"We're sailors, not landlubbers," answered the stocky man.

Rory caught Melissa's eye and issued a silent warning to stay away from the men. She nodded and settled on a rock near the pile of drying wood.

Rory studied the western sky. A slash of blue promised a fleeting patch of warmth. He approached the three sailors constructing a shelter out of the branches.

"I'm going to set a couple of snares. If one of you finds anything to fish with, I'd suggest you do so." He dropped to his haunches beside Melissa. "I won't be gone long, but I'd feel a lot more at ease if you came with me."

The shake of her head constituted more than a denial to accompany him. With each heartbeat, she pulled further away from him.

Melissa fingered the sailor's eyeglasses. The contrast of crude materials and fine workmanship might have been found in a museum. The lenses were suitable for her intent, though a disposable lighter would better have served her purpose.

Part of her marveled that she had survived so long without the countless technological advances she had taken for granted. Thinking about what she no longer had was more comfortable than contemplating who she no longer was.

Major Melissa Fuller lived on the cutting edge of scientific research. She had spent her life pushing the limits until she was able to float among the stars.

Yet the Melissa who blossomed in the light of Rory's countenance missed none of the trappings of technology. She had discovered more important things, like a garden, children, and a reluctant sense of belonging. She marveled that a woman as intentionally remote as she could experience such depth of feeling for the children of Freedom House. The bittersweet realization that she loved them slammed hard into her heart. Her love for Rory went even deeper.

All the more reason to get back to where you belong. He won't love you. No one can.

Major Fuller was afraid for the first time in years. In the

space age, she was safe from emotional risk. Here, she was vulnerable.

"I'll be damned." The wounded sailor propped against a rock beside her pointed at a curl of smoke rising from the pile of wood.

Melissa held the eyeglasses steady. The break in the clouds gave the lenses a strong sun to magnify. She needed every second of sunlight to dry the small bits of wood enough to set them on fire. Her gaze never wavered from the rainbow refraction burning tiny holes in her targets.

Using both hands, she shielded the fragile flame finally coming to life amid the smoke. She forced down the conflict posed by a past she had wished for so many times and now wanted to ignore.

With the single-mindedness that had carried her to the stars, she concentrated on building the fire. One step at a time, she would ensure survival.

How she had known what to do in the mountains with Rory lost its mystery with the return of her memory. Years earlier, she had learned how to live off the land during a rigorous course taught in the mountains high above Colorado Springs. As she did in all of the classes she attended, she had absorbed every important detail.

Carole Banning, a classmate at the academy and a participant in the mountain training, emerged into memory. The foolish woman had suggested they team up for the duration and help each other along. Carole had no idea what it took to survive outside the suburbs of Des Moines, Iowa, and her cozy family. Being a woman entitled her to no special consideration in Melissa's estimation.

"We have the option of teaming, Melissa. Why not?" Carole had asked.

"Because real survival is an individual endeavor. If I ever need to make it in the wilderness, I intend to do so. You won't be with me then, so I'd suggest you do the same."

"Survival is about a lot more than being dropped into some godforsaken place and living long enough for rescue to arrive."

"That's right, Carole. There may be no rescue other than the one you devise for yourself."

"That's not what I meant. I've watched you. If ever I met a person in need of a friend, a real friend, to share confidences with and laugh and cry with, it's you, Melissa. I'm offering to be your friend. If you let yourself, you might actually like me."

"I don't dislike you, Carole."

"I didn't think you did. You don't dislike anyone. You talk to everyone, only you never reveal anything personal. I want to get to know you. This is a marvelous opportunity. I'm not asking you to carry me through this course. I know the importance of it. And you're right—if we ever need to use any of this, we'll be on our own."

"Then we may as well do the course that way."

"If you ever think you might like a friend, Melissa, give me a shot. I won't let you down. Trust me."

Of course she hadn't trusted Carole Banning. Nor had she given the offer of friendship a second thought. When Carole finished the course in the same top echelon as Melissa, she thought she'd done Carole a favor by refusing the pairing.

Now, staring at the temperamental flame threatening to succumb to the adversity of damp wood and swirling wind, Melissa wondered if accepting Carole's overture would have harmed her. Sadly, she realized the years of protecting herself from other people's hurts had left her ignorant of how to be a friend. Carole represented another missed opportunity for learning one of life's essentials—friendship. How many others had she passed up? Her life had consisted of acquaintances and a military chain of command defined by rank and position.

Only when she forgot who she really was did the parts she had repressed venture into awareness. It boiled down to choices.

Recalling the social functions and work-related festivities she had attended made her want to weep with regret. The clarity of hindsight stripped away the bravado of the self-sufficiency she had clung to like a life raft. She had always attended alone, but in truth she had a date. His name was Loneliness, and his fidelity was unquestionable.

The woman who floated among the stars considered it a sign of weakness to need anyone. Certainly she did not want anyone to need her. So she shut out anyone who invited friendship.

The only obligations she had recognized centered on herself and the goals shaped in the Tibbenses' living room. She kept her sights on the heavens, and the opportunity to fulfill those dreams kept her on an unerring course.

Making dreams come true cost the dreamer something; the sacrifices made to achieve them became the yardstick of her commitment. Until today, she hadn't realized how much of her life she had abandoned in the process.

Belatedly, she wondered what had happened to Carole Banning after she left the Air Force Academy. If she was here now and offered a hand in friendship . . . Melissa let the thought fade. She had no better insight into the mechanics of being a friend now than she'd had when attending the academy. The difference made by knowing and caring for Rory heightened an inadequacy that she had not perceived in her former life. Isolation wasn't strength, she realized. It was merely loneliness.

Staring into the fire, she thought of her damaged vocal cords. They were only an inconvenience; her stunted emotions, encasing her personality like stainless steel, were a true handicap.

Chapter 17

MELISSA HUGGED HER knees under the protection of her mackintosh. Strong winds turned the fine spray from the waves breaking against the rocks into needles on her skin.

Since recouping her memory she had thought of herself as two people inhabiting one mind.

Major Fuller's iron will focused on the goal of survival. Her resourceful practicality forced her to eat the fare the men found.

Melissa considered the woman she could be by cultivating a blend of who she had been with who she'd become. It was a simple solution. The complexities of transforming herself into a self-confident, feeling, whole person were staggering.

Major Fuller loathed the notion. It conjured an abdication of control and implied vulnerability. The prospect spawned fear of any change.

But the change had already started. The choice of direction was real. In the twentieth century, Major Fuller had not cared what anyone thought of her beyond her professional competence. The fewer emotions she experienced, the better. The nineteenth-century Melissa explored the spectrum of emotions she'd discovered like treasures in a dark cave. Each one sparkled in the light, sometimes painfully. It mattered what others thought, particularly the injured men. She wanted them to understand they were important. What she could not convey with words, she imparted with a touch, a gesture, a forced smile. Holding her hand, first one, then the second had slipped into the arms of death.

"Take my specs, ma'am," the young man had whispered moments before his death. "I'll be gettin' a new set of eyes in the next life."

Now there were six survivors of the *Northern Trader*. Only she and Rory possessed the knowledge that kept them fed and sheltered against the damp, cool nights. While the sailors scavenged for seafood, she and Rory had set snares. They cooked the combined fare over the fire the men gathered wood for and kept burning. By day, the thick smoke from the unseasoned wood doubled as a signal for passing ships. By night, the blaze served as a beacon.

Rory had assured her of rescue. No ship entering the channel to Friday Harbor would ignore a signal fire. Mariners had an unwritten code considered above the laws and schedules of land-loving businessmen.

In Major Fuller's time, the men might have survived. A Coast Guard cutter would have rescued them when the storm broke yesterday. But this was a different place and time.

The second of two graves among the trees awaited the young man beside her. With a feeling of helplessness reminiscent of her childhood, she had witnessed death claim another victory. Melissa's fragile, soft side had tended the injured men and cried when her efforts could not save them. She wept for the men's families and friends when Major Fuller lamented their primitive circumstances. They both shared and detested a sense of futility.

"They're ready for Mr. Ramsey," Rory told Melissa.

She took a final look at the young man who had bequeathed his eyeglasses to her, then she accepted Rory's offered hand and rose. Together they followed the four sailors carrying Ian Ramsey's body up the embankment and into the trees. She and Rory stood aside while the sailors placed their mate in his final resting place, then filled in the hole. One by one, they mounded rocks over the grave and marked it with a cross hewn from broken branches.

After securing the burial cross with a few more large stones, they took their places on either side of the grave and waited for Melissa and Rory.

She had not expected to offer any prayers at the first graveside service in the pines. But the woman she had become since entering Rory's life refused silence. Her voice too fragile to risk, she had spoken with her hands and Rory had read her hands and interpreted her thoughts. As he spoke, tears had broken the dam of her lower lashes.

Now, for the second time in as many days, he waited across a fresh grave and watched her hands.

"Lord, please welcome Ian Ramsey into your kingdom," she began, then glanced up. Rory's intense concentration on her hands reminded her of how hard he had studied to learn signing while he conducted the business that kept his household and Freedom House solvent.

The solemnity of his tone turned the trees into a cathedral of lofty green spires. Instead of smoky incense, the clean aroma of evergreen and forest soil perfumed the air. A choir of treetops hummed with the wind. Overhead, low clouds flowed across the sky, breaking occasionally for the haze-dulled orb of the sun to watch.

"Ian was a better person than most of us. We ask that you treat him well, Lord. Before joining you, he considered his friends and fellow travelers in life. He gave his coat to Martin, who had no coat; his shoes to Lar, who lost one of his while fleeing the sinking ship; his trousers to Pegger, because his were torn; and his belt and hat to young Clarence, who had neither.

"I feel particularly privileged, Lord, that he entrusted me with his spectacles to start fires. Give Ian Ramsey new eyes to see heaven clearly, without the veils of human defenses and physical frailty." Her thoughts raced ahead of her hands. She stilled, waiting for Rory to catch up, appreciating his addition of the small words she omitted so the sailors understood.

"Show Ian how to choose the right path and not close his heart to those worthy of his caring. Show him who to trust and who will cut his heart with evil so vile that it cannot know your light."

Tears flowed down Melissa's cheeks. She could not stop them any more than she could silence the pleas surging from her soul.

She continued, vaguely aware of the silence from across the grave unable to quell the outpouring of her soul. "Show him how to love and how to be worthy of being loved, Lord. Heal his heart. Blend the two sides of him that are warring for dominance and make him whole. Give him strength to make atonement for the years of turning a blind eye to those in need of help.

"Help me, God. I'm so lost and I can't find the way to pull it together. I don't know how. I'm so frightened, Lord. You gave me back my fear and now it is overwhelming me. I don't know what to do with it. It won't go away. Is that the prize for my single-minded obsession? To live forever in this time, bereft of all that is familiar? In fear? Knowing what an empty shell I made myself? Knowing I never tried to change that which I hated?

"Is this my hell, Lord? To see what I was? I hurt no one by sins of commission. Are my sins of omission so great that I cannot find redemption? So heinous that I didn't even earn the right to die? Did I have an obligation to rescue those who came from where I came from? Was I supposed to be Mr. Tibbens? You took him and Melva, Lord, when I still needed them. Even today, I miss them. Yet you wouldn't let me join them when I fell out of the stars. Why, Lord? Why are you doing this to me? Was I so terrible to anyone besides myself? Why?"

Rory wrapped her in his arms and held her while she cried. "It will be all right, Melissa. Cry it out and it will be better."

Nothing would be all right again. Ever. All the tears in the ocean could not make it better, nor could they make her whole. The relentless war of conflicting identities raged whether she was awake or asleep. There seemed no way of blending the incongruities of her past with the present. In lucid moments, the imagery created by the word "asylum" showed where she belonged. Instincts for self-preservation honed over a lifetime refused such a retreat.

"Hold on to me, sweetheart. My heart is breaking with you."

A fresh torrent of anguish burst free inside her. She clung shamelessly to Rory as the only life raft in a sea of chaos, her fist absently clenching and unclenching against his mackintosh. The gentle way he rocked her eased her agitation. The multitude of conflicting emotions swirling around all her memories gradually settled. Once her tears played out, emptiness set in.

"Don't let go of me," Rory commanded, his arms tightening to the point of nearly crushing her against his chest. "Don't pull away from me again."

Her head shook in denial. "If you knew me better, you wouldn't be so kind."

The pressure of Rory's hand against her head made her look up. A ripple of gooseflesh ran down her spine. The misery raging in his gray eyes reflected hers.

"Melissa, listen closely. I don't care where you came from or who you were. I love you and I'll do everything I can to keep you. I want you. For the rest of our lives." He withdrew a pendant similar to his from his pocket and slipped it over her head. "This is the other half of the crystal I wear, just as you are the other half of me. Together, we are whole and much, much stronger than alone and separate."

He couldn't love her. There was nothing to love. "Don't—"

"No. Don't deny what's in my heart. Don't reject me if I haven't earned it. I'm not asking you to profess affection when you are clearly in turmoil over what has happened to you."

"You deserve—"

His lips brushed over hers and quelled further protest.

"Ah, sweetheart, what we want and what we deserve are often very different. Fortunately, we seldom get exactly what we deserve. What I want is you."

The warmth of his palms against her tear-dampened cheeks imparted a comfort that reached into her savage thoughts. For an instant she believed.

Then it passed. Conscience refused to deceive him by allowing him to consider the possibility of a life together.

She relinquished the bedrock of sanity his body represented. While she held on to him, nothing bad could happen.

But her nature wouldn't let her cling. She pushed back and raised her hands to speak.

"I am not who you think I am," she signed.

"You have remembered?"

"Everything." She hesitated before continuing. "Most things."

"What disturbs you so much that you withdraw from my company?"

She had not realized her actions hurt him until she saw the proof in his sad gray eyes. It seemed he searched for a way into her soul and a glimpse of the devils lurking there. "You are the last person on Earth I would ever wish to hurt. You are kind and generous to a fault."

A sad half-smile tugged at the corners of his mouth. "I'm a man who indulges in what pleases me. Nothing more."

"How did I get here, Rory?"

"You do not remember?" Puzzlement furrowed his brow. "I had thought you might tell me."

"I have discovered that I do not—" she paused, then corrected herself—"did not—believe in magic."

"So, you cannot believe me when I tell you Shelan's magic brought you to me."

What an endless circle of chaos. The linear logic of Major Fuller's training as an engineer rejected the idea of magic. To her, computers were magic. Cellular phones were magic. Space flight was magic. Technological magic, and very explainable. She looked at Rory again.

Falling out of space and plummeting to Earth and certain death only to wind up in 1887 was not explainable in any era.

"Magic is tricks."

Rory drew a long breath and let it out before continuing their conversation with his hands. "Some is. Sometimes magic is what happens between two people. Once in every so many lifetimes, it is something so powerful, so fantastic that no other word describes it. Shelan unleashed that kind of rare magic the night she summoned you."

Preposterous as it sounded, it was the only explanation possible.

Rory's hands moved slowly, as though reluctant to ask his next question. "Do you know where you came from?"

Nodding, she couldn't look at him, for she had no intention of revealing the time difference. Melissa had adapted well to her present environment and doubted that Major Fuller would betray her origins through deed.

"Do you wish to go back?" he asked aloud, his hands dropping to his sides.

"I cannot," she signed. Major Fuller sulked in despair.

"Will you stay with me?"

"I cannot marry you."

"You have made your wishes clear in that regard. I asked if you would stay."

"And do what?"

His hands came to life with a response. "Whatever you like. Work with the children. Maintain the garden. Give me a hand in the office. I have a great deal of work to reconstruct since I've lost my cases."

Fresh turmoil roiled through her. No clear answer formed.

"Do you hold the idea in such disfavor that you struggle with giving me an honest answer?"

Honesty. At the least, he deserved the truth. "The person I was wants to leave. She needs no one, Rory. But the woman I have become since the fairy ring never wants to relinquish you."

"Then I ask her to stay. Together we'll deal with the old you."

"She will not be banished. I am the sum total of all my experiences. She is a part of me."

"It is not my intention to banish her, Melissa."

"What is your intent?"

"To woo her. I want all of your heart. I'm a patient man and you are worth waiting a lifetime for."

Tears stung her eyes. How could she tell him it might take that long to sort out the chaos threatening her fledgling tender nature?

*   *   *

Five days after the sinking of the *Northern Trader* a passing
ship answered their signal fire. Calm seas and bright sunlight
facilitated the rescuers' efforts to land a dory and ferry them
to the mail boat.

Arranging passage from Friday Harbor to Fairhaven consumed another two days. Rory went nowhere without
Melissa. Since their graveside conversation, Melissa increased the distance between them by day, but she allowed
him to sleep beside her until their rescue. He considered the
change progress. He ached to hold her against his heart, dis-
pel the turmoil from her mind, and worship her with all the
ardor burning in his soul.

He marginally understood the complexity of her plight.
The confusion she revealed beside Ian Ramsey's grave had
wrenched his heart. Consumed by what raged inside her, she
never noticed that he stopped relaying her words well before
she made it clear she was speaking about herself.

Her soliloquy bedeviled him. The notion of being part of
what she considered a personal hell did not bode well for the
future he planned with her. Questions he wished he had
asked accumulated into piles taller than the trees. One in particular begged for an answer.

Over and over he pondered how a woman could fall from
the stars. If he had not seen the bright star hurtling toward
him on the mountain, then heard her splashing in the lake, he
might have dismissed it. But he hadn't actually seen or heard
her fall into the lake. In truth, he had no idea of how she got
into the water. The only notion more bizarre than accepting
magic as the reason for her presence was that of a woman
floating in the heavens until summoned to Earth.

On the second floor of the Friday Harbor Hotel, Rory lay
in bed and stared at the ceiling. The creaking floorboards in
the adjacent room assumed a familiar pacing rhythm. When
he could endure no more, he dressed and went to her room.

The door opened without protest. She had not thrown the
bolt as he had warned she must for her own safety. The blazing lamps chased away the night.

"Is it time to go?" she signed.

The late hour kept his end of the conversation silent. It would not do for anyone to hear his voice in her room. "We can go to the ship in three hours."

Dressed in a blouse and a practical skirt that didn't require a bustle, she resumed pacing. The neatly made bed had not a wrinkle, evidence that she had that not even tried to sleep. Her jacket and small tote holding her trousers and mackintosh sat on the bureau.

"Are you so eager for home that you cannot sleep?"

Instead of answering, she turned her back.

"Speak to me," he whispered, unwilling to let her raise the barrier between them any higher.

The woman who spun on her heel regarded him with an anger that sent a chill up his spine. Her rigid stance accentuated the fire blazing in her hazel eyes and the tension pursing her lips. The depths of the control she exerted to keep her fury harnessed astounded him.

"Home." Signing the single word pinched her brow and changed the anger into uncertainty. "I have no home."

He began to sign. "Yes, you do. With us. With me."

She shook her head in denial. "You collect the misfits and mistakes of the world. Which one do you consider me?"

"Neither. You are the woman I love."

"Wrong. I am both a misfit and a mistake. You cannot love me. I am incapable of love. Love can hurt you. The only person it is safe to love is yourself. No one else will look out for your interests. Their own will always come first." Bitterness twisted her mouth into a scowl.

"Tell me, do you love yourself?"

"I told you, I am incapable of love."

"I don't believe that."

"It doesn't matter what you believe. This is not a philosophical matter open for debate. We are not voting on it. I have looked at my past and know this truth with every fiber of my being."

Rory watched her face when her hands stilled. Her conflicting emotions showed in small facial twitches. He ached to gather her in his arms and soothe her turmoil, but he remained rooted to the spot. "You are afraid if you love, you will be spurned? Hurt? That is no reason to lock your heart away. We all experience anxiety in matters of the heart."

"Not you. You're so sure of everything you do. No one can worry about being hurt and enjoy as many aspects of life as you do. You find humor where there is none. You laugh when there is nothing amusing, then make it so. You reach out to those kids and never consider they will reject you or . . . die if you love them."

"There is a great difference between understanding your affections may be rejected and being so fearful of rejection that you refuse all forms of affection. Yes, people die. Children die. Even at Freedom House.

"Tommy had a younger brother when I brought him home. Toby took ill and died. Nothing Shelan or I did could save him. We brought a doctor from Fairhaven, but he couldn't save him either.

"We didn't stop loving Toby because he died. On the contrary, because we loved him, we grieved after he left us. We cried together and alone. And we were thankful we were able to know him at all."

Melissa went back to her pacing.

Rory folded his arms and leaned against the doorjamb. "You have loved deeply, or you wouldn't be so consumed by fear of doing so again. But it's too late, Melissa," he said. "Katy and Sandra have already wormed their way into your affections.

"And what of the Tibbenses? You named a star for him. He knew the secret, didn't he?" he answered softly.

"What secret?" she growled in a raspy voice.

"Why, the secret of love, of course."

She halted in front of him and opened her clenched hands. "What are you talking about?"

He smiled against the sadness growing inside him. "Look at you. You use your hands to speak in hopes of healing your throat so you may use it to speak again. You learned signing because you needed to. You practiced even when you were alone until you became proficient."

"What's that got to do any secret? Practice is practice. It leads to proficiency."

"That's right. The same is true of loving. It takes practice. You don't get it right every time and know the joy of having it returned. But that doesn't change the need for being loved.

"The secret is, the more you love, the more you can love and the more love you receive. Rejection is always rejection, and it inflicts pain on a vulnerable heart. But even rejection has a good side. You learn to love wisely. There are as many ways and forms of loving as there are stars in the heavens. Yet they don't shine with equal brilliance."

"Some do not shine at all."

Rory pushed away from the door. "Unfortunately, that's true. Could it be they are fearful someone may see their light, so they hoard it until it goes out? Then no one knows they were there."

"That's not what I meant. They burn out and have no light left to shine. Cold. Unfeeling. Dead stars of incredible mass."

"Then they burned once?"

"Very brightly."

"What consumed them until self-pity snuffed the light it would have pleased you so to see?"

"Self-pity?" Surprise brought a submerged anger into life. "You think I'm consumed with self-pity?"

"At the moment, yes," he answered, hoping she would unleash some of the venom simmering in her heart.

"I detest pity from anyone."

"You're very safe, since I doubt you'd receive any. Pity is seldom wasted on total strangers."

"Get out," she croaked. Anger turned her cheeks crimson and her eyes into shards of colored glass.

"And let you hide? I don't think so." He grinned, knowing he'd struck a deep nerve. "I don't pity you, Melissa, or anyone who can make children laugh while shopping for clothes. Like it or not, you gave the girls a gift of the heart that day. They had never had a reason to laugh like that before. You laughed, too. Maybe giving a little piece of yourself wasn't all that painful for you."

"Leave the girls out of this. You have no idea why I was drawn to them."

"No, I don't. Why don't you tell me?"

"Why don't you go to hell?"

Rory chuckled, wondering why she hadn't extended such an invitation sooner. Progress, he decided, had many faces. "I don't care for the climate, but it does seem a little chilly in here." He reached for the doorknob. "I'll be back when it's time to leave for home."

He let himself out without a glance at her wildly flying hands delivering a scathing retort.

Chapter 18

MELISSA YANKED A fistful of weeds out of the rich, dark soil. During her prolonged absence, they had overrun the herbs and flowers struggling for room in the gardens. Pent-up frustrations wreaked vengeance on the leafy, prickly intruders marring her once pristine gardens.

Self-pity. Who did Rory McCullough think he was to accuse her of such a petty, useless indulgence? The man didn't know self-preservation from self-pity. Hell, he'd never had to know the difference. He was a man—a big man whose size intimidated others at a glance.

In the aftermath of her venomous outburst, guilt took the sting out of the lies she told herself.

He hadn't always been a man.

She pictured him as a child sitting on his father's front stoop day after day. How in heaven's name had that neglected little boy become the gentle man she knew?

You're a better person than I, Rory McCullough, she admitted, then dug out the roots of another giant weed. *I would probably have hated the old man.*

Rory never wasted time on hate. He was too busy loving everyone or working himself to death so he could continue supporting the whole damn world, herself included. Who was going to look after him when he grew too old to continue?

No one. Those kids will do just what I did—get the hell out of here and never look back.

She stabbed her weeding tool deep into the damp soil, then rocked it until another weed popped loose.

She had no idea what had become of any of the countless kids with whom she had shared county dorms or foster homes. She consoled herself by believing she would have heard of any successes. Everyone expected her and those like her to fail, and most lived up to the expectations. Had it not been for the Tibbenses, she probably would have, too.

Their single act of heartfelt charity lay at the crux of a growing dilemma. Did she have an obligation to render the same kind of patient caring and encouragement to other children as the Tibbenses had lavished on her? With unrestricted love and patience, Henry and Melva had transformed her trouble-plagued life. After their deaths, the single-minded tenacity with which she pursued her lofty goal of going to the stars kept her out of harm's way.

Settling back on her heels, she appraised the medicinal herb garden. Delicate white horehound blooms basked in the sun and flourished in the sandy soil. The fragrance of rosemary mingled with that of meadowsweet. A turn of her head to the right brought the heady scent of mint. Beyond the aromatic leaves, licorice root awaited harvesting. In defiance of logic, witch hazel, marshmallow, and a dozen other herbs prospered in the garden as well.

A laugh tickled her throat. A decade of education and rigorous training had taken her into space. Now that she had crashed and burned, her sole responsibility lay in pulling weeds in someone else's mystical garden. And why not? The Help Wanted ads had no postings for astronauts. If she told anyone about how cluttered the sky would be a century from now, they would put her in an asylum for sure.

Her silent laughter loosened the grip of her practiced, sinister side. In this time and place, she had no need of her old guardians. What more could happen to her?

How could she be hurt any more than what life had already dealt? She had survived that pain and she would live through whatever else came her way. Of course she would. Death didn't want her or he would have claimed her in space or the lake. He'd had an excellent chance when the *Northern Trader* went down, too.

She exhaled hard. Perhaps death only claimed those who had exerted the effort or taken the risk to live. The rest be-

came lost souls, or perhaps ghosts that eventually slipped un-
noticed from the human masses.

She stared at the intricate root system of the weed in her
hand. Unlike the weed, she had a second chance to become
something useful to those around her.

The children of Freedom House . . . ah, maybe they
needed her as much as she needed them. They had had less
time to hone the art of isolation and hatred than she.

She resumed her weeding with a new vigor. Perhaps the
sheltered garden was more than it appeared. She began considering it a mirror of her life. In her case, the herbs and
flowers had grown in spite of the weeds she thoughtlessly
cultivated.

For each weed she pulled out of the garden, she practiced
exorcising portions of the bitterness weighing on her spirit.
Several hours later, the first glimmers of serenity emerged.

Placing her hands in the small of her back, she rested on
her heels and uncoiled into a slow stretch while surveying
her domain. The scent of fertile soil, fragrant herbs, and
tangy sea air scrubbed her senses. Strange how the beauty of
the garden registered once her obsession with a life far removed from here subsided.

More noises intruded on her private realm. She slid around
and sat firmly on the ground and stretched the kinks from her
legs.

Clad in trousers, Katy and Sandra weeded at opposite
sides of the garden. While absorbed in introspection, she had
not heard them working.

The clang of her weeding tool against a rock caught their
attention. Tentative smiles grew stronger as they approached.

"Are you angry at us?"

Melissa shook her tilting head. Leave it to Katy to speak
her mind. Reflexively, she signed, "Never at you. I'm tired
of being angry."

The girls exchanged puzzled glances, then looked back.

Melissa laughed silently, realizing what she had done. She
scrambled to her knees and embraced a girl in each arm.

Both immediately burst into tears and hugged her neck so hard it threatened to snap. "Don't cry, girls," she pleaded in a raspy voice thick with instant tears.

"We heard your ship sank and everyone died," Sandra sobbed. Her hand patted Melissa's back in mutual comfort.

"We thought we'd never see you again," Katy murmured, then sniffed. "Please don't ever leave us, Miss Fuller. I couldn't stand it if something really did happen to you or Mr. McCullough."

"We prayed every night, just like Mrs. Lindstrom told us to. I don't think we have any prayers left," Sandra wailed.

"I promised God, if He brought you home, I'd be good forever. I'd do everything Mr. and Mrs. Lindstrom said. I'd never argue with Roger again, unless it was really important. And I'd give him my dessert for a whole year," Katy moaned.

Sandra loosened her hold and gazed at her friend in disgust. "Roger? You're going to give Roger your dessert instead of me? Why?"

" 'Cause Roger and I argue the most. I really, really wanted God to bring Miss Fuller and Mr. McCullough home, so I had to promise something hard. How else would He know I meant it?"

The simplicity of Katy's logic amazed Melissa with its depth. And it touched her just as deeply. She was worth a year of desserts to a child with a sweet tooth.

Melissa placed a hand on each of their shoulders and pushed to her feet. "Don't make promises you don't want to keep, no matter what," she managed through the constriction of laughter in her tender throat.

Katy hugged her waist. "Having you home is worth all the desserts in the world."

Gazing down at the girls, Melissa gasped. She pushed them away, then lifted the ends of their hair. Their long golden-red and raven locks ended at their shoulders.

"We cut it like yours," Sandra said proudly.

"Mrs. Lindstrom evened it out for us."

"Yeah, then she gave us extra chores for a month," Sandra added.

"It was worth it." A mischievous grin spread the freckles dusting Katy's cheeks. "We cut it *before* we heard about the ship."

A surge of emotion overwhelmed Melissa. She gathered the girls to her in a desperate hug. Despite the traumas of their early childhood, they still reached out with an innocent invincibility. This time, their gesture captured her heart and held it fast.

Enough weed pulling. The garden of her heart was mending fine. Sniffing, she released them and caught their hands. With a wink and a smile, she nodded toward the fence, then hesitated.

Rory watched from the gate. His enigmatic expression made her wonder how long he had been standing there.

"It seems the clouds have parted long enough for you to find your smile," he signed.

She released the girls' hands and signed, "And a couple of rays of sunshine in the storm."

Nodding, he picked up the tools leaning against the fence and walked away.

She ushered the girls through the gate, determined to hold on to the seed of contentment growing among the thorns wrapping her heart.

"Will you teach us to talk with our hands?" Sandra asked.

Melissa nodded. She'd like nothing better than to spend hours teaching them and holding the balm of their laughter against the darkness lurking inside her.

Rory closed the door of his office. The sound of his footsteps on the wooden porch brought Melissa's attention.

"I thought you'd be out here," he said. Above the sea a cloak of stars stretched across the night. "The moon will rise soon."

In the island of serenity created by the night, he was drawn to her with a potency that fired his loins and set his heart hammering. As always, he tempered it before wrapping his arms over her shoulders. Eyes closed, he inhaled the familiar rose fragrance of her hair and wondered if her skin tasted of honey and roses.

"Some believe you can wish upon a star and it will come true," he whispered into her hair.

With a nod, she relaxed against him. He savored the gesture for a moment before asking, "Do you wish upon stars?"

Denial rocked her head against his chest.

"Too bad. Wishes become dreams and people have a way of trying to make their dreams come true."

She cleared her throat, then asked, "What is the biggest dream you ever dreamed?"

"This."

"I don't understand."

"This, Melissa. Standing here watching the sky, with you in my arms. The children snug in their beds at Freedom House where the Lindstroms won't let me spoil them beyond redemption. A year's worth of work waiting for me in the office."

He kissed the top of her head. "Only in my dreams, you come into my room and beg me to make wild, passionate love to you or you won't survive the night. I feel the fire of your desire in the intimate touch of your fingers. You make my soul want to fly." He tucked her head under his chin.

"Kindhearted sop that I am, I bow to your wishes. After we make love until we couldn't stand if the house was on fire, you tell me that you love me, that you'll stay with me for the rest of our days. Then we make love for the rest of the night and all the next day."

The laughter shaking her shoulders made him grin.

"I confess to indulging in that dream every night right before I go to sleep."

A jerky squeak escaped her throat, startling her.

"Was that a 'Yes, Rory, I'll make your dreams come true'?"

Still laughing, she shook her head.

"Then I've no choice but to keep on dreaming. What a gruesome fate to be in love with a woman who does not love me," he teased without conviction.

The laughter melted from Melissa.

"But you will, sweet Melissa. When you realize you trust me and I will never betray your precious trust, you will love me as a friend. Listen in here." His hand pressed against her left breast over her heart. "Sometimes the whispers of the heart are the most important sounds, but the most difficult to hear over the din."

She turned in his arms. In the faint glow of starlight, her eyes searched his face. The gentle touch of her fingertips on his cheek warmed him more than was safe.

"I have never known anyone like you," she said. "You shake everything I am . . . I believed. . . . You're like a mythical spirit invading my psyche. You won't let go until I see the world you paint through rose-colored glasses."

"Is it such a dismal place?"

"Oh, no. It is more beautiful and altruistic than I am capable of grasping."

"Sweetheart, we can make our lives whatever we want them to be." He longed to carry her into his bedroom and strip away her reservations with her clothes until all the barriers disappeared.

"I dream, too, Rory. We're in the circle and I have no fears, no inhibitions. Nothing matters except making love with you."

"It can be like that again."

"No. It can't. I can't. For years, I feared nothing, not even failure, because anything you fear can become real and cause a stumble. I thought of nothing beyond my next goal and the ultimate culmination of my dream. There was no time to care about others, unless I needed their cooperation.

"When you pulled me out of the lake, I was a different person, yet the same. The memories were gone, but not the instincts and habits of a lifetime.

"Now I'm changed. You softened me and opened doors I would have rushed past. You showed me a lighter side filled with laughter and simple pleasures I previously shunned as frivolous. But they weren't. The light surrounding you showed me the darkness of my soul.

"When my memories flooded back, I felt a nearly uncontrollable outrage. The new me was horrified by the callousness I built up over the years and embraced as though it was King Midas's gold." She cleared her throat, then swallowed.

"Sh-h-h-h. Too much talking."

"No, I must say this now . . . aloud . . . before I lose my nerve. Change is very difficult. Now, I have fear, too. Since I've been with you, I've experienced a life I would never have chosen. Thinking about anything other than achieving my next career goal didn't cross my mind. Giving back anything to those who helped me was out of the question, unless in a professional capacity. Those were dues I paid gladly."

The quaver in her raspy voice bespoke the price of overuse, but her need to speak aloud of the demons plaguing her kept him silent. His heart swelled with hope for a time when she would accept the generous spirit he perceived in her.

"I worked hard and placed a burden on no one. I thought I was a good person. The truth is, I was neither good nor bad. I was barely a person at all. I was empty of compassion, uncaring of the misery or joys those around me expressed. Locked inside was an anger at the world. And at myself. It came out before you found me. I was screaming in rage. Screaming so hard, I damaged my vocal cords.

"You are easy to love. If ever . . ."

The fingertips stroking his cheek lowered to her throat.

"Enough, sweet Melissa. It is my turn to speak." He cradled her face in his hands. The rising moon shone in eyes sparkling with emotion flowing from her and into him.

"When I look at you, I see a woman at a crossroad struggling with a choice of direction. I can't choose your direction—I can only pray it is the one I hope for you. And me. No one can know the full extent of another heart. I suspect that in telling me what you have tonight, you allowed me further inside you than you allowed anyone previously. You honor me, and humble me, with the treasure of your trust. My love for you would never allow betrayal.

"There is no hurry for us. We have heaven's time to grow

a love that will outlast the stars watching us." The cool, satiny feel of her forehead against his lips begged exploration.

Her slender fingers drew his hands away from her face. Leaning into him, she rose on tiptoe.

The brush of her trembling lips against his ignited the carefully restrained fires of passion. Heart thundering in anticipation of her kiss, he waited.

Her cool hand brushed his cheek.

He remained frozen with the need to hold her, to touch the core of her spirit and love her into the glorious light belonging only to them.

Her mouth found his with a tentative kiss, then lingered.

As soon as her arms slipped around his neck, he crushed her against his body, aching for her warmth, her passion, and the gift of her heart. The rhythm of their bodies spoke a silent message.

Rory deepened the kiss. She responded with a hunger that seized control of his raging desire. For just a moment he allowed her free rein. Too quickly she drew him into a sensual maelstrom, tearing at his determination for restraint. He lifted her, then held her against his arousal. The delicious rocking sensation she initiated against him sent his heart slamming against his ribs.

He absorbed the heat of her desire, sure if he raised her skirts and released his trousers, she would be his eagerly and willingly. Instead, he broke the kiss and clasped her tightly against him. The sounds of their ragged breathing matched the thunder in his chest. He wished the embrace around his neck was as permanent as it felt at that moment.

"Ah-h-h-h, Melissa. There are some things in which I'm not strong. If we were to succumb to the heat burning the resolve from my bones, I'd know the sweet ecstasy of being one with you again. You don't believe it possible we'd experience what we found in the fairy ring. It wouldn't be so sweet for you once the passion abated, would it?"

Motionless against him, she gave no answer. The truth required no confirmation.

"When Someday arrives, we will both know it. God help me, I want you as I've never wanted anyone or anything. But I want all of you, Melissa, with no regrets afterward, only the glow of our hearts lighting the night around us."

A small sniff followed by a familiar pulsing of her ribs tore at him.

"Don't cry. Please don't cry. I'm not strong enough to keep from kissing your tears away and making love to you until I see your smile of satisfaction."

The desperate hold on his neck eased. Reluctantly, he let her slide down his body until her feet touched the ground. She brushed her teary cheeks with the ends of her shawl, then gathered it around her like armor and folded her arms. Unexpectedly, she bowed her forehead against his chest over his heart.

Rory's fingers curled into steely fists. If he touched her again . . .

"For now, it is enough to know you want me, Melissa. There have been times since leaving Seattle that it seemed you wished me out of your life forever."

Her head rocked in denial on his chest.

"That's fortunate for both of us, because I won't be disregarded easily. I, too, am capable of single-minded pursuit, and your heart is my goal."

When her head lifted, a lopsided smile lit her eyes in the glow of the moon. "Are you sure we don't always get what we deserve?" she asked, her voice cracking.

He touched her lips with the tip of his forefinger. "Absolutely."

She kissed his fingertip, then turned toward the house.

He watched her in the moonlight, his body screaming with the agony of denied release. The night breeze washed over him without cooling the heat pumping through his veins.

After she disappeared into the house, he looked up at the sky. More often than not, when they viewed the stars together, he remained with them after she retired.

"What does she say when she speaks to you?" he asked Mr. Tibbens.

Mr. Tibbens twinkled brightly but kept her confidences.

Chapter 19

TONIGHT, AS SHE had every night for the past week, Melissa thought about Rory's dream before she drifted off to sleep. Erotic fantasies filled her sweetest nights. Knowing Rory slept down the hall and shared them heightened their impact on her senses each morning.

A pounding jolted Melissa out of a sound sleep. Groggy, she lit the lamp on her bedside table. Sliding into the wrapper she kept at the foot of her bed, she opened the door and started into the hall.

"Stay behind me," Rory warned, pulling a shirt over his partially buttoned trousers.

She followed him down the stairs and into the foyer, where she hung back a few paces. No good news came in the middle of the night. She hoped one of the children at Freedom House hadn't taken ill.

Rory lit the foyer lamp, then opened the front door.

An elderly couple carrying tattered traveling bags stood with a little girl between them. The sound of horses and a livery wagon faded into the night.

"Mr. McCullough?"

"Yes."

Melissa lit another lamp and inched forward, curious why anyone would pay a call at such an ungodly hour.

"I'm Abe Faulkner. This here's my wife, Agnes. Dr. Jacobson sent us." Abe pulled a heavily creased envelope from his jacket pocket and offered it to Rory.

"Come in." Rory took the envelope and threw the door wide. "Into the parlor and rest."

Taking her cue, Melissa hurried ahead and lit the lamps.

"Merciful heavens, what is going on? I heard Adam Clayburn's noisy wagon all the way from my bedroom." Pausing at the parlor door, Elmira tucked a loose cluster of hair into a bun.

"These folks have just arrived from Seattle, Elmira," Rory said, reading the missive from Pete. "Tea and a little something to eat might be in order, if you don't mind."

"Most certainly I don't mind. What a long way to travel, only to reach Fairhaven when everything is closed," Elmira said, then hurried to the kitchen.

"We don't want to be any more trouble than necessary," Agnes Faulkner protested.

"No trouble," Rory assured, then shuffled through the papers.

Melissa watched the little girl, whose age she guessed was between five and six years. The smudges on her face and the backs of her hands bespoke her need for a good bath. The rags hanging in layers from her frail shoulders were good only for the fire. White-blond hair pulled into a ponytail at the nape of her neck accentuated the frailty of the child's elfin features.

As though sensing the scrutiny, the girl lifted her bowed head and stared back.

Melissa smiled, inwardly wincing at the wariness in the child's deep-blue eyes.

"Read this," Rory snapped, thrusting the letter into her hand.

She glanced at him. The blood in her veins chilled. Anger as dark as any she could imagine stormed in his gray eyes. The scowl dragging down the corners of his mouth started at his forehead.

"I'll be right back."

Stunned, Melissa watched him leave the parlor, then looked askance at the Faulkners. Much as she wanted to question aloud, she had not dared use her voice since stressing it with Rory under the stars a week earlier.

Abe Faulkner pointed at the letter.

Melissa settled into a chair. Her mouth turned dry with revulsion as she read. Victoria Faulkner was eight years old, not five or six as her small size hinted.

As she read Dr. Jacobson's missive, familiar rage welled up from her toes. In near disbelief, she sought confirmation from the Faulkners. Each time her gaze slid to the child staring at her. With all the self-discipline she could muster, Melissa kept her expression impassive. None of the emotion clamoring inside leaked past the facade.

Elmira brought in hot tea, coffee, sandwiches, and poppy-seed cake sliced to fit small fingers.

From across the room, Melissa heard Victoria Faulkner's stomach growl with hunger. The child did not so much as glance at the food placed on the serving table in front of her.

Elmira offered a tray of damp hand towels to Agnes. "I thought you might want to wipe the road from your hands before you have a bite."

"You are most thoughtful. Thank you." Agnes took two towels and gingerly cleaned Victoria's hands.

Melissa's stomach churned. The dark splotches on the child's hands were old bruises, not dirt. Desperate to question the Faulkners, she looked around for Rory. He did not return for more than ten minutes. By then, the last of the food had disappeared from the platter.

When Rory entered the parlor, Melissa jumped to her feet. "Who did that to her? Who hurt that child?" she signed.

"Later," he growled at her, then handed some papers to Abe Faulkner.

Not ready to be put off, she grabbed his arm.

Rory straightened, facing her. "Later," he signed. "I won't question them in front of her. She's sitting there taking in every word we say. I won't treat her like she's not here or is less than the rest of us, someone insignificant enough to ignore."

Shamed, Melissa turned away. He was right. So right. In her outrage all she thought of was extracting vengeance on the barbarian who had hurt Victoria Faulkner. Long, long ago she had experienced a similar desire for retribution in a place of lopsided justice. Too young to deliver it personally, she had stood by while Pacho gave Horace Freeland a taste of what he unleashed on the foster children at his house. Pacho's death in an adult jail frustrated her taste for vengeance.

"Melissa," Rory called, snapping her reverie.

Contrite, she faced him. "You are right; I was callous."

"It doesn't matter. I'm keeping her. Will you help her?" he asked with his hands.

Exasperated he thought it necessary to ask, she pursed her lips and nodded. "Of course. She needs us."

"You. She may be afraid of me for a long time," he signed.

Sickened by the history of sexual abuse Pete Jacobson detailed in his letter, she nodded. Victoria would not take to strange men easily. "Then I will take care of her and teach her she has nothing to fear from either one of us."

The tension around Rory's eyes and mouth eased. He took her hand and led her to the Faulkners. At the couch, Rory lowered onto his heels and spoke in a soothing tone that belied his anger. "Victoria, this is Miss Fuller," he said softly. "Like you, Miss Fuller has a problem with her throat. Unlike you, there are times when she can speak a few words. Miss Fuller and your grandmother are going to take you upstairs and give you a bath."

The child didn't move.

Melissa tapped Rory's arm, then quickly signed a message for Victoria.

"Miss Fuller wants you to know you are safe here. No one and nothing will hurt you."

Victoria heaved a sigh, resigned to her helplessness in the situation.

Agnes urged the girl with a nudge. "It's for the best, Toria. These people can help you. Much as we want to, your grandfather and I can't keep you safe in Seattle."

Melissa offered her hand. "Please," she croaked, then swallowed hard at the twinge of discomfort low in her throat.

Toria's eyes narrowed, but she got up from the couch. Agnes Faulkner followed.

Melissa took the child's hand and led her up the stairs to

the bathroom. She filled the tub with warm, steamy water and dropped beads of a floral oil blend into it. The girl undressed, folding each tattered garment as she removed it.

Agnes examined the bathroom until Melissa helped the child into the tub. "Dr. Jacobson said you could teach her to talk with her hands. I had my doubts. But that's what you and Mr. McCullough were doing, wasn't it?"

Melissa nodded and started lathering Toria's hair. She avoided looking beyond the gray suds carrying grime from the child's scalp. Clusters of bruises in a rainbow of colors marked the child's malnourished body.

The tenuous balance of emotions Melissa maintained kept her on edge. How she wished someone had offered a safe place and bathed her battered body when she had endured similar abominations. She had believed the terror and degradation behind her, and it had been—until she read Dr. Jacobson's letter and looked into Toria's eyes. She saw herself at age six.

Melissa gritted her teeth against memories and the waves of gooseflesh surging up her arms and across her body. Nothing could change the heinous act that had robbed a little girl of her innocence. Whether a wharf in Seattle or the dank confines of Horace Freeland's closet, the emotionally debilitating aftereffects carried scars that lasted a lifetime.

She rinsed the girl's hair and worked up a second lather. Meanwhile, Toria scraped a washcloth against a bar of soap. The punishing vigor with which she rubbed her skin until it turned a bright pink made Melissa wince.

"We don't want her to be hurt no more. Dr. Jacobson said you'll protect her," Agnes stated. "Will you?"

Melissa met Agnes's imploring gaze and nodded firmly. With her last breath, she would protect this vulnerable child scrubbing the grime from her feet. In time, she would teach her how to protect herself.

"I, ah, don't mean you gotta do it personally, Miss Fuller. Women are at the mercy of men. There isn't much we can do in our own defense. I meant . . . Mr. McCullough. He wouldn't, well, ah, ever . . ."

Toria froze, her wounded gaze locked on Melissa.

Melissa's hands stilled as Agnes Faulkner's voice trailed off. Anger bubbled inside her. She rose, soapy hands on hips, and glared at Agnes Faulkner. "Never. He's a protector, not an abuser," she croaked.

Agnes did not quail in the face of her outrage. "I had to know. Toria is our only grandchild. She was lost to us for so long, it's hard on me and Abe giving her up for her own safety after just finding her.

"Abe and I are old and worn out. We can't protect her any other way, except by hiding her."

The painful sincerity and the tears in the old woman's bloodshot eyes touched Melissa. Without responding, she resumed her place beside the tub and went about rinsing Toria's hair. At all costs, she would make sure no one molested the child again.

"Tell me what you've learned about Victoria Faulkner," Melissa demanded, the crisp motion of her hands betraying her agitation.

Rory led her into the office and closed the door. Neither of them would sleep the last hour before dawn. He gestured at the desk chair, which she occupied reluctantly, as he leaned against his drawing table.

"Is she asleep?" Rory asked softly.

Nodding, Melissa balanced on the edge of the chair facing him. "In my bed," she signed. "Where are her grandparents?"

"In the room next to yours. They sail with the afternoon tide," he said, contemplating their destination. "I've asked them to consider remaining on the ship until it reaches San Francisco. I'm not convinced they're safe in Seattle, even without Toria."

"Why? What is so important about one little girl that places them in danger?"

Rory debated the wisdom of revealing all Abe Faulkner told him until he confirmed the story through Pete Jacobson. But during the interim, if she suspected he withheld anything, Melissa would badger him until she wrung the last detail from him. Resigned it was best she know, he nodded.

"Nine years ago Anne Faulkner, their daughter, ran away with the captain of a trading ship. She sailed with him for several years. During that time, Anne gave birth to Victoria without benefit of marriage.

"Abe's understanding was that the captain's wife showed up unexpectedly. As the consummate trader, the captain sold Anne, and Victoria with her, to another seaman."

"You can't sell people. That's slavery."

On occasion, Melissa's naïveté surprised him. "Laws apply only where people acknowledge their existence. At sea, on most of the waterfronts, a different set of laws is in effect. What you consider slavery, they consider working off a debt."

"What debts could she possibly have? If we're talking sexual favors for room and board, the captain shouldn't have had a complaint."

"I can't argue against your logic. All I know is, he found a way to make a profit and appease his wife at the same time. It didn't matter if it was at Anne's expense, nor did he apparently care about the fate of his daughter.

"Sometime during the past year, Anne ended up in a wharfside brothel." Rory drew a heavy breath and looked out the window. "Such places are terrible enough for an adult. For most of the women there, by whatever circumstance brings them, it is a final stop. The stench of unwashed bodies, stale liquor, and sex, and the filth stand out in my mind. The women live and work in cubicles not much larger than the size of a bed."

The touch of her hand on his leg drew his gaze from the window.

"You've been there."

"Once. That's where I got Orin. He was about two years old then. His mother had syphilis. One of my clients, or one of his acquaintances, sent me a note about Orin. Anonymous, of course. Few men admit to frequenting the dregs of the brothels, but many do, as is evidenced by the number of women working there.

"Pete and I found Orin bound to a board under his mother's bed so his presence wouldn't interfere with her customers. She was glad to be rid of him. Pete and Miriam Jacobson kept him for several months. We wanted to make sure he wasn't ill with the same disease before bringing him in contact with the children at Freedom House."

"How long did Toria live in that hellhole?"

"That's where the story gets complicated. Anne sent her to live with Abe and Agnes about ten months ago, close to the time she started working the wharf. Then, two months ago, Anne visited them. When she left, she took Victoria with her."

"Anne? The mother? Took Toria back to the brothel?" Melissa's eyes widened in disbelief. "After getting her away from that kind of life, she took Victoria back there?"

"Yes. Anne had some debts to pay and nothing to pay them with except her daughter."

A hardness forming around Melissa gave him pause.

She clenched her fists, loosening them reluctantly to sign. "And children are the easiest commodity of payment, aren't they? They have no rights. They have no redress. On the social ladder, throwaway kids rank somewhere below dogs and above cockroaches."

"The game has many players and multiple facets. She's fortunate she had grandparents who cared enough to get her out of there. As it stands now, Victoria Faulkner belongs to us."

Melissa regarded him with disgust. "She doesn't belong to anyone. She's a little girl, not a piece of property."

"Not according to what Abe Faulkner told me. When Anne took Toria back to the brothel, the Faulkners were frantic. They went to Pete and asked for help.

"Agnes has cleaned the building where Pete has his offices for years. She trusted him to give them good advice. He called in an attorney friend of ours. Eventually, they got a judge to sign permanent custody of their granddaughter over to them.

"But it didn't end with getting Toria out of the brothel.

The proprietor, Cyrus Horn, demanded they return her. A change in custody didn't pay Anne's debts. He wanted his money's worth."

"From Toria," she signed, color draining from her face.

"Abe suspects the bastard collected last month. Toria hasn't spoken since he and Pete and half a dozen armed lawmen rescued her."

"She may never speak again," Melissa signed slowly.

"Whether with her voice or by signing, she will speak. The sooner we draw her out of the isolation she has wrapped around herself, the quicker she'll heal."

"You never heal from something like that. It haunts you in the middle of the night and colors everything. You're sure it was your fault, no matter what anyone says. And the shame. The shame. She'll never feel safe or trust . . ."

Rory stared at Melissa for a long time after her hands dropped into her lap. A dark understanding he loathed took shape. Grimly, he doubted Melissa had had any refuge or offer of consolation as a child. Not then. Later, perhaps, in the loving tenderness generously given her by the Tibbenses.

"The man. He's going to look for her and the Faulkners, isn't he?"

Rory nodded, struggling to absorb the implications of her unintended revelation.

"Stop staring at me like I was a poisonous snake. I know that expression, Rory. Shock. Horror. Revulsion. I'll kill whoever comes after Toria by whatever means at hand before I let anyone touch her. So help me God, as long as I can draw a breath, no one will violate her again."

A sudden lump in his throat kept him quiet. He lifted her out of the chair by her shoulders and drew her into an embrace. How many demons vied for her spirit? Holding her tightly, he wished he could battle them for her, but, sadly, he knew he could not.

She stood rigid, with her arms at her sides, as though defiant and unyielding to his superior strength.

"Shock, yes. I suspected something other than the deaths of those you loved had hardened you early, but not anything so vile." He cradled her head against his chest and stroked her shoulders, wishing he had the ability to negate the power of old, ugly wounds and the scars coloring her perceptions.

"Horror, God, yes," he continued, aching for her. "Envisioning any child, you in particular, as a victim of that kind of brutality both horrifies and angers me beyond words. It also gives me some insight into the reasons behind your reaction to Victoria Faulkner. I believe you would protect her with your very life. The thought of your doing so does horrify me. I never want to lose you for any reason.

"Revulsion? Never for you, Melissa. Understanding, yes. I now understand why you trust so little and cannot make love without it." The disjointed pieces of the childhood she revealed began to make sense. Regardless of the memories Toria's presence dredged up, Melissa had found in her a kindred spirit, one she would do anything to protect from the revilement she had experienced.

"You can help her, Melissa, and maybe help yourself too. Better than anyone, you know what she faces and how to conquer it. If possible, show her how to take away the power that bastard still has to hurt her. I don't know how, nor would she be likely to let me get close enough to help if I did. You can reach her if anyone can. Give her some of the strength that drives you."

The light pressure of her arms at his waist told him her answer. He held her closer and continued stroking her head against his chest.

"Promise me something," she whispered, her voice breaking with the strain of emotion.

"Anything." He placed a kiss on the crown of her head.

"Tell no one what happened to her. No one. Ever."

"I give you my promise, Melissa."

The way her arms tightened and her body softened against his felt like trust. When he looked out the window, the sun was rising on a clear morning.

Chapter 20

ABE AND AGNES Faulkner wept when they kissed Toria good-bye. Expressionless, Toria tolerated their parting hugs and kisses. All the while her blue eyes accused them of yet another betrayal by their desertion.

During the days that followed, Melissa's insight into Toria's private world helped her coax the girl out of a co-coon thicker than the silence enveloping her. Melissa quickly discovered the difficulty of translating her desire to help into practical measures. Now that she ached to make a difference for Toria, she discovered the detachment she had honed over the years left her inept.

She drew on Rory's experience with the other children. He possessed an uncanny sense of what a child needed, of what people needed, she decided.

The third morning after the Faulkners' departure, Melissa awakened with the feeling she was being watched. She rolled onto her back and pushed up on an elbow. Toria stood at the foot of her bed.

She drew back the covers and beckoned for the girl to join her.

Toria crawled in, her cold feet seeking warmth, then darting away.

Melissa scooped the child close and rubbed her thin arms through the blankets. Lying spoon fashion, Toria lifted her hands from beneath the covers and practiced signing the alphabet they had concentrated on for the last two days. When she stumbled, Melissa hugged her, then made the proper sign. Once the chill left Toria, they sat up against the head-board. The girl exhibited an aching tenacity Melissa identified with. For now, the tunnel vision served her well in acquiring communication skills.

Aromas of a sumptuous breakfast filtered in under the door. Although her stomach growled, Toria refused to budge until she could run through the alphabet without help. The rudimentary reading skills learned from her grandparents encompassed only the simplest words.

Clad in a dress and shoes Sandra had outgrown, Toria accompanied Melissa into the dining room. Rory awaited with a cup of coffee, his hair damp from a morning swim in the ocean.

"Good morning, ladies. You are both looking lovely this morning." As was his habit, he seated Melissa, then Toria.

Melissa tried not to smile when Toria imitated her, smoothing her skirt. The child had reached a decision sometime during the night. This morning, she did not cringe when Rory loomed behind her holding her chair as an act of courtesy. However, she never took her eyes off him.

The plaid flannel shirt he wore with the sleeves rolled up midway reminded Melissa of their time in the mountains. The familiar warmth of her fantasies heated her cheeks.

"About time you lazybones came down," Elmira scolded as she brought in a tray loaded with breakfast. "The day's half gone."

Toria folded her hands in her lap and stared at them.

Elmira set the tray down. "What did I say?"

Melissa nudged Toria. Obediently, the child raised her head.

"Elmira is teasing us," she signed for Rory to interpret.

Elmira fisted her hands on her hips. "Young lady, when I am angry at you, you'll know it. I don't use any of that hand-talk, but if you're going to learn it, maybe I should too. That way there won't be any misunderstanding between us."

Melissa glanced at Rory and noted his satisfaction when Toria's chin rose higher.

"That's a tall order, Elmira." Rory reached for the platters on the tray.

"What? You think you and Melissa and the children are

the only ones who can learn it? Rory McCullough, I'm ashamed of you for doubting my intellect."

"It isn't your intellect I question, Elmira."

Melissa noted the tease in Rory's voice and the way Toria stared at him in wary fascination.

"And what is it you're doubting, might I ask?" Elmira placed a cup of hot chocolate in front of Toria.

"Why, your ability to keep silent. I've never known you not to have an opinion concerning how things should be done." He dished a poached egg onto Toria's plate. "I can't imagine you not wanting to improve on Thomas Gallaudet's system for communicating through sign."

Melissa laughed. Although he was teasing, Rory spoke the truth. Beyond Elmira's stoic veneer breathed a lovable, opinionated chatterbox.

"I most certainly will do no such thing." Elmira set the serving tray aside and took her place at the table.

"Where is Marvin?" Melissa queried.

"He went into town with a packet for the mail boat," Rory answered.

"Besides," Elmira continued, reaching for the eggs, "if I did find a way to improve on it, no one would listen."

Rory leaned closer to Toria, who regarded him with wide eyes but didn't draw back. "We all use it the way Gallaudet wrote it down. That way, Elmira can't change it."

The gleam in Elmira's gaze deepened Melissa's affection for the housekeeper. She wondered how many times Elmira and Rory had played word games for the children and suspected the number was high. Humor became a weapon he wielded against the shells built around their hearts.

"I miss the children," Rory said when he finished eating. "Would you visit them with me?"

Melissa checked Toria's reaction from the corner of her eye, then nodded. Perhaps it was time for Toria to meet the others.

Toria's eyes narrowed, her chin rigid below her clenched teeth.

"The children are eager to meet you, Toria," Rory told her. "Each of them lived with me when they arrived. Now they live at Freedom House with Mr. and Mrs. Lindstrom. If they continued living here, I wouldn't get any work done—at least not enough to feed us more than clams we dug up from the beach." Rory inclined his head and grinned. "We'd fish all the time. Read books on rainy days. Play games."

Melissa grinned, suspecting his explanation carried far more truth than Toria would believe.

"Then go," Elmira ordered, collecting the dishes. "You worked all night to get those plans ready to go on the mail boat. We won't have to resort to digging up clams for tomorrow's breakfast for a while yet."

Melissa started collecting dishes. Toria immediately followed suit.

"Go. Go!" Elmira waved them away. "Give me some quiet."

Laughing, Melissa gave Elmira a one-armed hug. The housekeeper afforded her a quick hug in return, then waved her away. Expecting Toria to follow, she started toward the door. Her heart caught in her throat at the sight of Elmira crouched before Toria.

"You are one of Mr. McCullough's children now, Toria. I am very pleased you are here to share your smile with us."

Toria opened her mouth. When the words remained locked in her head, she lifted her hands, but didn't know what to do. Helpless, she sought Melissa.

Melissa pointed to her own smile, formed over the tenderness welling up for Elmira. If magic had ever existed, it dwelled in the McCullough home.

Toria smiled at Elmira. The transformation of her elfin features made Melissa draw her lips between her teeth and bite down. Emotion filled her heart. Toria should smile all the time.

"By golly, you do have a smile," Rory boomed. "And a very pretty one at that. Come on. Let's go try it out at Freedom House." Not waiting for anyone else, Rory headed for the front door.

Melissa cast a grateful eye to an understanding Elmira and took Toria's hand. The girl had no time to ponder Rory's

compliment. Hand in hand, they ran to catch up with him.
His gigantic strides had already carried him down the walk.

They caught up near the side of the house. "It is too beautiful to be inside today," Rory said. "Look at that blue sky. If
the sun took a little nap, I bet we'd see Mr. Tibbens laughing
with us right now and wishing he could join us. Did he like
to fish?"

Melissa shrugged and grabbed his arm to slow them down.
Toria's short legs pumped just to keep up.

"Nope, can't slow down, Melissa. The day's not going to
wait for us." He scooped Toria up and hoisted her onto his
right shoulder. "Relax, girl. I won't let you fall."

Melissa met Toria's horrified gaze with an encouraging
smile. Though she questioned Rory's approach of treating
her as he did the rest of the children, she trusted his instincts.

Rory belted out a Gaelic song at the top of his lungs. The
birds fled. The trees moved not a branch. In the underbrush,
small animals scurried out of range.

When they emerged from the trees, Melissa asked why he
sang so loud.

"I have to make up for your silence. Someday, the three of
us are going make this walk and sing loud enough to let them
know we're coming before we clear the trees. Look." He
pointed at the side door of Freedom House. "Here comes the
greeting committee."

The children of Freedom House emerged in stair-step
order. Orin and Roger led the way, their arms waving and
pushing at each other. Katy and Sandra followed, both of
them giggling and waving. Tommy and Darin grinned from
ear to ear, their advanced years of thirteen and twelve denying the childish exuberance of their peers.

Melissa waved back, quickening her step to keep up with
Rory. She laughed when Rory began jogging toward the
children, then slowed and lagged behind, content to watch
him with those he loved. She saw the Lindstroms on the side
porch and returned their friendly wave.

"Who's going fishing with me today?" Rory lifted Toria
from his shoulder and set her in the midst of the children.

"I never catch anything," Orin complained.

"Why settle for a fish on your hook when you can haul in all that seaweed? Somebody has to weed the ocean so the fish can get to my hook." He ruffled Orin's blond hair.

"First, there's someone I want you to meet. It is my honor and privilege to introduce Miss Victoria Faulkner. You may call her Toria. When you all learn how to sign, you'll be able to speak with her. She hears just fine, so mind your manners, boys, and introduce yourselves." Rory backed away to Melissa's side.

She looked a question at him, but he shook his head and thrust his chin at the children. "Watch her reaction to them. It will tell us a great deal," he whispered so low she barely heard him.

With one hand on his belly and the other at the small of his back, Orin bowed. "Hello, I'm Orin Simpson. I'm seven and I've been here most of my life that I can remember, except for when I wasn't and I don't know."

Uncertain, Toria glanced over her shoulder at Melissa. She nodded her head once. Toria responded with a weak imitation of Orin's bow.

"I'm Roger Nutley. I'm nine. I'm never leaving here, no matter what." As an afterthought, he gave Toria a formal bow. "I've been here two years and I haven't been really hungry even once."

Toria's chin tilted down, then up as she scrutinized Roger. As though knowing she doubted him, he dug a cookie out of his shirt pocket and offered it to her. "Mrs. Lindstrom bakes these just for me. If you like it, there's a whole plateful in the kitchen. We'll get more before we go fishing, just in case we get hungry. Fishing with Mr. McCullough gives you a powerful appetite."

Toria took the cookie and bit into it.

"Do you like it?"

She nodded and opened her pocket.

"You don't have to save it. Honest, there's lots of food here."

Toria glanced at the bigger boys, then crammed the rest of

the cookie into her mouth before anyone thought to steal it. She gave Roger a deep bow.

"You're welcome, Toria."

A signal from Tommy sent Darin forward. The gangly strains of adolescence shot his height above the others. "Welcome to Freedom House," Darin said, bowing from the waist. "I'm Darin Calvert. I'm twelve, almost thirteen. I've been here three years. You never have to tell anyone what happened to you before you got here. See, we figure if you're here, it wasn't too good and we don't pretend otherwise. We watch out for each other, and we'll watch out for you, too, from now on."

Toria gaped at Darin, her eyes glassy with pent-up emotion.

Melissa slipped her hand into Rory's and drew strength from his reassuring squeeze.

"Miss Faulkner, I'm Tommy Beckwith and I'll be fourteen next month. As the oldest, I look out for the rest of kids here. So does Darin. He told you the truth, we do our best to take care of each other. We have a few rules that can't be bent even a little bit.

"First, no lying. Some of us used to survive by lying, stealing, and running as fast as we can. We don't need to do that here.

"The second, no stealing. Mr. McCullough makes sure we have what we need. I've been here six years. Any help I can give him or Mr. and Mrs. Lindstrom with chores, I do because I know how lucky I am to be here and not . . . somewhere else. They don't ask for much. It's up to each of us to help out.

"Third, do the chores I assign you. If you don't think something's fair, let me know. You might be right. Mr. Mc-Cullough taught us that an open mind is more effective than an open mouth chewing on bitter words.

"Fourth, is studying. Even though you're a girl, you have to learn as much as the boys. If you need help, one of us will give it."

Tommy grinned, his blue eyes bright as he dropped down

on his haunches. "Don't let that chin quiver, Miss Toria Faulkner. Mr. McCullough and Miss Fuller aren't going to leave you here today. In fact, it might be quite a while. See, we're all learning how to sign so we can understand Miss Fuller—and you, because you'll be learning with us."

Toria sniffed, then nodded. Slowly at first, then faster, she demonstrated the alphabet.

"E-F-G . . ." Rory said, cueing the children, who chimed in immediately.

". . . X-Y-Z."

The triumph of accomplishment lit Toria's face with a generous grin.

Tommy glanced at Katy and Sandra fidgeting beside each other.

"I thought you were going to talk her ears off," Katy chided.

Tommy gave her pigtail an affectionate tug, then winked at Toria. "Just one. I figured you two would do the rest."

Katy giggled.

"I'm Sandra Gigliotti. I'm Italian and I'm ten. So is Katy. Ten, that is." She poked a thumb in the redhead's direction. "We're sisters. I've been here five years, that's half my life. Katy and I have decided to marry the same man so we never have to leave each other."

Toria looked back and forth between Katy and Sandra.

"I'm Katy Wayne. I've decided to be Irish because they like red hair and green eyes." Katy drew Toria's white-blond braid over her shoulder. "You're Scandinavian. I can tell by your hair."

"Her name is Faulkner. That's Irish," Sandra corrected. "Or maybe English."

"Well, she can't be Irish. I am."

"She *can* be Irish."

"No, she can't. If she decides to be our sister, we can't have two Irish and one Italian. Everyone will wonder about you."

Sandra's brow knit. "You're right. Can you be Scandinavian?"

Toria nodded.

"Good. How old are you?" Katy persisted.

Toria held up her fingers.

Sandra nodded at Katy. "Eight is close enough. I mean, it's not like we're twins. Exactly. Do you know when your birthday is?"

Toria shook her head.

"Okay," Katy mused. "Mine is September seventh. Sandra's is November twenty-first. You can have October fourteenth. That way, we'll have a party every week for three months, then Christmas. Okay?"

Toria nodded.

"Oh, this will be famous fun," Katy said. "We need more girls here."

"You can arrange the rest of Toria's life down at the beach," Tommy said, laying a hand on Katy's head. "Mr. McCullough has come to fish."

Roger and Orin whooped and started for the outbuilding near the bluff where the fishing poles awaited. Roger veered toward the house, as Mrs. Lindstrom held the kitchen door open for a cookie detour.

"Come on, Toria. We can build a sand castle while they fish. They never catch much of anything, just get wet and laugh a lot." Katy took Toria's left hand; Sandra snatched up her right. Toria glanced over her shoulder as the girls led her away. A sudden smile told Melissa all she needed to know.

"How did you do this?"

"What?" Rory asked, his brows arched in perplexity.

"I grew up with kids nobody wanted. Where are the shells around their hearts? Where is their caution? Their fear? Anger? How did you do this?"

"I didn't. They did. Those who remember where they came from don't want to go back. They have love and acceptance here. They have each other, and all of them recognize Tommy's authority. Tommy was the most difficult. He worried the new kids would see him as less than equal because of his Negro parentage. They don't. Tommy's a natural leader with a tender heart. For that reason, I won't bring in a child older than Tommy. I hope one day he'll take on a few kids himself.

"Roger is a good example of self-motivation. He eats more than I do and is skinny as a fence post. He was so weak from malnutrition when he got here, he could barely stand.

"Trust me, these kids keep each other in line better than the strictest disciplinarian could. Respect breeds a helluva lot more cooperation than fear. They have both."

"And a lot of love," Melissa added.

"Thanks to Sven and Olga." Rory laughed and clapped Sven on the shoulder. "So you have a Scandinavian soon to come your way."

"Ya," Olga agreed, her blue eyes smiling brightly. "This week she'll be Scandinavian. Next week, they may decide she's German. Hello, Miss Fuller."

Melissa signed a hello. "Have they decided which boy they're both going to marry this month?"

Rory translated, then laughed.

"Last month was Darin. This month, it's Tommy because of his blue eyes," Olga said, ushering the four of them toward the bluff. "Next month? Depends on who they see in town."

Toria waited at the top of the bluff with Katy and Sandra.

"I put a bundle of clothing the girls have outgrown near the front door, Rory," Olga said quietly.

"Ya, she stayed up late sewing on ribbons and lace to make them look new. She is a great mother," Sven added, resting his hand on Olga's stout shoulder.

"The best," Rory agreed.

Melissa wondered why no little Lindstroms inhabited the house, then guessed that the couple could not have children. Where did he find the people he collected? Somehow, they all fit together like a jigsaw puzzle of a beautiful sunrise. Or a new life that drew on tragedies of the past to build something wholesome and positive.

Watching the three girls with their heads together and giggling over something secret, Melissa knew she believed in magic now. Rory McCullough was a magician if ever one drew a breath.

Chapter 21

"DON'T FRET. TORIA will be fine." Rory rolled a
drawing into a scroll and slid a rubber band around it. "Katy
and Sandra do an amazing job of interpreting what she
wants."

"I hadn't expected her to spend the night at Freedom
House so soon," Melissa signed. "She's only been here three
weeks."

"Consider it a triumph, Melissa. She knows you'll be here
tomorrow. Tonight she can be the Scandinavian member of
the Three Musketeers." Rory winked at her with an understanding smile. "Maybe next time they'll invite you too."

Melissa rolled her eyes and resumed her pacing, pausing
only to sign. "I don't want to spend the night at Freedom
House. I just . . ."

Rory rounded the desk and blocked her path. "You just
want to have a chance to love her? Heal her little heart and
your own as well? You can't give her what you needed at
that age; you have to give her what she needs. Right now,
it's a chance to grow and have friends. This is a new experience for Toria. She hasn't had many opportunities to play
with other children. She's hungry for their companionship
and the giggle sessions. Have you noticed how difficult it is
to be angry when you're laughing? She has."

"She can't hide from what's happened to her. It will fester.
Eat at her."

"The time hasn't come for her to look that much ugliness
in the face again. First she needs to believe that where she
came from is only a small part of the world. There are good
people who won't hurt her, who like her and want to extend

themselves on her behalf. Once she's had some laughter and friendship, she'll stand a better chance of seeing what happened in a light that doesn't shame her or make her feel she is less than she can be."

"Why do you have to be so damn smart? So right all the time?" she croaked.

Rory chuckled. "Is that what has you on edge?"

"Partly," she signed. The perpetual desire for the man within arm's reach was the main reason for her unsettled state.

"Sweetheart, Toria is the eighth child I've taken in. Considering her background, she has relatively few behavioral problems. Her inability to speak will either cure itself or it won't. We have no control over it. The rest?" He shrugged and folded his arms. "Trust the children. It's like a perpetual motion machine."

"There is no such thing."

"I'll take your word for that."

He'd take her word just like he took the word of an eight-year-old that she wanted to spend the night with Katy and Sandra. She had to admit Toria hadn't seemed coerced. Truth be told, her excitement had sent her skipping up the stairs to collect her nightgown.

"Maybe Toria is ready for a night away. But what if she isn't and she gets lonely? Sometimes she crawls into bed with me."

"She'll be sleeping between Katy and Sandra when they finally do sleep. I expect three tired little girls tomorrow afternoon when Sven brings her home." Understanding put a soft smile on his lips. "And perhaps one tired lady. You've adjusted very well to worrying about someone other than yourself. Careful—it becomes a habit."

Startled, she retreated a step. Since Toria's arrival, she hadn't had time to dwell on the conflicts that had been tearing at her since the wreck of the *Northern Trader*. Meanwhile, her angry, selfish side had sulked, meshing with her tender, emotional personality only when necessity dictated.

Absently, she fondled the crystal pendant around her neck.

She gazed into the carefully banked fire of desire in Rory's smoldering gray eyes, then smiled.

"Will you be working half the night again?"

"Four nights in a row is enough," he answered. "Another hour, maybe."

"It won't inconvenience you if I lie in the bathtub for a while?"

Rory swallowed hard. "No. It would do you good to relax before retiring."

Without another word Melissa went upstairs and prepared a bath. She needed time and a clear head.

Soaking in the steamy water scented with rose oil settled her thoughts. She grinned and drew her pearl-handled straight razor along her calf. The razor, a gift from Rory, was much finer than the one he purchased for himself after losing his old one when the *Northern Trader* sank. If she left the razor on the sink, he stropped it to a marvelous edge.

She admired her clean-shaven calf. Fortunately, she hadn't bled into a state of anemia before mastering the use of the blade around her knees and ankles.

After tremendous soul-searching and endless battles with herself, Melissa decided on a course of action. The skeptical Major Fuller balked but accepted the new direction of her life. Quelling, then gradually cultivating the favorable aspects of her old self might become a lifelong endeavor. However, she found things about her emerging self that she liked.

A little adjustment here. A little compromise there. Pretty soon, I might like all of the person in my mirror.

So, if magic was responsible for bringing her here—bizarre as it was, no other explanation existed—and the responsible party was gone. Rory had said she would never be back. That being the case, any hope of returning to the space age had gone with Shelan.

What if she had a choice of staying here or returning to the time in which Shelan found her?

Melissa smiled and shook her head. Tonight she was making her choice, perhaps the most important one in her life.

Tonight she wanted Rory to like what he saw.

*   *   *

Melissa rapped lightly on Rory's bedroom door.

"Come in."

A flurry of butterflies took flight in her stomach. She drew a solid breath, then opened the door, confident she wanted the love he offered. Rory leaned against the headboard on the near side of his bed. Three pink-and-white scars slashed through the silken forest of his chest hair. The crystal pendant, which he never removed, caught the lamp's glow and refracted a rainbow of light.

Melissa put her trembling hands behind her and softly closed the door. A deft flick of her finger sent the bolt into place with a sound louder than the sudden anxious acceleration of her heart. Engaging the lock confined her to the frightening risk ahead as surely as it shut out the rest of the world.

Rory closed the book in his hand without marking his place, then set it on the night table. His gaze held hers until her hands spoke.

"A wise man once said there were two sides to everything: adversity and opportunity. You are right about Toria. Her job is to reach, mine is to catch her if she stumbles. Tonight, I, too, want to reach. For you. For the magic I almost believe in." Silently, she narrowed the distance to the bed. With each step, she moved closer to heaven or hell. With all her heart she wanted to believe they could re-create what they found in the stone circle. Yet old doubts and fears harried her hopes and gnawed away at the shiny edges of her fragile optimism.

"Show me it's possible. Make love with me, Rory, for I don't believe I'll survive the night if you don't." Without waiting for a response and before she lost her bravado, she lifted the sides of her nightgown over her head. She stood proudly beside him, wearing nothing except the crystal, and let the nightgown fall from her hand.

Rory didn't move. The desire in his gray eyes spoke for him.

Aching for the bliss he promised they would share on this Someday, Melissa lifted the edge of the bedclothes and drew them over the rise of his elevated left knee. Her mouth formed a silent O as she unveiled the splendor beneath. Her dreams had failed to match the naked magnificence of his fully aroused body within her reach. Fascination heightened her desire and dimmed her anxiety.

She touched his toes, then trailed her fingertips up his straight right leg. Beneath the coarse, silken hair on his thigh, she felt the unmistakable ripple of gooseflesh across his warm skin. Her mouth suddenly became dry and her heartbeat quickened.

"Are you cold?" she whispered as her fingers splayed across his upper thigh.

"Not cold." Awe made his response a faint whisper.

"No, you don't feel cold," she said, unwilling to yield her treasure long enough to sign. When she collected the twin sacs of his sex in her hand, she heard the sudden hiss of his breath being sucked through his teeth. Desire shot through her in head-spinning waves.

"You feel warm." After a moment, she curled her fingers around his turgid sex. The proof of his great desire for her pulsed against her hand. The delicious ache in her loins begged for the throbbing erection she sinuously stroked. "Hot, actually."

"Very hot," he warned in invitation.

With a free fingertip, she touched the bead of clear liquid forming on the tip of his tumescent sex. The drop of moisture she spread in slow, widening circles glistened in the glow of the lamplight.

"Too hot." The strain in Rory's voice drew her gaze to his face.

With a deft motion that warned of his strength, he caught her up and lifted her over him, then rolled until he lay on top of her, his weight braced on his elbows. Wide-eyed, Melissa stared into his dilated gray eyes, brimming with raw passion.

"Much too hot," he growled, lowering his mouth to hers.

The taste of his desire sent Melissa grappling for a hold on him. With an urgency she didn't understand, she wanted him molded to her flesh, part of her heart, and inside her body.

The depth of her need manifested itself in her response to his heady kiss.

She drew the probing tip of his tongue over her teeth. The rhythm of his assault sent her hips rocking against him, seeking the physical union of the love she wanted to give him. Her hands took on a life of their own, exploring the sleek glide of muscle along his back and the swell of his buttocks.

Abruptly, Rory broke the kiss and stilled.

Stunned, she searched his eyes and felt the minute trembling of his body protesting against the immobility he imposed. Her gaze lowered to his mouth. Unbidden, the tip of her tongue ran over her bottom lip.

"Why?" Rory whispered as though in pain.

Comprehension dawned upon her slowly. The flutter of emotion independent from the desire ravaging her strengthened. He was going to force her to say words that fostered fear. Speaking them aloud made them more real than a private admission made in the dark of her room or under the stars. Saying them put her at risk of exposure. What if they made love and she didn't . . .

Mentally, she shook herself. She refused to consider it.

"Why?" Rory repeated, his tone softer, the tremble of his body mastered now.

"Because I . . . I want you as much as you want me." Why was it so difficult to say what he needed to hear, what she knew in her heart?

Rory shook his head, not accepting the obvious as a reason for her presence. Not one to mask his emotions, his resolve showed in the set of his jaw and his unblinking eyes.

"You're going to make me say it?" She tried swallowing the sudden lump in her throat. It remained. Desperate to soften the unyielding expression looming above her, she brushed aside a lock of brown-gold hair falling over his brow.

"I need you to say it. I want no questions later. No regrets, Melissa."

She closed her eyes and turned her face toward the gentle

stroking of the back of his fingers against her cheek. What was she afraid of?

When she opened her eyes again, she had her answer. In Rory's arms, the shadows of the past lost their potency. He wielded more power over her heart than her fear did.

"I trust you, Rory," she breathed in a shaky voice. In the silence ensuing, her admission boomed in her ears. When the echo quieted, a new freedom buoyed her heart.

"I swear to you that I'll never violate your trust, Melissa. I'd sell my soul to keep you from harm." He placed a light kiss on the tip of her nose. "I love you."

Her heart cried out that she loved him too, but the words refused expression. The admission made her too vulnerable. "Then love me, Rory. Give me . . ." The tender brush of his lips against her silenced her.

"I'll love you after I draw my last breath."

Her chin lifted in anticipation as he placed a line of kisses along her lower lip.

"I'll love you even after the stars stop shining."

The hand closing on her breast made her wildly crave more. "I need you . . . in my life . . . in my body." The sensation of the head of his erection against her inner thigh built her need for fulfillment.

"Now," she whispered urgently, clutching his shoulders.

"God help me, I wanted to go slow. Waited so long . . ." His mouth found hers.

The desire raging in Melissa rejected any notion of slow, leisurely lovemaking. The force that had seized her in the fairy ring captured her again. This time, the love she bore Rory heightened the need of their joining into oneness.

He shifted, allowing her to free the leg trapped between his. The tender invasion of his fingers found the core of her need weeping for him. The vibration of his groan rattled his chest against her sensitive breast.

The fire in her raced through her veins. She cried out when his lips abandoned hers, then she arched her breast into the heat of his mouth. Lost in a maelstrom of sensation, she writhed against his hand and mouth. She wanted to give him all she was and hold his love against her heart forever. Yet she was lost in the beautiful, agonizing pleasure he created.

"Rory," she squeaked as the tide of passion lifted her higher.

Rory made a response, then settled on his heels, lifting her as he rose until she sat on his folded legs. During a brief pause in his motion, she recognized in his eyes the wild glaze of a passion rivaling her own. He lifted her higher, then slowly lowered her onto his erection.

Melissa's neck arched. She gasped for air as the hot, delicious sensation of him entering her inch by pulsing inch seized what little remained of her senses. Nothing was as close to heaven as having him inside her.

The slow, calculated movement he allowed intensified her pleasure. She had denied him and herself for so long, she thought the exquisite sensation of having all of him might stop her thundering heart. She locked her hands behind his neck and held on. Bowing her spine thrust her breasts close to his face, and he caught a nipple in his mouth and suckled with his tongue, teeth, and lips. His greediness belied the slow, sinuous motion with which he controlled the marvelously agonizing penetration and retreat, then a slightly deeper invasion before his inevitable retreat.

The tension coiling within her tightened. Again, he lifted her a little bit, then lowered her until he was completely buried inside her. Melissa cried out and clutched his neck, pressing her body against his.

His lovemaking grew insistent as the tempo quickened in response to her unspoken demands. The sweet union glowed with love. She gave him everything—her body, her heart, her passion, her very soul—to cherish and consume at will. When she yielded the last vestige of herself, something more glorious than she had imagined possible assaulted her. The love she felt radiating from him knew no bounds.

"Oh, yes, sweetheart!" Rory drew a ragged breath. "With me," he rasped, seeking her mouth.

The invasion of his tongue claimed a complete possession, and he quickened the deep thrusts building to an unbelievable pleasure. Melissa held on, letting the surge of passion carry her higher and higher. He was with her, part of her. His love glowed in every cell of her body. She felt the first tremors of climax tighten and the sudden, uncontrollable spasm of his body finding and giving release.

Ecstasy swept through her with the force of a tornado, blowing the smallest cobweb of doubt out of existence. In the rapture, she savored his embrace. Their island of paradise shone with love. Nothing in her experience, not even floating among the stars, could rival the beauty they shared.

By mutual, silent consent, they lingered as long as they could in the heavenly time of their love. When she opened her eyes, the beauty she experienced without benefit of fairy rings or magic spells amazed her. An enigmatic smile crept across Rory's lips as she met the odd intensity of his unwavering gaze.

Still dazed, she removed his smile with a series of tender kisses, which he returned with thorough attentiveness.

Rory cradled her head against his cheek and tightened his embrace.

Melissa basked in the bliss dancing through her. Hugging his neck, rocking slowly with him, she lifted her mouth to his ear and whispered, "We were both wrong. This was clearly more . . . more fantastically beautiful than the magic circle."

"So you do believe in magic?" he teased, then chuckled, shaking them both.

"I believe in you, Rory. You are magic greater than anything I've encountered."

"I don't know about that. You're the one who let me live out my nightly fantasy." He kissed her shoulder. "Thank you for doing it that way." Very carefully, he laid her back on the pillows, then followed, never withdrawing the connection between them.

"Look," Melissa whispered, not quite believing. Sometime during their lovemaking, her pendant had slipped through the thong holding his and twisted. The twin quartz crystals had rejoined at their jagged facets where Shelan had broken them apart years earlier.

"Our hearts fit together in the same way." He settled over her. The crystals nestled between her breasts. "I feel your heartbeat and it matches mine."

Mesmerized by his soothing voice and expressive gray eyes brimming with love and hope, Melissa felt the strong pulse of his heart against her breast.

"We belong together, Melissa. I want to make love with you every night for the rest of our lives." He kissed the corners of her mouth, then used both hands to brush her hair from her face and hold it back. "Maybe in thirty or forty years we'll be able to go slow the first time."

"The first time?" Her brow knit in puzzlement.

Rory chuckled. "You surely don't for a moment believe we've finished? The sun is a long way from rising and we can both still walk."

The excitement glistening in his smile and eyes promised far more than his words implied. "In that case, I may not survive," she mused in a whisper.

Rory's laughter shook the bed. "Fear not, Mistress Melissa, I shall carry you to your bed before the household stirs. There you may sleep the day away."

"I don't think so, though I suppose this does make me your mistress. I never thought about being any man's mistress before." The notion sat crosswise to her self-image.

"Not my mistress, Melissa. I want you as my wife, the mother of my children, my partner in all things."

"Me, a wife?" Even further from the consideration of being a mistress was being a wife. "Marriage and children never crossed my mind after childhood."

Rory stiffened. "I see."

"I don't think you do. I never had any reason to believe I'd fall in love and want the domestic scene." Her throat gave a warning spasm she recognized as stress.

"Domestic scene?" he asked, his perfectly arched eyebrows rising. "What is that? A painting?"

Melissa shook her head and grinned.

"If you loved me, would you consider marrying me?" All traces of levity evaporated.

Melissa hesitated, then nodded. She would think about it. Seriously.

"Will you think about marrying me anyway? We're playing with fire here. If we create a child, I won't give you a choice—you'll marry me. Our child will know both of us. No one will have to buy him off the streets or—"

"Yes. You made your point."

"Yes, you'll marry me?"

"Yes, I'll think about it." Her answer eased some of the tension she saw in his face, but not all. "Did anyone ever tell you that you worry too much?"

"Some things are worth the trouble. I've always regarded the matters of a wife and children seriously."

Melissa cleared her throat. "Either you stop talking and we make love again or you're going to have to give me my hands. I'm done using my voice for the night."

The fingers entwined in hers and holding her hands beside her head tightened. "In that case, we're done talking—for now—unless you want to know what I'm going to do to you."

Biting her bottom lip to suppress a grin, she nodded.

Rory lowered his mouth to her ear. The intricate details of his erotic plans made her blush with anticipation as he hardened inside her.

Chapter 22

A CANVAS TARP painted with rows of circles dominated the center of the great room at Freedom House. Laughter rattled the windows. The girls and Melissa had donned their trousers for the occasion, and Roger had made a gift of an extra pair to Toria. A version of a game Melissa recalled from her childhood was the source of their laughter.

Sven spun the makeshift wheel. "Blue."

Left hand and both bare feet locked on their colors, Melissa ducked under Tommy, who balanced with both hands on red circles and a foot on a yellow circle. Just as she reached for the blue circle, Darin began teetering.

"Hold it," Tommy cried, laughing and struggling for balance between Melissa and Darin.

Melissa started laughing too. Her shaking back bounced against Tommy's ribs.

"Don't move so much," Darin pleaded. "I'm tipping."

The interwoven limbs vying for their designated color spots trembled as Darin struggled to regain his balance.

"Don't put your foot down, Tommy!" Roger warned from the sidelines.

"Darin's gonna fall," Orin called. "You look like a pretzel."

"I feel like one," Darin called back.

"You be careful, Miss Fuller," Olga warned. "If those boys fall, you'll be squished."

"Mr. McCullough will have to pick you up with a pancake turner," Katy giggled.

"Tommy put his foot down!" Sandra cried out.

"Need some help getting out of there, Tommy?" Rory asked, laughing.

"I think—" Before he could finish, he swayed, then toppled sideways and took Darin and Melissa with him.

Melissa broke their fall by bowing her back and stiffening her limbs. Feeling the burden of their squirming weight, she let them down easy. Good old basic and physical training had benefits neither NASA nor the Air Force dreamed of touting.

"Whoa, you're really strong," Tommy told her, then rolled away.

Slowly she signed, "Do I need a bath?"

A sudden quiet descended as the watchers followed her hands.

Rory and Toria exchanged a look, then grinned. Laughter again burst through the room.

Only Tommy didn't laugh. "Oh, no, Miss Fuller, that's not what I meant," he protested. "I would never imply such an insult."

He looked so horror-stricken that Melissa instantly regretted making a joke at his expense. She offered her hand to him.

Tommy immediately helped her to her feet. Before he could let go, she caught him in a hug and bussed his cheek, then smiled.

"You can joke with me anytime, Miss Fuller," Tommy said, then smiled. "You're a really good sport." His smile became a grin. "And strong, too."

Melissa drew back her fist and faked a punch to his arm.

"Oh, you broke it! You broke my arm. Look!" He stood lopsided, flicked his arm, and let it dangle from the shoulder as though detached.

Laughing silently, Melissa watched him, feeling her love for Tommy and the rest of the children expand her heart to the bursting point.

Toria jumped up, her eyes narrowed and darting from Melissa to Tommy, then back. She pushed at Tommy's arm.

It swung like a damp noodle. Color drained from her cheeks, and her jaw dropped as she stepped away from Melissa.

"Hold it, little one," Tommy said, then ended the charade by picking Toria up with his phony broken arm. "Good as new." He leaned close to her ear and spoke aloud, "She didn't even graze me. She might be strong, but she's a softy when it comes to hitting people she likes. I can tell. Sorry I scared you."

Melissa glanced at Rory, whose smile evaporated into an amazement she shared. There had been so many changes for the little girl since arriving at the McCullough home. The greatest was her trust of Tommy because of his size and authority.

When Tommy put Toria down, she skipped back to Katy and Sandra.

The parlor clock chimed the hour.

"It's time for me to take Miss Fuller and Toria home," Rory said, rising. "Say good night and wish me a safe trip. I'm off with the morning tide to Seattle."

"Mr. McCullough," Sandra started, rising from the floor with Toria and Katy, "promise you won't get on a ship when it's stormy. Please."

Rory dropped to his haunches before the Three Musketeers. "On that, Miss Italy," he flicked Sandra's nose, "Miss Ireland," he flicked Katy's nose, "and Miss Scandinavia," he flicked Toria's nose, "you have my most solemn promise. I won't be gone long, two weeks at the most." He gave each girl a hug, not allowing Toria time to shrink from his fatherly affection.

Melissa noted the tenderness Rory showered on the seven children gathered around him. He had a way of making each feel special.

Toria hung back, eyeing the bright canvas. The little girl took a deep breath, squared her shoulders, and approached. Her fisted right hand rose with her thumb across her fingers. She drew the thumb under her finger, then raised it.

"S-t-a," Melissa read silently.

Toria pointed at herself, then the floor.

"Here?" Melissa asked. "You want to stay the night and play longer?"

Toria's face brightened into a smile. She nodded, her blue eyes hopeful.

"Just tonight," Melissa whispered, understanding that Toria didn't want the children to continue playing the game without her.

A grin revealed her permanent teeth and a gap where her eyeteeth poked through the gums. "Thank you," she signed.

By the time the farewells ended, the clock had struck a quarter past the hour. Rory tucked Melissa's hand into the crook of his arm and strolled into the evening.

"You let Toria stay?" Rory asked when they entered the woods.

Melissa nodded.

"I hope like hell you have a selfish motive, other than something frivolous like letting her be a part of the children's games."

She laughed at his exaggerated leer, knowing full well Toria's absence provided an opportunity for her to spend the night in his bed. Sleep was the furthest thing from her mind.

"She asked. I couldn't say no," Melissa said in an almost normal tone. The tonics, prolonged silences, and judicious use of her voice had aided in her limited, slow recovery. Melissa maintained her silence around the children as an additional incentive to practice signing.

"Have you thought about marrying me?" The seriousness of his tone made her glance up. All traces of the evening's levity evaporated.

She nodded. She had thought hard on the matter. Although she was certain she was not carrying a child, the possibility loomed each time they made love. Thus far, luck had favored them—but luck was lousy birth control.

"Are there measures, I mean, things we can use to prevent conception?"

"Yes. We don't have any at the moment. Until you, there was no need to consider such things." He took her hand from his forearm and held it in his. The natural twining of their fingers heightened the intimacy of their conversation.

"Are such things available in Seattle?" she asked hopeful.

"Yes. I'll see to it while I'm there. However, prevention methods are far from perfect. No one will vouch for their effectiveness, though I'm sure something might be better than nothing. There is always a risk." He squeezed her hand. "I'd rather you married me because you want to, not because circumstances dictate it."

Sensing his reservations, she smiled at him. "Rory, you can bet the last drop of water in the ocean that I wouldn't marry you for any reason other than because I wanted to. I know how you feel about having a child out of wedlock, and I agree with you. My concern is having a family before we're ready."

"You're not ready?"

Melissa rolled her eyes and shrugged her shoulders. "Do I look like the stable pillar of the community ready to enter the mother-of-the-year contest?"

"I'm not sure I followed all that, but I gather you'd prefer to give us some time before starting a family." A subtle smile played at the corners of his mouth.

"Go to the head of the class, Mr. McCullough. There is still so much I'm trying to sift through. I lived in a very different place from anything you know, Rory. There are things I miss, things I would change drastically because I am changed, if I went back."

They walked in silence for a moment before Rory spoke. "Do you long to return?"

The advances in technology she'd never see again seemed endless. In this time, she'd never drive a car, microwave a dinner, phone for pizza delivery, or access the Internet. Here, the stars were out of reach. Memories tempered her losses. She had lived her dream in another time. Now she had a new dream and a future with Rory. Yet the countless avenues of progress made in the gap between the times pulled at her.

Fleetingly, she imagined Rory in front of a computer, plotting out his plans. How much more easily his work would go; he would have so much more time to play with the children he adored. But the two worlds would never meet.

Besides, though she would always yearn to walk in space, returning to the time in which her lifelong dream came true wasn't an option. And even if it were, leaving Rory and the children was out of the question. The woman she had become valued people more than things.

In the deep shadows cast by pungent evergreens, she saw the color fade from his face as she contemplated her answer. "I wouldn't trade this for all of the good things in the world I came from. I can't change what was, but I can continue changing myself. Because of you, I can make a small difference with the children. Instead of turning my back, I can participate. That in itself is a gift you've given me. One of many."

She stopped and met his searching gaze, then traced his jaw with her fingertip. "I worry your marrying me is a very bad bargain for you. I'll always be a little different, a bit avant-garde, you might say."

He raised his eyebrows skeptically. "More so than I?"

She tipped her head to the side and smiled. "Touché. But you're different in a beautiful, wonderful way. If I didn't know you, I could not be convinced you had ever walked upon this misery-infested world.

"Marrying you is not a question of whether or not I love you, Rory. I do love you with all my heart. It's just that we have it so good now, I don't want to spoil it with marriage."

Incredulous, Rory gripped her shoulders. "What the hell does that mean? You love me? My god, Melissa, if we were married, things would only get better. I ache to hold you every night, to awaken every morning with you at my side. I want to shout to the whole world that Rory McCullough loves Melissa Fuller and she loves him. Most of all, I want our names bound as tightly as our hearts are."

"How can you be so sure?"

"How can you not be sure? Will there ever be a man who loves you as I do?"

"No, and I will never love anyone but you." She slipped

her arms around his waist and laid her head on his chest. "Oh, Rory, why am I so afraid of commitment?"

The gentle stroking of his hand on her hair consoled her. "It is too late for fear. Your heart has already made the commitment."

She burrowed against his chest, realizing he was right. What did the words matter? She had traded her heart and soul for his. "I suppose you're right."

"You suppose?"

"You're going to drag it out of me, aren't you?"

"Yes, because we're going to do it right." He laid a kiss on the crown of her head, then unwound her arms from his waist. Nonplussed, Melissa watched him kneel on one knee and take her hand.

"Melissa, will you do me the honor of becoming my wife?"

Touched by the formality he preserved in the middle of the woods, she smiled. "Yes, my gallant Mr. McCullough, I will be your wife, your partner, your friend, and your lover. Will you be the same for me?"

"With every breath I take for as long as the stars shine." He kissed her hand, then lifted his face. "God, how I love you."

She bent and found his mouth, then slowly rose as he stood. The tender kiss quickly burned with the bright flame of passion.

Rory lay on his back and watched the stars through the skylight over the bed. If he hadn't built the portal to the heavens years ago, he would do so now for Melissa.

A satisfied smile parted his lips. The woman he loved curled against him, her head on his shoulder, her smooth, naked thigh slung across his sex. The possessive warmth of her arm draped his chest.

Shelan had brought him a woman to love and build a future with. When he returned from Seattle, Melissa would become his wife. This strange woman with more facets than the number of stars in the heavens loved him. The thought made him grin broadly at the stars twinkling overhead. Melissa did nothing in half measure. Loving him meant loving him with every fiber of her luscious body. He deemed himself the honored recipient of a love hoarded for a lifetime in anticipation of finding the right man.

The bounty of love once held captive in her heart by a fear he had glimpsed at odd times found freedom with the children. She identified with them and understood the dragons lurking beyond the safe harbor of Freedom House.

Rory had not believed any woman would want to share herself as generously as Melissa did now. The games she devised brought laughter and joy. The patience she maintained during instruction in signing grew every day, as did her affection for the seven children Rory considered his.

"You haven't slept at all," she murmured, nuzzling her cheek against his chest.

Now that she was awake, he did what he had longed to do for the past hour: run his hand along her thigh, over the swell of her hip, into the valley of her waist, then along her ribs. He lingered at her breast, feeling the nipple harden at his touch. The subtle response started the familiar changes in his body. He resumed the journey along her shoulder and down her arm until he caught her hand and lifted her palm to his lips.

"Sometimes I fear you are a dream," he whispered between kisses on each of her fingers. "If you are, I never want to wake up."

Melissa scooted forward on an elbow, then propped herself on his chest. "If this is a dream, take me with you when you wake. I couldn't bear to be left without you, Rory. You're my heart, my salvation. You've taught me more about how to live and love in four months than I learned in nearly thirty years. I love you, Rory. I need you in ways I'm still discovering and that sometimes frighten me."

Rory adjusted their positions until she lay atop him. "I never want you frightened." He framed her face in his hands. "But I want you always to need me." He brushed a kiss on her lips. "Always to love me. There is nothing I wouldn't do to make you happy."

Her arms crept up until her elbows slid over his shoulders. "You've already done your part. The rest is up to me. Though with you as my lover, my partner, my mentor, happiness has no chance of eluding me."

"God, how I love you," he murmured, capturing her mouth in a kiss that rose from his heart.

"You must. I haven't brushed my teeth yet," she said against his mouth, then laughed.

The desire ruling his loins wouldn't part with her for a moment. "Kiss me, my love. I sail in a couple of hours and should be dressing now. I'd begrudge your tooth powder anytime you gave it."

Her forearms cradled his head as she lowered her mouth. "Now that we've found each other, don't let anything happen to you, Rory. I'd be lost without you."

He spent no more time with words. The blaze of her passion took his desire even higher. He needed her now as fiercely as he had last night when they pleasured one another with a carnality reaching the limits of his wildest dreams.

Running his hands along her arms, shoulders, and down her ribs, he savored her exquisite contours and the erotic sensation of her breasts brushing against his chest. He filled his hands with her buttocks and answered the demands of her kiss.

Her inner thigh glided along the outside of his legs, her undulating hips seeking the prize he wanted to give her. He embraced her at the shoulders and hips, then rolled their bodies until he loomed over her and broke the kiss.

"We have one more position to exhaust before the night is over," he whispered.

"By all means."

The strength of her arm hooked around his neck always amazed him. He met her mouth and entered her slowly. The trip-hammer in his heart skipped a beat at her moist readiness for him. He deepened the kiss and yielded to their growing need to meld their hearts, bodies, and spirits into one.

He moaned into her sweet mouth. Immediately, her legs rose and locked around his waist. The sudden hard surge of her hips sent him plunging into her.

She gasped and broke the kiss.

"Sensitive?" he murmured, as the fire inside him raged.

"Marvelously so," she breathed back, her breasts heaving against him. "Don't stop."

The heaven enveloping him denied any possibility of such a superhuman feat. His mind bent to his body's will.

Watching her eyes in the faint glow of dawn leaking across the skylight overhead, he yielded the last shred of his control. Buried inside of her, he stilled. He swept his hand under her hips and held them motionless. The quiver of her impending climax matched the throb of his erection. The pulsations erupted in a burst of ecstasy that made her cry his name.

His heart soared. The sublime beauty of their pleasure burst with color and a sense of all-consuming love shared in spirit as well as body. The totality of his soul blended with hers. He savored the rapture with ever-increasing awe and basked in the glow they created. He clung to each color and fragment of bliss that made him believe he could fly among her stars if she so much as hinted she wanted him to do so.

When they reluctantly drifted back into reality, he held her tightly, never wanting to release her. Their ragged breathing stabilized while he stroked her taut back, buttocks, and thighs.

"I will miss you terribly. Don't be gone too long, Rory."

He kissed her shoulder. "If I don't get out of bed, I won't be going at all."

Slowly, as though fighting a natural impulse to remain entwined, she released him.

Rory drew a deep breath, then released it. "I want to marry you the day I get back."

She caught his face between her hands. "We may as well. We'll have a wedding night with or without the preacher or his paper."

"In my heart you have been my wife since the day I found

you." He brushed a kiss across her forehead. "But, I know seven children and an entire town who recognize nothing other than a formal, witnessed ceremony."

"Then we'll give it to them." She lifted the pendants once again entwined into solidarity. "But you must go so you can come back. Meanwhile, I will think of all the ways I want to make love with you." She untangled the crystals. "May I count on you to do the same? A little show-and-tell might be very interesting."

Rory chuckled, amazed again at the playful side of her erotic nature. "I assure you, you may count on it. And me." He kissed her nose, then extricated himself from their tangle of arms, legs, and rumpled sheets.

He lit the bedside lamp and went to his dresser. The partially packed valise sat on the floor.

"I was right," she mused.

He glanced at her, then froze. She stretched like a preening cat satisfied with the world. He had not expected to see such an expression from her for a long time yet. "About what?" he asked, realizing the awesome power of the love they shared.

"When you carried me out of the lake, I thought you were an Olympian god." She propped her head on her hand and gave him a dreamy smile. "You are."

Brimming with happiness so great he almost felt immortal, Rory chuckled. "If so, you are my goddess." Fleetingly, he wondered if a man could burst from joy.

Chapter 23

"DARIN AND TOMMY would benefit greatly from advanced instruction," Charles Markel told Melissa and Sven at Freedom House the following afternoon. "Both are bright, eager students. My compliments on the excellent study habits you and Mr. McCullough have instilled."

"Thank you, Mr. Markel. As for furthering their education, in the near future we have no teacher other than you." Sven's blond eyebrows rose.

"I've compiled a list of the studies they must master to continue their education," Charles Markel said. "I'm certain Mr. McCullough has many of the literature books and some of the history books in his personal library. He and I have discussed most of these works over the years. If he can make the time, I'm also certain he can tutor them in advanced mathematics. That leaves science."

"Are the textbooks available?" Melissa asked in a quiet voice.

Charles Markel's smile conveyed his pleasure at hearing her speak aloud. "I gave Tommy a list of them. But desire alone is insufficient for a complete understanding of the subjects."

Her recollections of her own education and the teachers she hounded with questions and explanations illustrated the truth of his words. "Science and math?"

"Yes. I have access to several of the textbooks they will need. Perhaps they can glean the basics, and then Mr. McCullough's tasks will be lighter."

Lighter? If Rory undertook tutoring Tommy and Darin as Mr. Markel was suggesting, he would never have time to sleep. "Or perhaps we can find an alternative," she mused.

"My obligations in Fairhaven seem to grow each year. I have spoken with Mr. McCullough about the need for an advanced tutor. He has assured me he is pursuing the matter." Markel looked from Sven to Melissa. "For a man such as I am, Miss Fuller, teaching the children here at Freedom House is most rewarding. I would like to continue aiding in their education for many years.

"This place is a font of hope. The changes I've seen in these children . . ." Respect lit Markel's bright brown eyes. He pushed his glasses up on his nose as though to see the present dilemma more clearly.

"We'll work something out," Melissa promised.

"Thank you for understanding." Markel collected the children's papers and put them in his satchel. "The new one, Toria, will be a welcome challenge. I've never taught a child who didn't speak before. She is eager to expand her reading skills and to learn to write." Markel smiled knowingly. "Of course, catching up with Orin and Roger will be a challenge that I expect Sandra and Katy will relish helping her meet."

"Natural competition is good for them. They push each other as much as they help one another," Sven said.

"It shows in their work, Mr. Lindstrom." Markel started for the schoolroom door, then paused. "I have time this evening to bring the science texts Tommy and Darin will need."

"That's most generous of you, Mr. Markel," Sven said. "Could you arrange to stay for supper with us, too? Olga would enjoy your company, as would the rest of us."

Markel's grin sent his glasses sliding down his nose again. "That is an offer I cannot let pass. Thank you." He resumed his progress toward the door. "And I do love to watch Roger eat Olga's remarkable cuisine."

Melissa smiled, liking the schoolmaster even more for his understanding of the children's idiosyncrasies.

"Rory has no time. He cannot oversee Tommy and Darin for their studies," Sven mused after Charles Markel departed.

"No, he can't. I'm glad we're in agreement. However, I can." The notion unleashed a passel of butterflies in her stomach. She had the education, the knowledge, but not the methodology to share it effectively. "I'll need help."

"My knowledge of higher mathematics and science is quite limited," Sven admitted. "I am better at getting the children to study than studying myself."

"That's what I need from you, Sven. I have the academic background." More than anyone in this time dreamed. The trick would be sorting out the difference between what she accepted as common knowledge and that in the textbooks. The eleven decades of scientific advances would take some winnowing. If she started with the basics, she would have time to do it.

"You have attended a university?"

"Please don't look so shocked." Smiling, she examined the schoolbooks on the side table. Then, she faced Sven decisively. "We can do this. Between the two of us, we can. Poor Tommy and Darin will be my lab rats."

Doubt tugged Sven's thin lips into a frown. "Lab rats?"

"That means I'll experiment on them. They can help me acquire some teaching skills that will benefit the rest of the children when they advance. Oh, Sven, I don't know anything about teaching, but I'm willing to give it a try."

"Then we will do it. Rory will help too, when he returns."

"When he returns . . ." He'd been gone since yesterday morning, and already it felt like a year. When he returned, her first thoughts would have nothing to do with children, other than possibly conceiving one—if she hadn't already. The beautiful memory of the physical love they shared the night before his departure left her weak-kneed. Yes, she would marry him, have his children, and build a future with him. Rory was a dream she had never dared reach for in her old life. Now he was the center of her world.

"When he returns," she repeated, "instead of problems, he's going to find some solutions already in place." She smiled at Sven. "And we're going to provide them. I'll work with Tommy and Darin on math and science. When you can spare the time, I'd appreciate it if you'd drop in and give me some pointers on how I might teach them effectively."

Embarrassed, Sven shook his head. "I think you will do fine, Miss Fuller. They will speak up if they do not understand something. Mr. Markel encourages questions."

Realizing the enormity of the task she was undertaking, Melissa drew a deep breath and let it out. "All right." The tickle in her throat warned she had reached her limit of speech for the day. She massaged her throat and eased some of the tightness.

"Ah, no more talking." Sven stacked the books Melissa had examined earlier. "Shall I get Tommy and Darin and you can surprise them? They will enjoy the prospect of having you as a teacher."

She nodded, grateful for his sensitivity about her speaking ability.

Thinking to combine the subjects in practical application, she started writing an equation on the blackboard. Even before she finished, she erased it, her head shaking in disbelief. Today Albert Einstein was only eight years old. Toria's age. The Theory of Relativity lay a long time in the future. *Talk about jumping the gun,* she chided herself silently. Throwing out the important aspects of science like atomic theory, electronics, and the principles of aviation engineering left her wondering how much she really knew about the scientific transitions that had changed the world before the age of technology.

She raised the chalk, hesitated, then wrote a series of basic algebraic equations. Before she could begin teaching Tommy and Darin, she needed to find out what they knew. The science aspects could wait until she reviewed the books Mr. Markel brought when he returned for dinner.

Absorbed in the processes of creating equations of increasing difficulty, she covered the blackboard.

"Gosh, Miss Fuller, do you know the answers to all of those?"

The awe in Darin's question sent her spinning on her heel. She hadn't heard the boys enter the schoolroom and take seats at the study table. A sudden excitement made her grin as she nodded. She set down the chalk and signed, "You will, too, in a while. Show me how much you understand."

The boys exchanged dubious looks, then rose.

"Mr. Markel lent us an algebra book." Tommy took the chalk. "We read the first two chapters, but . . ." He shrugged and his voice trailed off. He wrote the answer to the first equation, then handed the chalk to Darin, who studied the board for a moment before answering the second.

The boys put their heads together and whispered to each other. When they decided on an answer, Tommy wrote it on the board. Both looked expectantly at her for confirmation.

Something inside Melissa soared. Watching the pair reason out the correct answer delighted her. She nodded, then pointed at the fourth equation and raised an eyebrow.

The doubt they exuded told her they had reached their limit.

"Okay," she whispered, then erased the board while they resumed their seats. Satisfied she knew where to begin the next day, she changed tactics when she faced them again.

"The ancient Egyptians and Babylonians were the first ones to use algebra in building their civilizations," she signed slowly, giving them time to understand. "Every enduring civilization since then has relied on those principles and added to the body of algebraic knowledge."

She nodded at Tommy's raised hand.

"All the things you wrote on the board . . . Do they have practical use? Even more than Latin?"

Inwardly, Melissa groaned. In this time, Latin remained an essential subject. She nodded. "Mr. McCullough uses algebra, geometry, trigonometry, and probably some calculus in his work." The way their eyes lit up with heightened interest provided her with a direction for the brief history she planned.

Melissa pulled up a chair and launched into the contribution of the Greeks and the Pythagorean theorem. The questions she encouraged led to a discussion that continued until Orin poked his head into the room and announced that Olga would be putting supper on the table shortly.

She sent the boys off to do their chores, then made notes on what they had discussed. By sharing her hard-won education, she could make a positive difference in their lives. Instead of feeling like an isolated outsider focused on a dream of walking among the stars in a different time, she could be an insider with children similar to those she had known growing up.

The last veil fell from the corner where her old cautious self lurked. All that remained were the scars of healed wounds. Bit by bit, the anger she harbored for years had melted in the brilliance of the love she found with Rory and the children. The power of it had conquered the fear of betrayal and a thousand injustices with their lingering miasma of bitterness. Rory was right—the more she loved, the greater her capacity to love.

Melissa put down the pencil and wished she could run to Rory and tell him what she had learned. She chuckled silently. He had been right. Again. She could not love with the depth of her heart and embrace hatred simultaneously.

"Miss Fuller?"

Melissa glanced up to see Sandra in the doorway.

"We can't find Toria. She was with Katy and me a little bit ago. We thought she was with you, but Tommy said . . ."

Melissa stood up so quickly that the chair toppled backward. "When did you last see her?" she asked, her voice cracking.

"Maybe half an hour ago. Mrs. Lindstrom asked Katy and me to fetch eggs from the henhouse. Toria doesn't like going in there. So we left her by the big tree that hangs over the cliff."

Melissa crossed the room in long strides. *Dear God in heaven, if Toria fell . . .*

"She didn't go down the cliff," Sandra said. Her wide, worried eyes searched Melissa for assurance. "We looked over the edge."

"Not in the house?" Melissa signed too quickly, then repeated the question slower. Dread blossomed with every tick of the clock in her head. The thought of Toria lying injured, helpless, unable to cry out for help chilled her to the marrow.

"No."

"Tell Mr. Lindstrom. We must find her."

"Katy went to tell him when I came here."

"Keep looking, Sandra." Melissa rushed down the hall and out the side door. Anxiety increased with each running step toward the big tree. Toria wouldn't run away, wouldn't just disappear, certainly not from her or anyone at Freedom House. The child found the dense forests daunting. Even when they played hide-and-seek, she found nooks and crannies near the safety of the house, never in the trees, thickets, or underbrush.

Melissa stopped abruptly at the tree. The top of the ancient giant overlooked the bluff. A long, heavy branch extended inland as though counterbalancing the gnarled evergreen. At the base, a sawed-off limb supported two dolls propped against the trunk. They faced each other as though engaged in silent conversation. Wreaths of tightly braided white and yellow flowers circled their heads. A third wreath lay in the grass. Closer to the bluff in a clump of tall grass, Melissa found the third doll. Toria's doll.

Fear churned in Melissa's stomach.

What if Toria had wandered down the bluff?

Melissa repeatedly swallowed the acid clawing its way up her throat, then licked her dry lips.

Toria didn't swim. If she had ventured too near the water, a wave might have snatched her from the rocks. At visions of her frail body dashed against the jagged shore a pain shot through Melissa's chest.

She hurried around to the steps leading down the bluff, silently thanking Rory for carving them into the stone and wishing he was here. Holding her skirts high, she grabbed the thick rope bolted into the cliff face as a safety banister and descended. *Please, God, don't let me find her floating in the water. Don't take her from us,* Melissa prayed.

Large waves warning of an autumn storm still out to sea splashed against the rocky jut beyond the sandy beach. Eye-

ing them as she navigated the uneven steps and the canted
rock path, she viewed them as formidable tentacles lunging
at her. The rumble of the ocean and the gathering gray
clouds taunted her.

At the bottom of the rough path, she paused and squinted
at the sand. A stiff wind had obliterated any sign of foot-
prints into uneven ripples. She wished for neon arrows or a
sign to pop out of the sand and give her a direction, even if it
was back the way she had come.

The cynic in the corner of her mind emerged. *A woman
who can't call out, searching for a little girl who can't cry
for help. What possible chance is there of finding her?*

If she's here, I'll find her, she fired back, tucking the back
hem of her skirt into her front waistband to get the yards of
material out of the way. Her heart hammering, she took a bear-
ing on where the tree ought to hang over the lip of the bluff,
then dashed across the sand. The boulders littering the beach
at the jut formed a hazardous ridge that broke the gravel and
sandy beach on the other side.

Melissa navigated the obstacles, careful to remain close to
the cliff face where Toria might have fallen. She lost sight of
the mark where the tree should be as she rounded the farthest
point.

Waves of increasing intensity broke over the rocks. The
spray drenched her. The mist filled her nostrils with the salty
scent of the approaching storm. As she started around the far
side, a bright piece of red and white bobbing in a tidal pool
caught her attention. She jumped into the knee-deep water
and pulled a hair ribbon from the swirling pool. A wave
slammed against the rocks behind her and showered her. She
stared at the ribbon draped across her fingers. It was the
same one she had retied in Toria's hair after lunch.

Her chest tightened. The churning in her stomach intensified. "Please, God. Not Toria. Please," she whispered. She
fisted the ribbon and scoured the rock crevices for any sign
of the girl.

The next wave sent her scrambling over the rocks. She

searched the crannies and tidal pools where Toria might be clinging for life.

Gradually she made her way to the gravel and sandy beach on the northern side of the outcropping. High overhead, the giant branches of the misshapen tree waved in the wind. Her throat burned with the need to cry out Toria's name.

Toria wasn't on the north side of the jut. Perhaps she lay further down the beach in one of the numerous rocky alcoves. Melissa darted along the waterline, her feet soggy against the gravelly beach crunching under the hard soles of her shoes. At the next rocky thrust into the sea, she slowed, searching what she could see of the beach on the other side. No Toria. She resumed scouring the rocky crevices and the tidal pools.

A rock bounced against the boulder on her right, then splashed in a tidal pool. Melissa straightened and looked around. She had just about decided that the wind or a crab had loosened it when a second one clattered down the jut.

She peered up.

Toria emerged from a narrow opening too small for anything larger than a reed-thin eight-year-old to wriggle through.

Relief so vast that she sagged against the nearest boulder washed over Melissa. Toria was safe. Unharmed. With a silent prayer of gratitude, she watched the child descend, unmindful of the cold spray of breaking waves at her back. Once Toria was within reach, Melissa helped her the final few feet.

Haunting, wide-eyed terror seized the child's ashen face when she turned. Stunned, Melissa fought back the gooseflesh rippling her skin. Immediately, Toria gave the danger signal and pointed down the beach. Without waiting for a response, she inched around the rocks.

Filled with questions, Melissa followed, trusting the girl's instincts, though she could not fathom what dangers stalked them, other than the autumn storm whipping the waves into a frenzy.

As they climbed onto the beach, a man emerged from a cluster of boulders at the base of the cliff.

Whirling in retreat, Toria ran into Melissa, who caught her with both hands. "He won't hurt you," she promised in a raspy whisper.

The panic in Toria's eyes as she struggled to get free loosed an old anger in Melissa.

She gave Toria a shake, demanding the child's attention.

Chest heaving, eyes wild like those of a trapped rabbit with the hot breath of a cougar ruffling its fur, Toria froze.

"Do you know him?"

Her chin quivering, she gave a barely perceptible nod.

Melissa glanced up at the man advancing on them. Confidence oozed from his stocky form.

"Oh, God," Melissa breathed. "Is he the one?"

Toria's mouth opened and closed as her shoulders rose in response to the approaching man.

"Is he the reason you can't speak?"

Toria nodded.

"Hold on to her, ma'am. She's a tricky one," the man called over the noise of the waves.

"Get back into your hidey-hole. Hurry. Don't come out until I say." Melissa stepped forward and thrust Toria behind her.

"Hey, don't let her go. I've had the devil's own time finding her." The man quickened his step, and Melissa heard Toria scrambling over the rocks toward safety.

Melissa took a deep breath, then cleared her throat, hoping that her voice would hold for the confrontation ahead.

"Who are you and what do you want with that child?" Melissa maneuvered to block the only boulder providing easy access to the elevated outcrop. *Climb, Toria, climb. Get yourself safe and stay there.*

"She's mine," the man insisted, his whiskered cheeks pink with exertion. "She was stolen from me. I've had a . . . difficult time finding her again."

Melissa loosely laid one forearm atop the other crossing her abdomen and tried to appear calm. Her entire body was a hairsbreadth from a physical attack. *Time,* she counseled, *give Toria time to get up there to safety.* "I see. And who are you, sir?"

"Cyrus Horn, her legal guardian so designated by her dear deceased mother and the court in Seattle." Horn threw his hands up in exasperation. His narrow blue eyes snapped with anger. "Look what your delay has cost. She's crawled back into those rocks and won't come out. You let her go back up there. Now go bring her down. My patience is wearing mighty thin with that child. She's becoming an incorrigible runaway."

It required all the restraint Melissa possessed to refrain from spitting on the brothel owner. She gazed into the depths of Horn's blue eyes and envisioned the brutal rape of little Toria. A revulsion that had been fermenting for more than two decades surged through her. "Really," she managed without choking on her antipathy for Horn.

"Yes. Go get her," he seethed between his yellow teeth.

Melissa shook her head and waited. She recognized him as a brother under the skin of Horace Freeland. She'd waited more than twenty years to settle the score as Pacho had tried to do. Cyrus Horn, like Horace Freeland, preyed on children and women: the weaker the victim, the greater his excitement.

"Toria Faulkner isn't going with you, not now or ever. You have no legal claim on that child and you damn well better consider yourself lucky to be breathing clear air and not in jail. You got away with hurting her before, but never again."

"Look, lady, I'm trying to be nice here." He withdrew a packet of papers from his inside coat pocket. "These here papers give me rights to her. Her ma owed me. I'm just claiming what's mine. Now go get that piece of fluff and bring her down here. Whatever you're accusing me of didn't happen. And I resent like hell you telling lies about me. That girl can't talk, so quit pretending like she said anything."

"But she can talk."

"Like hell she can." Horn grabbed Melissa's upper arm and pushed. "Go get her down."

"Take your hand off me, or I'll break every finger on it. And enjoy it."

Surprisingly, Horn released her and retreated a step, but not before giving her a shove.

He returned the packet to his coat pocket. "Like it not, bitch, Toria's coming with me. Let's see how much she likes you." He withdrew a Colt pistol from under his coat at the back of his waist and pointed it at her. "Come on out, Toria, or I'm going to make your friend pay."

"I won't let you do this," Melissa warned, all the agitation and fear gone. The cold competency of practiced detachment for a mission settled over her. This time her task was not just to fix a billion-dollar satellite, it was to save a little girl, which she considered far more important. Regardless of the consequences, Major Melissa Fuller would not fail Victoria or herself.

Chapter 24

"STAY WHERE YOU are, Toria," Melissa called, then stiffened against the stab of pain in her throat.

"I said get down here, brat," Horn demanded over the wind and waves. He drew back the Colt's hammer and carefully adjusted his aim at Melissa's heart. "Or I'm going to shoot your friend. How much do you like her?"

Melissa watched him, never doubting he'd shoot her. And at six feet, he wasn't likely to miss.

"If you make me shoot her, Toria, I'm coming up there and taking you out of those rocks, even if I have to cut you to pieces. Either you leave with me now, or neither one of you is leaving this beach."

The sound of stones bouncing down the rocky face communicated Toria's decision. Melissa accepted the complication without a flicker of emotion. The fingers of her left hand spread in readiness on top of her right forearm. She curled the first two joints of her fingers on her right hand and tucked her thumb against her palm.

Stones clattered over the boulders as Toria squirmed out of her sanctuary. The crashing waves filled the air with fine mist.

Melissa watched Cyrus Horn with practiced eyes. Arrogance led to carelessness, and Horn possessed an abundance of both. Although the gun barrel never wavered, his gaze was distracted by Toria navigating the hazardous rocks.

With an expertise gleaned from the mean streets of her childhood, Melissa assessed Horn. She considered him a lazy man better at ordering others to do his bidding than at taking action himself. The casual way he held the pistol betrayed a lack of respect for the weapon and his opponent. She gambled that he also lacked the reflexes to shoot spontaneously.

The sound of Toria's hard-soled shoes slipping on the gravel-strewn rocks grew louder as the waves retreated for another attack on the shore.

"Move," Horn sneered at Melissa.

She captured his vile gaze but held her ground in front of the last boulder leading from the outcrop to the beach.

"I said: Move! Let the girl get down."

Melissa did not so much as blink.

"You think by not moving you can stop me? Nothing stops me, bitch. That girl is mine. Mine. Her ma owed me, and I'll use her any way I want. I'm damn tired of hunting for her and havin' her stolen from me by interfering, meddling people who think they got a right to her."

Toria was a few feet behind her.

Horn's glassy eyes narrowed to a squint. "A quiet little girl like Toria is a great asset in my business. She's going to make me a lot of money."

"In a brothel? She's only eight years old," Melissa said calmly, watching his eyes.

"Damn right. When I get tired of her, she'll be taking her ma's place, only for a lot more money because she's young and fresh. There are those who'll pay a very tidy sum for sweet, tender flesh. Now get out of the way so she can get down. I'm taking her, and there's not a damn thing you can do about it. These papers," he patted his breast pocket, "say it's all legal and proper."

Left-handed, Horn lunged, intent on yanking her aside.

Melissa countered swiftly by driving her curled fingers into his solar plexus and twisting the gun out of his grasp with her left hand. The ferocity of her swift retaliation caught him unprepared. Clutching his chest, he doubled over and staggered backward several steps.

"Keep moving backward," she warned, shifting the Colt to her right hand and clearing the way for Toria's descent.

His chest heaved while he gasped for breath. Startlement flared into a rage that turned his ashen face a bright crimson.

The hatred burning in his narrowed eyes concentrated on Melissa. "Bitch. If you think I'm going away just 'cause you got my gun—"

"You're going. Now. Alone." She felt Toria clutching her skirt.

"It ain't that simple. She's got business for me. I've been through a lot of trouble to find her and I've taken steps to keep her. I got the law on my side now. You can't keep her from me."

"The law," Melissa spat. "What sort of law is on the side of a pervert like you?" The memory of countless injustices sanctioned by layers of authority clouded her derision. For an instant, Cyrus Horn's hate-filled face became that of Horace Freeland.

"Who else has a better claim than me? I can prove I married Anne. That makes me the girl's stepfather. Family." Triumph and hatred dripped from his words. The lethal gleam in his eyes when his gaze settled on Toria sent the child trembling in fear against Melissa's leg.

"Anne signed custody over to her parents. You have no claim. Now get out of here and don't ever come back."

"The Faulkners ain't going to contest a thing." His confidence became a sneer, curling his upper lip. "Dead people don't object to anything. Victoria is mine, and there's no one to say otherwise."

The wall of detachment shuddered with her grim understanding of the reason for his confidence. "You killed the Faulkners? Both of them?" she rasped, her voice growing fainter against the roar of the ocean.

"Let's just say they won't be hiring any more nosy lawyers, nor will they object to me claiming Victoria." Horn grinned, delighting in the game he was playing. " 'Course, some men would say anything if someone was holding a gun on them. You can't be sure, can you?"

"There you're wrong. I know the truth when I hear it," Melissa whispered.

"The truth is, if you force me to leave without Toria, I'll be back for her. With the sheriff. I'm getting her one way or another." He stopped rubbing his chest and glared at her. "And when I do, I'm paying you back. I'll burn that damn house and you, with those other brats inside it. Nobody will know it was me, except you." Malevolence oozed from every pore.

"You would really do—" *Oh, yes, he would. And enjoy it.*

"When you're trapped inside, you'll know who it was you tried to foul up. When they're screaming and the flesh is burning off your bones, you'll be sorry you ever crossed Cyrus Horn."

Melissa studied him. She weighed his intent with a cold, logical detachment. She had not a flicker of doubt that Cyrus Horn would carry out his nefarious promise.

"Why don't you just give me the girl and we'll both be on our way?"

"Toria stays with me."

"Are you willing to trade your life and those of the other kids to keep Toria?"

The sudden, intense shift of his gaze focused all her instincts on a razor edge. The waves breaking against the rocks sounded far away. The stench of fear and excitement made her nostrils flare.

She felt more than saw his hateful sneer. "No," she warned. The sudden tension between them made the air she inhaled feel like fine glass.

The eyes always betray. Where they go, the body follows. Only the most savvy fighter knows not to give himself away with a telltale glance. The words of a young street fighter who never lived to be an old one burst into her awareness.

The casual manner in which Horn's right hand dipped into his coat pocket barely registered. The sense of detachment isolating her from the emotions a hairsbreadth away kept her staring into his eyes.

Horn quickly stepped back and pulled his hand from his pocket—holding a derringer.

Melissa's right hand tightened on the Colt. The pressure depressed the trigger, and a single shot reverberated above the waves pummeling the shore.

The force of the bullet jolted Horn backward. He sprawled lifeless on the gravelly beach, a small hole in his coat directly over his heart.

Melissa stared at him for a long time, the Colt poised for a second shot. Eventually she felt Toria clutching her shirt and sobbing. She hurled the gun into the ocean.

Holding the girl's trembling shoulder, she thumbed away the tears streaming down a faint dusting of freckles. "It's over, Toria. You're safe. He'll never bother you again."

Toria sniffed and nodded. "I love you," she signed.

"I love you too," Melissa signed back.

The sobbing child threw her arms around Melissa's neck as though she would never let go. Melissa hugged her for a long time before lifting her up from the beach.

"Let's go home," Melissa croaked in a barely audible whisper. She stared at the still form of Cyrus Horn. The shiny derringer had fallen from his open fingers into the sand. The foamy edge of a wave lapped at the weapon and dampened his sleeve. It was as though the sea abhorred the vermin on the beach and immediately tried to cleanse the stain of ugliness. She met Toria's knowing gaze with a fresh sorrow. Soundless, Toria hugged her in reassurance. Her chin held high, Melissa looked to the top of the bluff hiding Freedom House.

Four figures stood at the edge: Sven, Tommy, Mr. Markel, and a man she thought might be the sheriff. How long had they been watching?

The foursome met Melissa and Toria at the top of the path the children used to get to the beach. The stranger approached immediately. "Miss Fuller, I rode out here today to warn Mr. Lindstrom that he would have to turn Victoria Faulkner over to Mr. Horn. Now I'm going to have to arrest you for his murder. Will you come peacefully?"

"See here, Barstow," Sven said, coming to life, "you can't arrest her."

Barstow shook his head. "I have no choice. All four of us," he pointed at Toria, "and the little girl, saw her kill a man in cold blood."

During the long trek around the final outcrop and across

the beach to the steps, Melissa was anticipating what sort of justice she'd receive. Experience prepared her for the fate Sheriff Barstow advocated with his proclamation of murder. She expected no impartiality and knew of few instances of real justice handed down by the legal system. No one she knew survived when *The Man* pointed a finger. Resignation leaked from behind the wall containing the maelstrom of volatile emotion. They had seen her kill Cyrus Horn and could just as easily say murder as self-defense. Truth be known, whether or not he had reached for his pocket gun, she knew she'd do it again to protect Toria and the children of Freedom House.

"What will happen to Miss Fuller?"

She met the confusion in Tommy's blue eyes brimming with sudden tears. "Take care of Toria," Melissa signed. "She needs a strong shoulder."

"Give her a minute," Sven demanded of Sheriff Barstow.

"There's a storm blowing in. The sooner we get back to town—"

"For crying out loud, Barstow, give her a minute with Tommy and Toria. She's not going to hurt them and there's nowhere for her to run," Charles Markel argued.

Barstow shrugged and retreated a step.

Melissa motioned to Tommy, then crouched in front of Toria. Fresh tears of anguish streamed from the girl's eyes.

"I want promises from both of you," Melissa signed.

Tommy knelt beside her and Toria to complete the small circle. "Mr. McCullough will—"

She cut him off with a hand motion. No one was going to rescue her. She had killed a man in self-defense. The reasons for Cyrus Horn's presence on the beach were something Melissa never intended to divulge. Perhaps Sheriff Barstow and the others had seen enough to realize that Horn was about to kill her, but she shot first.

"My fault," Toria signed. A fresh flood of tears ran down her cheeks and dripped from her jaw.

"No. Never. You promise me you won't think that. I made a choice. It was mine. Not yours. I pulled the trigger. If I hadn't, he'd have killed me, then taken you. I wouldn't let that happen, Toria." More than anything, she didn't want Toria scarred by guilt for something over which she had no control.

Toria's hands fisted at her sides.

"Toria, this was my choice. I made it for me. I never asked you. Will you try to love yourself as much as I do?" Tears stung Melissa's eyes when Toria's pale blond head bowed in promise.

"Take care of her while I'm gone, Tommy. It shouldn't take too long to give the sheriff a statement and clear this up." She searched Tommy's expressive blue eyes and found nothing but misery.

"I will." He glanced at Toria, who lifted her gaze to his. "We both know the same demon. He likes little boys too. Is that her devil on the beach?"

Melissa nodded. "Tell no one about his connection to her. If they knew in Fairhaven . . ."

"We know," Tommy said aloud. "Does Mr. McCullough—"

She waved all mention of Rory aside, unable to cope with the consequences of her actions as far as he was concerned. "He cannot help me. I got myself into this; I'll handle it. That too is my choice."

Out of words, bursting with emotion, she grabbed the children. Tears flowed through the three-way hug. She kissed each tear-dampened cheek. "Take care of each other. I love you all," she rasped. "I'll be back soon."

She stood and lifted her chin when she met Sheriff Barstow's agitated gaze. After a farewell nod to Sven, then Charles Markel, she walked up to the sheriff.

"My horse is in front of Freedom House, Miss Fuller. You understand you're under arrest for murder, don't you?"

Melissa nodded and extended her hands, expecting the cold steel of handcuffs around her wrists.

"Do I need to put handcuffs on you?"

Melissa shook her head. The notion of her being arrested

for murder would be traumatic for the children. Seeing her cuffed and taken away would be even worse.

"We'll saddle a horse for you," Barstow said, taking her upper arm and starting for Freedom House.

Melissa shook her head and pointed at him, her voice gone.

Barstow inhaled deeply, then let it out slowly. "All right. We'll ride double. It isn't far to town. The last thing I want is a scene with half a dozen crying children I'll have to pry off of you."

Melissa stared straight ahead. The barrier restraining her tumult needed only a single assault before it crumbled. Gone was the hard heart tempered over years to form a shell impervious to the suffering around her. Love had dissolved it and leached out the bitterness as it flourished.

She mounted the horse without a glance at Freedom House. The house that love built reeked of Rory. She couldn't think about him and maintain any shred of composure.

Heavy rain pelted them on the way to Fairhaven. Although Sheriff Barstow shivered against her back, the chill did not touch her. Instead, she held a cloak of detachment around the fragile veneer that kept her together.

Melissa sat on a hard pallet in the Fairhaven jail. At the clank of the outer door lock opening her spine stiffened. The time for tears had ended. She'd cried herself dry during the sleepless night.

Sheriff Barstow unlocked her cell door. "I'm taking you before Judge Murphy. I explained to him you'd lost your voice and could tell your story with a paper and pencil."

From the sound of it, she had no story to tell, but she appreciated the sheriff's attempt to ensure what he considered a fair hearing.

"Judge Murphy has a soft spot for what Rory's doing with those kids. I know whatever motivated you to shoot Horn centers on Toria Faulkner. Now is the time to give your reasons. Murphy doesn't want to sentence you to prison or to hang any more than I want to see you at the end of a rope."

With bowed head, she accompanied Sheriff Barstow to the courthouse.

"Damn. Why didn't you look up and see us standing there?" Barstow seethed on the way. "Why'd you have to shoot him in front of us? Why didn't you just give him the girl? He had a legal right—"

Melissa stopped short and glared at Barstow. Fury heated her until her cheeks burned.

"Never mind. Tell your story to Judge Murphy. If he decides to hang you, I'll see you get a good rope." He led her into the courtroom.

The surrealistic nightmare ensnaring her receded as she recited the mantra of her name, rank, and social security number. The girl who had escaped gang bullets, drugs, and the dangers of the streets to float among the stars would meet an ignominious end on the gallows after all. Like the countless faceless minions before her, she'd lived up to society's expectations.

As the court proceedings droned on, she smiled at herself. The woman slated for the hangman's noose wasn't the same one who had traveled to the stars. This one had a heart capable of far more than circulating her blood.

"Miss Fuller," Judge Murphy boomed from the bench.

Melissa lifted her head to the visage of stern Josiah Murphy peering down at her from behind a bench that obscured his bulk. Sharp gray eyes the same steely color as his hair regarded her through a pair of thick spectacles.

"It is my understanding you've suffered a throat injury that impairs your ability to speak. Is that correct?"

Melissa nodded.

"It is also the contention of the prosecuting attorney that you killed an unarmed man with malice and forethought. Is that correct?"

Malice and forethought? No, not that. She stared back for a moment before writing a response. *He had a pocket gun, a little derringer. Had to shoot or be killed.*

"You're pleading self-defense when you were holding the

Colt?" Judge Murphy glanced around the courtroom. "Have you engaged an attorney, Miss Fuller?"

Melissa shook her head.

"Do you need time to do so?"

Again, Melissa shook her head, then wrote another note. *I threw the Colt I took away from him into the sea. The derringer was in his right hand.*

Murphy read the note, then set it aside. "Is it your intention to plead guilty?"

"Your Honor," Sheriff Barstow interjected.

"Clem, you have something to say on her behalf? You're supposed to be with the prosecution."

Sheriff Barstow fingered the brim of his hat. "I know Josiah. But there's something here that sits crosswise with my lawman's instincts."

"Did you see this woman shoot a man?"

"Yes, sir."

"Was the man armed?"

"From where we were standing on the bluff, he didn't appear to be. My deputy didn't find any weapons when they brought him up the cliff."

Melissa stared at the tabletop. Years of hard use had turned the oak grain as black as her prospects of a defense. No weapon. What had happened to the derringer?

She hadn't imagined it. There really had been a derringer. She remembered the foamy edge of a wave closing around Horn's outstretched hand. If the sea had claimed the gun . . .

"She doesn't deny shooting him in front of five witnesses. You found no gun near Horn. What's the problem, Clem? It sounds pretty straightforward to me."

It did to Melissa, too. If she were Judge Josiah Murphy, she'd sentence her to hang without a moment's hesitation.

"That's what bothers me. The little girl saw and heard the whole thing. She didn't act . . . There's something more to this. I wouldn't feel right about letting this woman be labelled a murderess without finding out what went on down there. For that matter, I'd like to know more about Victoria Faulkner and Mr. Cyrus Horn too."

"What are you asking for, Clem?"

"Time, Josiah. This woman's going to plead guilty. She won't speak to anyone."

"I thought she couldn't speak."

Melissa felt Judge Murphy's scrutiny but twitched not a muscle.

"Can't, won't—what's the difference. Hanging a woman, even one I saw kill a man with my own eyes, isn't going to sit well with the townfolk. It's going to make Fairhaven look pretty bad to the rest of Washington Territory. We've got hard enough times. Let me do some investigating and see what I can dig up."

Judge Murphy leaned over the bench. "Let me get this straight. You saw her kill an unarmed man, yet you don't want her to plead guilty?"

Melissa looked directly at Sheriff Barstow, then shook her head. She didn't want his help, his intervention, and definitely not his investigation. The only thing his questions would do was hurl Toria into a sea of guilt.

Tommy will protect her. The certainty in his blue eyes burned in her mind.

"That about sums it up, Judge. I need to find out why she killed him or what happened to the gun she says he had. And I think the little girl can tell me. I'd also like to find the pocket gun, if it exists." Barstow shrugged. "It could have happened just like she says, Josiah. We didn't get there until damn near the minute she shot him. Seems to me, if Horn had a pocket gun and pulled it while she was holding him off with the Colt, that turns this case into a horse of a different color. The little girl's the key."

Melissa wrote a quick note, then handed it to Sheriff Barstow.

"I think you're right. Talk to the girl." Judge Murphy gestured at the note. "What's it say, Clem?"

Sheriff Barstow heaved a heavy breath. "It says, 'Toria can't speak. Can't read or write well enough to communicate. Leave her be. You can only hurt by probing.' "

Melissa glared at the judge, willing him to end this farce of a hearing.

"I'm going to give you a week, Clem. Then we'll have a trial and, if need be, hang her the next day." Judge Murphy glared over the top of his glasses. "Unless you find something to change our minds."

"Two weeks," Sheriff Barstow insisted.

"I'm not haggling for timber acres. I'll give you ten days."

"Thanks, Josiah. I'll be leaving for Seattle in the morning."

"Why? Who's going to look after your prisoner?"

"Hal Johnson can watch after her. I'll deputize him." Sheriff Barstow slapped his hat against his thigh. "Cyrus Horn came from Seattle. I intend to start finding out what's what by talking to the judge who signed the papers Horn showed me. They gave him guardianship of Victoria Faulkner. She sure didn't seem upset about Miss Fuller shooting him." Sheriff Barstow exhaled loudly. "Now, I gotta ask why a judge would hand over a little bit of a girl like her to a man like Horn."

Melissa closed her eyes and prayed Barstow did not make a complete connection with the brothel. What was done couldn't be undone. Revealing the abominations of Toria's past to the whole town tainted any chance the child had for a normal life. This time and place put a premium on chastity. Emotionally, Toria had never known an innocent day. Physically, she had been violated in ways that most *good* people didn't admit existed.

"I can see that this does not meet with your approval, Miss Fuller," Judge Murphy said.

Melissa scratched a note to him.

Judge Murphy read it, then scowled at her. "No, Miss Fuller, a ten-day postponement does not violate your constitutional right to a speedy trial. Where'd you hear such drivel?"

"I'll find Rory McCullough while I'm in Seattle," Sheriff Barstow added. "He may be able to lend some insight. At the least, he'll want to know what happened here."

The impact of an invisible fist into her belly weakened Melissa's knees. She sat down hard and began the mantra of name, rank, and social security number. She wouldn't think about Rory. Seeing his eyes. Feeling his shock and disillusionment. She refused to acknowledge the future she was giving up to protect Toria and Freedom House. She didn't want to look Rory in the eyes and feel all she was losing crash down around her, because she would do the same thing again.

She had the easy part. If Sheriff Barstow brought Rory home, what would he do after he watched her hang?

Chapter 25

DURING THE TEN days Melissa inhabited the small Fairhaven jail, the sun hid behind roiling gray clouds. At last the steely clouds fragmented. The stars peeking through seemed especially bright. Tonight it seemed they glittered with an extra brilliance to compensate for their long absence. Or perhaps they shone with special intensity because she would probably join them in another day or so.

Life's ironies made her smile at the heavens. The last time she had faced certain death, bitter anger had owned her soul. The swift death promised upon entering Earth's atmosphere meant incineration to nothing more than ash streaking across the morning sky of the West Coast. At the time it had seemed a grave injustice. Yet for the woman who was Major Melissa Fuller it was an appropriate end, devoid of sentimentality or tender feeling.

In a little over four months she had flipped her strengths and weaknesses. It required far more strength to risk her heart and love than to withhold all emotion in pursuit of lofty goals and personal detachment.

The first glimmers of dawn snuffed the starlight one glittering point at a time. She supposed she was as ready to die as a person got. Self-responsibility formed the backbone of her character. If she needed anyone's forgiveness before climbing the stairs to the gallows, she thought it might be Rory's. The coward in her didn't want to see him or acknowledge the full magnitude of losing the future he had believed possible.

She clutched the crystal representing his heart and held it until it grew hot in her hand. If she had to return from the

grave as a ghost, she would find a way to soften the blow of
her death. This time, no magic woman would jerk her head
out of the noose and lay it on Rory's magnificent chest.

Purple morning light turned orange with the sunrise over
the mountains. Never in her life had Melissa been more cog-
nizant of time. The river of minutes rushed down the water-
fall of hours and into the sea of days receding with the tide.
The autumn nights seemed shorter instead of longer; it
seemed as though the hours had put half of their minutes on
sale and someone bought them all.

The clank of the outer jail door lock startled her. Surely
Hal Johnson hadn't come to see if she'd escaped in the middle of the night when he had all the keys.

She leaned against the wall and waited.

In the eerie glow of the swinging lantern, she saw Sheriff
Barstow and a companion. Her heart lurched into her throat.
Only Rory towered over men of average height with such an
imposing presence.

Wordless, Sheriff Barstow unlocked her cell and held the
door for Rory to enter. He stood motionless until the sheriff
bolted the door, then left, closing the outer door.

"Melissa," Rory breathed and took a step forward.

Instinctively, she raised a hand to hold him back. If he
touched her, she would shatter into a million shards, like the
irreparable dreams of their future.

"Release me from my promise concerning Toria."

She shook her head in the chilled light brightening the
lone window. "It would change nothing. I killed him, Rory. I
won't barter the only chance Toria has at a somewhat normal
life for any reason. I won't take her down with me."

The anguish in her chest squeezed her heart like a tear-filled
handkerchief. "I don't want to die, especially not now that I've
found you. But to tell anyone about Cyrus Horn . . . what he
did to her . . . to use her as an excuse . . . I can't give her up to
the fate we both know would haunt her all her days at Freedom
House and follow her as an adult . . . I can't do it. Even if I
could, what good would it do me? They believe I'm guilty of
shooting him in cold blood."

"Melissa."

With each step closer to her, the torment in his gray eyes and the lines of strain etched into his unshaven face deepened. The misery seeping from him touched her own. Tears pooled and spilled across the dam of her lower lashes. "Please don't come closer, Rory. If you touch me, I'll disintegrate."

"Then take me with you and we'll disintegrate together. Let me hold you." He gathered her into his arms.

Sobbing, she melted against him, her heart starving for his nearness, the solidity of his power, and the assurance of his strength. Love flowed from him with every breath. Love for her.

"I won't let you die," he whispered into her hair. "I won't lose you. Not now—not like this."

She lifted her head and he captured her face in his hand and covered her mouth with a tender kiss that immediately burned with passion. Unable to get enough, he broke the kiss and started again, deeper, more intense in the demands each made on the other. She tasted him, let him explore her, all the while running her hands over his face, through his hair, and along his neck and shoulders to reassure her aching heart he was really here. The tempo of his barely controlled kisses stoked the fires of his love. She returned his kisses with the hunger of pent-up love and burgeoning sorrow. Meanwhile, tears of joy and sorrow, flowed down her cheeks. The false assurance of forever became the frenzy of a few precious moments alone in the painful beauty of their love.

He held her face between his hands. "I want you home, in bed with me, and naked against my heart.

"I'm in a helluva position. They can't find the gun, so no one believes self-defense. The only other chance I have of gaining their understanding and your release lies in betraying you and Toria.

"If I keep silent, they'll hang you. Either way, I lose you. We lose." He brushed her hair from her forehead. "I won't break that trust, Melissa. But I won't stop anyone from revealing what they know. Including Toria. Do you think she wants to grow up knowing you died to hide a shameful secret for which she is blameless?"

Melissa's heart twisted. "No. She's innocent. I won't throw her to the lions. They'll see her as a bastard raised and used in a brothel. Make her understand, Rory.

"Nothing changes the fact that I killed Cyrus Horn. He would have killed me if I hadn't pulled the trigger. I'd do it again, Rory. God help me, even though it cost me you, I'd do it again." Sobs wracked her body. There was no time for anything except the naked truth. If he turned from her in disgust, so be it.

"I want to know what happened out there. I'd rather you tell me than Toria."

She froze. "You'd subject her to telling bit by painful bit?"

Rory nodded, his jaw clenched in resolve. "Yes. I want to know what made you carry a gun down there and shoot him. I want to know all the reasons. From the looks of it, I'll have years to think about them, to try and find some sense to all of this. You've taken a stand that doesn't leave room for me beside you. Make me understand, Melissa. Don't close me out and leave me with nothing but questions and broken dreams. I know you love me. Help me."

"Dear God in heaven, how I love you, Rory. You're my only regret this time. Forgive me."

"You know I'd forgive you damn near anything."

The feel of his lips against hers sent a fresh flood of tears down her cheeks.

"Tell me what happened," he whispered.

"It's a long story."

"It appears we'll never have as much time as we do right now."

He deserved the whole truth, without omissions. He needed to understand that the woman he loved was capable of using every means available to defend herself and those she cherished.

Rory followed her hands in the light streaming through the window. As she related the events on the beach, sounds of the town stirring to a morning routine broke the silence of the dank cell.

"The gun belonged to Horn?" The revelation sparked as much optimism as amazement. "I'm baffled. How did you get it and why, then, did Clem lock you up?"

Melissa nodded.

In rapt fascination, he concentrated on her hands as she described how she wrested the Colt from Horn. Upon learning of the threat against the children of Freedom House and her conviction that Horn meant it as a promise, anger and an awesome understanding dawned. Either way, Horn had put her in a losing position and meant to catch her off guard and shoot her. How easy Horn's claim of self-defense would have been—she had held the Colt. But Horn had known too little about Toria's unyielding protector.

"What happened to the derringer?" he mused, proud of her despite the pain her actions brought them both and those they loved.

"I don't know. His hand was open after he fell. I saw the derringer lying on his fingers as the waves came up the beach," she answered aloud. "Maybe the ocean buried it. Maybe someone picked it up. Maybe it disappeared by magic. I don't know."

"It has to be somewhere. We'll find it and that will vindicate you." Already, he had plans for the children of Freedom House and the small cadre of people who accompanied him from Seattle.

Melissa rose and went to the window. "There are things I should tell you. About myself. About where I came from. I want you to know before it's too late."

"McCullough," Sheriff Barstow called from the outer jail door.

"Yeah?"

"You about done in there?"

"No."

He watched Melissa turn away from the window. Ten days in this dank cell had leached the color from her face.

The hours of lost sleep and confinement left purple half-moons beneath her eyes.

"I'm sending Hal for her breakfast. You want some?"

Food was the last thing on his mind. "Sure. Thanks." Perhaps if he ate, she would too. The way her dirty, wrinkled clothing hung on her, she probably hadn't eaten more than a few bites each day.

"Have you seen the children?" she asked tentatively.

Rory shook his head. Her forlorn expression ducked into shadow when she bowed her head. All he had thought about since Sheriff Barstow found him at Pete Jacobson's house four days ago was her. "Sheriff Barstow and I rousted Hal as soon as we got off the ship. He said you weren't letting anyone visit you. Why not?"

"Why, Rory. They don't need to see me in here." Her hand swept the confines of her cell. "Let them remember me as I was, not . . ." She lifted her stained skirt. "Not like this. A filthy animal in a cage."

Rory found no solutions to the most important dilemma he'd ever face. Melissa expected a death sentence from Judge Murphy. She might be willing to forfeit her life in exchange for Cyrus Horn's life, but he wasn't. Horn wasn't worthy of cleaning her chamber pot. Later, Rory would find a way out for all of them. Now, he would spend every minute possible putting her at ease.

"Tell me what you want me to know, Melissa. I want to learn all there is about you."

She resorted to signing, as though she feared being overheard and incurring even more censure.

"When you look up at the stars at night and see them shining, you'll know I was once up there." An enigmatic smile softened the fatigue around her eyes. "I come from a time in the future when we walked in space. We floated above the Earth at speeds and altitudes beyond your wildest imaginings. Growing up, that was my dream. That was what I lived for, what kept me going during the roughest of times after Henry and Melva Tibbens died. Without them there would have been no dream. I probably wouldn't have made it through puberty. I'd have given up. Run away. Lived on the streets and ended up whoring for drugs by the time I was ten."

He didn't understand all of what she meant, but at last he comprehended the core of her motivation to protect Toria. Shivers of revulsion ran over him. She was Toria's Henry and Melva Tibbens.

The clank of the outer door opening interrupted her monologue. Hal brought breakfast, which Rory insisted she eat, though he had no appetite.

When she resumed signing, he absorbed the details of her story and gradually understood the woman who had denied involvement for so long. The tenacity that had carried her through life and out to the heavens daunted him. His respect for the difficult changes she'd undergone in her relatively brief time with him knew no bounds.

"When you fell out of the heavens . . . what year was it?"

"1998."

Not trusting his voice, he signed. "About a hundred and ten years from now. Shelan found you that far away?"

The first genuine smile touched her lips. "Must be, because I wasn't looking for her. Are you going to tell me you accept me saying I'm from the future just like that? No reservations? No doubt or qualms?"

Aching for the warmth and comfort of her, Rory enfolded her in his arms. "Believing in magic was the tough part. But Shelan didn't leave me much choice when she gave you to me. If she can pull a woman out of thin air, one I love with all my heart and every corner of my soul, believing she brought you from another time is not difficult," he whispered. "That's not a mystery like what happens to the love we feel for one another when we're both dead."

The feather touch of her fingertip in the cleft of his chin grated against the two-day whisker growth darkening his face.

"That's easy," she whispered back. "We take it with us. When I was falling to Earth, I was angry. I thought I'd done everything right. I'd achieved. I'd succeeded. But I wasn't much of a person. I didn't know how to love or how to accept love. I had no love to take with me, and I saw eternity as a cold, lifeless desert—like my soul.

"You changed everything, Rory. You showed me what kind of awesome strength it takes to love unselfishly. You've given me a gift beyond measure. I won't be angry when I face death again."

He quickly kissed her parted lips. For just a little while, he wanted to postpone confronting the dire realities beyond the cell walls and the fate Judge Murphy promised to deliver after the hearing tomorrow.

"McCullough," Sheriff Barstow called from the outer cell door.

"Yeah?"

"It's noon. You gotta go. Can't let ya stay any longer. Sorry."

"Give me five minutes."

"Five minutes," Barstow agreed.

Rory molded their bodies together, aching to draw her physical essence into himself and hold her safe for the rest of his life. "I love you, Melissa. You own my heart."

"I love you, too, Rory, for as long as the stars shine."

He kissed her, reining in the desperate passion clouding his thinking.

"I don't want you to come when . . . if they hang me. I don't want you to see if I am not brave enough . . ."

He felt her tears dampen his shirt. The rocking of her head against his chest betrayed her doubt.

"You've done what you had to do. So will I. I won't let them hang you or send you to prison, Melissa." Alarm brought her head up. "Nor will I violate your trust." He kissed her nose. "I get the definite feeling Major Melissa Fuller doesn't believe in second chances."

"She doesn't. Not on matters of trust."

He nodded at the warning. "Do you trust me, Melissa?"

"With all my heart."

Sheriff Barstow opened the outer door.

Rory indulged in a final kiss that would have to satisfy them both until he thought of a way to extricate her from the hangman's noose.

Rory spent the next hour with Judge Josiah Murphy. If Sheriff Barstow had discussed the results of his findings in Seattle with Judge Murphy, neither man acknowledged it. Rory had hoped for an ally in the lawman when court convened for Melissa's hearing the next day. He left Fairhaven as ambivalent about Barstow's position as he was doubtful of Melissa's chances for acquittal.

When he reached home, Elmira met him at the door. Her usual neat appearance accentuated the strain of worry and sleepless nights in the deep care lines around her eyes and mouth.

"I've seen to settling in Dr. Jacobson, Mr. Brockbannon, and the two children he brought," she informed him.

"Thank you, Elmira." He set his work case aside and proceeded toward the stairs with his luggage.

Elmira touched his arm. "Have you seen her?" Her normally strident question was a whisper rife with an aching desperation Rory shared.

"Yes. She looks like hell. Would you gather clean clothes and toiletries for her? I'm going back to Fairhaven this evening." He squeezed her hand, then started up the stairs.

"They will allow you—"

"I don't give a damn what they allow. I'm seeing her again tonight." He took the stairs in twos, feeling the press of time. "Where's Toria?"

"She's been staying at Freedom House since—since they took Miss Melissa. Tommy won't let her out of his sight, except at night when she sleeps with Katy and Sandra." Elmira wrung her hands. "Rory, is there anything we can do?"

He paused on the landing. "Yes."

"Good! We'll do anything you think will help, and pray it is enough. Thank God you're finally home."

"I'll be down in twenty minutes. Would you ask Pete and Calvin to meet me in the library?" Brockbannon had no school, no funds, but he'd acquired two deaf mutes who were in desperate need of a place to live and study. Seeing a way to help them all, Rory had offered Freedom House in exchange for Brockbannon's services as the teacher he needed for the advanced subjects.

He had intentionally omitted any mention of Dr. Jacobson's and Mr. Brockbannon's presence to Melissa. The news of Brockbannon's arrangement would have uplifted her spirits.

However, she'd have considered Pete Jacobson's presence a threat to Toria. If she knew he was here, she undoubtedly would try to extract a promise of silence from him, too.

When Sheriff Barstow found Rory at Pete's Seattle home and revealed Melissa's plight, Pete had insisted on accompanying Rory. Before leaving the Jacobson home, Barstow had spoken little of his plans. In retrospect, Barstow's tight-lipped attitude both worried and encouraged Rory. His and Pete's efforts to locate the Faulkners had been unsuccessful. In light of Melissa's revelation about Horn removing all impediments to possessing Toria, he had a bleak suspicion of why.

Rory bathed and shaved. When he saw Melissa again, he wanted to impart an air of confidence and a smidgen of hope. While he dressed, he contemplated ways of revealing what had happened on the beach between Melissa and Cyrus Horn without violating her trust.

In the library, Pete and Calvin waited with long faces.

A methodical logic and a knack for detail made Rory successful in sorting out the potential trouble spots. He sifted through the details, turning them over in his mind and examining what lay beneath the dilemma at hand. He gathered papers from his office, then entered the library.

"Gentlemen, tomorrow we're going to put on a defense for Melissa," he announced.

"An architect, a doctor, and a teacher?" Calvin set aside his empty coffee cup. "What we need is a skilled attorney."

"No time," Rory muttered. "Besides, what lawyer would believe in her like we do?" He studied the morose expressions on their faces and the eyes that refused to meet his. "Like I do."

"What kind of defense can we possibly present in a court of law? Five people saw her kill him," Calvin said, searching the library table drawers.

"Paper is in the center drawer," Rory told Calvin.

"Four people saw a small part of what happened on the beach, but heard nothing except the gunshot," Rory continued. "The fifth person saw and heard everything that took place. I've sent Marvin to fetch Toria and Tommy."

"What do you have in mind as Melissa's defense?" Pete pulled out a chair and joined Calvin at the table.

"How about the truth? Self-defense." He was teetering on the edge of Melissa's trust and could go no further than what she had told Judge Murphy.

"Do you know what happened down there? Did she tell you?" Pete asked softly.

Rory settled hard on the wooden chair. "Therein lies the rub, gentlemen. She told me everything. Unfortunately, even if she had looked up and seen the witnesses on the bluff, it wouldn't have made a shred of difference. It really was self-defense."

"Can't you tell the story in court tomorrow?" Calvin asked.

"No. First, it isn't direct testimony. I wasn't there. Judge Murphy might bend a few rules, but he won't break them. There's another wrinkle. If I violate Melissa's trust, I lose her.

"What we have, gentlemen, is a doctor," he gestured to Pete, "who has not made promises of secrecy concerning Victoria Faulkner's life before Freedom House. You sent Toria here and made sure all the legalities of custody were firm in Seattle.

"Judge Murphy said Horn had guardianship papers for Toria in his pocket. I asked him to postpone Melissa's hearing until we can ascertain whether they are legitimate. If they are, that makes the papers the Faulkners signed with me the day they left Fairhaven worthless."

"Horn's papers are forgeries," Pete said, a flush of color brightening his jaw. "I'm sure of it. We couldn't take Toria out of Horn's hellhole until we got the custody issue settled. Horn probably knew a dozen counterfeiters and forgers. No judge would give someone like him custody of a child."

"I hope not," Rory said slowly, confident Pete would do well on Melissa's behalf. "Sheriff Barstow is holding whatever answers he found in Seattle very close to his chest. He never mentioned Horn's guardianship claim on Toria when he found me at your home, Pete, or during the voyage home." Rory pondered for a moment before focusing on the teacher taking notes on the other side of the table.

"Calvin, you're the most impartial man here."

"I wouldn't call me impartial, Rory."

"Tomorrow you're going to become Melissa's attorney of record."

Calvin set down his pencil and slowly gazed from Rory to Pete and back. "Look, I—"

"Pete can't. We may need him as a witness. That leaves you. I'll help you. You know that. Besides, you're the most qualified to interpret Toria." Rory ran his fingers through his hair. "Damn, we've got a woman who won't defend herself. A missing derringer. Four witnesses to what appeared cold-blooded murder. And we have an unsettled child who knows the entire story but can't speak and can't write well enough to communicate. In the corner we have a sheriff who may or may not hold answers that will benefit our side."

Rory studied his friends. "Think we can get the charges dismissed?"

"Not a chance in hell," Calvin said, shaking his head.

"I won't let her hang or go to prison," Rory said calmly.

"Then we'd better get busy laying some strategy and hope like hell Barstow is on our side," Pete said. "Meanwhile, let's get the kids down to the beach. If Melissa said there was a gun, there was, and we need to find it." Pete rubbed his chin and thoughtfully met Rory's gaze. "We need that gun. The waves couldn't have carried it too far or the sand buried it too deeply."

"Melissa is due a piece of good luck," Rory mused, heading for the door at the sound of Tommy's voice in the foyer.

Chapter 26

THE FIRST HINT of morning lit the eastern ridges. Soon golden sunlight would brighten the morning sky and hide the stars. Melissa craned her neck to catch a glimpse of Mr. Tibbens through the narrow, barred window and the imperfect glass distorting the heavens.

"You once told me to give someone else a chance when I grew up, Mr. Tibbens. Now I have. When I see you in the heavens, I can meet you without shame," she whispered. "I understand so much, so late."

"But not too late, Melissa Fuller."

Melissa spun in the direction of the melodious voice. She hadn't heard the outer door open. The dim glow of the lantern hanging on the wall outside her cell illuminated an alluring woman nearly as tall as she. The strange woman stood proudly within the narrow confines of the cell.

"How did you get in here? Who are you?" Astonishment quickened Melissa's heartbeat.

"Getting inside a prison cell is seldom difficult." The woman raised her arms. Flickers of light caught the iridescent shimmer of colors in her shawl. The faint song of crystal bells chimed with each movement. "I am Shelan."

Melissa gaped in amazement. The magic woman who had brought her across time and made plants grow in impossible places stood before her. When Melissa gathered enough composure to close her mouth, she approached Shelan, then tentatively touched her shoulder. Warm flesh and bone. Breathing, living. "You are real."

The lilt of youthful laughter mingled with the distant echo

of Shelan's bells against the dank walls. "Quite." Shelan lit a lantern and hung it from the bars on the cell door.

Melissa continued staring at the mystic, enthralled. Shelan's beauty glowed in her raven hair and smooth, creamy skin. Heavy black lashes framed clear azure eyes that had seen through time and found whimsy in the world around her. "You're very beautiful."

Again Shelan laughed. "My beauty is a reflection of Rory McCullough's spirit, Melissa. In the course of my life, I've discovered very few mortal women worth envying. Were I of such an ilk, I would envy you, Melissa. Rory has given you his heart, which I surmise is quite aching at the moment. Forsooth, I never anticipated Rory losing you to a hangman's knot or the rot of a prison cell. He will not be whole if you meet such a dreadful fate."

Still reeling from the appearance of a magic woman she had never thought to meet, Melissa shook her head. "What is done cannot be undone. In the grand scheme of the universe, perhaps my real purpose in this life was achieved on the beach with Cyrus Horn. The woman you plucked from the sky . . . I don't think she would have fought for Victoria Faulkner or the children of Freedom House."

"Possibly not." Shelan waved a long-fingered hand in the air. "However, I know nothing about the intentions of the Highest Powers. In my scheme, saving the world, even the one at Freedom House, was most definitely not the reason I brought you here. I summoned you for Rory, not to save the children. Rory does that quite well by himself.

"You were not easy to find. His wishes for a wife were far more complex than he imagined."

Melissa laughed her silent laugh. "I still cannot fathom being transported across time just to be some man's wife. I would never have agreed to anything so absurd—if you had asked."

Shelan cocked an eyebrow. "You do not wish to wed Rory?"

"With all my heart, I wish for nothing else. But that won't happen now. The woman you brought here wouldn't have considered marriage. Because she couldn't trust . . . was incapable of trusting, she was blind in so many ways." Melissa glanced at the window. The first glimmers of morning snuffed all but the strongest stars. Soon they too would fade. "The woman I am now loves Rory with all her heart and trusts him without question," she concluded.

Shelan sighed and sat on the pallet. "You are much like Rory in your unbending commitment to what you hold dear."

The question that had nagged her for months escaped in a whisper. "Why me, Shelan? Why me?"

Shelan leaned against the wall. Shimmers of color from her brightly patterned skirt flowed like silken water around her. "Because you were dying without having glimpsed the goodness in your spirit. Your potential was not easy to unveil.

"You were like no one else I've touched. Seldom have I encountered a heart as closed as yours was when I reached out to you, Melissa. There have been others I have seen meet death with anger and bitterness. You went even further and flaunted your outrage. But what made the way you faced death very different was your complete lack of fear."

Melissa recalled every second of the plunge toward Earth. Now her self-centeredness was a source of embarrassment. The only person she had thought about in what should have been her final moments had been herself. Then, who else could she have considered? No one had touched her life in any way that mattered for a long time. Guiltily, she met Shelan's knowing gaze.

Shelan nodded slowly, as though understanding how Melissa viewed the changes still unfolding within. "You needed Rory to show you how to change your anger to love and your bitterness to compassion. As with all growth from change, no one, not even Rory, could do it for you. You discovered your true heart by yourself."

She looked away from Melissa a moment before continuing. "I had doubts you would take the risk and understand the beauty of what Rory offers you. It appears that I needn't have given it a second thought. There is little middle ground with you, Melissa, as is evident from the predicament in which I find you. And Rory."

"How did I get from up there"—Melissa glanced at the brightening sky—"to the lake without a trace of my old time? How did you bring me here? Why didn't I die?"

Shelan laughed, tilting her head back. "How did I bring you to Rory? Ten years of saving my magic made me very powerful. The vows of my coven bind me to repayment of all great acts of kindness bestowed on me. No companion in my long life has equaled Rory's pure generosity and goodness. He wanted a wife, Melissa. What he needed was a lover and soul mate who shared his visions for the children he collected."

Genuine affection mellowed Shelan's intensity. "I thanked Rory for the gift of his generous spirit and my forced abstinence from magic by giving him you."

"You can't give one person to another." Melissa's cheeks warmed under the tolerance she saw in Shelan's patient smile.

"That is true—to a point. You gave yourself to him. You knew in the circle he was the love of your heart. Yet when the spell wore off, all the defenses you put in place during your lifetime rose in denial. Oh, you were strong, and stubborn, Melissa. Had I not obscured your memories of other times and places, you might not have given one another even the one night. Beautiful, was it not?"

Melissa swallowed hard. "You were there? Watching?"

The crystal bells sang with Shelan's laughter; her azure eyes sparkled with delight. "Not watching. I could feel it in the vibrations of the spell. He loved you even then, Melissa."

Remembering their night of wild, uninhibited lovemaking in the circle sent two tears coursing down her cheeks. "Will I miss him after I am dead? Is there a way to stay near him from, from the other side?"

"Ah, Melissa, you are not dead yet. Nor do you have to die. That's why I'm here."

"A little over four months. Such a short time," Melissa

said, turning toward the window. "Yet, I cannot imagine life without Rory or the children."

"If you try, you can."

"Why didn't you come sooner, Shelan?"

"Until today there was time. Now . . . I've come to give you the choice I didn't offer before. I can send you back, Melissa. Would you like to go?"

Melissa wheeled around from the window. "Back to what? A satellite plunging into Earth's atmosphere? I think I prefer the hangman's noose or a cell where I'll rot with a few good memories."

Shelan clucked her tongue in reproach. "If you wish me to send you back, please trust you can resume the life I plucked you from without the peril that sent you into disaster." Shelan poised her forefinger and thumb within a breath of each other. "This much difference keeps you safe. Surely you must realize if I can send you back, I can deflect a small rock this tiny a little bit."

Melissa closed her eyes and relived the fateful moment when the satellite took on a life of its own. A fraction of an inch might have made the difference between a hit and a miss. Life and death. Who she was and who she'd become. Rory and oblivion. "It doesn't matter now, does it? I'm here. Death is death."

"Are you afraid?" Shelan asked softly.

"Yes," she whispered. "And no. I don't know what I feel beyond an oppressive sadness."

"There are forces beyond your comprehension at work. Returning you to the place in time moments before you fell to Earth requires great magic.

"I have the power, thanks to Rory. What I cannot manipulate is the tide of time. Until tomorrow, it ebbs sufficiently for me to send you back. After that . . . the tide changes. You may go today, tonight, even early tomorrow morning, if you wish.

"Only for this brief period can I return you to your former place in time. Yes, there would come other opportunities

when the forces would allow me to send you back, but not
for a while.

"Like all things, there are absolutes that cannot be ignored.
Such are the covenants binding me. If you go, you can return
to the stars again. You can continue the course you charted
early in your life and sacrificed everything tender to attain. Is
that not what you wanted?"

Melissa weighed her options carefully. A few weeks ago
the scenario may have tempted her. Even now, a slight tug
drew her thoughts toward old dreams. But she had fulfilled
those dreams and walked among the stars. Now she had different dreams. "If I returned, my heart would remain with
Rory. By then, his bones would be dust in a grave. Rory and
I would live out our days aching for one another with no possibility of ever touching again.

"And the children. What of them? They would believe I
ran away. I cannot let them down like that." She rushed to
the pallet and sat beside Shelan. "Is there no other way?"

"Sadly, no. I cannot interfere with the present. I could
bring you to Rory in the circle only because mortal death
would have claimed you in another moment."

The compassionate sweep of Shelan's cool hand against
her damp cheek unleashed a flood of tears. "I can't go back,
Shelan. I am a coward. Even if I could live with the censure
of running out on the children, I could not live day after day,
year after year, knowing that Rory . . ." Her teary gaze
sought understanding in Shelan's compassionate eyes. "I
love him. I can't leave."

"And you won't defend yourself by revealing what Cyrus
Horn wanted from the little girl to buy a chance at living?"
Shelan's raised eyebrow imparted a censure of its own.

"They don't believe I killed Cyrus Horn in self-defense
because they can't find his gun. They think I stalked him,"
she said. "I made a promise to keep Toria safe. To the best of
my ability, I'll keep it. She finally has a home with people
who care about her. At Freedom House no one will sell her,
use her, or beat her. As it is, the children are eyed with skepticism when we go to town. Not by everyone, but by those

who seem to hold the reins of power and set the social rules for acceptance. If the townfolk knew of Toria's past, for her to grow up anywhere near Fairhaven would be hell. I fear she would become the way I was. That isn't living, Shelan. It's existing in a cold darkness more complete than the void above Earth."

"Is it possible you fear too much for Victoria and sell her short in the shadow of those fears?"

Melissa sniffed and wiped her cheeks with her fingers. "You sound like Rory."

Shelan straightened her shoulders and grinned. "Why, thank you. Answer my question."

"I don't know. I just know I won't gamble with her future."

"But you already have, my dear. You've wagered she isn't strong enough to fight for what she wants, which is you alive, not dead or in prison. Conversely, you've stacked the odds in a manner that weighs heavily on her being better off without you. Is she? Have you nothing to teach her? No means of guiding her through difficult times? No motivation to impart?"

"How dare you sit in judgment of me! You've played with my life, my fate, and now you condemn what is probably the noblest deed I've ever done? Oh, Shelan, you are truly a witch. Why are you asking me all these questions?"

"Ah, yes, Melissa, I am a witch. And I'm asking these questions because you are running out of time. It is serious business playing with people's lives and futures. I did not undertake extending yours without great consideration of every foreseeable consequence. I merely ask you to do the same."

Shelan took Melissa's right hand and ran a fingertip over the calloused pads. "You had no choice in coming because I gave you none. Understand, Melissa, I give you one now. I will return before dawn tomorrow for your answer."

"Save yourself the trip. I'd rather die where I've known love than live without any possibility of touching it again.

You have my answer, Shelan. It won't change by tomorrow morning no matter what happens today."

"Not even if I offer you oblivion from remembering this time and place? Not even if I folded time to the second before that metal thing you were holding on to began wobbling and speeding toward Earth?"

Oblivion. A giant eraser sweeping over the most beautiful part of her life. "No, Shelan," she answered slowly. "My heart would never forget Rory. And what of him? Would it the same for him and the children? Would they . . . forget me, too?"

Shelan shook her head sadly. "Alas, I cannot give them oblivion."

"You have your answer with my thanks, Shelan. Oblivion at Rory's expense holds no appeal. I've come too far in finding out how to live as a real person to return to my old ways." Melissa captured Shelan's hand. "Truthfully, I don't think I like the old Melissa Fuller very much, but there is much about her that I admire and respect. Her strength and stamina help me even now."

Melissa rose, head shaking. "I sound like a schizophrenic. It's all me. Me. Melissa Fuller. The good, the bad, and everything in between." She braced her hands on the sides of the barred window and stared out. "All those elements are like the sea and land around here. Some of it is deadly, yet spectacular in its beauty. The weather is the personification of its moods, happy and sunny or angry and stormy. Before you brought me here, I never saw anything around me the way I see it now.

"I want to live, Shelan. I've never wanted more out of life than I do right now. I could have had it all . . . Rory, children of our own, Freedom House." She closed her eyes against the anguish she felt. "All I had to do was give Toria to Cyrus Horn. Instead, when he made a threatening move I shot him. I didn't wound him or disarm him. I blew a hole though his damn heart in front of four witnesses."

"Aren't you forgetting Toria?"

Melissa's head rocked against the cold wall. "No. To her, I

ended her worst nightmare. I slew her devil, her bogeyman, and he's never coming after her again. And I guess I vicariously obliterated the last of my own demons when I pulled that trigger." Horace Freeland couldn't roll back the clock and make her six years old again. He couldn't steal into her room in the middle of the night and whisper that she was a whore who seduced him, her foster father, and it was now his right to use her. Horace Freeland had finally died with Cyrus Horn.

At that moment of realization, she felt freer inside the tiny cell than she had for more than twenty years. She lifted her head to the light streaming through the distorted glass. Never had she seen life so clearly.

"I'll be back before dawn, Melissa."

"My answer will be the same. They're going to have the trial today. Tomorrow—well, tomorrow will take care of itself. And me."

"We will see," Shelan said from the other side of the cell door.

"Some of us will," Melissa murmured, suddenly tired beyond reason.

Laughter rippled from the walls. "Ah, Melissa, Melissa. Have you so little faith in the man you love? Do you truly believe he will allow any mortal to take you from him?"

A sudden chill sent a shiver along her arms. "Dear God in heaven. I don't want to ruin his life and all he's worked for with the children. I couldn't bear it."

"Rory's actions are as far beyond your influence as yours were beyond his on the beach." A sad chuckle floated from beyond the outer door. "The human condition is a source of constant amazement, and occasional amusement."

After a long time Melissa turned away from the window. In the morning silence it seemed Shelan's visit was nothing more than a waking dream conjured by a desperate mind. The sun climbed high in the sky. Her untouched breakfast waited on a tray Hal had left on her hard pallet. Strange, she had not heard him enter or leave.

Noises mingled with voices beyond the outer cell door. Melissa turned back to the window. Wisps of clouds caught on the mountains. She closed her eyes and returned to the fairy ring. A hundred details flooded her memory: Rory massaging the aches from her body, the flash of desire in his gray eyes, the tender concern he showered on her like sunlight, the image of him walking into the lake, his quick laughter and the delight he found in the most improbable things. Eyes closed, she could almost hear the way he laughed deep in his chest while they made love. He had been so patient with her. Waiting, knowing she trusted him and loved him long before she admitted it to herself.

When had she fallen in love with him? Right now, she couldn't imagine not loving him.

"Miss Fuller?"

Hal's tentative call broke her reverie. The bleakness of the present crashed down with an oppressive force. "What is it, Hal? Time to go?"

"Your lawyer is here."

"I don't have a lawyer."

The clank of the outer door lock opening sent her forehead against the wall. Why couldn't they leave her alone?

"Yes, you do, for whatever good a schoolteacher will do in a court of law."

At the familiarity of the voice, she tightened her grip on the bars over her head. Was there no end to the humiliation? "You can't help me, Calvin."

"Perhaps not, but I'm going to try and you're going to help me try." The resolve in his voice bespoke the weight with which he regarded his task.

"I can't help you." Talking about what happened and why was a waste of time.

"Turn around, Melissa." A tremor shook Calvin's voice. "Look me in the eye and tell me you're giving up without a fight."

She heaved a deep sigh, prepared to do as he bade her. However, when she turned, the words died in her throat. Beside Calvin Brockbannon, Tommy held Toria's hand.

Dressed in their best clothes, they would have looked like angels if not for the tears streaming down Toria's cheeks and falling on the lacy bib of her blue-and-white-gingham dress. Melissa's heart twisted when Tommy silently patted her teary cheeks with a handkerchief. Toria's sad blue gaze remained locked on hers.

"Why did you bring them?" Melissa signed faster than either Tommy or Toria could interpret. "Couldn't you have spared us this? I don't want the children remembering me as a prisoner."

Calvin stiffened, then set down his briefcase and signed just as rapidly. "They're part of this. You didn't ask for it. Neither did they. There is no changing it."

"I don't want them in the courtroom," Melissa said aloud. "Please take them home."

"Judge Murphy said we have to be here," Tommy said. "So did your other lawyer."

"No," Melissa seethed, then resorted to signing. "This is wrong. Wrong! Why is there even a hearing? They didn't believe me before. Why not let them do what they wanted to do ten days ago and be done with it? They don't want the truth; it's inconvenient, complicated. Don't you know you can't change the minds of any authorities that don't see believing you as being in their best interests? I wield no influence. I have no money. No power. Therefore, I will get no justice. That's the way it is. I accept how things are. Why can't you do the same?"

The rest of Tommy's earlier pronouncement settled hard in the nest of her confusion. "What do you mean, my other lawyer? I haven't engaged one lawyer, let alone two. What is going on here, Calvin?"

"A sincere attempt at establishing a proper defense under the law."

"There is no defense they are willing to accept," Melissa whispered. "They've already decided I'm guilty."

"Exactly what you are guilty of?" Calvin resorted to signing, moving too quickly for the children to follow. "We all know there is more to what happened than what the men saw from the bluff. There is much more to Cyrus Horn, too. For all our sakes, cooperate with what we're trying to do here."

A small sniff escaped Toria. Melissa's heart sank even more.

Calvin cleared his throat, then spoke softly. "Sheriff Barstow will escort the four of us to Judge Murphy's court in a few minutes. The children wanted to make sure you were well before going."

The sorrow emanating from Tommy and Toria turned her heartbeat into a sluggish thud. Each time a fresh tear slipped down Toria's cheek, the weight pressing on Melissa's spirit grew heavier.

She crouched in front of the door and reached for Toria's hand through the bars. The child's skin was silky beneath Melissa's calloused fingers and palm. "No matter what happens, you just remember I love you. Every one of you at Freedom House."

The outer door latch clanged the sound of release. "Good morning, Miss Fuller. Looks like we got ourselves a fine day for a hearing." Sheriff Barstow's greeting boomed into the cell. He threw the outer door wide and entered. With each step, Melissa's heart thudded faster. She had thought herself ready for whatever lay ahead, resigned to her fate, and prepared to meet her maker. The unrelenting blue stare of the little girl with the quivering chin drew her back. The rush of agitation quieted. With every fiber in her being, she knew she was doing the right thing.

Chapter 27

"M ISS FULLER, PLEASE accompany me to chambers." Judge Murphy heaved his bulk up from behind the justice bench.

Beside her, Calvin rose and collected the stacks of papers he had laid out in a neat array.

"You stay here, Mr. Brockbannon."

Melissa glanced at Calvin, who returned an encouraging, if somewhat ineffectual, smile. Rising, she quickly scanned the courtroom. Two pairs of hopeful blue eyes met her gaze. In the row directly behind the defense table Dr. Pete Jacobson examined his cuticles. Although he was impeccably attired, his feigned nonchalance did nothing to bolster her confidence. Charles Markel lifted his chin in a show of defiant support.

The ever impassive Sheriff Barstow gave her a slight nod from his seat behind the prosecutor's table. Abbot Pearson, the young man prosecuting the case, took a sudden interest in the tips of his shoes when her gaze swung his way.

Rory's absence registered with keen disappointment. It seemed impossible he would miss this last chance for them to see one another outside the confines of metal bars and dank walls. More amazing, he had allowed the children into the courtroom without his attendance.

She paused to ask Calvin if something had happened to Rory. Before she could speak, Judge Murphy called out, "Come along, Miss Fuller. Let's see if we can't wind this up before dinner time."

His cavalier remark served as a poignant reminder of how much she had inconvenienced the judicial process by taking up valuable time despite her simple, straightforward acceptance they found her account of events unbelievable. Dutifully, she rounded the defense table and followed Judge Murphy through the door guarding his chambers.

The judicial sanctum boasted a cluttered table, two chairs, and rows of bookcases with shelves sagging under the burden of law tomes. A single window of distorted glass in need of washing filtered the late-morning sunlight. Standing in the far corner and leaning against the wall, Rory awaited, his arms folded across his chest. Her heart leaped with joy at the sight of him.

Judge Murphy lumbered past the bookcases, then settled heavily into the massive wooden chair on the business side of the table.

"Close the door and sit down, Miss Fuller."

Melissa glanced at Rory, wondering why he was in Judge Murphy's chambers and not out in the courtroom with Calvin, Pete, and the rest of the important spectator-witnesses. Absently, she obeyed Judge Murphy's order.

"I suppose you're wondering why I brought you in here." Judge Murphy fingered a stack of neatly scripted papers.

"It has crossed my mind more than once in the last two minutes," she answered cautiously, then risked a glance at Rory. The intensity of his gaze registered in every pore.

"I see your confinement has had the benefit of restoring your voice, for which I am glad, since it will shorten this hearing considerably if at least one of the people involved can speak."

"Would you please elaborate on what you mean by 'one of the people involved'? To my knowledge, I'm the only person charged with a crime." Her gaze rose, then locked on Rory's stormy eyes.

"Be that as it may, Miss Fuller, you involved Victoria Faulkner when you shot Mr. Horn in front of her." The chair creaked under Judge Murphy's considerable weight as he tilted it onto the back legs. "Apparently, a great deal occurred before the men on the bluff arrived just in time to see you pull the trigger on Mr. Horn."

Judge Murphy's calloused fingers rapped against the two-day growth of stubble on his jaw. "Now, I want to hear everything that happened. You're going to elaborate on every salient point and omit nothing. Is that clear?"

"Judge—"

"It goes no farther than this room, Melissa. For God's sake, tell him all of it," Rory demanded in a chilled voice never rising louder than a whisper.

The anguish he emanated mirrored her own. They had come so close to weaving the threads of their improbable dreams into reality. Rory wasn't ready to let it go. For him, as well as herself, she bowed to his wishes.

"Before I say a word about what happened on the beach, I'll have your personal word, Judge Murphy, that nothing said here today leaves the confines of this room." The way his gray eyes narrowed bespoke his indecision over taking offense at her demand.

"You have my word, Miss Fuller. Please, speak freely."

Still, she hesitated. With all her heart she believed any mention of what actually happened with Cyrus Horn would jeopardize Toria's future. If she did not shelter the child . . .

"Tell him the way you told me, Melissa." Rory moved away from the wall, and the light in his stormy gray eyes struck her soul, begging her cooperation in this slim chance of avoiding the gallows.

"Believe me when I say I have never had more to live for than I do now, Judge Murphy. Nor have I ever had more to protect." She settled back and braced her elbows on the arms of the chair. Her loosely folded fingers alternately tented and dropped as she spoke. She started with her search for Toria, leading her to the tree and the abandoned dolls. The child would never have left her prized possessions unless something dire had happened.

Once the words began flowing, Melissa relaxed. While her story unfolded, she looked directly into Judge Murphy's eyes. Unlike Rory, Josiah Murphy was an expert at masking his emotions. When she finished, she sat back and dropped her hands into her lap.

Judge Murphy remained silent for a long time. "I have two questions, Miss Fuller."

Melissa lifted her eyes and cocked her head. "Only two?"

Murphy harumphed and leaned back in his chair again. "First, did you understand Mr. Horn to say he killed the Faulkners?"

"He did not specifically say so, but he made sure I understood he had done just that. They were the only impediments he knew of concerning Victoria." She glanced at Rory. "He was wrong. I know Mr. McCullough took some legal actions of his own to ensure guardianship of Victoria Faulkner. This was what her grandparents had requested—protection for Toria. And, in turn, themselves. They were afraid of Cyrus Horn—"

Rory withdrew the papers he had drawn up the day the Faulkners arrived with Victoria. "These guardianship papers are quite legal. I believe you know Judge Thompson and will recognize his signature."

"Earl scribbles his name, he doesn't sign it," Judge Murphy muttered while examining the papers. "So you knew Horn's papers were forgeries, Miss Fuller?"

"Yes. I had seen the original documents the Faulkners gave to Rory. It is difficult to say for certain how the legal system works or doesn't, in some cases," Melissa said carefully. "But that wasn't why I killed him, your Honor."

"Did you kill him because you believed he would burn Freedom House down and the children in it, Miss Fuller?"

Melissa sighed. "I'm not a noble person, and I'm not very good at self-sacrifice. In truth, I've lived a self-centered life, until recently. What I found at Freedom House . . . Well, I wouldn't have let Cyrus Horn destroy it.

"But the truth is, I never had to make a decision. He made it for me when he reached into his coat pocket for the little derringer he was going to shoot me with." She glanced at Rory and felt the weight of truth lifting from her shoulders. "But you're right in predicting what I might have done if he had not thought he could get away with it. I wouldn't have let him sneak back in the middle of the night and burn Freedom House down with the children inside. Nor could I trade their lives for Toria's by giving her to him."

"You're still protecting her, aren't you?" Judge Murphy asked softly.

Melissa nodded, then ignored the question. "On the beach, I ran out of options. I didn't see anyone else down there trying to help Toria, or me. I'm damn good at protecting myself. Mr. Horn underestimated me. He expected me to wilt. When I didn't, he decided to play the ace tucked in his pocket. I acted out of reflex, just as any man might do.

"The last thing I considered when I went looking for Toria was that I'd end up killing a man."

Murphy flipped the edges of the neatly penned papers in front of him. "Do you know what this is, Miss Fuller?"

Melissa studied the thick sheaf of papers, then shook her head. "No, but I have a feeling you're going to tell me."

"Mr. McCullough, Dr. Jacobson, and Mr. Brockbannon exhibited the patience of Job. The account Miss Faulkner gave of what occurred on the beach, and a great deal more, is contained in these pages." The old oak table groaned as Judge Murphy leaned toward Melissa. "I understand why you wished to protect her by remaining silent. However, understanding motivation is only part of my job. Since the dawn of time, people have committed murder with purely honorable intentions. In order to mete out justice fairly, I had to know all the truth."

Judge Murphy's broad chest expanded with an audible breath. "I know you have not seen Victoria before this morning, by which time this information was already in my hands. Therefore, I am certain there has been no collusion. Your stories are identical, so I believe I have found the truth. Justice cannot be served without it.

"I don't know what happened between Cyrus Horn and Victoria, but I can imagine it was the stuff her nightmares are made of. I'm not going to ask about those nightmares." He coiled the papers into a roll, slid a rubber band over both ends, then offered it to Melissa. "I gave you and Mr. McCullough here"—he gestured at Rory—"my word Victoria

Faulkner's association with Cyrus Horn would not be aired in court. You're right, Rory. The child has enough to over-come without making her a sideshow."

His promise of confidentiality sent relief flooding through Melissa.

Judge Murphy pushed his chair away from the table. The grating of wood on wood pierced the air. "I believe we can return to the courtroom now. This case does get more inter-esting by the moment."

Melissa clutched the papers to her chest for a moment, then handed them to Rory. "I know you'll take care of this and her." Searching his pain-filled eyes, she forced a smile. "I trust you, Rory." She put the testimony in his hands know-ing she should never have doubted he'd find a way to defend her without compromising his integrity.

"Coming, McCullough? Miss Fuller?" Judge Murphy waited at the door.

Melissa squared her shoulders and managed a feeble smile in the face of the misery scoring the lines around Rory's eyes and mouth. "Thank you," she whispered, barely containing the depth of emotion testing her control.

Outside the chamber silence reigned. The anxious stares of the spectators stirred a prickling sensation along Melissa's skin. She caught Toria's unwavering gaze and found hope burning in her blue eyes. Tommy watched her with a confi-dence bolstered by the responsibility of being strong for Toria, whose small hand filled his.

Assuming her place next to Calvin, she felt relief when Rory pulled up a chair beside her at the defense table.

"Sheriff Barstow, I gave you ten days to satisfy your law-man's itch about this case. Have you done so?"

"Your Honor, the prosecution intended to present its case by calling Charles Markel to the stand first," objected the young prosecutor.

"If this were a trial, that would be your right, Mr. Pear-son. However, this case has some unusual and sensitive as-pects that I don't intend to explain to you," Judge Murphy boomed.

"You can't withhold evidence from me." Pearson's face flushed crimson with outrage.

"It isn't evidence unless I say it is, Mr. Pearson. Now let's get on with this inquiry." Judge Murphy pushed his glasses up his bulbous nose, then motioned to Sheriff Barstow.

"Inquiry? What happened to the trial?" Pearson started to rise from his chair.

"It's premature for a trial, Abbot. Just have a seat and listen. You might hear something interesting." Judge Murphy pointed his gavel at the sheriff. "What did you learn in Seattle, Clem?"

Sheriff Clem Barstow withdrew a packet from his inside coat pocket. "I visited Judge Blankenship in Seattle. His name appears on the guardianship papers we found on Cyrus Horn. Judge Blankenship had never seen the papers, nor had he heard of Cyrus Horn or the Faulkners. He confirmed Miss Fuller's original contention that the papers Cyrus Horn showed us were forgeries.

"I got to wondering how this young girl"—he gestured at Toria—"came to be here in Fairhaven in the first place, and why she is the center of so much attention."

Fearing that Sheriff Barstow was about to reveal Toria's origins, Melissa started to rise. "Your Honor—"

"Quiet, Miss Fuller." Judge Murphy lifted a finger and nodded at Clem Barstow. "The court is aware of the circumstances surrounding Miss Faulkner."

Clem heeded the warning with a nod, then cleared his throat.

"No, the court is not," Pearson again started to his feet. Immediately, Judge Murphy waved him back to his chair.

"Abbot, let's just hear what Clem has to say. If I think you need to know more, we'll discuss it later." Judge Murphy met Melissa's worried gaze. "Continue."

"The deeper I checked into Cyrus Horn's activities, the more it reminded me of a maze of slug trails." Barstow leafed through the papers in his left hand. "When I paid a call to the Seattle authorities, I got an interesting surprise, Josiah. Seems they wanted to talk with Mr. Horn. However, they weren't upset upon learning that wasn't going to happen. Turns out they think he killed an elderly couple." Sheriff Barstow glanced at Toria, who looked back with clear blue eyes. "Abe and Agnes Faulkner were this young lady's grandparents. It appears that Cyrus Horn murdered them about two weeks ago. That makes it right before he came up here."

The bottom fell out of Melissa's nervous stomach. Horn had told the truth. He had killed the Faulkners and thought he had removed the last obstacle to claiming guardianship. She looked at Rory, who refused to meet her eyes. When she glanced at Toria, only the slight quiver of her small chin betrayed the depth of the loss of her grandparents. Melissa stared at the table in front of her. Apparently, Sheriff Barstow's revelation was news only to her and the prosecuting attorney.

Brimming with anxiety, Melissa squeezed her tightly laced fingers and pressed her hands into the tabletop.

"This is circumstantial and not germane to whether or not Miss Fuller committed murder," Pearson protested.

Sheriff Barstow shifted his weight to his left foot. "There was a helluva lot more than circumstantial evidence, Abbot. The Seattle authorities had a cold, hard case against Cyrus Horn. If Horn had known he'd been seen leaving the Faulkners' home by a neighbor and two deliverymen, I seriously doubt we'd be here today. He would have kept traveling." Barstow handed the packet of papers to Abbot Pearson.

"Why did he want this little girl?" Pearson demanded, perusing the papers.

"That's not the issue before the court," Judge Murphy growled.

Exasperated, Abbot Pearson slammed the papers onto the table. "Perhaps you'd clarify exactly what is the issue before this court? What am I prosecuting, Josiah? I thought it was murder."

"Then pay attention, Pearson. This is not a trial. It is an inquiry. The issue is whether or not Miss Fuller acted in self-defense when threatened by a known killer who would kill not only her and the girl, but the rest of the children and in-habitants of Freedom House. This court adheres to the strictest interpretation of the law with regard to the safety of children, especially children who have endured and survived things that most of us would cower at facing."

Melissa stared at Judge Murphy, not quite sure what she'd heard. A sense of detachment settled over her.

Hope.

She'd given up any semblance of believing in the possibility of a reprieve.

"Josiah, five people saw her kill a man. Are you going to—"

"Four people arrived at the top of the bluff just in time to see Miss Fuller defend herself. Mr. Markel!"

Charles Markel stood, hat in hand. "Yes, Judge?"

"Where was Miss Faulkner at the time Miss Fuller found it necessary to shoot Mr. Horn?"

Looking straight at the judge, Charles Markel answered immediately. "She was clutching Miss Fuller's skirts and out of Mr. Horn's reach."

"Is that what you saw, Clem?" Pearson asked the sheriff.

"I'd say that was an accurate description. We weren't up there for more than a half a minute before she fired," the sheriff answered slowly, his gaze narrowing on Melissa.

"Did you see Mr. Horn with a weapon?" Pearson pressed.

"Can't say that I did or didn't, Abbot. He fell into the waves. The tide was coming in with the vengeance of the storm that knocked us around that night. Horn could have had a weapon and lost it when she shot him. Things are sel-dom as clear-cut as they seem at first glance. You know that as well as I. My instincts say she shot him for cause and in defense of the little girl." Clem nodded at the children staring up at him. "Miss Victoria Faulkner."

"What we didn't know then, Abbot, was that the papers Horn presented to me and Judge Murphy were phony. Miss Fuller, she knew. She'd seen the papers giving Abe and Agnes Faulkner full custody of their granddaughter. They, in turn, assigned guardianship to Mr. McCullough."

"That true, Miss Fuller?" Abbot Pearson asked thoughtfully.

"Yes, Mr. Pearson," she answered softly.

"The only protection between Victoria Faulkner and that vile murderer Cyrus Horn was Miss Fuller," Calvin said, rising. "Given what we now know about the man, is it not perfectly reasonable to believe Miss Fuller's contention of self-defense? The waves could easily have buried Mr. Horn's second gun in the sand—or pulled it out to sea. In either case, we're not likely to find it.

"In that light, I move that all charges against Miss Melissa Fuller be dropped and a finding of self-defense be entered and approved."

"Abbot? Any objections?" Judge Murphy cocked an eyebrow in mock patience.

"Lots, but I don't think it will do me any good, will it, Josiah?"

"No. This one you're going to have to take on faith."

Abbot Pearson gathered up the papers strewn across the prosecution table. "Anyone but you, Josiah, would have to give me a helluva explanation. But you're not going to, are you?"

"No, Abbot, I'm not. Have you ever known me to render a verdict I didn't consider fair?"

"No, Josiah. That's why I'll let it pass. Go ahead."

"Miss Fuller, please rise."

Melissa rose unsteadily to her feet. Along with her, Rory, Calvin, and the rest of the spectators in the courtroom stood.

"It is the finding of this court that you acted in self-defense and in the best interest of a child entrusted to your care." The sharp rap of the gavel reverberated through the room. "Case dismissed. Go home, Miss Fuller."

Melissa stared at Judge Murphy, hardly able to believe her ears. For a moment no one moved. The courtroom shimmered in her vision. She was free. Free!

Dimly, she heard the courtroom door bang open and a surge of commotion.

Rory gripped her hand claiming her full attention. She

looked up into his serious gray eyes regarding her with an intensity that touched her soul.

"We found it!" Darin called out, trailing Sven and Olga Lindstrom and the other five residents of Freedom House. Martin and Elmira brought up the rear of the procession.

Melissa and Rory turned toward the door.

"Your Honor," Sven called out from between the defense and prosecution tables, "please. We have found the little gun Mr. Horn tried to use on Miss Fuller. The sand and storm had shifted it against a rock and buried it."

"Give it to Mr. Pearson. He can close out his paperwork and we can all be about our business. Thank you, Mr. Lindstrom and the esteemed residents of Freedom House. But, you are too late."

A silence so complete that Melissa could hear her heart beating descended.

"Miss Fuller has been released and is free to go. I'll ask all of you please to keep an eye on her so she stays out of trouble." Judge Murphy nodded at Calvin. "Court is dismissed."

"Judge Murphy," Rory said, his gaze never flickering from hers. "We might have an easier time of keeping Miss Fuller in line if you'd agree to marry us?"

"I've never known marriage to help a man much in that area, Mr. McCullough. However, if you have a license, I'd be happy to give you both a life sentence."

Rory reached into his coat pocket and pulled out a paper. "Right here."

"You really believed we'd win," Melissa whispered, awed by the depth of his faith.

"If a man can believe in magic, surely he can believe in the triumph of love over adversity." He grinned, then winked. "And just in case no one else did, I have a wagon waiting for us loaded with everything we'd need to live in the mountains. You didn't for a moment believe I'd let anyone take you from me?"

"Rory McCullough, I love you." She threw her arms around his neck.

"Then marry me so we can go home and show each other how much we missed one another," he breathed into her ear.

A slight tug on her skirt forced her to release Rory. She scooped Toria up and hugged the child, who cried softly on her shoulder.

"All right, everybody line up for a wedding," Judge Murphy ordered.

Basking in the light of Rory's love, Melissa stood beside him, answered at the appropriate times, and pledged her heart and life to him. The pendant lying between her breasts warmed her flesh with the promise of their hearts and souls joining forever.

Rory lowered his head. Smiling, Melissa parted her lips in sweet anticipation. In all of heaven's time, no kiss was sweeter, more passionate, or imparted a more total commitment.

"Take me home," she breathed, eager for privacy and the fulfillment that his kiss promised.

"Whatever you say, Mrs. McCullough." He picked Toria up and carried her on his forearm. "Melissa McCullough. Has a rather nice ring, don't you think?"

Toria nodded, then smiled for the first time in more than ten days.

Melissa smiled back, finally understanding that heaven was a state of mind, not just a place in the stars. Heaven was love, and Rory, and the children.

Epilogue

THE HEADY SCENT of roses and gardenias perfumed the late-evening air. The large blooms swayed in the ocean breeze. The prolific bushes flourished under Melissa's patient, nurturing care.

She wandered toward the berry arbor and glanced at the stars peeking down one at a time. The advanced stage of her second pregnancy in four years made her cumbersome as well as cautious.

Smiling at a sudden flurry of kicks, Melissa slid her hand over her round belly. "Easy, young lady, or there won't be much left of me by the time you meet your father and brother."

"That's no young lady you're carrying, Melissa."

Startled, Melissa glanced in the direction of the voice. In the shadows beyond the berry arbor, a woman in brightly colored garb smiled at her.

"Shelan."

"Aye."

Melissa grinned. "Have you come to play devil's advocate again?"

"I think not. And your days of choosing the direction of your destiny are over." Shelan smiled knowingly. "You were not in the cell when I returned as I had said I would."

"I made my choice before you left me."

Shelan nodded. "You chose well in the face of adversity. You are worthy of Rory's generous spirit and loving heart."

Melissa reached for the magic woman's hand and clasped it in both of hers. "Did I ever thank you for bringing me here? For the opportunity of learning how to live from the heart? For giving me Rory?"

The breeze caught Shelan's youthful laughter. "You are both happy. That is all I care about."

"I thank you now, Shelan. I never believed such happiness existed this side of heaven. And I do believe in magic." Melissa laughed, her great belly rippling the folds of her loose dress.

Shelan touched Melissa's cheek. "There is no magic under the heavens as powerful as love."

Gazing into the mystic's clear blue eyes, Melissa knew the truth came from Shelan's heart, which was wise with the learning of generations.

"There is your magic, Melissa." Shelan laughed and watched a scene over Melissa's left shoulder. "I have used nearly all my ten years and ten days allowed with Rory. However, I've saved a couple of days so I can return now and then—if he does not see me.

"Be well, Melissa. Be as happy as you have made him."

She turned to where Shelan's glittering gaze shifted. "Oh, I am happier than I ever thought possible."

Rory entered the garden carrying thirty-month-old Josiah on his shoulders.

"Tibb. Tibb," Josiah said, pointing at the polestar Melissa had long ago dubbed Mr. Tibbens.

Love swelled her heart. A woman got only so many chances in life. She thought she had used all of hers in search of something more beautiful and glorious than any fantasy. She turned to tell Shelan so, but the magic woman had disappeared.

"Come again, Shelan," she whispered into the night.

"When the time is right," came a whisper on the breeze.

Melissa extended her hand to her husband and felt her world complete when he took it.

"See that bright star." She pointed at a glittering point of light in Ursa Major. "It's called Rory, and it watches over us every day and night all year long."

"Like Da?" Josiah asked in amazement.

Melissa met Rory's tender smile with one of her own. "Like Da."

Rory drew her close, then kissed the top of her head. "I love you, Mrs. McCullough."

The familiar excitement of anticipating his touch and the intense concentration of his love rippled through her. Each day it strengthened. She smiled at him, basking in the magic of the night and the love they shared.

"I love you, too. I never thought Someday would be so glorious."

Rory grinned at Melissa. "And we've just begun."

Melissa slipped her hand inside his and squeezed. "So we have," she murmured with a glance at the stars. It seemed that Pacho, Rashad, Chandra, Kate, and Delvin could see her and applauded in approval.

TIME PASSAGES

__CRYSTAL MEMORIES__ Ginny Aiken   0-515-12159-2

__A DANCE THROUGH TIME__ Lynn Kurland

                                              0-515-11927-X

__ECHOES OF TOMORROW__ Jenny Lykins   0-515-12079-0

__LOST YESTERDAY__ Jenny Lykins   0-515-12013-8

__MY LADY IN TIME__ Angie Ray   0-515-12227-0

__NICK OF TIME__ Casey Claybourne   0-515-12189-4

__REMEMBER LOVE__ Susan Plunkett   0-515-11980-6

__SILVER TOMORROWS__ Susan Plunkett   0-515-12047-2

__THIS TIME TOGETHER__ Susan Leslie Liepitz

                                              0-515-11981-4

__WAITING FOR YESTERDAY__ Jenny Lykins

                                              0-515-12129-0

__HEAVEN'S TIME__ Susan Plunkett   0-515-12287-4

__THE LAST HIGHLANDER__ (7/98)

                 Claire Cross   0-515-12337-4

VISIT PENGUIN PUTNAM ONLINE ON THE INTERNET:
http://www.penguinputnam.com

Payable in U.S. funds. No cash accepted. Postage & handling: $1.75 for one book, 75¢ for each additional. Maximum postage $5.50. Prices, postage and handling charges may change without notice. Visa, Amex, MasterCard call 1-800-788-6262, ext. 1, or fax 1-201-933-2316; refer to ad # 680

Or, check above books   Bill my: ☐ Visa   ☐ MasterCard   ☐ Amex _____ (expires)
and send this order form to:
The Berkley Publishing Group   Card#_____

P.O. Box 12289, Dept. B   Daytime Phone #_____ ($10 minimum)
Newark, NJ 07101-5289   Signature_____
Please allow 4-6 weeks for delivery.   Or enclosed is my: ☐ check   ☐ money order
Foreign and Canadian delivery 8-12 weeks.

Ship to:

Name_____   Book Total $_____
Address_____   Applicable Sales Tax $_____
                                        (NY, NJ, PA, CA, GST Can.)
City_____   Postage & Handling $_____
State/ZIP_____   Total Amount Due $_____

Bill to: Name_____

Address_____City_____
State/ZIP_____